Family Secrets

"Readers looking for a compelling drama and dynamic family relationships will be thrilled with Ms. Bowden's newest offering."   *—Romantic Times*

"A riveting plot . . . draws readers in from its opening page . . . craftily building suspense."
—Winnipeg Free Press

"An intriguing plot filled with a collection of interesting characters. Bowden drops the clues one by one, keeping interest constantly burning."
—Affaire de Coeur

Homecoming

"The very talented Susan Bowden consistently demonstrates her special ability to peer deep into the hearts and souls of her all-too-human characters. The complex family relationships and conflicting emotions of this novel make for compelling reading."   *—Romantic Times*

"A long, leisurely read with finely crafted, memorable characters."   *—I'll Take Romance*

Also by Susan Bowden

Bitter Harvest

Forget Me Not

Say Goodbye to Daddy

Sisters at Heart

Family Secrets

Homecoming

HOUSE
OF
SHADOWS

SUSAN
BOWDEN

A SIGNET BOOK

SIGNET
Published by New American Library, a division of
Penguin Putnam Inc., 375 Hudson Street,
New York, New York 10014, U.S.A.
Penguin Books Ltd, 80 Strand,
London WC2R 0RL, England
Penguin Books Australia Ltd, 250 Camberwell Road,
Camberwell, Victoria 3124, Australia
Penguin Books Canada Ltd, 10 Alcorn Avenue,
Toronto, Ontario, Canada M4V 3B2
Penguin Books (N.Z.) Ltd, Cnr Rosedale and Airborne Roads,
Albany, Auckland 1310, New Zealand

Penguin Books Ltd, Registered Offices:
Harmondsworth, Middlesex, England

First published by Signet, an imprint of New American Library,
a division of Penguin Putnam Inc.

First Printing, April 2003
10 9 8 7 6 5 4 3 2 1

This book is dedicated to the countless people of Barbados whose welcome was as warm as the weather, and, in particular, to Wilber Lorde, the superb driver and guide on my travels throughout the island.

Acknowledgments

My sincere thanks to my editor, Genny Ostertag, whose diligence and insight have greatly enhanced this book.

PROLOGUE

Peverill Hall, 1950

The wind roared in from the Atlantic, bending the palm trees to its will, ocean surf pouring over the coral reef, pounding the golden beaches. The old house tensed, steeling itself for the onslaught. Its massive limestone walls had withstood far worse storms than this. Hurricanes had toppled its decorative chimneys, torn down mahogany and palm trees, flattened the fields of sugarcane beyond its gardens, but for three centuries the walls of the house had remained strong and invincible.

She sat on the bed, the blinds drawn down over the window in case the glass should crack and blow in on her. The lights had gone out almost an hour ago, and the candle on the bedside cabinet guttered in the wind that somehow found its way into the room.

Heart pounding, she wrote feverishly, knowing that she had very little time left to complete the note. *I'm in the bedroom with the door locked,* she wrote, digging the pencil into the paper, *the lights are gone.* Her head jerked up. She was sure she'd heard the stairs creaking. She scribbled frantically. *I hear his footsteps on the stairs. I will try to hide this from him and hope you will find it. Take care of my precious, darling son. Pray for me.* She could hear a scraping sound outside her door. *Oh, Jesus Lord save me he is at the door*

She sprang up, her eyes wildly searching for a weapon, but all she had were her nail scissors, and they were in the dressing table drawer across the room.

Now he was hammering on the door. "Come on, sweetheart," he pleaded, his voice muffled. "Open the door."

She dropped to the floor and rolled beneath the bed. Breathing fast, she pushed back the small coconut mat and pressed down on one end of the floorboard, wedging it with a corner of the mat. She opened the tin box and thrust the two sheets of paper inside. Then she lowered the floorboard, making sure it clicked into place, and pulled the mat back over it.

"Open the door, you stupid bitch," he yelled, "or I'll break it down!"

Her mind raced. Should she try to drop from the window onto the front porch? No, it was too far. She could break her neck. Besides, he'd still be able to catch her. Knowing that she didn't want to be trapped beneath the bed and dragged out, she rolled out from under it and darted across the room to the dressing table. But before she had time to open the drawer and grab her scissors, the door crashed open and he was lunging across the room toward her.

"Jesus Lord, save me," she cried out, but in the flickering light of the candle she caught the glint of metal in his hand . . . and in that moment she knew that she would never see her family again.

CHAPTER
ONE

The turbulent late September weather swept in from the south across Lake Ontario, whipping the pewter water into white-capped waves and pounding downtown Toronto with heavy rain. The crowd gathering at the glass-fronted gallery on Bloor Street jumped from taxis, dashed from cars, fighting to shield themselves from the rain with puny, wind-tossed umbrellas.

Inside the gallery, Patrick Grayson presided, standing not too close to the entrance. No need to look too eager. Let people seek him out. But he stationed himself near enough to the doors to be able to personally greet anyone of importance. And there were plenty of them. He'd made sure of that.

After he'd welcomed the minister of foreign affairs and steered him across the room to another group of politicians, Patrick drew Vivien aside, his face and shaven head flushed with excitement. "I told you, darling," he shouted above the babble from the people milling around the small space. "I told you you'd be a whopping success."

Vivien gave him a wan smile, wishing herself a thousand miles from here. Despite the excited chatter around her, imposter syndrome was fast setting in, as it always

did when one of her exhibitions opened. One day, she
was certain, she'd be found out. Some prestigious critic
would blow the whistle on her. Perhaps this was the
time. She'd open the review section of *The Globe and
Mail* on Saturday to find a scathing review. *Vivien
Shaw's photographs are derivative . . . a striking lack of
originality. She should return to her roots as a regional
newspaper photographer.*

Her agent, Frieda Siemens, squeezed her arm. "Stop
panicking."

"Is it that obvious?"

"Not to anyone else, but I know you too well."

"I keep telling you," Patrick said. "You're a very
clever girl. You also look absolutely stunning in that
dress. The green goes so well with your dark hair."

"What would I do without you both? My wonderful
support team," she told them.

"Of course we are. That's our job. Oh, my goodness,"
Patrick said, his voice rising, "there's Genevieve Suarez.
Don't move an inch, darling. Let her come to you. She'll
be thrilled to meet you."

Frieda brayed a laugh as he darted forward to greet
the famous fashion designer. "I'm going to work this
crowd," she said. "Give me a shout if you want me."
She strode away, her broad figure clad in black velvet
trousers and white ruffled shirt carving a way through
the crowd.

Left alone, Vivien turned slowly to survey the exhibition of photographs that represented two years of her
life. CANADIAN FACES: THE NEW MILLENNIUM proclaimed
the banners, but in fact she had taken most of the photographs in the two years that had completed the twentieth
century. Two years of traveling back and forth across
Canada by plane and train and car. As far north as Nunavut. As far south as Windsor. East to Newfoundland,
west to Vancouver Island. She'd learned more about her
own vast, beautiful country than she could ever have

dreamed of knowing. About its people, their hopes for the future, and, particularly in places where mines were closing and fish stocks depleting, their yearning for the past. Now the fruits of her journeys hung on the walls of Patrick's fashionable gallery. Portraits of Canada and Canadians, the mainly black-and-white format stark against the white walls. However, she'd balanced the collection with some color landscapes and a few pictures of people in brilliant ethnic costumes to surprise the observer.

The gathering far exceeded Vivien's expectations. "We'll invite the cream of the crop," Patrick had said several months ago when they were planning the opening. "We'll make it so exclusive that everyone who is anyone will be clamoring for invitations."

When Vivien had protested, saying that most of her photographs were of ordinary working Canadians and that they should be represented, too, Patrick jumped on the idea and decided on a second opening night, with free refreshments and food for anyone who cared to come. Great publicity. But tonight was strictly for the champagne crowd.

Heaven forbid the two should mix, thought Vivien wryly, recalling how she'd had to fight Patrick to make sure her pictures of Toronto street people, their eyes wary and cheeks hollow, were not tucked away in some shadowy corner of the gallery. Hungry people on Toronto's streets was too close to home for this fashionable crowd.

Patrick had also made sure that copies of the book that had been printed to tie in with the exhibition were piled on little tables throughout the gallery, the glossy covers gleaming beneath the bright beam of the halogen floodlights.

As she gazed around, she caught her mother's eye and smiled across the room at her. Her parents had been cornered by Sabrina, Patrick's assistant, who was intro-

ducing them to a woman with flame-red hair. Vivien
knew that her mother and father were even more nervous than she was, if that were possible. Frieda had
made sure that they were kept away from her for the
earlier part of the evening until her nerves settled. Her
father gave her his little punch-of-the-fist sign to signify
Hang in there. She acknowledged it with a quick grin
and then turned away.

A tall man in a dark suit with a tight mass of gray
hair like steel wool was admiring one of her favorite
pictures, while talking animatedly with the younger
woman beside him. The picture was one of several Vivien had taken in a primarily black community in Toronto: four small girls dressed in their Sunday best
skipping rope, while two older boys—also black—
dressed in baggy pants, leaned on a chain-link fence,
jeering at them.

On impulse, Vivien moved across the room to join
them in front of the photograph. The woman turned, her
brown eyes widening when she saw Vivien. She appeared confused, unable to speak. Then she recovered.
"This is a fine picture, Miss Shaw," she said. "I've been
a fan of yours since your first exhibition."

"Thank you." Vivien frowned slightly, wondering if
they had met somewhere before. She didn't recall having
done so, but the woman seemed to know her.

"I'm Janice Greene, a curator at the Royal Ontario Museum," the woman explained in the slightly singsong accent
of the West Indies. "I've been following your career for a
long time." She turned to the tall man beside her. "This
is Mr. Marshall of the Barbados consulate."

"Wesley Marshall," the older man said, holding out a
large hand to Vivien. She felt her hand gripped tightly
and then he turned back to the picture on the wall. "I
know little about photography," he said, "but to me
this"—he indicated the photograph—"is more than just
a picture. It is art."

Warmed by his enthusiastic reaction, Vivien smiled. "It's one of my favorites."

"Taken in Toronto?"

"Yes. The boys were skateboarding on the church steps after the service, and the girls were skipping rope."

"Nothing bad happened?"

"Oh, no. The girls' parents were nearby, chatting together. I think they were members of the choir and had come out from church a little late. So the girls just took out their rope and started skipping."

"But the boys hadn't been in church?" he asked, a small smile tilting the corners of his mouth.

"No. They were at that age when they say, 'No way are we goin' to church, man.' "

"It's all there, in the picture."

"I didn't want it to appear menacing," Vivien said a little anxiously. "Just . . . normal interplay between girls and boys. They didn't mean any harm."

"That's what's so good about it."

She grimaced. "I'm afraid some people will say it's a bit too Norman Rockwell."

"Rubbish! Our boys are depicted in criminal acts so often that they begin to see themselves only that way. It's good to see them as normal children." He turned to Janice Greene, who had been silent but listening intently. "You were right," he told her. "Miss Shaw's work is superb."

"I imagine you live in Toronto if you're at the consulate here?" Vivien said to him.

"That's right. I've been here for three years now. Of course, I have a home on my island as well. I have known Janice's family for many years." He hesitated. "I don't want to take up your time now, Miss Shaw. I can see you're in great demand."

He was right. Vivien could sense people hovering just behind her. And now Patrick was at Mr. Marshall's elbow with Genevieve Suarez. The gallery owner grimaced with impatience as he waited to pounce on Vivien.

"Perhaps I could speak to you later?" Wesley Marshall said hurriedly. "There is something I would like to discuss with you. Professionally," he added. "You came highly recommended by Mrs. Greene."

"Really?" Vivien was intrigued. She waited for some further explanation from Janice, but although the woman's eyes were alert, she seemed reluctant to say anything more. "That sounds very interesting."

"Later," Mr. Marshall repeated with a smile. Taking Janice's elbow, he eased her away into the crowd.

Very much later, when nearly everyone had left, Vivien had forgotten her brief conversation with the man from the Barbados consulate.

It had been a long but extremely successful evening. At least that was what Patrick told her. Vivien was too weary, and also slightly buzzed from several glasses of champagne, to make an assessment. All she knew was that her feet were killing her. The delightful—and horribly expensive—concoction of high heels and thin strips of matte-gold leather she'd bought on impulse were not intended for long-term standing.

She sank into one of Patrick's chrome and black leather chairs, releasing a sigh of relief. She smiled at the sight of Patrick and Frieda sitting in a far corner, knee to knee, an open bottle of champagne on the floor beside them. As usual, they were amicably arguing. How lucky she was to have them.

Her parents beamed down at her. "So?" she said to them. "What do you think?"

"It was absolutely marvelous," her mother gushed, her English accent still dominant after more than thirty years in Canada. "Your best opening ever."

Her father nodded. "Good turnout," he said in his usual low-key way, but she could tell from his smile that he was pleased and—even more important—proud.

The knot in her stomach loosened. Her parents' ambivalence about her work had tempted her not to ask them to come to this exhibition—they had been far happier when she'd been a photographer with the *Winnipeg Free Press,* taking pictures of politicians, local car pile-ups, or the occasional blizzard—but she knew how hurt they would have been had she not invited them to the opening.

"Peter didn't come," her mother said.

Vivien tensed again. "I didn't think he would." She tried to keep her voice light.

"You did send him an invitation?" Even though she and Peter had been divorced for two years, her mother had not given up on the hope that they might get together again.

"Leave it alone, Ellen," Vivien's father said beneath his breath.

Ellen colored and murmured, "Sorry," to Vivien.

"No problem. I didn't think he'd come. Peter always hated my 'artsy crowd,' as he called it."

Just then Vivien caught sight of Wesley Marshall sitting in a quiet corner of the gallery, immersed in one of the exhibition books. "Mr. Marshall," she called to him. "I'm so sorry. I'd forgotten all about you. Come and meet my parents."

He crossed the room to join them.

"Where's Mrs. Greene?" Vivien asked him.

"She had to leave. She asked me to tell you how sorry she was not to speak to you again, but that it had been a great pleasure to meet you."

Vivien found Mr. Marshall's deep, mellifluous voice and slow, measured tones extremely soothing after the high-pitched babble of this evening's crowd. "I'm sorry I wasn't able to say good-bye to her." Vivien turned to her parents. "Mr. Marshall is from the Barbados consulate in Toronto," she explained. "My parents, Ellen and Matthew Carlton," she told him.

"Carlton?" Mr. Marshall repeated.

"Yes, unfortunately there is another professional photographer called Vivien Carlton—actually Vivian with an *a*—so I kept my married name, Shaw, even after my divorce."

As her parents shook hands with him, she noticed how pale her father was, dark smudges of shadow beneath his eyes. Was he okay? Abruptly she said, "There was something you needed to discuss with me, something professional?"

"That is right. I realize this comes somewhat out of the blue, as it were, but Janice has told me all about you and your work, so I was well prepared. In fact, I have already discussed this with other people . . . the minister of tourism in Barbados, for instance."

Discussed what? Vivien wanted to ask. But she recognized that Mr. Marshall was not a man to be rushed. "We have been considering for a while," he continued, "that there is a great need for a good book about Barbados. We have many little histories and some excellent fiction writers, like George Lamming, of course—"

"And Austin Clarke," Vivien added.

"Of course, Austin and Cecil Foster, both of whom live here in Canada and are among our foremost Barbadian ambassadors. But still we feel the need of a . . ." He hesitated. "I hope you won't be offended by this, but what we need is a high-quality coffee-table book about Barbados. One with splendid photographs of the island's beautiful places: the sandy beaches and the great houses. The Bajan people themselves. And, of course, our unique chattel houses."

"Chattel houses?" Vivien asked.

Wesley Marshall laughed. "Obviously you have never been to Barbados." His dark eyes gleamed. "You must be in need of a holiday after all your work on this marvelous exhibition. Why not come and visit our beautiful island? I will have to finalize it with my government, of course, but you would be our guest. Tourism is now one of our main industries and essential to our island's prosperity. This book would be both a souvenir and a selling point for Barbados."

A coffee-table book? Vivien wasn't sure if she should feel insulted. Obviously Wesley Marshall did not intend it as an insult. She could certainly use the money. Since the divorce from Peter, money had been tight. Traveling throughout Canada had been costly. She'd have to sell a great many of her pictures and a great many more copies of her books to keep solvent. But what would a glossy souvenir picture book do to the reputation she had painstakingly built as a serious photographic artist?

Vivien's mother broke in. "Forgive me for interrupting, but weren't you talking about going to Europe in the fall, Vivien?"

"I said I might." Vivien was surprised and annoyed by her mother's rudeness. Also, apart from his nervous habit of clearing his throat, her father hadn't spoken a word since Wesley Marshall had joined them.

"Well, Miss Shaw?"

"I'm not a coffee-table book or pretty calendar type of photographer," Vivien said bluntly. "If I did agree to this assignment, I wouldn't be photographing only the touristy beauty spots. And I'd insist on freedom to choose what should be included in the book."

"That goes without saying. I am fully aware that you are not a calendar photographer," Mr. Marshall said, his tone austere. "I have seen your work, remember?"

Vivien realized she had offended him. "Wouldn't it be better to engage someone who is more . . ." She sought for a tactful way to put it. "Someone from Barbados who would have an intimate knowledge of the island?"

"We hope to engage one of our leading Barbadian writers to collaborate on the book."

"Have you someone in mind?"

"We have."

There was a hesitancy in his voice that puzzled her. "Who is it?"

"Let us say that the writer we have in mind is a creative artist of your own stature. We would prefer not to divulge his name until we are certain he will undertake the project."

So this unknown writer might perhaps share her qualms about doing a "coffee-table" book. "I would prefer to know who my collaborator will be before I agree to take on the project."

"That is understandable. We will do our best to let you know. Whoever the author is, he or she would write about Barbados from his or her own perspective. And you would look at the island with that unique ability and freshness I have seen here tonight in your pictures. Our island is very beautiful, imbued with a history unique in the West Indies."

"You are very persuasive, Mr. Marshall," Vivien told him, smiling. She considered for a moment, trying to blank out the annoying jangle of her mother's keys in her purse.

Ever since she had finished her work on this millennium project she had felt drained, empty. She longed to get out in the field again, her canvas bag of equipment slung over her shoulder. Yet, as always, she had no idea what her new venture would be. To be able to embark on something new and totally fresh was extremely tempting.

"I will think about it and let you know," she told Mr. Marshall, careful not to show him that her interest was already engaged.

"And if I do not hear from you, may I call you?"

"Certainly. Give me one of those cards, would you, Mom? I'll write my number down for you, Mr. Marshall."

Her mother stared at her as if she hadn't understood.

"Could you pass me one of those cards, please," Vivien repeated, an edge to her voice.

It was her father who handed her a gallery card from the black ceramic container without looking up at her.

"Thanks." Vivien scribbled her telephone number on the card and handed it to Mr. Marshall.

"I can call you here, at this number?" he said.

"Yes, but I promise I'll get back to you as soon as I've made my decision."

"Here is my card." Mr. Marshall took one from his wallet and handed it to Vivien.

"Thank you. I'm glad you enjoyed the exhibition."

"It was my great pleasure, I assure you." He shook hands very formally with her and both her parents and then walked to the door, pausing only to exchange a few words with Patrick and Frieda before he left.

During the entire conversation, Vivien had become increasingly aware of the tension emanating from her parents. They'd barely spoken to Wesley Marshall. What on earth was wrong with them?

Seeing how stiffly her father walked across the room, she wondered again if he was okay. He'd been having some angina problems recently. She hoped this evening hadn't been too much for him. Oh, God, she sighed to herself, would there never be a time when she wasn't worrying about her parents . . . and they worrying about her?

As she caught sight of the rain lashing against the gallery windows, the thought of escaping from the gloomy onset of winter to sunny, carefree Barbados became even more enticing.

CHAPTER
TWO

Patrick had arranged a limo to take them home to Vivien's apartment. "Can't have my star charged with driving while impaired with the best Mumm's," he'd said, when Vivien had protested. But the champagne's effect had worn off long before they reached home, and so had the excitement of her success. Her father's silence and her mother's nervous attempts to cover it up were ruining the evening for her.

Eventually, when they were only a few minutes from her apartment, she cut into her mother's chatter. "What was that about?" she demanded.

"What?" her mother asked, looking startled.

"All that stuff when Wesley Marshall joined us. If I didn't know you better, I'd have said you two were racist."

"Of course we're not racist." Her mother drew herself up, her spine stiff with indignation. "How could you say such a thing?"

"Then what exactly was going on?"

Neither of them responded. Vivien saw her mother's glance slide to her father, who sat pressed against the side of the limo, staring out the window as if he were desperate to escape.

Vivien leaned forward. "Dad?" she demanded.

He turned his head, but glanced away from her. "I'm not feeling too good. Damned angina, that's all. Sorry if it spoiled your evening."

Vivien's mother patted his hand and then took it and gripped it in hers. "We didn't like to say anything," she said, giving Vivien a wan smile.

"I wish you had." Vivien was immediately aware of the sharpness in her voice. "I'm so sorry, Dad," she hurriedly added. "I didn't realize you weren't feeling well. It was probably all the people and the excitement in the gallery."

"It was very hot in there."

"Yes, it was." Vivien was swamped with guilt. "Should we stop by a hospital, just to make sure you're okay?"

"No need," her father said. "I've taken my pills. I'll be fine." He turned his head away again to stare out the window.

"Are you sure?"

"I'm sure."

"Okay." Vivien sank back into the cushioned seat. She dreaded being trapped in her small apartment with both of them. Although she was concerned about her father, she was glad they were going home tomorrow.

How often in her life had this happened? Plans canceled, special outings spoiled because of something that had upset her father. The difference was that in those early days it was never anything tangible or physical, like angina. It wasn't that he ever lost his temper; he just withdrew into himself.

Once they were back in her apartment, she tried hard to hide her resentment. If she'd been on her own, she might well have finished the evening off with a large brandy, gone to bed, and pulled the quilt over her head. But then, she thought as she went into the small den to open the sofa bed and change into warm pajamas, if she'd been on her own she'd have felt elated, excited, not engulfed by this wretched pall of gloomy disappointment that always seemed to end their family excursions.

"Can I make some tea?" her mother called from the galley kitchen.

"I'm just coming." Vivien came out, pulling down her pajama top. "You sit down. I'll do it." Then she saw that her mother had already put the kettle on and set cups and saucers and teapot on the tray. The perpetual mother.

But when she carried the tray into the living room, Vivien could understand why her mother had tried to keep busy. Her father was still off in that secret world of his own, his eyes fixed on the copy of *The Globe and Mail* he held open before him, but Vivien could tell from his faraway expression that he wasn't actually reading it.

"Tea, Dad?"

He shook his head, not even bothering to lower the newspaper.

"Okay." Vivien bit into the piece of cake her mother had brought her. "Your fruitcake is as delicious as always, Mom."

Her mother beamed. "I'll send you some more when I get home."

Years ago, Vivien used to enjoy her mother's fruitcake. Now she hated it, but she did her best to eat the piece of rich, heavy cake to please her. As she worked her way through it, tension pervaded the room. She swallowed the last crumbs down with a gulp of hot tea.

"That was a nice-looking man Sabrina introduced us to," her mother said, to fill the silence.

"Which one?"

"Raymond, I think his name was. Is he a friend of yours?"

"Raymond is Jane's husband. Jane was working at the hospital tonight, so Raymond came instead."

"Oh." Her mother's round face sagged with disappointment. Ever since Vivien had broken up with Peter, she had never stopped trying to find her a new husband.

"Are you seriously thinking of taking on this job?" Her mother's question came at her without warning.

Vivien stared at her, then quickly recovered herself. "Yes, I'm seriously considering it. I know the project's not quite my thing, of course, but—"

"Exactly, dear. It really isn't. In fact, I thought that man had some nerve asking a famous artist like you to take photos for some touristy book."

"Famous artist or not, I need assignments, Mom," Vivien said crisply. "As long as I have the final say about what goes into the book, I don't mind."

"But what about this writer you'll have to work with? You know nothing about him."

If she hadn't been so weary, Vivien might have laughed aloud. What did her mother think, that she was going to be carried off by white-slave traders? "You heard what Mr. Marshall said. He's one of the leading writers in Barbados. That's good enough for me. Besides, I can go there for a few days, check it out, and then decide against it, if I want to."

Her mother perched on the edge of her chair. "Isn't it the storm season there at this time of the year? I'm sure Barb Edwards told me they had hurricane warnings there when she went last fall."

Vivien gave her a grim smile. "Just think of all those wonderful storm pictures I'd get. Waves crashing on the beaches, shutters being ripped off—"

Her father flung the newspaper on the floor. Anger sparked in his dark eyes. "Can't you see how worried your mother is?" he shouted.

Vivien was surprised. Her father rarely lost his temper. "I'm sorry, Dad, but I think you're both overreacting. If you hadn't been there when Mr. Marshall spoke to me, I'd have just called you in Winnipeg and told you I was off to Barbados for a week on assignment, and you would have said, 'Fine. Have a great time.' "

She wasn't so sure about that. They both tended to be anxious and overprotective with her, particularly when it came to traveling alone in remote locations. But the Caribbean was hardly remote.

Her father's face had been ashen pale before, but now it was mottled with red. "Sometimes you can be extremely irresponsible, Vivien. You have no idea who this man Marshall actually is. You seem to have swallowed his line without any question . . ."

"For heaven's sake, I'm not a child, Dad. I can check it on Monday, can't I?"

He stared at her, breathing heavily, searching for words. "You are far too impulsive," he said at last.

Her mother took her cue from him. "What about dengue fever?" she demanded. "I'm sure I read that they have mosquitoes that carry dengue fever in the Caribbean now."

Vivien had had enough. "Okay. No more talk about the horrors of traveling," she said briskly. "If you both had your way, I wouldn't go farther than Vancouver. If you'll excuse me, I'm dead tired."

"Vivien, we are only trying—"

"It's been a long, stressful week for me. I'm going to pour myself a brandy and go to bed. If you need more blankets, they're in the closet. Anything else you need?"

Her mother shook her head.

"Okay. Just help yourself to anything. You know your way around here. And don't hesitate to call me if you need me. Night, Mom." She hugged her mother and then bent to put her arms around her father's shoulders. They were as tense as wooden planks. "Night, Dad," she whispered. "It meant so much to have you here for the opening. Hope you feel much better by the morning." He lifted his head. As she bent closer to kiss his cheek, she was dismayed to see that his lips were quivering.

"Night, sweetie," he whispered.

"Be sure to call me if you need me."

Unable to stay in the room one minute longer, Vivien

turned away and hurried down the hall to the den, knowing that it would take her a long time—and more than one brandy—to get to sleep. They're leaving tomorrow, she reminded herself. Then she must get away.

The thought of a week on a tropical island with some fairly easy, lucrative work thrown in was heaven. She'd speak to Frieda, discuss it with her. If Frieda thought it was a good idea, she'd accept Mr. Marshall's invitation, and tell him she was available to leave as soon as everything was arranged.

The following morning, as soon as she got home from taking her parents to the airport, Vivien called Frieda at her home to tell her about the Barbados idea. Frieda had been her agent for the past five years. She was far more than an agent. Friend and counselor, she had guided and supported Vivien through those difficult times when she'd first come to Toronto, without a job and with very little money.

To her surprise, Frieda was all for her doing the Barbados book. "What have you got to lose?" she shouted down the phone. Frieda was rather like a burly sergeant major, but her hectoring was balanced by great warmth and kindness.

"I'm concerned that doing this kind of book will harm my image as a serious photographer."

"That's a load of crap. Any exposure is good, as long as you retain artistic control and the book will be printed by reputable art publishers. Of course, it also depends on the quality of the text. But you can leave all that stuff to me," Frieda told Vivien. "That's what you pay me for."

"I'd prefer to speak to Mr. Marshall myself."

"Sure. Fine. You do that, but then get him to call me. He can put me in touch with whoever is going to be in charge of this project. Then we can get down to business."

Vivien smiled to herself after she ended the call.
Frieda was worth every penny of her fifteen percent.
But her smile faded as she thought again of her parents,
particularly her father. What was it about Barbados that
made him so irrationally anxious?

CHAPTER THREE

By the third week of October, when the leaves had started to fall and Vivien had scraped the frost off her windshield a few times, it was all arranged. She would fly down to Barbados and stay there for a week—all expenses paid, as a guest of the Barbados Ministry of Tourism—and then, once she'd had the chance to check things out, she'd sign a full contract to do the book.

Her only problem had been that they still hadn't engaged a writer for the project, but Frieda had persuaded her to accept the deal. "They've assured me they're negotiating with a high-profile writer. Besides, who cares? Your pictures are what will sell this book."

Two days before she was due to leave, Frieda called her. "I've got your partner's name," she said, without any greeting.

"What?"

"It's me, Frieda," Frieda shouted.

"I know that, you idiot," Vivien said, laughing.

"I've been able to screw the name of your writer out of them. They've faxed me from Barbados."

"About time. Who is it, the writer, I mean?"

"A David Moreton. Ever heard of him?"

"No, I haven't."

"I looked him up. Very impressive. Literary novelist. Won—or short-listed for—several literary prizes. Professor of Literature at the University of the West Indies."

"Well, that's a relief."

"He's written three novels, plus edited a couple of collections of short stories by Caribbean writers."

"I wonder what he's like."

"Who cares? I don't suppose you'll even meet him. He'll probably just send you a copy of his text when it's ready."

"I sincerely hope not. Wesley Marshall talked about us being collaborators, and that's the way I want it to be."

"Want me to call him to confirm that you will be consulting with this David Moreton?"

"No, I'll do it." Vivien released a sigh. "Then I'd better call my parents to tell them I'm definitely leaving on Saturday."

"I take it that they've accepted that you're going by now?"

"Sort of. Not happy about it, of course. You know them. They always make such a fuss when I go away." But it was different this time, Vivien thought uneasily. This time there was a sense of desperation about their protests.

"They need to get a life," Frieda said. "Every time I meet your mom and dad, I thank God I'm not an only child."

"They've been worse than ever this time."

"You don't need the hassle. Don't call them—just go."

Vivien groaned. "I'd like to, but I couldn't. Especially now that Dad has this angina problem."

"Good luck. Call me later and let me know how it goes with Mr. Marshall, okay? Gotta go."

Frieda rang off before Vivien could say any more. She glanced at her watch. She was due to lecture on digital versus traditional photography at Hart House in an hour. That gave her enough time to call Wesley Marshall. However, when she dialed his number at the consulate, she got his answering machine with a message saying he'd be away for a few days and to leave a message for his secretary.

"Damn!" Vivien muttered. What was the point of leaving a message if he wasn't there? She'd been given a name and a contact number at the Barbados Ministry of Tourism and a driver was to meet her at the airport when she arrived.

She hesitated and then reached for the telephone again, tensing her shoulders as she steeled herself to say good-bye to her parents.

So all the travel brochures and guide books were right, thought Vivien, as her plane approached Barbados. The weather was perfect, the sky a brilliant blue with only a few puffs of white cloud. Somehow her mother's repeated warnings of storms and hurricanes at this time of the year had lodged in her mind, but as the plane descended, the sun blazed down on a vivid turquoise sea.

It would be good to move again after sitting for almost six hours, but she hadn't wasted time during the flight. She'd read an abridged version of the history of Barbados, trying to cram in as much information as she could before she arrived. She'd also read David Moreton's long introduction to a short-story collection he had edited. She didn't want to appear totally ignorant when she met him. His credentials were impressive: winner of the Commonwealth Writers Prize and a guest lecturer at Oxford University, among other accomplishments. There was an ironic tone to his writing that made her smile, but it also caused her to wonder even more why a renowned writer would engage himself in creating a text for a coffee-table picture book.

I'm not going to worry about it, she told herself as she

hurriedly stowed away the books and her bottle of water
in her bag. She was here to enjoy herself, make some
money, and immerse herself in a totally different
environment.

This one was certainly different, she thought later on,
as she waited for her bag in an area open to the outside.
She'd imagined that Barbados Airport would be quiet,
relaxed, but the baggage retrieval area was as chaotic as
those in most North American airports. The difference
was that here the echoing enclosure was filled with the
music of a calypso band and the good-natured shouts
from the porters, and the air was steamy hot . . . the
tropical atmosphere a combination of moisture, rich
earth, and ripe vegetation.

Carefully placing her precious equipment bag at her
feet, she was about to lug her soft-sided bag off the
carousel when she heard someone behind her say,
"Allow me, Miss Shaw."

Vivien spun around to find Wesley Marshall standing
behind her. "What are you doing here?" she said, surprised but also delighted to see him.

He nodded to the porter beside him to take her bag.
"I decided to come home for a few days, so that I could
be here to greet you." He gave her his broad smile. "A
little surprise for you."

"It certainly is." So pleased was she to see a familiar
face that she felt an impulse to hug him. "I called you
in Toronto but got your machine."

"Forgive me. I should have called you before I left
Canada. Let me drive you to your hotel, get you settled
in," he said as he led the way to the exit. "Then, if
you're not too tired from the journey, perhaps you
would care to come for dinner tonight at our home? My
wife, Sarah, is very much looking forward to meeting
you."

"That's very kind of you . . . and your wife." Actually,
Vivien had hoped to be able to crash out, have a light
meal, get to bed early.

"I've invited David as well. I thought you would like to meet him."

So much for Frieda's suggestion that the writer would merely send in his text for the book. "Oh . . . that's great." Vivien knew that her response was cool, but she would have preferred not to meet her collaborator until she'd read more of his writing and also done more research on his homeland. She would also have preferred to spend a day or so exploring the island for herself, getting the feel of it, before they met.

"What if I decide not to take the assignment after I've spent a week here?" she asked him bluntly. "Won't that make it rather awkward, with David Moreton, I mean?"

Wesley frowned. "I don't think so. You see, David, too, hasn't made a definite decision to take this on. It will probably depend on how well you get along together."

"Who's assessing whom?" Vivien asked, an edge to her voice.

Wesley looked amused. "Let's say it's a mutual assessment. Would you prefer to postpone it? Perhaps you feel too tired?"

"Of course not." Vivien felt she'd been offered a challenge, and she wasn't about to run away from it. "I'd love to come to dinner. And I'm really looking forward to meeting David Moreton."

Wesley cleared his throat. "I must warn you, David can be a . . . a little formidable at first."

"Really? In what way?"

"Ah, here we are," Wesley said, indicating the large black car at the curb. As soon as the driver saw them, he opened the rear door and Vivien slid into air-conditioned comfort.

"I feel like some visiting dignitary," she told Wesley as he sat beside her.

"You are," he said. "Very much so."

She smiled in response. She had hoped to pursue the topic of David Moreton, but the driver's presence was a

deterrent. As they set off on the journey to her resort
hotel on the east coast, she sat back, only half listening
to Wesley's smooth voice describing the places they were
passing. She gazed out eagerly, first taking in the ram-
shackle buildings around the airport, then the lush
greenness beyond it, fields where black-bellied sheep
grazed, palm trees swaying in the hot tropical breeze.

After a while they left the highway and the roads dete-
riorated. In places they were so badly pitted with potholes that the driver didn't even try to avoid them,
letting the well-sprung car bounce in and out, swerving
occasionally to dodge the larger holes that could wreck
a wheel.

"We are famous for our roads," Wesley said with a
wry smile.

"I can see why."

"The government is addressing the problem," he
added.

None too soon, Vivien thought.

Now they were passing through a more rural area.
Large fields spread on both sides of the narrow road, the
rich earth covered in fresh, green, shoulder-high shoots.

"Sugarcane," Wesley told her.

Vivien was surprised. "I was expecting it to be much
taller. One book I read said it was so tall you couldn't
see where you were going."

"It varies. This is the new crop. We have recently
harvested our summer crop. Now the new one is growing. By the end of the year, it will be tall again and all
the tourists will be getting themselves lost." Wesley gave
a throaty chuckle.

They passed a bus stop, where a group of young girls,
chattering like a flock of birds, waited for a bus. They
were dressed in a school uniform of blue tunics and crisp
white blouses, some of them with their hair plaited in
neat pigtails. Apart from their dark faces, it could have
been a scene from rural England.

Occasionally the car passed little communities of small, brightly painted houses and a larger building, which Wesley told her was the local rum shop or bar. Men sat on the plain wooden benches outside, their faces glistening in the heat.

In less than half an hour, the car swung through the open iron gates of the Ocean Sands Resort and drove slowly down the extended avenue of large palm trees. Vivien sat forward, eager to see as much as possible. "This is so beautiful," she said, taking in the shady gardens and the hibiscus hedges covered with brilliant yellow blossoms. She felt herself relax beneath the spell of the moist heat and exotic scents. Yet she also felt a stirring of uneasiness at being cut off from the real Barbados beyond the security gates. Despite the lush beauty of the place, she had the feeling she would not find the real Barbados here.

"The resort should not be too busy at this time of the year," Wesley said as they drew up before the imposing main building. "Most British and American children are back at school now." He guided her up the steps into the hotel office to register.

A young man, expensively dressed, heavy gold chains about his neck and wrists, was arguing with the desk clerk. The man's wife, clad in silk shorts and top, watched him. "I want one of the special rooms in this building," he demanded.

"I'm sorry, sir. As I've told you, there are none available," the desk clerk told him.

"I want to see the manager." The man spoke like someone used to getting instant attention. A pop music star or a sports idol, Vivien conjectured.

"He's engaged at the moment," the clerk said frostily.

"But I'm from Jamaica, man," the man protested.

"Well, that don' make no difference here," the clerk drawled. The lapse from his previously crisp and perfect English into the local vernacular made Vivien smile. She made a mental note, which she would later transfer to her notebook, about the dichotomy of the formal and informal speech. "Please excuse me, sir," the clerk said, reverting to formality. He turned from the irate guest. "Can I help you?" he asked Vivien.

Still muttering about insisting on seeing the manager, the man retreated to the lobby.

Within a few minutes, Vivien had registered. A mechanized cart drove her and Wesley to one of the resort buildings. They were then taken to a large room on the third floor with a balcony that overlooked the pool and, beyond it, the ocean.

"Is this to your liking?" Wesley asked anxiously, as if he sensed her hesitation about the resort.

"It's lovely." Vivien surveyed the room, the cool tiled floor, the fresh white and pale green colors, and the comfortably cushioned white rattan chairs. "I'm not used to such luxury," she hurriedly explained. "When I was on the road for my Canadian project, I stayed with ordinary people . . . bed-and-breakfast sort of thing."

"I understand," Wesley said, but Vivien wasn't sure he did. He checked the clothes closet, opening the door, peering inside.

"It's great," she assured him.

"Good. Forgive me for checking. Experience tells me that sometimes there are not enough hangers in hotel rooms. Now I will let you rest. I will send the driver for you again at six o'clock. He will meet you outside the main building, where reception is. Will that be suitable for you?"

"Perfect."

"I am glad. We want you to feel at home in Barbados." Wesley gave one last anxious glance around the room, then shook hands with her and left.

As the door closed behind him, Vivien released a sigh of relief and threw herself onto the king-size bed. Much as she liked Wesley Marshall and had been glad to see him at the airport, she would have preferred to experience her first impressions of Barbados alone, not to have had to filter them through his constant stream of explanation. This was a working holiday, and she'd hoped to make notes during the journey to the hotel, even take preparatory pictures.

She frowned, wondering why a stranger—however kind and avuncular—would go to so much trouble to make sure she had arrived and was safely settled into her hotel room. For a while, she'd felt like a child traveling alone, being met—and carefully watched.

You're getting as paranoid as Mom and Dad, she told herself. Shaking her head, she jumped up, grabbed her bag, and took out her loose-leaf daybook. Time to make a few notes while things were fresh in her mind. *Hibiscus hedges,* she wrote. *Kids in uniform. Rum shops. Potholes!*

Tomorrow she'd put on shorts and a T-shirt and rent a car so that she could escape from the resort, explore, and get the feel of this island. Tonight she would have to dress up, put on her social face, and be entertained.

And meet her collaborator, David Moreton.

She felt a thrill of anticipation. Although she'd wanted to get all the preparatory work done first, to appear as knowledgeable about Barbados as possible, it would also be exciting to meet this writer, establish a connection with him from the very start.

She also felt a qualm of concern. She was confident about her ability as a photographer, but this would be the first time she'd be working with an established writer. In her previous books, her photographs had spoken eloquently for themselves. This time, she suspected, from having read some of his writing, if she wasn't assertive, she could end up being merely an illustrator of David Moreton's words.

"No way," she muttered, flinging herself off the bed. "We'll be equals, or they can forget the whole thing."

Once Vivien had hung up her clothes and had a shower, she began to feel more relaxed. Wrapping herself in the thick white bathrobe, she lay down on the bed, hoping that an hour or so's sleep might refresh her. She lay there, concentrating on the surge of the Atlantic Ocean, the constant soothing *coo* of the small brown doves she could see through the open glass doors, perched on the railing of her balcony. Gradually, her body grew heavy, and she let herself drift away.

As soon as Wesley let himself into his apartment, he shut himself away in his office. Although his wife wasn't home from the university yet, he thought it best to make sure she wouldn't walk in and overhear him. Sarah did not approve of what he was doing.

He punched in the number. The phone rang twice and was then picked up. "Hello?"

"Wesley," he said succinctly. "She's here."

He could hear the release of breath at the other end. "Good. What—"

"I don't want to talk now. Sarah might come in. We'll talk tomorrow."

"Right. See you later, then."

"Yes." Wesley set down the receiver and then mopped his face with his white handkerchief. He had set the wheels in motion. What happened now was in God's hands.

CHAPTER
FOUR

Vivien was waiting at the front entrance of the hotel at six o'clock, as planned. She'd decided to wear the new lemon-and-black jungle print skirt with a black top. As she watched the other guests passing by, dressed in shorts or swimsuits, she was very much aware of being just another one of the mainly white tourists staying here.

Sitting on the hotel balcony, she had heard all kinds of accents as people passed by: British, American, French . . . She'd also read the lineup for this evening at the activity center. A local children's choir and a steel-pan band. Very atmospheric, she was sure, but whether it represented the real Barbados was another question. She'd read that there was an old house nearby that was an important part of the history of Barbados. She looked forward to touring the place with a local guide, but even that, she imagined, was only a small part of this unique island's colorful past. There must be more to Barbados than steel-pan music and ancient colonial houses.

She decided then and there that she should ask Wesley about moving to a bed-and-breakfast place somewhere outside the exclusive gates of the Ocean Sands Resort.

A sleek, black car drew up before the hotel with Wesley's driver at the wheel. She gathered up her bag and her compact Leica camera, and ran down the tiled steps.

The Marshalls' home was in an apartment complex in the busier part of the island, near Bridgetown. "We'd prefer to live in St. Philip or St. James, but having our home here makes it easier for me to get to the airport, when I commute from Canada," Wesley explained, having welcomed Vivien in the foyer of the complex. "My wife still teaches some linguistics courses at the university, so she spends more time on the island than I do."

When they reached his apartment, his wife, Sarah, came down the wide hallway to greet Vivien. She was almost as tall as her husband, elegantly dressed in a forest-green long silk dress, her thick gray hair coiled around her head like a coronet. "Welcome to Barbados, Miss Shaw," she said, her voice deep and musical. "Please come in."

Vivien followed Sarah down the hallway and into a large, airy living room that looked out over the bay. Caribbean art brightened the white walls, and exquisite coral limestone carvings stood in small niches. Vivien wanted to examine them more closely, but people were waiting to meet her: a man and a white woman of her own age, and an older man, in his fifties perhaps. As she entered, they turned in anticipation to look at her. Outside, on the terrace, stood another man, his back to them. For a moment, everyone seemed to freeze. No one moved. No one spoke.

Then Wesley said, raising his voice, "David, come and meet Vivien Shaw, the renowned photographer."

Vivien flinched. Announced in Wesley's booming voice, it sounded too much like a flourish of trumpets for her liking.

David Moreton turned, about to come into the room. Then he halted abruptly, his smile fading. The dark eyes that had seemed ready to echo the Marshalls' welcome narrowed.

He stepped inside the open glass doors but did not advance any farther into the room. His gaze slid past Vivien to fix itself stonily on Wesley. "*This* is the photographer you've chosen for my book about Barbados?"

Vivien felt anger rising in her at his scathing tone. What was his problem? Surely Wesley had told Moreton that she was a woman. And what was all this "my book" business?

Wesley stood his ground. "I told you that Miss Shaw is one of the finest photographic artists in the world. And she is."

"You certainly did tell me that, but—"

Vivien stepped forward, prepared to do battle. "Didn't Mr. Marshall tell you I was a woman?"

David Moreton turned to her with perceptible reluctance. "I have no objection whatsoever to working with a woman, Miss Shaw," he said coldly, carefully enunciating each word. "What my good friend Wesley omitted to tell me was that the renowned Canadian photographer he had chosen to work on a book about Barbados, a Caribbean island that has a ninety-five percent black or mixed population, was a *white* woman."

Vivien could feel the blood rush into her face, then heat surging through her body. The room had gone very quiet and felt airless, as if all the oxygen had been sucked out of it. Wesley touched her arm, but she drew herself away and stood, holding herself erect, confronting the man in the doorway.

"That was very rude, David." The voice was Sarah Marshall's. "Most especially as Miss Shaw is our honored guest." She might have been chiding an unruly child.

David Moreton inclined his head in Sarah's direction. "You are right. I was extremely rude," he admitted, to Vivien's surprise. "I apologize, Miss Shaw. It is not your fault, but Wesley's, that you were chosen for this book. If you will permit me, I shall try to explain to you why—although you are undoubtedly a fine artist—you are not the right person for this particular project."

"I don't think that will be necessary," Vivien said in a glacial voice. "You've already made it perfectly clear. I'm white." She lifted her chin. "I've heard about reverse discrimination but never experienced it before now."

"Why should you have? You live in a white world, where you belong, where you are accepted. Our people have struggled for centuries to assert ourselves, to be in control, against a tiny but powerful white minority."

Vivien heard a heavy sigh from behind her, but she had no idea where it came from. She stood, tense as stretched steel, waiting for David Moreton to finish his diatribe.

"When Wesley and I discussed the creation of this book, we agreed it would be not only for tourists but also for the people of Barbados to enjoy. That it should reflect a Barbados of which its people could be proud, not merely a glossy volume of pretty pictures for holiday makers to take home and put on their glass-topped tables—"

"And that was exactly what I told Mr. Marshall," Vivien broke in, her breath coming fast. "That I was not a coffee-table book photographer. That the photographs I chose for this book would reflect the reality of the places and people on this island."

"Exactly," Wesley said. "That is what Miss Shaw told me. Now, David, excuse me, but we have other guests waiting to meet her."

David seemed not to have heard him. His penetrating gaze fixed on Vivien. "Ah, but however gifted Miss Shaw might be, these places and people would be seen through a white perspective. Alien eyes."

Vivien took a step closer to him, fighting to remain as

cool as he appeared to be, despite his hostility. "They would be the eyes of a fellow human being, seeing your beautiful island with a fresh perspective."

He flashed his dazzling smile at her, but there was no corresponding warmth in his dark brown eyes. "Forgive me, but I am sure that we have several supremely talented photographers in Barbados with an intimate knowledge of our island and its people. Someone who could take just as pretty pictures as you, Miss Shaw."

It was a deliberate challenge.

"I think we should change the subject," Sarah said firmly. "Wesley, dear, take David away to cool off before we eat. Please come and meet our friends, Miss Shaw."

Vivien hesitated, unwilling to leave the fight unfinished, but her instincts told her that this was a battle that would not be easily won—on either side. She wasn't sure she wanted to become embroiled in it. She loathed any kind of conflict, yet the example of her father retreating into his shell to escape from the most minor of arguments had taught her not to run away from a fight but to stand her ground. Although she was tempted to tell them all to get lost, march from the room, and catch the next flight home to Toronto, she knew that would be seen as giving in to this infuriating man.

"We'll talk about this later," she told David, accepting the challenge.

She turned . . . and for a fleeting moment felt a spasm of panic when she saw that she and the one younger woman were the only white people in the room. Now, for the first time in her life, she realized how it must feel to be a member of a minority group, to live in a society where you were different from everyone else.

"I am so very sorry," Sarah Marshall said in a low voice in her ear as Wesley stepped out onto the terrace with David, sliding the glass door shut behind them.

"Please don't be." Vivien summoned up a wry smile.

"He does have a point," she conceded, "even if his timing was rotten."

"Yes, well, let me introduce our friends to you." Mrs. Marshall indicated the white-haired older man, who inclined his head to Vivien. "This is Mr. George Collins from the National Cultural Foundation."

"Welcome to Barbados, Miss Shaw. We must apologize—"

"Please don't say any more about it."

"Don't you worry. Leave it to us. We will work it all out."

No, thought Vivien. *I will work it out.* They'd have to get a new writer. She couldn't possibly work with such an arrogant, antagonistic man. If they refused to engage a new writer, she'd be flying back to Canada tomorrow.

"May I introduce my assistant, Celeste Beaton?" Mr. Collins said, indicating the younger woman.

Vivien shook hands with the attractive young woman whose black hair curled crisply around her head. Despite the breeze from the ceiling fan, Celeste's face glistened from the heat. Her palms, too, were moist. "Welcome to our island, Miss Shaw," she said, squeezing Vivien's hand fervently.

"Thank you." Vivien had thought Celeste was white, but now that she was closer to her, she saw that her skin was the color of creamy coffee, her eyes a dark caramel.

"This is my husband, Joseph," Celeste said, introducing the large young man, who looked as if he could be a linebacker on a football team.

Joseph grinned as he crunched Vivien's hand in his. "You are most welcome to Barbados, Miss Shaw."

Trying not to wince with pain, Vivien drew her hand away. It tingled from his tight grip.

"Excuse me," said Mr. Collins. "I'm going to act as umpire outside." He slid the glass door open and went out, closing the door behind him.

"Now you have met everyone," Sarah Marshall said.

"If you will excuse me, Miss Shaw, I will leave you in Celeste's good hands while I check on the dinner."

Vivien felt a knot of tension at the back of her neck. "Thank you" was all she said.

Celeste indicated the couch, and Vivien sat down with Celeste beside her. Although the glass door was closed, it was hard to ignore the raised voices from the terrace. Vivien was acutely aware that the men outside were arguing about her, about her participation in the project that was the only reason for her being here. What a bizarre situation . . .

She was prepared to go through this farce of a dinner, to be as polite as possible, but, afterward, she was determined to get the matter settled tonight, however long it took.

"David was wrong to speak to you in that way," Celeste said in her soft childlike voice, when she realized that Vivien was preoccupied.

"Do you know David Moreton well?"

"Not really, but Joseph went to school with him."

Joseph grinned. "David was into mind stuff; I was into sports." Vivien could believe it. Joseph Beaton seemed out of place in this elegant room, yet there was a quiet confidence about him that suggested a contented nature. When Celeste took up the conversation, he seemed quite happy to pick up a copy of the *Barbados Nation* and settle himself in a chair in a corner of the room, reading.

Celeste leaned forward eagerly. "Wesley said there was a large crowd at the opening of your exhibition in Toronto, Miss Shaw. How I wish I could have seen it!" Her eyes glowed. "He promised to lend me a copy of your book."

"I hope you enjoy it," Vivien said politely, finding Celeste's enthusiasm a little overwhelming.

"I have already. He showed it to me in the office." Celeste took a deep breath. "The photographs are superb. I wonder . . ." she hesitated, with a little grimace

of embarrassment, then continued, "I wonder if you
would like to come to my home for tea one day, so that
my mother and grandmother could meet you?"

Vivien didn't know what to say. "I'm not sure—"

"I know you're not going to be here very long, but it
would be so wonderful if you could come."

There was such an air of intense expectancy about her
request that Vivien couldn't resist. Besides, it would be
a great opportunity to visit a Barbadian home, perhaps
take some pictures. "I'd love to come," she said, smiling.

Celeste clapped her hands together like a child. "Oh,
I am so glad. Joseph!" she said, raising her voice to
reach him behind his newspaper, "Miss Shaw has said
she will come to tea with us. Isn't that wonderful?"

He lowered the paper. "Good," he said, grinning at
them. "Let me know when, and I will pick you up,
Miss Shaw."

Although she was rather taken aback by Celeste's fervor, Vivien couldn't resist the Beatons' warmth. "Please
call me Vivien, not Miss Shaw."

To her surprise, Celeste's eyes became watery, and she
felt her hand squeezing hers. "That is so kind of you."

Vivien wasn't used to such warm demonstrations of
friendship from strangers. She was inclined to think that
Celeste was some kind of celebrity groupie, yet her
warmth seemed genuine, if a little too intense.

To her relief, Sarah Marshall came back into the room
to announce that dinner was ready, summoning the men
from the balcony while Vivien and the Beatons moved
into the dining section of the large room. "What a beautiful table," Vivien said, gazing at the long, highly polished expanse of wood laid with exquisite crystal glasses
and white-and-gilt china.

"Thank you. It was a wedding gift from Wesley's
grandmother, made from Barbados mahogany." Sarah
turned. "Ah, there you are," she said as her husband,
David, and George Collins reentered the room. "David,

come sit beside me," she ordered, pointing to the chair beside hers.

"So you can keep an eye on me, make sure I behave?" he teased, smiling his thousand-watt smile at Sarah.

"Precisely," she responded, pointedly enunciating each syllable.

Vivien envied the easy rapport between them. Possibly David Moreton was a charming, intelligent man. Still, he had a hang-up about white people and she didn't think anything would change that. *I'd sure as hell like to get the chance to prove to him that I'm the best person to do this job,* she thought, gritting her teeth as she stared down at her place setting. But she didn't want to work with David Moreton on this book, did she? So how was she going to prove anything to him if he was pulled from the project?

She looked up from the table . . . to catch him watching her intently. For a brief moment their eyes locked. Then she turned away to speak to George Collins at her side.

The dinner was probably delicious, but to Vivien everything turned to sawdust in her mouth. She was so tense that the chilled consommé, followed by goujons of local fish and then roulades of pork in a creole sauce with fragrant rice all seemed to taste the same.

Throughout the meal the tension in the room was tangible. The Marshalls and their friends worked hard to smooth the situation but skirted around the issue that was uppermost in all their minds. It all had a weirdly surrealistic feeling.

The evening dragged on interminably. Vivien didn't need to be reminded of the time by the rosewood clock on the sideboard. She was painfully aware of each minute as it ticked away.

Eventually, though, as she was sipping iced coffee on the wide terrace, accompanied by the constant buzz of the insects, it was not she but David Moreton who cracked first.

"This is ridiculous," he said, sliding back his chair and jumping up as if he'd suddenly exploded. "We have to settle this."

"Now is not the time," Wesley said in an undertone.

"Of course it isn't," Sarah agreed, frowning at David.

"I'm sorry, but I think he's right," Vivien said, firmly setting down her glass on the ceramic-topped table. "I for one want some kind of decision made before I go back to the hotel." She glanced at her watch. "And it's now almost ten o'clock."

"Wouldn't it be better to leave it until tomorrow?" Sarah said. "When you've had a good sleep?"

"That's right," Celeste said. "Everyone sees things differently after a good night's sleep."

Vivien was surprised by Celeste's earnest tone. What did she care? "I don't think a night's sleep is going to make any difference. Mr. Moreton is determined not to work with me. And, obviously, that makes it impossible for me to work with him." This time she did not avoid looking at David Moreton. "One of us will have to back out of the project."

"And you think it should be me?" he asked, his voice rising in incredulity.

"Why not? You're the one making the objections."

Sighing, Wesley shook his head. "If you both insist on discussing this tonight, I suggest we go into my study."

He reluctantly led the way down the hall into a smaller room lined with books, and they followed him. It was cozier, more relaxed than the rest of the apartment, and Vivien imagined Wesley being able to kick off his shoes, put up his feet on the desk in here, which would probably not be permitted elsewhere by his regal wife.

Although Vivien sat in the chair Wesley indicated, David refused to sit. He paced like a caged panther to the window and then turned to face them. "I would remind you again, Miss Shaw, that my objections were not to you personally, but to your . . . lack of the necessary background for this book."

"That sounds far less racist than *I object to her because she's white,* but it comes to the same thing, doesn't it?"

"Hardly," he said with a shrug, "but if that is how you want to interpret it . . ."

His nonchalance infuriated Vivien. Again, heat suffused her face, but Wesley broke in before she could respond.

"Now, let me say one thing here. I chose you, both of you, because you were the best people for this project. David is a writer of great sensitivity, with a passion for the history of the Bajan people. Vivien . . . I hope you will not mind me calling you Vivien," Wesley said, with a little nod in her direction.

"Of course not," she murmured.

"Vivien is a gifted artist, with a keen eye for the unusual, the uniqueness of people and places. However, neither of you really knows much about each other's work."

"Oh, surely Miss Shaw read all my literary work before she agreed to come to Barbados?" David drawled, his voice dripping acid.

Vivien smiled at him. "For one thing, Mr. Moreton, I was not told who the author of the book was to be until this past week. For that reason, I only had time to read one of your introductions to a short story collection."

"I see." He said no more, but the little smile suggested that it hardly constituted much of an effort on her part to know his work.

"And what have you seen of my work?" she demanded.

"There's no reason you have to make a decision tonight," Wesley said hurriedly.

"Which one of us are you talking to?" demanded David.

"Both of you. Spend some time together. Discuss what

this book would mean to you. See if you can find any common ground."

Vivien hesitated. She didn't want to work with this man. Yet, at the same time, she wanted to prove to him that art could transcend the color of one's skin.

"I could find a suitable photographer tomorrow," David said, determined to fire the last salvo, but now it sounded petty. He seemed to recognize that himself and, in what appeared to be a small gesture of surrender, he sank into a chair, stretching out his long legs, and gazed out the window.

Vivien stood. "It's obvious that we're not getting anywhere, and it's been a long day." She gave Wesley a weary smile. "If you don't mind, I think I'll go back to the hotel."

"Where are you staying?" David asked.

"The Ocean Sands."

He rolled his eyes. "Ah, the pride of the all-inclusive tourist resorts with the innocuous but free-flowing rum punches."

"I prefer staying in bed-and-breakfast places myself," Vivien said, bristling. "But Wesley kindly booked me there," she added hastily, not wanting to hurt her host's feelings.

"It is one of our best hotels," Wesley protested.

"I'm sure it is," David said. "But you certainly won't see much of the real Barbados there. But then, what's new? Most of the tourists who stay in these resorts don't set foot outside the gates, except to go to and from the airport."

Vivien had had enough. She picked up her bag. "I have a beautiful room with a large comfortable bed. At the moment, that's all I'm interested in."

"I'll drive you there. I live on the east side of the island."

Vivien was taken aback. She didn't want to be confined alone in a car with this man. She was about to tell him that Wesley's driver would take her back, but Wesley jumped at the idea. "Good thinking. The hotel's on David's way. He lives a short distance from Bathsheba, north of the hotel."

Within a very short time, Vivien found herself racing along the highway in a canary-yellow Mustang convertible, the night wind blowing against her face. She sat as far forward as possible, resisting the impulse to clutch the side of her seat. Although David's eyes were fixed on the road, one hand casually moved the steering wheel and the other hand drummed on his thigh to the reggae beat issuing from the stereo.

He glanced at her. "Relax. I could drive this road blindfolded. That's the trouble with living on a small island. You travel the same roads over and over again."

"You live here year-round?"

"Not anymore. I also teach at the university's campus in Jamaica. And I spend a few weeks in England, doing some West Indian literature courses at Oxford University."

"So you travel a great deal."

"Lord, girl," he drawled. "I does get around some. I's a college boy, you see."

Vivien wasn't sure whether she should take him seriously or not. Then he laughed. "You sure is uptight, girl," he taunted her. Vivien was beginning to realize that Barbadians had two languages: their very correct, almost old-fashioned English and their colorful colloquial tongue, which they used between themselves or when they wanted to tease people.

"Can you blame me," she retorted, "considering your reaction to me this evening?"

"No, I suppose not. But seeing you was a shock. Wesley was sneaky. He knew how I'd react, so he never even hinted that you were white." He shook his head. "I have known Wesley Marshall since I was a small boy.

I still cannot fathom why he chose a white woman from Canada for this book."

Vivien's shoulders tensed. "I'd prefer not to discuss that subject again tonight."

He glanced sideways at her. "We'll have to deal with it sometime soon."

He was right. A short time ago she'd been determined that David Moreton would have to go. But now she felt an increased desire, almost a feeling of excitement, to prove to him how well she could fulfill Wesley Marshall's faith in her.

"Who is Frank Worrel?" she asked, catching sight of a large sign at a roundabout.

"He's a famous Bajan cricketer."

"Oh," Vivien said dismissively.

"Cricket is not only a sport in Barbados, Miss Shaw. It's a religion, an obsession." He didn't add that if she was from Barbados she would have known that, but it echoed in his voice.

"Did you know all those people at the Marshalls'?" she asked, quickly changing the subject.

"I knew them all except George Collins."

"Celeste mentioned that you went to school with her husband."

"Yes, Joseph and I were at school together. And on the subject of cricket, Joseph Beaton is a member of our international cricket team. A famous batsman. He also freelances in Australia and England."

"Oh, I see." But she still couldn't understand why Joseph and Celeste had been at the dinner. "I don't know too much about cricket, but I know more than most Canadians. My parents were born in England, and my father used to play the game when he was a young boy."

"It wouldn't be too popular in Canada, I suppose, with your perpetual winter."

She twisted sideways to confront him. "I'll have you

know we have extremely hot summers and beautiful falls in Canada and—"

He was laughing at her again. "I know that." He sighed and shook his head. "If we are even going to think about working together, you will have to stop taking me quite so seriously, Miss Shaw."

She was very aware of how close they were in the confines of the car. Biting her lip, she stared straight ahead. Then, returning to the previous conversation, she said, "I suppose the only reason the Beatons were asked to dinner is because Celeste is George Collins's assistant."

"She certainly didn't contribute much to the conversation."

"How would you know? You were out on the terrace most of the time before dinner. In fact, Celeste asked me to come and visit her home for tea."

David cast a quizzical look at her. "Did you accept her invitation?"

"Yes, I did."

"Good. Bajans are very hospitable people. She would have been hurt if you had refused to go."

Vivien was glad she hadn't told him that one of her reasons for accepting was that it would enable her to visit a Bajan home and possibly get some pictures. It might have sounded a little too cold and calculating.

Once they'd passed the airport, the road became more rural. It was a dark night and the sugarcane fields closed in on them on both sides, making Vivien feel claustrophobic.

"Okay?" David asked when she shivered involuntarily.

"Of course," she responded brightly. The car sped down the narrow road, bouncing in and out of the potholes. "I thought I'd rent a car," she said breathlessly. "But now I'm not so sure."

David laughed. "Sorry. Want me to slow down?"

"Would it help?"

"If you mean the potholes, trying to avoid them would make it even worse. You'd feel as if you were on a roller coaster."

"It's not just the roads. I don't think I could find my way around at night. All these little roads and no lights to read the signposts."

"Even if you could read them, it wouldn't do you any good. You'd have to read a map at the same time." He grinned at her, teeth gleaming in the darkness. "Getting lost is part of the charm of Barbados. Why not ask Wesley to find you a driver to use while you're working here?"

She heard him catch his breath, as he realized too late what he'd said. Vivien knew a sense of triumph and let a few moments pass before she spoke again.

"Why do you want to do this book? After all, it's not exactly your kind of thing, is it?"

"No, but I would like it to be something better than Wesley proposes. I have no idea why he and George Collins suddenly decided to take on this project, but it is time that people find out more about our island— other than Brits knocking back inferior rum punches and getting red as lobsters on our beaches."

"So you decided to take it on."

"Better me than someone else."

He certainly wasn't modest, thought Vivien. "Then why were you so reluctant to do it?"

"Because it's going to take a great deal of juggling of my work."

"Surely not. A few dozen captions?"

She couldn't see his face, but she sensed that he was not at all amused. A strained silence hung between them, which she was reluctant to break lest he lash out at her. It was a tropical silence, filled with the screech and rustle of birds, the perpetual zizzing of what she'd been told were not insects but tiny frogs, and the rush of hot wind blowing against them. The scents and sounds and moist heat of this exotic environment were alien to a Canadian woman born and bred on the prairie, used to hot dry summers and icy winters. This place filled her with a feeling of anticipation, a tingling of excitement. It was a different world.

"Why do you want this job? Money?" David suddenly asked her in a cool voice. "After all," he added, "it's not your sort of thing either, is it?"

"No, it's not. Yes, partly the money," she had to admit. "My Canadian book cost me more in traveling expenses than I shall probably recoup from the book and photograph sales combined."

"It was a labor of love."

"Right."

"That's what I'd like this Barbados book to be." He turned to her. "Maybe now you understand why I was shocked when I saw you. How would you have felt if your writer had turned out to be a black guy from the Caribbean, who'd never set foot in Canada before?"

"I wrote my own captions."

"But that's the problem," he yelled, slapping the steering wheel with the heel of his hand. "This is not going to be a book of pretty photos with captions."

They were back where they'd started. "Not pretty photos," Vivien retorted. "However, it was my understanding that Wesley wanted the photographs, not the text, to be the main part of the book."

David started to slow down on the winding road as they approached the resort's iron gates. "Then he doesn't need me." He halted at the porter's hut. "Give me your key-card to show him," he said abruptly.

Vivien handed it to him, and they were waved in.

"What made you choose this place to stay?" David asked as he turned into the drive lined with large palm trees.

"I told you before, it's not my sort of place," she said,

exasperated. "I didn't choose it. Wesley offered to have me stay at his place, as his wife would be there, but I said I'd rather not. I need my space. I suggested a B-and-B, but he said he'd book me into a hotel in a quiet area. I hadn't realized until I arrived that it was a resort."

"I prefer this side of the island, but you won't learn much about Barbados shut behind the gates of a tourist resort, however attractive it might be. If you are staying on, you'll need to get out into the island, talk to the people."

"I fully intended to do so. I would remind you that the original arrangement I made with Wesley was to stay a week before I made a definite decision."

"Good idea." David pulled up before the main section of the hotel. Before she had time to open her door, he had jumped out and opened it for her. He held out his hand. "Good luck." She felt the firm, brief clasp of his hand on hers, and then he strode quickly back to the driver's side of the car.

"Thanks for the ride," she called, but she doubted he'd heard her. The car roared off, leaving her standing there, her mind filled with unanswered questions.

CHAPTER
FIVE

Vivien awoke abruptly the next morning to shrieks of laughter coming from the nearby outdoor pool. Dragging on her robe, she slid back the glass doors. Immediately, she was engulfed by the moist heat. She stepped out onto the balcony, flinching as her bare feet met the searing tiles.

Below her stretched an expanse of lawn sloping down to the beach. Beyond it was the ocean, a wondrous turquoise merging, once past the reef, into a rich navy-blue. She had never seen such a range of colors, not even in Hawaii.

The pool—and the bathers who had woken her—were to her left, the umbrella-shaded tables and chairs that surrounded it already filled with holidaymakers in various stages of dress, or undress, from full-length sarongs to the skimpiest of thong bikinis. The pool wasn't nearly as inviting as the multihued ocean and the white beach that bordered it. Once she'd organized her day, she promised herself she'd make her way down to the beach and explore.

Feeling ravenously hungry, she reached for the menu. She'd order room service rather than having to wait to eat until she was showered and dressed. Before long she'd decided on fresh papaya to start, followed by scrambled eggs, breakfast rolls, and coffee. She was about to dial room service when the phone rang.

"So, how ya doing?" It was Frieda.

"Fine. I was about to order breakfast and eat it out on my balcony, looking out over the palm trees and azure sea."

"Get lost. It's raining, mixed with snow, here."

"What's new?"

"So, you fixed up okay?"

Vivien hesitated. She didn't feel like explaining the intricacies of what had happened last night. At least not until she'd had some coffee to wake her up. "Can I call you back after I've eaten?"

"Sure. But I'm going out at ten, so make it snappy."

"I don't even know what time it is."

"Must be nice!"

"It is."

"It's ten past nine."

"Okay. I'll call you back before ten."

Vivien was about to set down the phone when Frieda asked, "Something wrong?"

However careful she was, Frieda could always sense when something was going on. "I'll tell you when I call you," Vivien said firmly and put the receiver down before Frieda could ask any more questions.

It struck her that she should call Wesley before she got back to Frieda, but she was determined to eat before she did anything else. Besides, she wasn't sure she wanted to speak to Wesley. Not yet, anyway.

Putting everything else out of her mind, she concentrated on ordering her breakfast. It arrived less than fifteen minutes later, borne by a beaming member of the staff who bade her a cheery "Good morning, Miss Shaw" as she set the tray out on the balcony table. "There's this morning's copy of the *Nation* for you to read," she added, setting the folded newspaper beside the tray. "Is there anything else you would like?"

"No, thank you. That looks great," Vivien said, signing the bill.

"Now, you have a specially good day," the young woman said, sounding as if she really meant it.

As the door closed behind her, Vivien felt heartened by the woman's cheerfulness. The sense of foreboding she'd experienced when she'd spoken to Frieda receded as she started in on her breakfast, relaxing in the sun's rays. She was enjoying her second cup of coffee when she checked her watch and saw that it was nine forty-five. With a reluctant sigh, she set her cup down and went back into the room.

"So, what's going on?" was Frieda's first response to her call.

"Why should anything be going on?"

"I can tell. You hate the hotel? You don't like the vibes? It's too humid? You feel no inspiration? What?"

"Am I really that neurotic?" Vivien asked, laughing.

"No, not you. Just artists in general." There was a long pause. "So . . . what is it?"

"Oh, God, Frieda," Vivien groaned, dragging one hand through her unruly hair. "It's not the hotel or the vibes. I *hate* David Moreton."

"Your writer?"

"That's just it. He's not *my* writer. He wants this to be some great literary project of his own, with me merely illustrating his immortal prose."

"And?"

"I told him I thought he was going to write captions for my photographs."

"You didn't!" Frieda's shriek of laughter was so loud Vivien was sure she'd damaged her eardrum.

"It's not that funny," she yelled.

"Yes, it is," Frieda said, still cackling. "Talk about wounding the poor man's ego."

"It damn well needs some wounding. He's the most arrogant, egotistical—"

"Hold on! What the hell did he say to you to make you so mad at him?"

"He told me he wouldn't work with me because I was white." Just repeating it made Vivien's stomach squirm.

Frieda whistled. "Surely not as baldly as that. He must have sugarcoated it a bit."

"No, that's what he said. He had no objection to working with a woman. Just not a white woman."

"Well, I suppose at least he was honest, which is more than most people are about such things. Did he try to explain himself?"

"Of course. When he was driving me back to the hotel—"

Frieda's voice rose again. "You mean you let him drive you home after he'd—"

"I didn't have much choice. He tried to explain, asked me how I'd feel if someone from the Caribbean who'd never been to Canada before had written the text for my book."

"He's right, you know."

Vivien resented Frieda's capitulation. "Maybe he is in theory, but in practice he was rude and arrogant, and it was excruciatingly embarrassing."

"So when did all this happen?"

"At dinner at Wesley Marshall's home."

"So he's in Barbados?"

"Yes. He met me at the airport and invited me to dinner with him and his wife. David Moreton was there."

"So . . . what you going to do? About the project, I mean."

"Last night, I felt like getting on the first plane home, but now I'm having second thoughts. It's so beautiful here, and the few people I've met have been so kind and welcoming. I feel I should give it a chance."

"Why not give it a chance, then? You haven't committed yourself or signed a full contract yet."

"David Moreton, that's why not." Vivien glared down at an innocuous face on the front page of the newspaper, imagining it was David Moreton's arrogant face in front of her. "There's absolutely no way I could work with him," she said vehemently.

"You're sure about that? I mean, you'd be willing to give up this project rather than work with the man?"

Vivien hesitated. "If I have to."

"You don't sound too certain to me."

Vivien sighed. "I want to do this project. There's more to this place than just gorgeous beaches and rum and calypso music. Everyone I've met seems so proud of their island. I want to discover the real Barbados."

"Well, you have a week to decide, right?"

"And, dammit, I'd like to prove to the high-and-mighty Professor Moreton that an artist doesn't have to have lived in a place for years to be able to capture its essence."

"Quite right."

"That a combination of imagination and curiosity can bring fresh perspective to one's work." Vivien was on a roll. "After all, Nunavut and Newfoundland were far more remote and different to me than this island is, and I think I managed to capture some of their magic in my pictures."

"Did you tell Moreton that?" Frieda asked.

"He didn't give me the chance."

"Then they'll have to find a new writer, won't they? After all, it's the pictures that will sell this book, not Moreton's deathless prose. Besides, if he has such a huge ego, telling him he was to write captions for your pictures will have put him off already. Want me to speak to him or his agent before I leave for Frankfurt?"

"No. I can deal with him—if I have to."

"Okay, that's good. I've gotta go. Don't forget I leave

for Frankfurt tomorrow. You have my number there, don't you?"

"Yes. You gave it to me before I left."

"Good. Keep in touch. Let me know what happens. And you can send some of that sunshine up here."

"No, I want it all. Bye, Frieda—and thanks."

"Okay."

Determined to get down to the beach, Vivien took a quick shower and got into the new sleek black swimsuit she'd bought before she left. As she surveyed herself in the mirror inside the closet door, she was glad she'd kept in shape during her extensive travels for her last project. And her skin would soon tan to a deep brown in this sun.

She was about to gather up her camera and books when the phone rang again. Now what? She was tempted to let it ring, in case her parents were calling her, but she picked up the receiver. "Yes?" she said tentatively.

"Good morning, Miss Shaw," Wesley's voice boomed in her ear. "We have to talk."

Vivien took a deep breath. "Can it wait? I'd planned to go down to the beach."

"I can meet you there, if you like."

Although this was his island, the image of the stately Wesley Marshall clad in shorts on a beach was an incongruous one.

"When?" Vivien asked.

"Right away. I'm at the reception desk."

He obviously meant business.

Vivien sighed, her dream of sunning herself and reading all morning ebbing away. "Okay. Why don't we meet at one of the bars?"

"Too noisy. There's a pleasant garden area with seats near the restaurant. If it rains, we can go inside. I will order drinks. What would you like?"

"Something exotic. Fruit juice: pineapple, mango . . ."

"Rum?"

Vivien laughed. "No, thanks. Too early for me. See you shortly."

As she pulled on a long-skirted cotton sarong over her swimsuit, Vivien's heart was pounding. Wesley had been almost abrupt with her. Tying the rope belt around her slim waist, she gazed out to the rolling surf beyond the beach. Despite David Moreton, she knew that she really wanted to do this project. A few days' free vacation wasn't going to be enough for her.

Drawing in a deep breath, she grabbed the black cotton bag containing her book and camera and left her room.

She found Wesley sitting on a wooden bench beneath a large tree covered in bright orange and yellow blossoms. He rose to his feet as soon as he saw her.

"What a gorgeous tree!" she exclaimed. "It has different colored flowers. I've never seen anything like that before." Automatically, her hand reached down to draw her camera from her bag. "Excuse me for a moment."

"It's a pride of Barbados," Wesley said, resuming his seat. As she took several photographs from different angles, she was aware of him in his long-sleeved white shirt, watching her intently, his arm spread out on his dark suit jacket draped over the back of the bench. For a large man, he had singular grace. She was reminded of David, who had the same physical grace but not Wesley's gracious manner.

"I ordered a tropical punch for you," he said, moving his panama hat so she could sit down. He indicated a tall glass filled with juice and garnished with mango and starfruit on the wooden table before him.

Vivien took a sip. "Wonderful," she said, savoring the blend of tropical flavors. She turned to confront him directly. "You came here to speak to me, not to talk about trees and tropical drinks."

Wesley nodded, his eyes wary. "David called this morning. He told me he was pulling out of the project."

Vivien felt a leap of adrenaline in her chest. "I'm sorry to hear that," she said, her voice calm. "But it was obvious from his reaction that he couldn't work with me." She gazed down at the camera in her lap. "I can understand why, of course. But to be honest, I felt both humiliated and angry at the way he attacked me last night. He could have said what he had to say privately instead of embarrassing me. I imagine he made everyone else in the room feel embarrassed, too."

"You are right, of course." Wesley inclined his head solemnly. "David has always been too impulsive." He hesitated, his eyes fixed on the ground, then he cleared his throat. "The trouble is, Miss Shaw, the ministry will only finance the project if David is engaged. He has the name, the reputation in Barbados that will give credence to this book."

"And I haven't?" Vivien demanded.

"Elsewhere, you do. But in Barbados, it is David's name that is well-known."

"So . . . what are you saying? That David Moreton will not accept me, so I'm off the job?"

Wesley shuffled his feet. "That is not my choice, but it is the National Cultural Foundation's project, under the direction of the Ministry of Tourism. I was only the instigator."

"Perhaps you should have made that more clear when you first approached me." Vivien's eyes flashed. "The way you spoke, I thought the decision was in your hands."

He looked pained. "The idea came from . . . me. However, the project had to be approved and financed by the ministry. Once they were brought in, it was not in my power to dictate terms to them."

Vivien sat on the edge of the bench, the icy glass clenched between her hands. "So, you want me to leave today?"

Wesley looked shocked. "Not at all. The arrangement

was that you stay for a week, all expenses paid. That remains."

Vivien banged her glass down on the table. "I can't really see the point of my staying here if I'm off the project." She turned away so Wesley wouldn't see her disappointment.

His hand gripped her clenched hands for a fleeting moment, then drew away. "I want you to do this book. David is being stubborn. Having made himself look a fool, he won't back down. He also told me that there's no way you could work together after such a bad start. That you would never forgive him."

Their eyes met. Vivien frowned at him over the top of her sunglasses. "So now he's using me as an excuse." She saw the pleading look in his eyes. "Don't tell me you're suggesting I go to him and tell him I forgive him?"

"Something like that." Wesley's grin was sheepish.

"He insults me in a room full of people I don't know and I'm supposed to go to him and beg him to work with me? You're kidding, right?"

"Merely hoping."

Vivien sprang up, grabbed her camera, and swung her bag over her shoulder. "Well, you can forget it, Mr. Marshall. Count me out. I'd try to change my flight so I could leave today, but it's probably too late. I promise you, I'll be out of here tomorrow morning."

He scrambled to his feet, looking, for the first time since they'd met, inelegant in his haste. "Please don't go. You *must* stay."

The intensity in his voice puzzled her. "Why must I?"

He laughed it off. "To save me embarrassment, I suppose." His large shoulders lifted in a shrug. "I've made rather a mess of the whole thing, haven't I?"

He looked so wretched, beads of sweat shining on his forehead, that Vivien felt sorry for him. "Never mind. You'll find someone else for your photographs. Someone

who knows Barbados well," she added with a tinge of
bitterness.

The intensity she'd heard in his voice was now in his
dark eyes. "I wanted *you* to do this," he said.

Vivien stowed her camera in the bag. "Thank you for
your faith in me. I'd have done a good job, you know."
She looked around her. "I'd have liked to get to know
the island." She shrugged. "As it is, I'll have been a one-
day tourist."

"Please stay on for a few more days. Sarah and I can
show you the island."

Vivien shook her head. "Thanks, but I don't think
so."

"If you'd prefer, I could provide you with a car and
a driver so that you could be totally independent."

"It's not that I don't want to be with you, Wesley,"
she assured him. "I'm just very disappointed. All I want
to do is get out of here."

He put on his hat, gathered his jacket from the bench,
and stood up. "I can understand why."

He looked so dejected that Vivien couldn't bear it.
"All right," she said. "I'm not staying on," she added
hastily, seeing the spark of optimism in his eyes, "but
I'll accept your offer of a car and driver for this afternoon. That way I can see a little bit more of Barbados
before I go home."

He gave her a broad smile. "Good. But please permit
me to drive you. It would be my pleasure to show
you—"

"No," she said firmly. "You'll only try to persuade me
to stay on. Normally, I'd rent a car and drive myself,
but I'd rather not get lost when I have so little time. If
you'll arrange a car and driver for me, I will pay for it."

"Please, Miss Shaw!" He looked so pained that she
knew she'd insulted him.

"All right. Thank you." She held out her hand to
shake hands with him. "And thank you for inviting me

to Barbados. One day I'll come back again as a proper tourist."

"Why not stay on and take some photographs? You never know . . ."

She looked at him quizzically. "Maybe I'll publish a book to rival David Moreton's?" she teased him. "Is that a wise suggestion, Mr. Marshall?"

"Perhaps not." He sighed heavily and took out a neatly folded white handkerchief to wipe his forehead. "Very well. I will send you a reliable driver. Would two o'clock be suitable?"

"Perfect. Time for the beach and a light lunch. What places would you recommend for me to see? Don't forget I don't want to see only the usual tourist attractions."

"You won't be able to see much in one afternoon. I'd suggest staying on this side of the island and going up the east coast. Visit Bathsheba. Maybe one or two of the great plantation houses, like Sunbury."

"Yes, I definitely want to see one of those. And isn't there an old college somewhere near here?"

"Codrington College. It's a theological college for Anglican clergy. A very tranquil spot."

"Good. I can do with tranquil today."

Their eyes met.

"I'm very sorry about this," Wesley said simply. He seemed deeply disappointed.

"So am I."

"I'll drive you to the airport tomorrow."

"No need. I can take a taxi." She saw that he was about to protest. "Please. I'd prefer it that way."

Inclining his head, he shook hands with her again, his large hand crushing hers. Then he lifted his panama hat to her and walked away across the lawn to his waiting car.

As soon as Wesley had driven through the hotel gates, he picked up his cell phone. "She insists she's going home," he said, without preamble, as soon as his call was answered. "I did my best."

"Damn David."

"I agree. But I should have foreseen it. I suppose I was so determined to get her here that I didn't consider the possibility of his attacking her like that."

"That was the problem with having to involve the ministry. There must be something else we can do to keep her here. To have come this far . . ."

"I know. Leave it to me. I'll try to find a way to stop her leaving the island."

CHAPTER
SIX

When Wesley had gone, Vivien slumped down on the bench, her bravado ebbing away. Angry disappointment overwhelmed her. Because of one arrogant, egotistical man she'd lost an important project, one that could have advanced her international career. And now she had thrown away her chance of spending time on this beautiful island. She was already regretting her hasty decision not to stay on but was far too proud to admit it to anyone but herself.

She sat there, staring gloomily at a group of children turning cartwheels on the grass, trying to decide what to do next. This was her only morning on the island. To spend it relaxing on the beach would be a terrible waste of precious time, wouldn't it?

The sun beamed down, filtering through the branches of the pride of Barbados spreading above her. *Rest, relax,* everything around her seemed to be saying.

Damn David Moreton, she thought, her gloom lifting. She was determined that he wasn't going to spoil her time here. She jumped up and marched down the pathway to the beach of white sand stretching below.

* * *

In fact, her time at the beach wasn't wasted at all. Not only did she get some spectacular shots of the broad expanse of white sand, shaded by palm trees, and the brilliant turquoise sea, but also some great people pictures. A sunburned Englishman, his belly hanging over his too-tight swimming briefs, happily playing cricket with a small cluster of local boys, using a green plastic spade stuck in the sand as a makeshift wicket. A chambermaid in a red velvet hat whom she'd passed on the way to the beach and who'd happily allowed her to take her picture and then went on with her work sweeping the pathway, with a warm "Now, you take it easy, honey."

After a while, she put away her camera and used her carryall bag as a pillow, stretching out on the striped beach towel she'd bought at the hotel store. She tried to read the *Mini Rough Guide to Barbados,* but the combination of heat and the constant swell of the surf forced her eyes shut, the sunlight dancing on her closed lids.

She awoke with a start, to find herself in total shade. Grabbing her watch from her bag, she saw to her horror that it was almost one o'clock. Yikes! She still had to change her flight, shower, eat lunch, and be ready for the car to pick her up at two o'clock.

Scrambling to her feet, she shook out the beach towel, slipped on her beach shoes, and hurried up the steps. On her way back to her room, she encountered a group of people on the pathway, all craning their necks and pointing at the stand of palm trees at the rear of the beach.

Ever curious, she couldn't help stopping. "What's going on?" she asked a little girl whose long blond hair had been plaited and beaded.

"Green monkeys," the girl replied. "See?" she said, pointing. "There's two swinging across from that tree."

There were far more than two. A swarm of green monkeys were scaling the trees and swinging from one to the other. Intuitively assessing the light, Vivien attached the telephoto lens to her camera and snapped off six or seven pictures.

The girl beamed up at her as if she felt responsible for the success of the pictures. "Like me to take one of you?" Vivien asked her. "Is that okay?" she asked the girl's mother, who was standing nearby, eyeing her as if ready to pounce if she made another move.

"Sure."

The child immediately posed, one hand on her hip, with an unnatural smile.

Used to dealing with children, Vivien adjusted the girl's stance and managed to place her naturally with a hibiscus bush behind her, its luxuriant blooms of bright yellow echoing her blond hair.

Having extricated herself after promising to leave a copy of the photograph at the hotel desk for them, she made a dash to her room, peeled off her beachwear, and stepped into the shower, relaxing under the warm flow of water as she shampooed the sand out of her hair. When she was younger, she'd longed for a long, sleek look, but at times like this she was grateful for having wash-and-wear hair. A dab of conditioner and a tug of the comb and she'd be fine.

When she'd pulled on shorts and a T-shirt, she picked up the receiver to call the airline about changing her flight to tomorrow, but something stopped her. *I'll do it later,* she told herself. That way she could keep her options open.

She downed half a glass of Banks, the excellent local beer, and ate half a slice of pizza from the bar at the nearby pool before tearing off to the central hotel building, arriving a few minutes after two.

She approached the reception clerk. "I'm expecting a driver and—"

"Miss Shaw?"

"That's right."

"Your driver's sitting on the bench at the foot of the steps. His name's Spencer."

"Thank you."

When she came out again, a slightly stooped man of about sixty, wearing a pale blue, short-sleeved shirt, was waiting for her. "Miss Shaw?" he asked. When she'd confirmed that she was, he led the way slowly to his car.

To Vivien's surprise, it was not a comfortable sedan like Wesley's but a small, rather battered van. When she went around to the front passenger seat, she was ushered politely—but with a small frown—to the rear of the van. As she was swiftly learning, in Barbados everything had its correct place, and hers was in the back, not beside the driver.

"Mr. Marshall tell me you want to go to Bathsheba, right?" the driver said once she was settled into her seat.

"That's right." She hastily scanned the list she'd made on the beach. "And Sunbury House and Codrington College . . . Will there be time for both, do you think?"

"Depends." Spencer was a man of few words.

"On what?"

"How long you plan to stay lookin' around."

"Of course. I'll try not to be too long anywhere. I've only got this afternoon."

Spencer raised one grizzled eyebrow but said nothing as he shifted gears and started off.

Despite her qualms about Spencer's efficacy as a tour guide, by the time they were on the open road, Vivien realized that Wesley had not made a mistake. For one thing, it was easy to see out all the van's windows. For another, Spencer's lack of the usual tour-guide chatter enabled her to think and concentrate on everything she was seeing. Most of all, Spencer's driving was exemplary. Somehow he managed to maneuver around the potholes and bumps without slowing down, and she sensed from the relaxed yet alert set of his shoulders that he knew exactly what he was doing.

She should have known Wesley could be relied upon to choose the right man, she thought, settling back into her seat and opening her map.

"This is the parish of St. Philip," Spencer said as they drove away from the coast into the interior of the island. He pronounced it "*sin* Philip." "Sunbury first." It was a statement, not a question. Spencer was in charge, and Vivien was happy to have it that way.

As soon as they joined the highway, the ride became smoother, making it easier to take pictures from the moving van. She leaned forward as they passed a highway restaurant called Chefette. "I think I saw another Chefette like that when we drove in from the airport."

"Could be. Lots of Chefettes here. No McDonald's."

"No McDonald's? I don't think I've ever been anywhere in the reasonably civilized world that doesn't have a McDonald's."

"Barbados doesn't. Only Chefettes." He grinned at her triumphantly in the mirror. She smiled back at him. The overwhelming if understated pride in their country seemed to permeate the people's everyday lives, despite their slave-based colonial history.

Sunbury Plantation was, she soon discovered, a prime example of the other side of that history. Set in extensive grounds, the house was not as grand as some of the larger stately homes she'd seen in England, but it had a simple elegance and was beautifully furnished with both imported furniture of the nineteenth century and several locally made mahogany pieces. Outside in the garden, she came into contact with the massive trees that, she was told by the guide, provided much of the wood for the local furniture.

She took dozens of pictures at Sunbury.

"What a beautiful house," she said to Spencer as he slid the van door open for her.

"Hmm" was his close-lipped response.

These houses could not hold the same attraction for

the majority of Barbadians, she realized. Many of them were the descendants of those who had built them with sweat and hard labor, who had literally slaved in their sugarcane fields and factories and in these very houses.

The young women showing them through the house had seemed genuinely enthusiastic, but that was their job, after all. Did they really care, or did they harbor a simmering resentment about these beautiful plantation houses?

I shall probably never find out, Vivien thought. She felt a twinge of sadness as she settled back into the van. The more she saw of Barbados the more she wanted to learn about this unique island. With its English names and schooling and graceful old houses, it was, in some ways, more English than England itself. She knew, from a recent visit, that England was fast becoming more Americanized than its own inhabitants realized.

"What are those?" she asked suddenly, having caught sight of three structures towering above a field of young, green sugarcane. "They look like oil rigs."

"That's what they are. Powerful lot of petroleum herebouts."

"Amazing." She looked back at the rigs, thinking how incongruous they looked in this rural part of the island.

"Bathsheba next," Spencer told her. "Then, if there is time, Codrington."

The drive to Bathsheba was a long, circuitous route through the interior and then down, down until they were at sea level again. She was surprised at how unspoiled this stretch of the coastline was.

As she stood on the plain of springy turf above the beach, the wind blowing against her, watching the surf pounding the beach, she shivered at the thought of a row of high-rise hotels where now stood an attractive little restaurant with large shuttered windows, which the woman who'd served her iced tea told her were called jalousie windows.

A young woman in a bright cotton dress approached

her to offer a tray of cheap imported jewelry, but her sales ability was as inferior as her wares, making it easy for Vivien to smile and say, "No, thank you," without feeling too guilty. As the girl retreated, Vivien called after her. "But I would like to take your picture."

Beaming, the young woman returned to shyly pose with her tray of trinkets, the rolling sea and surrounding hills a magnificent backdrop to her simplicity and natural beauty. When she'd finished, Vivien handed her ten Barbados dollars, but she shook her head, backing away. "I always pay my models," Vivien insisted and put the money on her tray.

The girl giggled and, folding the bill neatly, slid it into the leather pouch at her waist. "Thank you very much," she said, and, before Vivien could ask her some questions about herself, she had glided away to a small group of tourists who'd arrived in a minivan.

Despite the strong breeze blowing in from the Atlantic, the heat was intense, the sun beating down on them. Vivien could feel sweat trickling between her shoulder blades. She would have liked to spend more time in this beautiful unspoiled spot, but time was rushing by. She made her way back to the van, glad that Spencer had kept the air-conditioning on.

As they drove away, she saw a few villas perched way up high on the hillside, their large windows facing the ocean. "How wonderful to live there," she said to Spencer. "Lucky people. Are they holiday villas?"

"Some. Some local people."

"This is a lovely place. I'd like to come back here."

"Tomorrow?"

"I wish. Unfortunately, I'm flying home tomorrow." Yet, she chided herself, it was ridiculous not to stay and see more of the island when she'd come all this way, wasn't it?

"Too bad." Spencer sounded genuinely sorry. Probably because he'd be glad of the work, she supposed.

"Do you get a lot of driving jobs?" she asked him.

"Not so much now."

"Why's that?"

"Too many all-inclusive resorts. Tourists don't leave them."

"You mean they just stay in the resorts the whole time?"

"That's right. Fly in from England or Canada or any place, go to the resort, then fly home." His shoulders lifted and fell. "No drivers needed that way."

"I can't imagine coming here and not wanting to see more of this beautiful island."

Spencer shook his head as if he, too, found the ways of tourists unfathomable. "Codrington now?" he asked.

"Do we have time?" The sun was slowly descending. Vivien glanced at her watch.

"Yes. You will see only the grounds. You cannot go inside."

"Oh, I thought I could go into the buildings."

"It's a college for Anglican priests," Spencer reminded her sternly.

"Oh, I see. Okay. As long as I can get some pictures."

She sat back, wishing she'd bought a canned drink to take with her from the restaurant in Bathsheba. Her throat was parched and, despite the air-conditioning, her shirt was glued to her back.

More and more she was regretting having to leave the next day. Now, she began to seriously consider staying on, but at her own expense. That would mean she'd definitely have to leave the resort and move to a B-and-B. Not only because of the cost. The few hours she'd spent with Spencer had convinced her that she wanted to stay with local people who could share their knowledge of the island with her.

They had driven for almost twenty minutes when Vivien caught sight of a wooden sign at the side of the road, half hidden by overgrown hibiscus bushes. BED AND BREAKFAST, she managed to read as they drove past, and, beneath, the enticing words AFTERNOON TEAS.

"Stop," she shouted to Spencer. He slowed down but did not come to a full halt.

"There's a sign back there, but I couldn't see a building."

Spencer kept going as if he hadn't heard her.

"Could you please stop for a minute?"

With obvious reluctance, he drew the van to the side of the narrow road.

"There must be an entrance. Can we go back?" Vivien asked him.

He murmured something, but the words were unintelligible.

"Sorry?" Vivien said.

"That's Peverill Hall," he said.

"What is it?"

"Old plantation house."

"Is it open to the public?"

"Doubt it." He shifted the van into gear, ready to take off again.

"Hold on a minute," Vivien said, his reluctance piquing her curiosity. "I'd like to see this Peverill Hall, if it's open."

Muttering beneath his breath, Spencer reversed and then turned the van around to drive back to the sign. It hung on a rusty chain from a tall stake hammered into the ditch. "Too late," Spencer said, his face beaded with sweat.

"I don't see any times on the sign," Vivien said firmly. "Besides, it's not too late to ask about staying there. Let's try."

But Spencer made no move to start up the van again. His strange behavior only served to stir Vivien's interest even more. Was it some sort of superstition that made him fearful of this place? She was tempted to ask him but decided that it would only embarrass him. She was not about to force him to go in against his will.

"Do you know how far it is to the house from here?"

"Why?"

"Because I intend to walk there."

His eyes widened, so that the whites grew enormous in his dark face. "No way, Miss Shaw."

"Well, if you won't drive me, that's the only way I can get in." She was careful not to let any note of complaint creep into her voice.

"No way you're going in there."

"Well, yes, there is," she said quietly, "but I don't mind walking in by myself. Perhaps you could go get a drink somewhere and come back for me. Even if they've finished serving tea, I'm sure they can give me a cold drink."

"Plenty of cold drinks here," Spencer said desperately, pulling out a cooler from beneath an old blanket.

"Okay, give me a beer." He handed her a can of Banks, and she tucked it into her backpack. "I'll need it after I get there, in case it's a long walk to the house."

"I can drive you someplace else for tea," Spencer said.

Vivien hid a smile. Spencer didn't give up easily. "Thanks, but I really would like to see the house."

Not wanting to waste any more time, she dragged on her backpack and jumped down from the van. Spencer rolled down his window. "Meet you back here in about an hour," she told him. "Okay?"

Their eyes locked in a battle of wills.

"Get in," Spencer said, gesturing with his head to the back of the van. "I'll drive you and I'll wait for you, but don't say I didn't warn you."

"Warn me about what?"

He shook his head. "Get in," he said impatiently, like a parent tiring of a headstrong child.

Vivien did as she was told. With a spinning of wheels and kicking up of dust, Spencer turned the van into the narrow lane. Vivien was left with the uneasy feeling that it might be wiser to trust someone who knew this area better than she did.

CHAPTER
SEVEN

The lane was so narrow and so pitted with holes that even Spencer's skillful driving could not avoid them. Perhaps he wasn't trying. All Vivien could see was the back of his neck, but his shoulders were stiff with resentment. She felt badly for asking him to drive where he did not want to go, especially when their day together had been so amicable until now, but she had, after all, offered to walk in to Peverill Hall by herself. And something beyond mere curiosity told her that she *must* see this place that was so mysteriously, perhaps intentionally, hidden from the road.

The van jounced along the lane, dust settling on the windows. The trees and bushes that crowded in on them appeared not to have been cut for a very long time. Vivien was reminded of the forest in "Sleeping Beauty," growing up over a hundred years. She smiled to herself at the thought of Spencer as an improbable, aged prince slashing through the growth with his van.

She slid open her window and breathed in the scent of tropical blossoms. White flowers bloomed on gnarled trees. Hibiscus branches covered with dark pink blossoms brushed gently against her arm, without scratching. She had the strange sensation that the shrubs and trees and the songbirds were welcoming her, inviting her into this hidden place.

"Have you been here before, Spencer?" she asked him, to break the uncomfortable silence.

"Only once. That was enough." As if to emphasize his point, he turned on the radio loud enough to make more conversation impossible. The calypso was raunchy and noisy, drowning out the birds' chatter.

The lane widened into a driveway with a dilapidated white fence that was badly in need of paint. And so was the house that stood at the end of the driveway, but no lack of paint could mar its classical beauty. As they drove up to it, Vivien felt as if a hand had taken hold of her heart and squeezed it, releasing it slowly.

"My God, how beautiful!" she breathed.

A shallow flight of forest-green tiled steps led up to the paneled door, which was closed. Even the slatted jalousie windows on the ground floor were closed, which seemed strange on this steamy hot day, yet she felt no sense of being shut out. It was as if the house were inviting her to come in, to open up the doors and windows to allow fresh air to blow through. How glad she was that she'd ignored Spencer's superstitious nonsense.

"Looks like no one's here," she said to Spencer.

"Could be," he said, with his shrug that meant *Keep me out of this.* "Shall we go now?"

"I'll try the bell." Vivien got out of the van. This time Spencer made no move to help her but sat there motionless, resting his arms on the steering wheel.

Vivien mounted the steps, noticing the carved stone lions that guarded the ancient house. On the wooden door frame was an old-fashioned rusty iron bellpull. She pulled it and heard a satisfying jangle from within the house. At first there was no response, but when she pulled the bell again, a dog started barking furiously and did not stop.

"Shut up, you stupid animal," a man said, and with a rasp of locks and turning of a key, the door was opened by a white man with gray, thinning hair. He was trying to hold the door and restrain the barking Doberman pinscher at the same time.

"Hi," Vivien said. "I saw your sign."

"Sign?" The man's expression was vague, as if he'd forgotten they'd ever had a sign. "Oh, about bed and breakfast. I'll get my wife."

"I was also interested in the tea part," Vivien said. "A cold drink would be fine," she added hurriedly, sensing his reluctance.

"I'm sure we can give you more than that. Come on in." He held the door open wider. "I'll put Marcus away in the back. Noisy brute, but he makes a good watchdog."

Vivien was tempted to ask him why he would need a good watchdog when the house was so well hidden, but she didn't.

He led her through the verandah into a formal front room that took her breath away. Her hand instinctively sought for her camera bag. She was itching to start shooting. "I can't believe how beautiful this is, tucked away out of sight. How old is the house?"

"It was built in the seventeenth century."

"Amazing. I hadn't realized there were houses that old on the island."

"Oh, yes. St. Nicholas Abbey in St. Peter, farther north, dates back to Jacobean times. Some, like Peverill and Sunbury, were built in the heyday of King Sugar, some even earlier. Alas, those days are no more."

"No more sugar plantations?"

"Some, but not many. It's been hell keeping this place going for me and my family before me. But things are looking up for us at last." He didn't elucidate. He rubbed his hand on the side of his jeans and held it out to Vivien. "I'm Paul Hendley, by the way."

"Vivien Shaw, tourist." His hand was rough from hard manual work.

"I'll put Marcus away and get my wife."

"I should go and tell my driver that I'll be staying for a little while."

"Do that. We'll show you the rest of the house, if you like."

"I'd love to see it." Vivien turned to go out. "I'll see if Spencer wants to come in."

"Spencer?"

"My driver. He might like some tea."

"Doubt it. He'll probably take a snooze while you're here."

It wasn't exactly a no but near enough for a warning bell to go off in Vivien's mind. Maybe this was another, uglier side to Barbados she hadn't yet encountered. "I'll tell him I'm staying."

She went back outside, across the shady verandah and down the steps. She noticed that Spencer was anxiously watching the door, but as soon as he saw her come out he rested his head on his arms. As she approached, he turned down the radio.

"They're going to give me tea and show me the house," she told him.

He glanced at the large steel watch on his wrist. "I have another customer soon."

"Oh, I thought you said I had you for the rest of the day."

The way he looked away told her he had no other customer lined up.

"I promise I won't take long. Would you like some tea?"

He looked surprised and then grinned at her for the first time in what seemed like ages. "I've got drinks in here." He patted the cooler.

"Something to eat?"

"No, thank you, Miss Shaw. Don't you worry about me." The grin faded. "Just take care of yourself."

"I'll be fine. Back soon. You won't be too hot out here, will you?"

"No'm. I won't be too hot." He chuckled openly, laughing deep down in his chest. She smiled back at him. She could still hear him chuckling to himself as she went back up the steps.

A fiftyish woman in a creased cotton skirt and a white, short-sleeved blouse waited for her inside the front door. "I'm Marian Hendley. I'm so sorry we didn't hear you," she said with an anxious smile. "We were out at the back, trying to prune some of the bushes. It's a constant battle." Wearily, she ran her hand over her gray-blond hair, which was tied back in a ponytail. "They tend to take over so fast if you don't keep cutting them back." She spoke with a strong English accent.

It sounded as if she disliked the place and would prefer to live somewhere else.

Vivien gazed again at the high ceiling with ornamental plasterwork, the old landscape painting and a tarnished gilt-framed mirror each in a recessed alcove, the elegant curving staircase. "This is one of the most beautiful places I've ever seen."

"Oh, it certainly is." Marian sounded less than enthusiastic. She ran her hands down her cotton skirt to dry them. Despite the ceiling fan's lazy spinning, it was very hot in the house. "I'll bring you your tea on the verandah. There's a breeze out there."

"That would be great. Don't go to any trouble. Tea or a cold drink would be fine."

"Nonsense. We don't get many people stopping by, but when they do come, they get a proper English tea served to them."

Vivien was tempted to respond that if they were to cut back the bushes that half covered the sign, and also make the lane seem a little less forbidding, they might get more customers.

Again, when she went out to the verandah, she caught Spencer anxiously watching the door, but as soon as she came out, he ducked his head down and pretended to be dozing. What was it about this place that he didn't like? To her, it was an exquisite relic of a bygone age. She wondered how long it had been in the Hendley family. She sat on the cane-backed chair, contentedly lulled by the chirp of birds and insects.

After a while, both Hendleys came out, Marian to spread a delicate lace cloth on the wrought-iron table in front of Vivien, and her husband bearing a tray with a silver teapot and a cup and saucer of delicate china with an oriental floral pattern. After he placed the tray on the table, Paul nodded his head in Vivien's direction and then returned to the house.

"I've got scones in the oven. Here's some cucumber sandwiches to keep you going." Marian put down a plate piled high with tiny sandwiches of thin slices of cucumber on sliced bread. "I made the bread this morning," Marian told her, "so I couldn't cut it as thin as it should be."

Vivien took two of the tiny sandwiches and put them on the china plate. "This looks wonderful. I didn't expect anything like this. Reminds me of England." She took a bite of one of the sandwiches. It was cool and moist.

"Of course it does," Marian said, as if that went without saying. "Most of us came from England, including those who came centuries ago."

Vivien noticed that Marian spoke as if only white people had come to Barbados.

"I hadn't realized that until I read about it in the guidebook. I guess that's why all the Barbadians speak with an English accent."

"Except when they speak among themselves. Then they revert to their own way of speaking, and hardly anyone can understand it."

Maybe that was why *they* did it, thought Vivien. She cringed inwardly at this example of the *us and them* mentality, but objectively she could understand Marian's feelings. Being part of such a small minority on an island might make anyone feel a little defensive.

"What part of the States are you from?" Marian asked.

"I'm from Canada. Toronto."

"Oh, I am sorry. I thought—"

"That's okay. We're all part of the same continent, right?"

"We are part of the Commonwealth," Marian said firmly. "Barbados and Canada have the same queen."

Vivien ate the rest of her sandwich in one bite. She didn't like to say that she rarely thought about the queen. To her, the entire royal family was an anachronism, but it seemed that some people here still clung to that colonial heritage stuff.

Marian ran a hand over her faded hair and stood up. "The scones should be ready."

"No rush. There are plenty of sandwiches left."

"Scones aren't worth eating unless they're fresh and hot," Marian said as she hurried away.

Left alone, Vivien ate another cucumber sandwich and surveyed the garden in front of her, which was a mini jungle; close by were those trees with gnarled branches laden with delicate white blossoms, their scent drifting to her on the faint breeze. To her left, an elderly gardener was pruning a hedge of scarlet hibiscus with an electric trimmer. The high-pitched buzz grated on her ears, marring the tranquil atmosphere.

Marian returned with a large plate bearing four golden scones. "I'm so sorry there's no cream. Only butter and jam."

"That's fine." Vivien took a scone, opened it up, and spread the steaming center with butter and then yellow jam from a crystal jar.

"That's mango jam. I made it myself."

"Delicious," Vivien said, biting into the scone. She wished Marian would either go away or sit down and eat something with her, rather than standing there watching her. She seemed anxious to please and obviously enjoyed having someone to chat with. "I see you have a gardener," Vivien said, nodding toward the older man.

"Gardener?" Marian turned her head. "That's Paul's father, Thomas. He owns Peverill Hall."

Sensing the bitterness in Marian's tone, Vivien hurriedly changed the subject. "What kind of tree is that, with the white blossoms with yellow centers? I'm afraid I'm really a novice when it comes to tropical plants."

"Plumeria. You can smell it from here. Plumeria, magnolia, frangipani . . ." A complaining note entered her voice. "I get migraines from all those heavy scents. I keep telling Paul I have allergies, but he takes no notice."

Vivien realized she'd been right in her initial assessment of Marian Hendley. "You mean you'd like to move somewhere else?"

To Vivien's embarrassment, Marian's eyes filled with tears. "I'd give the world to go back to Yorkshire, but Paul won't hear of it. He's lived here all his life, and he'd never give it up. A year or so ago, I thought there was a chance he might leave, the place was doing so badly, but now . . ." Her voice trailed away.

"Now?" prompted Vivien.

"Now there's no way he'll leave."

"Why's that?"

Marian looked at her, startled. "Sorry. Not supposed to talk about it."

"Of course." Seeing Marian's confusion, Vivien hastily changed the subject. "You do bed and breakfast here, too?"

"That's right," Marian said eagerly. "Do you need a place to stay? We had a couple of Americans from Idaho here for the last two days, but they left this morning."

Vivien's heartbeat quickened. "I'd really love to, but I may be flying back to Toronto tomorrow."

"How long have you been here?"

Vivien grimaced. "This is my second day."

"I don't believe it. And you're going back tomorrow. Why?"

"It's a long story." Vivien gave her a rueful smile. "I was going to do a job here, but it didn't work out."

"What a shame. Can't you take a few more days just to explore the island? It is beautiful, you know. You could stay here. It's very quiet, away from the noisy tourist area." She seemed pathetically eager for Vivien to stay.

Vivien sat, the fragrant scent of the blossoms wafting to her, the sweet trilling of a nearby songbird in her ears. *Stay,* the bird seemed to say, *stay.*

There was something magical about this place. It was such a contrast to the attractive but bustling resort. No screaming youngsters splashing one another, and everyone else, in the pool. Just peace and beauty and Marian Hendley's excellent food. It was the sort of place she liked. The thought of staying here, of using it as a base for a few extra days, was extremely tempting. Vivien was eager to set up her camera, to capture this beautiful house and its magical surroundings.

"Could I think about it? I've told the hotel I'm leaving tomorrow, so I'll need to stay there tonight."

"You could call me tomorrow morning. I'll keep the room for you." Marian gave a nervous laugh. "Silly me. You'll want to see it first, won't you?"

"Okay." There was no harm in looking, was there? Even if she decided against it once she'd left Peverill Hall's magical spell. She stood up.

"Don't you want another scone?" Marian asked.

"Sorry. I filled up on the sandwiches. After I've seen the room, I really must go. Poor Spencer will be fed up waiting for me."

"That's his job," Marian said, surprised. "I'm sure he's overcharging you, like they do all the tourists."

Vivien bit back a retort. No point in antagonizing her if she was really thinking about staying here.

Marian led her back into the house and up the stairs. "There are four bedrooms. Our room and the little room that was the nursery are at the back." She showed her the nursery and then led her down the hallway to the front of the house. "This is the guest room," she said, opening the door.

It wasn't large and the brass bed took over at least half of the room, but it was freshly painted, the walls pale lemon and the woodwork gleaming white. A cane-backed chair with a faded tapestry cushion and a round, glass-topped table had been placed beside the large, paneled sash window. On the bed was an old but still charming white linen cover.

"It's lovely," Vivien said.

"The bed's old, but the mattress is new, so you won't be sleeping on dried corn husks or sugarcane leaves, as they did in the old days." Marian laughed.

The room was small but inviting. Vivien thought about sitting by the window in the evenings, writing in her journal, the tropical night sounds in her ears. She felt she would be at home here.

On the way out, they passed the door of the fourth room, which was closed. "That's the master bedroom, where Paul's parents sleep. It's the largest bedroom, of course," Marian added pointedly. "Sorry, can't show it to you. They don't allow anyone in there, not even me. They keep it locked." Her face flushed. "They say I peek and pry into their things."

Vivien felt sorry for her, having to live with people she disliked so much.

"Do you have any children?"

"Yes, one daughter. Sharon's married with two children, a boy and a girl, and lives in North Carolina."

Marian's face brightened. "I sometimes visit her and the children there."

"With your husband?"

"No." Marian sighed. "He can't leave this place, you see. The house would be overgrown if he left it for even a week."

They returned to the verandah, where Marian forced another cup of tea and a scone on Vivien. She had to refuse a piece of walnut spice cake with coffee icing.

"I'll keep it for you for tomorrow," Marian said.

Vivien wrote down the telephone number and paid the eight Barbados dollars Marian charged her for the tea. "That doesn't seem enough for such great food," she told her. But Marian assured her that Vivien's visit had given her such a boost she'd have been happy not to charge her anything.

Paul Hendley came around from the back of the house to say good-bye, but the man working on the bushes did not even turn his head to look as Vivien got into the van.

"Sorry I was so long," she told Spencer, who looked a little disheveled, as if he had been dozing in the driver's seat.

"No problem," he told her, eyeing the Hendleys as he spoke. He switched on the air-conditioning again and started up the engine. "You okay?"

"Of course I'm okay. Why shouldn't I be? I had a great tea and saw the upstairs part of the house."

A quiver jerked his shoulders. He started up the engine. "Let's go."

"Just a minute." Vivien opened the window on her side. "I'll call tomorrow and let you know, okay?" she told Marian, who was standing on the bottom step.

"Please do," Marian said, a note of desperation in her voice. Both Hendleys raised their hands in farewell as Spencer swung the van around and drove as fast as he could back down the lane.

CHAPTER
EIGHT

As they drove away from Peverill Hall, a strange reversal happened. Now it was Spencer who was eager to talk to Vivien about her visit, asking her what she'd seen, whom she had talked to, but Vivien was reluctant to discuss it. The more distance they put between them and Peverill, the more Spencer's mood lightened and hers darkened. Vivien felt as if her mind had been short-circuited. A variety of thoughts jumped and spat like static in her brain.

Why hadn't she taken some photographs before she left? As if in a slide projector, the pictures snapped one by one through her mind: her first view of the house coming at her through the trees, the elegant front room, the little nursery with its antique cot and white crocheted coverlet.

She became aware that Spencer had asked her something, and she had no idea what he'd said. "Sorry. I didn't hear you."

"I said, we coming close to Codrington. You still want to see it?"

Vivien had to drag her mind back to the present to recall what Codrington was. "No, thanks. I think I'd rather get back to the hotel. Besides, you have that other customer, don't you?" she added, an edge to her voice.

She immediately wished she could retract her words when she saw Spencer rub the back of his grizzled neck with embarrassment. "We'll be at the hotel soon," he muttered and put his foot down on the gas pedal.

She wanted to press him for his reasons for not wanting her to go into Peverill Hall, but she didn't want to embarrass him further, so she devoted the rest of their time together to asking him questions about the island and how it had changed in his lifetime, what the advent of independence from Britain in 1966 had meant to him. Taciturn though Spencer was, she was able to glean from him the simple story of a lifetime of hard work, a long marriage blessed with many children and grandchildren—several of whom had gone on to university—and, most of all, deep faith. He pointed out his church to her when they passed it on the road to the hotel. The plain stone building stood opposite a field of sugarcane.

"We have to keep the doors open for the service on Sundays," he said proudly. "Too many people to fit them all inside."

As they drove through the hotel gates, Vivien wondered how long this old way of life would survive, how long before overdevelopment—or the blight of drugs that had struck Jamaica—came to this smaller island and changed it irrevocably. Not too soon, she prayed. And selfishly, not before she could capture these old ways— as well as the new—with her camera. Another year or two might be too late. Peverill Hall could be sold and pulled down, in its place a high-rise hotel or a shopping mall for the huge influx of tourists. After all, the Atlantic coast of Barbados had not yet been exploited, and Peverill was on prime land close to the ocean.

"How much do I owe you?" she asked Spencer when he pulled up at the hotel.

"Mr. Marshall paid me, Miss Shaw."

"Oh! Then I'd like to give you this from me." She handed him a bill for twenty Barbados dollars, but he shook his head.

"Mr. Marshall gave me extra," he explained.

"This is from me," Vivien insisted and leaned forward to slip the bill into the pocket of his blue shirt.

He gave her a wide grin and a heartfelt "Thank you, Miss Shaw."

She hesitated and then said, "If I were to stay on for a few more days, would you be able to drive me around the island?"

He nodded and gave her one of his cards, which bore only his name, SPENCER YARDE, and his phone number.

"If I don't stay on, I'll give you a call about driving me to the airport tomorrow, okay?" Vivien said.

"If I'm free," he said cautiously.

They shook hands and she watched as the van moved slowly down the drive. When she went into her room she checked her telephone. The message light was flashing red. When she called the operator, she was told she had three messages on the answering machine.

The first one was from her mother, asking her to call back as soon as possible. Her father was worried because she hadn't been in touch. That was all she needed, having to deal with her parents and explain why she was returning to Canada so soon. The second message was from Wesley, asking her to call as soon as she got in. To her surprise, the third was from David Moreton, asking her to give him a call.

She thought she had finished with David Moreton. For a moment she hesitated, then, intrigued, she dialed the number he had left in his message.

"Dr. Moreton's office," a woman's voice said.

"This is Vivien Shaw. I'm returning Dr. Moreton's call."

"Oh, yes, Miss Shaw. Dr. Moreton asked me to give you his home phone number." Vivien wrote it down. "He left more than half an hour ago. He should be home by now."

Vivien thanked her and then sat, gazing at the beige

phone, wondering if she should call. She didn't want *Doctor* Moreton to think she was eager to speak to him. If he was calling her to back down, what would she do? Even if he apologized, how on earth could she work with this man? If she accepted his apology too easily, might it not create an imbalance of power between them that would bode ill for the book?

However, her encounter with Peverill Hall had made her even more keen to stay on. Surely it wouldn't hurt to speak to him—as long as she could keep her cool. She punched in the number and waited, her heartbeat speeding up.

"David Moreton."

"Vivien Shaw," she said crisply. "You called me."

"Hi, Vivien. How was your day?"

"Pretty good," she replied warily.

"I don't know if you're staying on here or not . . ." He let the sentence drift away.

"I haven't decided yet."

"Either way, how about dinner tonight?"

"With you?" The words were out, complete with incredulous inflection, before she could stop them.

He laughed. "Yes, with me."

Vivien wanted to say, *Are you sure you want to be seen out in public with a white woman?* But she didn't—that would only add fuel to the fire.

"I thought if it was your last night on Barbados, you should get a taste of decent Bajan food."

"I already did, at Wesley's home last night, remember?"

"So you did. I prefer to forget last night."

It was the nearest thing to an apology she'd probably get.

"I imagine you haven't had time to see Bridgetown yet."

"No, I had a few hours out this afternoon, but stayed on the Atlantic side of the island."

"My side. Did you visit Bathsheba?"

"Yes. It's so beautiful there."

"I'm glad you like it. What else did you see?"

"Sunbury House."

"Of course, the tourists' delight. All those beautiful old colonial plantation homes built by slave labor."

She didn't rise to the bait, but something around her heart lurched at this reminder that Peverill Hall would also have been built by slaves.

"I didn't have time to see Codrington College."

"It's worth seeing. The grounds are beautiful. It was originally another one of those sugar plantation estates, of course."

"Using slaves?"

"Probably. So what about it? I thought we'd go to Brown Sugar, one of our best restaurants."

"I'd like that," Vivien was surprised to hear herself say.

"Or we could eat Baxter's Road chicken—the Bajan equivalent of Kentucky Fried, but much better, of course. Or fried flying fish at Oistins Market."

"The Brown Sugar restaurant sounds fine."

"Good. Pick you up at six-thirty, okay?"

"Fine." She didn't know what else to say. Should she ask him if he'd changed his mind about the book, to clear the air before they met? No, better to deal with that over their meal, although it sounded like a recipe for indigestion.

She dialed Wesley next, but there was no reply at his office. She decided not to call his home. Better to wait until she'd met with David. That way she could tell Wesley the outcome of their meeting.

She sat hovering over the phone, circling the third and last message she'd jotted down on the notepad. Did she really want to call her parents? No, but she'd better do so or there'd be another frantic telephone call from them. Once her father got into one of his anxious moods there was no escaping. She dialed the number, and her mother picked up on the first ring.

"Hi, Mom," Vivien said.

"Are you okay, sweetie? Your father has been worrying himself sick about you."

Vivien sighed to herself. "I can't think why."

Her mother gave a nervous little giggle. "Oh, you know your father. He's—"

"Yes, I know him. I also know I'm negotiating a difficult assignment here and I am thirty years old. I'm not going to check in with my parents every day. You can tell Dad that from me, okay?"

Her mother sniffed and blew her nose. "I'm sorry, dear. I kept telling him you'd be fine, but he insisted I call."

"Let me speak to him."

"I don't think that's a good idea."

"And I don't think it's a good idea Dad getting you to do his dirty work when he's got himself into a ridiculous state of worry about me."

"He's been feeling a bit low since we got back to Winnipeg." Her mother's voice dropped to a whisper. "He hasn't been in to work for several days."

Vivien could feel the knots forming in her stomach. She drew in a deep breath and released it slowly. "Sorry, Mom. I have to go. I have a meeting in less than half an hour and I have to change." She just could not face any more of her father's mood swings. Increasingly she had been concerned about how long it would be before her mother cracked under the strain of coping with him. Then Vivien would have to deal with both of them.

"Okay, sweetie. I'll tell Dad that you're fine and not to worry, right?"

Her mother's bright voice didn't deceive her a scrap. "Right. Bye, Mom." Vivien put the phone down firmly.

Vivien had hoped that her father's bouts of depression might diminish as he grew older, but, on the contrary, they seemed to be getting worse. She had moved to Toronto, made a new life separate from her parents, married Peter, then divorced him. Made another new life. But you couldn't divorce your parents. She mused, as she often did, about what it would be like to belong to a so-called "normal" family. Well, one thing was certain; she would never know.

She realized that she'd been sitting staring at the phone, thinking, for far too long. She had to shower, wash her hair, which was sticky and bushy from the heat. And what was she going to wear?

"It's not a date, you idiot," she muttered to herself as she checked over the few clothes she'd brought with her. She chose the leaf-green cotton, which went well with her olive-toned skin.

As the hot water poured down on her body, she thought about the evening ahead, bracing herself for the fact that it was probably going to be confrontational, challenging, not at all relaxing. The short drive back to her hotel with David last night had prepared her. Then why, she asked herself, was her apprehension mixed with a tingle of excitement? Was it because she liked a challenge? Of course she did. Her work was a constant challenge: going out into the unknown, befriending strangers, capturing their souls on film.

David Moreton would make a marvelous subject, she thought as she was toweling herself dry. A strong, handsome face, the full mouth, sensitive hands with long fingers, the tall, lithe body, and all that energy emanating from him like electricity. She allowed herself to linger on the thought of how he would look without clothes—until she felt heat flushing her face. She was thinking solely as an artist, she told herself sternly, but the reaction of her body to her thoughts told her otherwise.

"Hello, Vivien!" she admonished herself in the steamy bathroom mirror. "This is the man who openly objected to you because you were a white woman, remember?"

But even Frieda had said he did have a point. The

difference was that David voiced his feelings, whereas most people nowadays covered their prejudices with political correctness.

Vivien released a long breath. It was certainly going to be an interesting evening.

David was fifteen minutes late. Vivien was beginning to think she'd been stood up when his Mustang swooped in, pulling up to the front of the hotel with a squeal of brakes, so that people turned around to look.

Head high, Vivien descended the steps from the hotel verandah. David sprang from the car to open the door for her. He was so full of energy that Vivien wouldn't have been surprised to see him vault across the car to get to the other side.

He grinned at her. "How you doin' this fine evening, Miz Shaw?"

"Great, thanks."

"Sure am glad to hear it." He met her daunting look with a grin. "Okay, okay, I promise to be good." He slammed her door and then went around to the driver's side and really did vault into his seat without opening the door.

Vivien tried hard to keep a straight face, but laughter burst out of her and once she started she couldn't stop.

"What's so hilarious?" he demanded as he drove away.

"You are."

"I know that," he said, laughing himself now. "But why?"

"You reminded me so much of Sidney Poitier in *Lilies of the Field*."

His eyebrows rose. "Because we're both black and you can't tell us apart?"

"No. Because he had the same sort of energy and did the same daft things."

"Daft?" he teased.

"Yes, daft. I can't help it that I have British-born parents, can I?"

"I didn't know that."

"There's a lot of things you don't know about me," she retorted as he left the hotel behind. "I don't put everything in my resumé, you know. But I don't suppose you've read my resumé. I mean, once you saw I was a white woman that was it, you—"

"Can't we get past last night? I thought I'd already explained why I'd reacted that way."

"You did. But it still bothers me that someone would just take a look at the color of your skin and reject you without even trying to get to know you, find out who you are beneath that skin."

"Now perhaps you know how we feel when we're in the white man's world."

Vivien slumped in her seat. "I guess you're right."

"There are places where it doesn't matter a damn that I've got a Ph.D. in English literature and that I've been published and read all over the world and that I teach West Indian literature at Oxford. In a pub in London or a Greyhound bus in Tennessee, some drunken, illiterate jerk who left school at fifteen still thinks he has a right to insult me and call me dirty names based solely on the color of my skin."

Vivien couldn't think of anything to say so kept quiet.

"But the fact that these things happen and they hurt makes my rudeness to you last night even more reprehensible."

Vivien was so surprised she didn't dare look at him.

"That's why I wanted to see you again. To apologize. People who know me would tell you that it's a rare thing, an apology from David Moreton, so I sincerely hope you will believe me when I say how sorry I am for the way I greeted you yesterday."

"Thank you." Vivien kept her gaze on the dark road unfolding before her.

"However, I have to tell you I still think that to choose a non-Bajan person from Canada was a major mistake on my dear friend Wesley's part."

Vivien sat up straight, lifting her chin.

"Have I spoiled the apology now?" he asked.

She turned to look at him and gave him a faint smile. "Not really. I've had some time to think about the whole thing, put it into perspective."

"And?"

"You do have a point."

"Thank you kindly, Miz Shaw."

"But I still think you should give me the chance to show you I can do this project."

"Why?"

"Maybe to prove to you that we're all human beneath the skin and we can respond to humanity, with its joys and cruelties, whatever our race."

"That all sounds very fine in theory, but by and large in practice it's a load of crap."

"And you are an expert in the evaluation of people, I suppose," she said, flinging the words at him. "It's my experience that writers are great at inventing people, but not so good at actually interacting with them. It's so much easier to communicate through the written word, or over the Internet, than to actually get out there and meet people. To smell their smells. Some people in the Arctic wear the same parkas for years and they eat uncooked fish so their bodies smell of it. That's getting to know real people, Mr.—sorry, *Doctor*—Moreton. Not sitting at a keyboard conjuring them up in an air-conditioned office, dressed in chinos and expensive sports shirts."

Silence met what she realized had been quite a diatribe. He sat back in his seat, one hand nonchalantly steering the car over the potholes. Spencer's driving was infinitely better and more comfortable, but she was fast discovering that David was not a person who made you feel comfortable.

A slow smile spread across his face. He glanced across at her and then back at the road. "I like you, Miss Shaw. You give as good as you get."

She released a sigh. "I don't want to fight even if you

do. This is probably my last night in Barbados. If what you want is an intellectual battle with me, I'd rather you took me back to the hotel, please."

"You're right. This was supposed to be a relaxed evening, but the problem is I find you very stimulating."

There it was again, the sexual undercurrent that she'd felt last night. Did he do it deliberately, or was it the unconscious behavior of a very sexy man? She didn't know nor did she want to know.

She turned in her seat. "So, what's it to be? Drive me back to the hotel or a pleasant evening? I have lots of questions to ask you about Barbados."

"I'm not sure I'm the one to ask, considering I spend so much of my time away from the island nowadays. And in response to your question, I'd prefer to spend the evening with you, but I cannot promise not to disagree with you sometimes. It's the way I am."

"Okay. Let's give it a try." She settled back into her seat. "I'll start with a question about you, if you don't mind."

"Not at all."

"How do you get on with your students?"

"Depends on which students we're talking about. Students in Barbados, Jamaica, Oxford?"

"Are they all so different?"

"Indeed they are. Barbados students are still reasonably respectful to their elders, Jamaicans are more rambunctious, but the Brits have this superior attitude that you have to prove yourself to them before they'll respect you. Of course, not all the students at Oxford are British."

"So do you adapt your classes to fit the different students?"

"Not unless I am getting a lot of aggro from them. They just have to adapt to me. It doesn't take long."

She began to think that it wasn't really arrogance with him but supreme self-confidence. Must be nice to feel that way about yourself, she thought.

He, in turn, asked her about her work, and before she knew it they were entering the outskirts of Bridgetown, passing some older buildings with ornamental grillwork and decorated gables and then several modern government buildings, fronted by lawns and trees.

Before they reached the center of town, David parked the car and walked her across the road to the covered entrance of the restaurant. Brown Sugar was not very large, but its open aspect and dimmed lighting, with tropical plants and soft Caribbean music, gave it the atmosphere of a lush garden.

David was greeted effusively by the staff. "We have your favorite table, Dr. Moreton," he was told, and they were led to a table in a quiet corner, away from the main bustle of the room.

Vivien looked around. "I love this."

"Good. There are many good, perhaps more upscale, restaurants here, but this one has authentic Bajan food and a pleasant atmosphere." He leaned back in the cane chair, smiling at her. "Pleasant was what you asked for, I believe."

"It was, and this is more than pleasant. Thank you."

They ordered drinks, a mai tai for her, a beer for him, and when they came, he said, "Tell me about yourself."

"You mean my professional self?"

"No. I can read that in your resumé. Or on your Web site." He eyed her over the top of his glass as he lifted it to his lips.

She could tell that he'd already checked her Web site. "There's not much to tell, really. Born and raised in Winnipeg, the center of Canada. My parents were British. No brothers or sisters. I wasn't very academic, but I did love art and fell in love with photography when my father brought me my first camera for my twelfth birthday. Fine arts degree at the University of Toronto. That's about it."

"Are you married?"

"I'm divorced." She swirled her drink in its glass.

"What happened?" he asked.

"That really is my business."

"Any children?"

"No," she said curtly. "Let's change the subject, shall we?"

"I don't mind if you want to ask me personal questions."

"Why should I?"

"Surely we should know more about each other if we are going to work on this book together."

Vivien sat bolt upright. "You told me last night you were not going to do it, remember?"

"That was before I read more about you, looked at reproductions of your work."

She looked at him quizzically.

"Wesley gave me a copy of your new exhibition book," he explained.

"And?"

"It is fine work. I particularly enjoyed the pictures of the Inuit people at Rankin Inlet and Baker Lake."

Vivien couldn't help smiling. "It was forty degrees below zero when I was there the first time. My breath kept fogging up the lens."

"There's an element of another world about the pictures."

"But then I went back in the summer and found flowers everywhere, there, above the tree line." Suddenly realizing she was getting carried away with her enthusiasm, she subsided, giving him a wry grin.

"You must agree that Wesley rather sprang you on us all as a big surprise," David said, almost apologetically. "As it was, I knew very little about the project. And suddenly here comes Wesley flying back from Canada with you in tow. No one has ever heard of you, yet you are to work with me on this big assignment to create a *gor-geous*"—he pronounced the syllables individually—

"glossy book about Barbados. If I didn't know Wesley better, I would have said he had the hots for you."

"Thanks a lot!"

"Sorry. Just saying it was all rather strange."

Although she would never admit it, she secretly agreed with him. It had all happened so suddenly that she hadn't had much time to think about it herself, but David was right. It *was* strange.

"It came as a surprise to me, too," she admitted.

"What made you accept his offer? Chance of a free vacation?"

Vivien gave him a searing look. "That's insulting."

He held up his hands. "Okay, okay. I admit that was nasty. Forgive me." His smile disarmed her.

"I must admit I was attracted by the thought of spending time here on this lovely island, but my main reason was that it was another challenge, something different. However, to be honest, it wasn't until I saw the island that I felt I really wanted to get to know the Barbados behind the tourist resorts and the calypsos—"

"You think calypso is a form of frivolous entertainment created for the white tourists?"

"Whatever it is, I'm sure you will set me right."

He ignored her sarcasm. "Calypso is a very important part of the West Indian culture. In the early days, calypso was a safe way of getting at the colonial regime through the medium of music and humor. A means of making subversive political statements by Afro-Caribbeans. If you will excuse me, here's a fine example of my concern about a non-Bajan person working on this book."

"I would be taking photographs of people singing calypsos. You would be writing the—"

"Captions?"

She felt herself blushing. "Sorry. I regret saying that last night, but you do have a habit of goading people into saying things they later regret. No, you would be writing the text. That is, *if* we were working on this book together, and that's still highly unlikely."

David's response was interrupted by the waiter appearing to take their order. "Will you allow me to order for us? I'd like you to try several Bajan dishes."

Vivien lifted her shoulders. "Okay."

David rattled off several things, Vivien catching a few, such as flying fish and cou-cou, creole fish, steamed okra. "And we'll finish with your coconut pie, of course." When the waiter left, David turned back to Vivien. "Why?"

She frowned. "Why what?"

"Why do you think it's highly unlikely we'll work on the Barbados book together?"

"For one thing, because you said so." Vivien sighed. "We've been over this before. I'm not going over it again. Let's just say we got off to a bad start and we're not compatible, okay?"

"But incompatibility can often create sparks that makes for freshness and originality, don't you think?" He rubbed his palms and long fingers together as if generating fire from them, his eyes glowing with amusement.

Vivien forced herself to look away from him. "I find conflict a waste of energy," she said, turning her fork over and then back again.

"You are afraid of conflict."

"Now we're getting personal again. Maybe I am afraid of it. Aren't most people?"

"You are not most people. You are an artist . . . and a damned good one. You should harness conflict and make energy from it, not feel that it drains you."

To her horror, Vivien felt her lips trembling. What the hell was wrong with her that she was allowing this— this stranger to get to her this way? Her eyes clouding over, she scraped back her chair and stood up. "Excuse me." She looked around wildly for an exit, a place to hide, before she gave herself away.

He stood and grabbed her wrist, holding her. "What is it? Are you okay?"

Her eyes darted fire at him. "Let go of me," she said in a harsh whisper. People were turning to look at them. He immediately released her. "Excuse me, please."

Bending to pick up her bag, she headed in the direction of the exit, leaving him standing there. She halted at the reception desk.

"Can I help you?" the hostess asked.

Vivien hesitated. Her heart was still pounding and what she really wanted was fresh air, escape, but instead she said, "The ladies' room?"

Fortunately, the hostess pointed in a direction away from the dining room. Vivien had no desire to walk back in there to face the searchlight beam of all those eyes, at least not until she had regained her composure a little.

"You're far too sensitive," Peter used to tell her. "Your bloody parents have a lot to answer for."

That was all she needed, Peter in her head at this moment!

"Get lost," she said out loud, so that someone coming out of the ladies' room turned to look at her. Great! She really was drawing attention to herself. She turned around and went outside instead. Standing beneath a banyan tree she watched the cars rush by.

Either I go back to the hotel right away, she thought, *or I stay and make the best of the remains of the evening.* Which was it to be?

If she dumped David and got a taxi back to the hotel, that would put an end to any chance of doing the book. If she stayed . . . An image of a white-painted house with a wide verandah swung into her mind. Peverill Hall.

If she stayed, she could move to Peverill, make it her work base, far from the tourist resorts and the seething beaches. Excitement built within her. If she stayed at Peverill, she could explore the house and the grounds, capture the soul of the place on film.

But most of all she realized that she was excited at the possibility of working with this challenging man. He was right. Incompatibility—if harnessed properly—could create originality. "Sparks," he'd said. A little shiver of excitement ran across her shoulders.

"Concentrate, you idiot!" she muttered to herself.

The question was, if they were to work together, could she keep her emotions in check whenever his arrogance got to her? It was something they'd have to discuss, although she wasn't sure how to approach it. What they definitely would not discuss was her reluctant realization that it wasn't only sparks of anger she felt with David. *Grow up!* she told herself. The project was the important thing, not a fleeting pulse of attraction to an undoubtedly fascinating man.

If there was to be any hope of doing this project, this evening was probably the last chance she'd have of coming to some sort of agreement with him.

Straightening her shoulders, she pushed open the door and went back into the restaurant.

CHAPTER
NINE

When David saw her approaching the table, he shot back his chair and jumped up. "I thought you might have gone back to the hotel."

"Almost."

He came to her side of the table to pull out her chair. The perfect gentleman. When he sat down opposite her, she could see the concern in his eyes. "Are you okay?"

She nodded.

"I don't know what upset you. It was something I said, but I don't know what exactly."

"I told you I didn't like conflict," she said quietly, "but it seems to be something you do like. I guess we have to accept that we can't change each other, so let's stop trying, okay? We're strangers. For now, let's keep it that way and have as amicable a dinner as is possible, in the circumstances."

"Pleasant?"

"That's right. Pleasant."

"Have I persuaded you to stay on in Barbados?"

"I wasn't aware that you'd been trying to persuade me. Quite the opposite, I believe."

"Now who is not being pleasant?" he said, with a lift of his black-winged eyebrows.

She had to smile. "Okay. How about we keep away from the personal for now?"

"Okay. I will try to answer all your questions about Barbados, without being in any way personal."

"Great."

"So fire away. Oh! Here's the food coming. Hold your fire for a moment."

"Wow!" Vivien breathed as the waiter and his assistant set down several dishes on their table. She held up her hand. "Wait! Don't do anything." She reached down into her bag and pulled out her camera, adjusting it for the reduced light in the dining room. "Look at those gorgeous colors," she said, snapping picture after picture.

David grinned. "Want me out of the way?"

"Please." People were turning to look again, but now she didn't care. Now she was in her professional mode, lost in the delight of the textures and colors of the food and background of the golden cane table and chairs.

She gave a huge sigh after the orgy of picture taking and sank into her chair. "Sorry about that. I couldn't resist it. I hope the food won't be cold," she added anxiously.

"Who cares? It was quite an experience watching you. You're as intense in your work as I am when I'm writing." It was a compliment.

They talked throughout the meal, she answering his questions about her photography career, David expanding on the history of Bajan food, both Afro-Caribbean and English, and how the two had mixed, so that cou-cou and bread-and-butter pudding appeared on the same menu. Vivien wished she'd taken notes. She told him so as she started in on her dessert.

"Don't you worry. I'll be putting it in the book," he assured her.

She looked at him quizzically but said nothing as the first few mouthfuls of her dessert alerted her taste buds to the contrast between the tart spiciness of the main-course foods and the extreme sweetness of the creamy coconut pie.

"I don't think I'll be able to eat another thing for a week," she said with a satisfied sigh when she'd finished it. "You were right. The food here is superb."

"Good. Want to call it a night or would you like to go somewhere else?"

"That depends. No more food," she said hurriedly.

"Lord, no. Feel like some music?"

"Depends," she said warily.

"On what?"

"I'm not in the mood for reggae or steel-pan bands tonight."

"I should hope not. Do you like jazz?"

He kept surprising her. "I love traditional jazz. Not so keen on the modern stuff."

"Ah, we'll have to educate you. How about blues?"

"I like blues."

"Like?" He shook his head. "There's a small place in St. Lawrence that usually has some blues playing. Want to try it? It's only a short drive from here."

Vivien hesitated. She was at last feeling relaxed. For now, her worries were in a hazy no-man's-land called Canada. As far as she was concerned, they could stay there. "Sounds great."

David was right, the place was definitely small. A dimly lit bar serving snacks as well as drinks, with a three-piece combo playing mellow music. When Vivien said she was thirsty, but didn't want any more alcohol, he ordered Cokes for them both. "I have to drive you home safely," he said.

The band struck up a slow, smoky blues number, and David held out his hand. "Let's dance."

Vivien loved dancing, but she hadn't danced with any-one since the separation from Peter. Come to think of it, she hadn't done much of anything, other than work, since her divorce. After a moment's hesitation, she took David's hand and followed him to the small circular dance floor.

He was an excellent dancer, but the slow number didn't call for any special moves. He held her not too close, but close enough for her to feel his supple body against hers. When they finished, he pulled her closer for a brief moment, and she felt a rush of irrational desire to stay there, with her body pressed against his.

As the next song started, she told him she was feeling tired and would rather just sit and listen. He nodded and said, "Fine," without trying to change her mind, but from then on he seemed more reserved.

A short while later, when she saw him glancing at his watch, she took the opportunity to suggest that they call it a night. Again, he didn't try to persuade her to stay on. He asked for the bill, but when it came she grabbed it before he could. "My turn," Vivien said. "You paid for that wonderful meal." There was a cover charge, but the bill was minuscule compared to the restaurant's.

As they drove back across the island to the Ocean Sands, they spoke hardly at all, both wrapped up in their own thoughts. Yet the electricity from the dance floor seemed to hang between them.

When they reached the resort, David drew up short of the hotel and made no move to get out of the car. Vivien turned to him to thank him.

"Can we talk for a few minutes?" he asked.

"Of course," she said, surprised. She waited.

"Not here. I'll park."

He stopped in the parking lot. "Let's go to the beach," he suggested.

"Okay."

The dark pathways were lit by flickering torches, but even in the semidarkness she was acutely aware of how many white people there were around here, in proportion to people of other races.

Was David aware of this, too? she wondered. Silently, he drew her down a pathway leading to the beach, where they found an empty bench. They sat without speaking, the surf pounding in their ears.

"You've never dated a man who wasn't white, have you?" David said after several minutes had passed.

Vivien shook her head. "No."

"Nor even danced with one? Before me, that is."

Again, she shook her head. She felt somehow ashamed to admit it.

"Was it okay for you? The dancing, I mean?"

She didn't look at him. "You know it was."

"I thought it bothered you."

Oh, yes, it had bothered her, but not in the way he meant. "I hadn't danced with anyone since Peter and I separated."

I've lived the life of a nun since Peter and I separated, she could have added.

He sighed. "I thought—"

"You thought it was because you're not white." She didn't want to say the word *black.* He might be offended by it.

His next question surprised her. "Can we work together on this book?" She had expected him to pry further into her feelings about dancing with an Afro-Caribbean.

"Maybe you have to answer that one yourself."

"I think we can, but we're both going to have to work bloody hard at it."

"I always work hard at any of my projects," she said.

"I'm not talking about work; I'm talking about us. The conflict thing. We can't avoid it." He scuffed his feet in the sand. "We're bound to disagree about some things. Can you take that?"

"I think I can." She drew in a deep breath. "As long as you don't think it's something to do with race, rather than just two human beings disagreeing."

He was so quiet she thought he was mad at her, but then she felt his hand take hers and squeeze it. "Very astute, Miss Shaw." He got up. "Time I was going."

Vivien glanced at her watch and sprang up from the bench. "Yikes! I forgot to call Wesley. Now it's probably too late."

"Wesley's not an early bird. Use my cell phone." He fished out the small phone from his pocket.

"Thanks, but I can call him from my room. He'd left a message for me earlier, but he wasn't there when I called back."

"Do you mind me asking what you will tell him?"

"About the book, you mean? I intend to stay on for the rest of the week, as we'd originally arranged, and make my final decision then."

"You don't believe in making hasty decisions, do you?"

"No, not usually. I realize that it's frustrating for you, not knowing immediately." She looked directly at him, but in the semidarkness it was hard to read his expression. "Please tell me honestly, do you still feel that I'm not capable of doing this book?"

"Of course you're capable. I never said you were not. All I said was—"

"Okay, let's not go through all that again. Let me put it this way. Would you be less concerned about the project if I had a lot of input from you . . . I mean, if you could spend some time explaining things to me, showing me around the island . . ." When he didn't respond, she added, "But, if you're too busy with your work, don't worry. I know that fall is usually the busiest time at university."

"I had made arrangements, rescheduled some of my classes, when Wesley told me the photographer was coming in."

"What he didn't tell you was that I was white," she said with a faint smile.

His own smile was wry. "I never thought to ask him. Took it for granted that you were a Bajan Canadian."

"Sorry about that."

"Not your fault."

"I think I've found a place to stay." Her heart thumped hard in her chest. For some unfathomable reason she'd avoided telling him about Peverill Hall until now. "I don't want to stay here after tonight. You may recall that you told me I'd need to move from a resort hotel to be able to get to know the island better."

"It would be a good idea, but if you're comfortable where you are—"

"It's not my kind of place. I usually prefer staying with local people, not in hotels, if I can. When I was out exploring this afternoon, I discovered the most enchanting place, a centuries-old house called Peverill Hall. I'm sure you must know it." She expected him to make some sarcastic comment about her wanting to stay with white local people and hurriedly added, "It was the first bed-and-breakfast sign I saw."

"I seem to recall the name, but there are several old plantation houses in Barbados. Some of them are almost derelict, some being kept up by the Barbados National Trust. Others are still privately owned."

"This one's still private, I think, but looks as if it's fallen on hard times. I had tea first and then the woman there showed me around. It is the most beautiful place, David. Lovely old woodwork—"

"Probably riddled with termites."

"Oh, don't be such a cynic. I fell in love with the place."

"So I gather. Even in the darkness your eyes are glowing. So, this is why you want to stay on in Barbados, not because of the book, or the chance of working with me, but because of a crumbling old plantation house."

He was laughing at her, she knew, but although it wasn't the only reason, the house *was* one of the reasons for her wanting to stay. "I'd like to find out more about the place."

"Why don't you ask the owners?"

"I intend to do so. I think I'll call them tonight and tell them I'm moving in tomorrow."

"Sorry, I'm not free until late tomorrow afternoon, or I'd help you move."

"That's fine. I can get a taxi."

He walked her back to the hotel entrance. "Do you have a number where I can get you at this new place?"

She rummaged in her bag for the piece of paper with Peverill Hall's phone number on it. "Sorry, I must have left it in my room."

He drew a card from his wallet and gave it to her. "Call me. If you get the machine, leave me your new number at—what was the name of the place again?"

"Peverill Hall."

He frowned. "Definitely sounds familiar, but I just cannot place it." He held out his hand. "Thank you for a great evening."

"Thank *you*. I had a really good time."

"Despite all the conflict?"

She chose not to respond but smiled back. He was still holding her hand. Slowly, she drew hers away, then held it against her side, rubbing her thumb back and forth across the tips of her fingers.

When she entered her room, she saw that the red light on her phone was blinking. When she checked in with the operator, she found that Wesley had left her another message, asking her to contact him as soon as possible. But when she tried his number, he still wasn't there, so she left him a message, saying she would call him first thing in the morning. She told him she'd decided to stay on for the rest of the week and that she'd had dinner with David. That was all. Let him stew about that overnight. Serve him right. It was obvious that Wesley liked to keep his cards close to his chest. Time he was treated the same way.

Then she tried the number at Peverill Hall, but there was no reply and no answering machine. As it was not quite ten o'clock yet, she tried again, twice, but although she let it ring more than a dozen times, there was still no reply. She imagined the phone ringing through the old house. Through the airy hallways and the dining room, with its long mahogany table, and up the gently curving stairway to the bedrooms. They probably went to bed early there. She didn't recall seeing a television anywhere or an antenna on the roof.

Disappointed not to get it all settled before she went to bed, Vivien set the receiver down and decided to call again in the morning. After all, Mrs. Hendley had said the room was vacant, hadn't she? She could only hope that no backpacker or cyclist had come upon the place by chance and was now sleeping in the little bedroom with the brass bed at the front of the house.

Not until later, when she was cleaning her teeth before she got into bed, did she realize she hadn't told David about Spencer's irrational fear of driving into the Peverill Hall estate.

It just didn't make sense.

She'd have to arrange a taxi for her move tomorrow. She wasn't about to impose that ordeal on Spencer again. However, she certainly hoped she could discover why he'd been so afraid of a house where she'd felt so comfortable.

CHAPTER
TEN

Vivien's sleep was disturbed by a series of weird dreams featuring a supernaturally tall David Moreton, wrapped in a long black cloak, pursuing her down the shadowy elongated halls of Peverill. She awoke a few minutes before seven o'clock, glad to escape and yet with a strange sense of loss. Her first rational thought was that she must call Marian Hendley, but it was far too early to call anyone. Breakfast started at seven. Although she wasn't at all hungry, she'd pass the time by getting some coffee, fruit, and cereal. Then she'd come back and make her phone calls. Marian Hendley first and then Wesley.

She walked along the pathway, past the pool, which was already filled with a group of noisy young men playing a rowdy game with a Frisbee, but she no longer cared. If all went well, she'd soon be away from boisterous holidaymakers, settled into the beauty and peace of Peverill Hall.

There was a long line for breakfast. She was tempted to grab a muffin and a mug of coffee from the urn on a table by the door and drink it outside, but she should eat some fruit as well. All around her were several varieties of British accents: London, Midlands, Scottish . . . Despite their years in Canada, her parents' accents had remained very English, especially that of her father, who was almost pedantic with his emphasis on using the right words and grammar. But that was Dad for you.

"Table for one?" the hostess asked. Since the divorce, Vivien had grown used to the pitying glances people gave her when she ate alone, but she wasn't about to stop dining out because of society's continued emphasis on couples and families. She was shown to a table in a corner, next to a middle-aged couple who were arguing. The woman, in a fluorescent-pink running suit, was complaining to the server about the doves and small black birds that flew in through the open windows to land on their table or the backs of their chairs, scavenging for crumbs. Her husband said he enjoyed seeing them. "You don't get that happening in Middlesborough," he told his wife. "You always have to complain about something, don't you?"

Vivien decided it was better to be alone than to be part of a couple that started every day with a fight. Peter had always been short-tempered in the morning.

She chose some papaya and savory plantain pancakes, wolfing the food down so that she could get out of this bustling madhouse.

When she'd finished, she made her way back to her room. The elevator seemed to take ages to rattle down to the ground floor and then she had to wait while a family with three small children loaded onto it. On the third floor, they all disembarked and she started off down the corridor, only to find the door to her room open and the chambermaid inside, cleaning.

"Damn," she muttered.

"You want to come in, honey?" she was asked. "Come on in. I can work around you."

"I'll sit on the balcony until you've finished."

"Okay. Oh, I was meanin' to ask. That book you left by the basket. You mean to throw it away?"

It was John Le Carré's latest novel, about the pharmaceutical industry in Africa. "Yes, I've finished it."

"Mind if I take it? Books are mighty expensive here."

"Of course."

"Thanks. Very kind of you, honey. My name is Cora. If you have any more books, I'd be glad to take them from you," she said with a chuckle.

What a fascinating place Barbados was, where a member of the hotel cleaning staff seemed just as pleased to get a book as she would be to get a tip.

As soon as Cora had closed the door, Vivien got out the piece of paper with the number for Peverill Hall and dialed it. This time she got through after two rings. "Yes?" a man said abruptly.

"Is Mrs. Hendley there? I was speaking to her yesterday about a room."

There was a loud clatter in her ear, as if the man had dropped the receiver on a table. She heard him yell, "Telephone!" and the next thing was Mrs. Hendley's voice breathlessly saying, "Hello?"

"Sorry to call so early," Vivien began. "This is Vivien Shaw. You remember I was there yesterday and—"

"Of course. How could I forget? I did enjoy your visit."

"You said you had a room available."

"Indeed we do. Is it for you only?"

"That's right."

"Well," Marian's voice dropped, as if she didn't want someone at her end to hear, "we usually like to have a couple so we can charge for two people, but I—"

"I'll be happy to pay a little more to make up for that," Vivien said hurriedly.

"I wouldn't ask for it," Marian said, lowering her voice almost to a whisper, "but it's my father-in-law, you see. As I told you, he owns the place . . ."

"That's fine."

"How many days shall I book you in for?"

"I'm not sure, but let's say four days for now."

"Wonderful! And you can always extend it if you want to."

"That's right."

"When shall we expect you?"

Vivien thought about that. "I'll need to pack, pay my bill, get a taxi."

"Oh, that's right, you don't have a car. You really need a car here, as we're so far away from anywhere. There is a bus, but it's not very frequent."

"I'll probably rent a car, but I can leave that until tomorrow. I'll get a taxi from here."

There was silence on the other end . . . then, "You're staying at the Ocean Sands, right? Tell you what. I have to pick up some groceries this morning. Why don't I stop by on my way home and pick you up?"

"That's very kind of you. Are you sure it's not taking you out of your way?"

"Not at all. Shall we say around eleven o'clock?"

"Perfect. I'll wait for you on the hotel verandah, so don't worry about being on time. I can always read while I'm waiting."

"Fine. I'm so pleased you're coming to stay. It gets pretty lonely here at times. Men don't understand things like that, do they?"

"No, that's true," Vivien said automatically, although she wasn't quite sure what Marian meant. She hoped she wasn't going to monopolize all her time by talking.

When she put the receiver down, she sank back into the rattan chair with a feeling of relief mixed with exhilaration. She was going to stay at Peverill Hall, explore its gardens and extensive grounds, seek out every nook and cranny of the ancient house.

What on earth was a cranny? she wondered, smiling to herself. David would probably know. She felt a rush of warmth as she thought of dancing with him last night, his body against hers. *Enough!* she told herself. *You are here to work, not to exercise an overheated imagination.*

Switching back to the present, she picked up the receiver again, this time to dial Wesley's number.

"Wesley Marshall here," he said, his rich voice booming down the line.

"It's Vivien."

"My dear Miss Shaw—"

"Vivien," she insisted.

"Vivien. We seem to have kept missing each other. I began to think we would never speak again. Did you get my message this morning?"

She saw it now, the red light blinking on the phone. "I am sorry, Wesley. I didn't check."

"I tried you about twenty minutes ago. You were not there."

"I was having a quick breakfast and then had to wait while my room was cleaned."

"Well, I managed to get part of the information I needed from David. He tells me you had a pleasant dinner with him last night. Sounds like progress in the right direction, yes?"

Vivien grimaced. It remained to be seen what exactly "the right direction" meant. "Let's say, we've agreed to give it a try."

"That's marvelous." Like David, Wesley pronounced all the syllables of some words, drawing them out for emphasis. It seemed to be a Barbadian thing, this intrinsic pleasure in words. "I am so happy to hear it." He waited for her to say more.

"To be perfectly honest, Wesley," she blurted out, "I didn't want to get in touch until David and I had met again. It seemed to be the best way to decide the whole thing. After all, there was no point in continuing with the project if we loathed each other on our second meeting."

"But you did not loathe each other?" She sensed a hint of amusement in his voice.

"Let's just say I think we might be able to tolerate each other. Dr. Moreton is"—she hesitated, not liking to criticize Wesley's friend—"very self-confident," she finished.

"That is a good way of classifying David. A very diplomatic way, if I may say so."

"He's rather exhausting, isn't he?" Or did she mean exhilarating? "I'm rather a quiet person. He is not."

"Ah, well, you know what they say about opposites attracting."

This is not an interracial dating service you're setting up, Mr. Marshall, Vivien felt like saying but didn't.

"What did you think of Brown Sugar?" he asked.

"I loved it. Excellent food and atmosphere."

"I am glad to hear it. So," he continued, "do you plan to stay on there, at the Ocean Sands?"

"No. Actually, that was my main reason for calling you. I'm moving to a private bed-and-breakfast."

"Oh, where?"

"An old plantation house called Peverill Hall." Was it her imagination, or had there been a sharp intake of air at the other end of the line? She barreled on, ignoring it. "We were driving along this road— By the way, I never thanked you for Spencer. What a terrific driver he is. It was a pleasure—"

"Did you say Peverill Hall?" Wesley said, breaking in.

"That's right. You must know it, I'm sure. A beautiful old place with—"

"I know it. I would strongly advise against you staying there," he said vehemently.

"Why? It's a beautiful spot. And Paul and Marian Hendley seemed very friendly. What's wrong with it?" she asked aggressively, prepared to do battle to defend Peverill.

"It does not have a good reputation," Wesley said, picking each word carefully.

"How do you mean? The place is spotlessly clean. It can't be the food. The tea I had there was excellent."

"I have my reasons for advising you not to stay there."

"Sorry, but I've set my heart on moving in. It's a wonderful spot. I can't wait to take photographs of the house and the grounds. Have you been over it yourself?"

He ignored her enthusiasm. "Have you met Thomas Hendley?"

"He's the owner of Peverill Hall, isn't he? Marian Hendley's father-in-law. No, I didn't actually meet him when I was there yesterday, but he was in the garden, pruning some trees and bushes. The place is overgrown with—"

"The house does not have a good reputation," he repeated stubbornly.

"What does that mean? Do they steal from their paying guests while they're asleep?"

"Perhaps."

She thought of Spencer's fear of driving into Peverill. "That reminds me. Spencer was extremely reluctant to take me onto the property. I had to threaten to walk in by myself, and even then I could tell he didn't want to go there." A nervous tingle ran down her spine. "Don't tell me the place is haunted."

"So it is thought, yes." Wesley seemed eager to accept this explanation. "That's why local people are reluctant to go there."

"What kind of ghost haunts it?"

"I have no idea," he replied curtly. "As I said, it has a generally unsavory reputation."

"I gather that you include the owner, Thomas Hendley, as part of this unsavory reputation?"

"And his wife. I understand there are the four of them there, plus their daughter, Sharon."

"I didn't see Mrs. Hendley senior, and Marian Hendley told me that her daughter had moved to North Carolina."

"Ah, yes. Now I recall that Sharon married an Ameri-

can and moved to the States. The elder Mrs. Hendley is
a semi-invalid. I understand she is rarely seen."

"May I ask where your negative information about
the house and the family came from?"

"One has one's sources, especially in an island the size
of Barbados."

"I'm sure one does, but I have to wonder if these so-
called sources aren't repeating some kind of rumor that's
become inflated through the retelling."

"I assure you that is not the case, Miss Shaw." Wesley
sounded annoyed.

"But you haven't actually told me anything of sub-
stance, other than rumors that the place and perhaps the
people who own it have an unsavory reputation. And it
might be because they rob people. Or it could be because the house is haunted. But you don't have any
more definite reasons, right?"

Wesley cleared his throat as if he were about to tell
her something, but nothing came. Then he said, in his
most formal tone, "I think you should trust me to be
telling you the absolute truth when I inform you it is
not a good idea for you to move to Peverill Hall."

"Thank you for the warning, duly noted, but until you
can give me something more tangible, it's my plan to
move there today. Mrs. Hendley is picking me up from
the hotel at eleven o'clock."

"You are not getting a taxi there?"

"No. She suggested she'd pick me up on the way
home after grocery shopping. Pretty mundane stuff,
right? Or do you think she's planning to have me robbed
and my throat cut en route?"

Dead silence.

"Wesley? Are you still there?"

"Yes, I am here."

"Okay. Wanted to make sure."

"I was hoping we might meet sometime today. You,
David, and I."

"Could we make it tomorrow instead? I'd really like to get settled in first, maybe take some pictures, make notes. I want to visit the public library in Bridgetown to do some research, so I could do that as well tomorrow."

"The university library is best."

"Good. Then maybe David can take me there," she said briskly, trying to ignore Wesley's patent disapproval. "But I prefer to make it for tomorrow." She was not about to have her plans spoiled by some island gossip that had been blown all out of proportion.

As soon as he had rung off, Wesley dialed another number. "You are going to find this very hard to believe."

"What?"

"She has found Peverill."

"Oh, my God! How could that possibly have happened? You must have mentioned something about it to her." The tone was accusatorial. "It can't be just coincidence."

"Apparently it was."

"That is very hard to believe. How did she find it? Was she driving a rental car?"

"No, Spencer was driving her. I organized it myself."

"Perhaps you let something slip to Spencer."

"Of course not! I intend to speak to him right away, ask him what happened."

"You should have stayed with her."

The usually calm Wesley exploded. "For the Lord's sake, I cannot keep the woman under lock and key, can I? But I haven't told you the worst. She has decided to stay in Barbados, which is good, but she intends to move into Peverill today and take a room there."

"Oh, dear God! What are we going to do?"

"Perhaps we should tell her the truth."

"All of it, you mean?"

"Yes."

"No! We agreed. We cannot tell her everything. We agreed; she is never to know!"

"I warned you this idea of yours would never work," Wesley said.

"There is one thing we must consider." The voice had turned contemplative.

"What?"

"This might turn out to be a positive thing. Perhaps we could use it to our advantage."

"How?" Wesley demanded. "All I can see are the dangers."

A heavy sigh. "You're right. We cannot expose her to any harm."

"Should we put an end to the whole idea?" he said. "Send her home without going any further?"

"Let me think about it. I'll speak to the others."

"Meanwhile?"

"Meanwhile, you must do all you can to persuade her against moving into Peverill."

"Too late," Wesley said. "She's moving in this morning. I tried, but she's very stubborn."

"Then we can only hope that they make her so uncomfortable at Peverill that she leaves of her own accord."

"And pray to God they don't find out who she is."

CHAPTER
ELEVEN

The hotel receptionist took Vivien's cancellation without protest. She was told that her bill had been looked after, including the extras. *Thanks, Wesley,* she thought. She wondered if she should get in touch with David before she left but decided against it. She'd call him from Peverill Hall once she'd settled in.

She was almost packed and ready to leave when the phone in her room rang. Marian was calling to say that her father-in-law needed the car, so Vivien would have to make her own way to Peverill. Marian sounded furious, as if she'd been deprived of a rare treat. Though surprised that Marian didn't have her own car, Vivien had a bellboy take her bags downstairs and, within minutes, was on her way in a taxi to Peverill Hall.

This time her driver was a hip young guy in a tight black tank top that displayed his impressive pecs. The radio in his 4x4 blasted raunchy reggae and, unlike Spencer, he drove so fast over the uneven road that Vivien felt her teeth were going to fall out.

Once they turned off the main road from the hotel, she had to direct him to Peverill. Fortunately, she'd followed the map on yesterday's return journey and committed it to memory. As it was, the driver zoomed past

the turnoff and had to screech to a halt and reverse back
to it when she called to him to stop.

"Whoa!" was all he said when she directed him down
the narrow lane, branches brushing across the windshield. It had rained heavily before dawn and the sky
was still gray with dark clouds. At the end of the lane
was the impressive house. In her vivid dreams last night,
it had appeared wavering and fluid, as if it lay at the
bottom of the Atlantic Ocean that surged at the foot of
the nearby cliffs, but now it was solid, looking as if it
could survive another three hundred years.

Yesterday the house had been basking in the late afternoon sunlight, but today it was in shade. Its walls
were gray, not golden, which gave it a more ominous
aspect, with the dark shadows of windswept branches
moving across its coral stone walls and shuttered
windows.

The taxi driver carried her bags up to the verandah
and then looked around. "Anyone supposed to be
here?" he asked.

"Yes, they're expecting me." She paid him and waited
for him to go. "Thanks very much."

He glanced around apprehensively. "Man, this is some
creepy place. You want me to wait with you?"

"No, that's fine. Thanks again."

"Okay," he said, shaking his head. He jumped back
into the 4x4 and sped off down the driveway, breaking
branches as he went. Moments later, she heard the
squeal of tires as he turned onto the road at the end of
the lane.

Now she was alone with the house and the people
who lived in it.

The main door was closed and, as she discovered
when she tried the handle, locked. She was surprised
that no one had come out when they heard the taxi
driving in. It was not exactly a warm welcome. She
pulled the bell-pull on the paneled door . . . and waited.

No response other than the bell's jangle inside the house. Strange. After all, they were expecting her. She tried pounding on the door with her fist, but soon gave this up when her hand became sore.

Had there been an accident? A sudden illness? Surely Marian Hendley would have contacted her again if that were the case.

Leaving her bags on the verandah, Vivien made her way around the side of the house. In the stone wall that divided the front of the grounds from the back, she found a dilapidated door made of woven cane and pushed it open. She had to wade through plants and weeds almost waist high to get around to the back. The vegetation was even more oppressive at the rear of the house, looking as if it were seeking to subsume it.

By the back door was a small clearing, paved with limestone, and there she found Marian, hanging out wet sheets on a line that stretched from the knotted trunk of a banyan tree to a hook in the larger tree that gave shade to the rear of the house.

"There you are!" Vivien couldn't entirely hide the edge to her voice. "I thought everyone must be out."

Eyes wide, Marian Hendley spun around, almost dropping the end of the sheet she was struggling to get over the line. "Oh, it's you."

"Sorry if I startled you, but I couldn't get a reply when I rang the bell and knocked."

"I'm so sorry. You can't hear anything when you're out here. All these damned trees muffle the sound." She glanced around and then bent her head toward Vivien and said, lowering her voice, "They should all be cut down or cut right back, at least, but he won't hear of it. Says he likes the place exactly the way it is." She straightened up. "Hang on, I'll just get this sheet up properly, then I'll let you in."

"Need some help?"

"No, thanks." Marian smoothed the wet sheet over the clothesline, the weight making it sag, and then wiped her hands on the old-fashioned wraparound apron she wore. Vivien could recall her grandmother wearing something similar when she'd visited Britain as a child, staying in the Somerset farmhouse where her mother had been raised. Her grandmother's floral apron had been so threadbare it was hard to determine the original colors. As she thought of it, Vivien conjured up the aroma of fresh-baked floury scones, taken piping hot from the Rayburn oven and then slathered with butter.

She hadn't seen much of her grandmother. Her father didn't like traveling, and his mother was afraid of flying all that way from Britain to Canada.

Marian heaved up the large wicker basket filled with dry towels and clothing, balancing it on her hip, and led the way through the back door into a small stone-flagged room, which might, thought Vivien, be best described as a scullery. Beneath a small window was a deep porcelain sink with rusty taps. Alongside an old electric washing machine were an ancient mangle and a huge zinc vat, with four flatirons on a shelf above the table.

"Sometimes the electricity goes off," Marian explained when she saw Vivien eyeing everything. "They belong in a museum. But then this whole place *is* a museum, isn't it?"

Vivien wasn't sure how to respond. "I think it's a beautiful house," she said. "I'm looking forward to taking some pictures." She breathed in the musty smell of dampness, which she hadn't noticed yesterday. The paint on the walls was peeling off in several places, leaving patches of bare stone.

"I'll just dump this down here," Marian said, setting the heavy basket on a trestle table. "Then I'll show you up to your room."

"You're busy. I can find my own way. I left my bags on the front porch." Vivien saw that there was another basket filled with dry washing on the table. "Can I help you fold those?"

"Of course not! You're our guest," Marian said,

shocked. Perspiration beaded her face. She took off her apron and wiped her face with it. "Let's get your bags and I'll take you upstairs."

As they went down the passageway to the front of the house, Vivien caught a glimpse of an elderly woman sitting in a wooden rocking chair in a small back room, which would probably have been called a parlor in the old days. She could hear the squeak of its runners as the woman rocked it back and forth, back and forth on the polished wood floor.

"Who is that?" the woman called out as they passed by the open doorway.

"This is Miss Shaw, Mother," Marian told her. "My mother-in-law," she whispered to Vivien as she kept on walking toward the staircase.

"Come back here directly. Don't you be so rude!"

Marian sighed. "Sorry," she whispered to Vivien. They backtracked a few paces to the open doorway. "This is Miss Shaw, Mother."

"Come in." It was an order, not an invitation.

Rolling her eyes at Vivien, Marian stepped inside, nodding to Vivien to follow her.

"Marian has no manners," the elder Mrs. Hendley said. She was a wizened little woman, her gray hair in a neat bun and her tanned face wrinkled like a prune. She wore glasses perched on the end of her nose, and her age-spotted hands were engaged in mending a pillowcase. "Where are you from?" she demanded, not looking up from her sewing.

"Canada."

"Big country, Canada. Whereabouts in Canada?"

"I was born in Winnipeg," Vivien replied. "I live in Toronto now."

"Hmm. What brings you to Barbados?"

Vivien hesitated, not wanting to take part in an interrogation. "Part holiday, part work." That was enough for this nosy old woman to know. It wasn't Marian who lacked manners, she thought.

"Work? What work would you do in Barbados?"

"I'm a photographer."

Mrs. Hendley looked up from her sewing. "A photographer?" Her watery blue eyes narrowed. "Hope you're not one of those people who takes pictures of our treasures so that thieves can steal them."

"Of course she's not." Marian jerked her head at Vivien, indicating that they should leave. "I'll take you up to your room."

"Enjoy your stay at Peverill, Miss Shaw," the older woman said, her voice muffled as she bent her head over her work again.

"Thank you, Mrs. Hendley," Vivien said, glad to leave.

"Don't take any notice of her," Marian said as they retrieved Vivien's bags from the verandah. "She gets more senile every day."

Vivien wasn't so sure. The eyes might have been watery, but they were also sharp. She must be careful not to venture into rooms where Mrs. Hendley senior was or, she sensed, there would be trouble.

The guest room was smaller than she remembered, but it had a large window looking out through a canopy of leaves so it would be fairly cool in the evenings. Now it was stifling.

Setting the smaller bag on the floor by the bed, Marian went to switch on the fan that stood on the white-painted dressing table. "Sorry there's no ceiling fan in here. We have them in the front room downstairs and in the two larger bedrooms, but that's all."

"That's fine. I don't expect I'll be in much during the day, and I imagine it gets cooler at night."

"Sometimes. But this is the stormy season, and they're forecasting a storm brewing up. If there's no wind, it gets terribly humid and oppressive. Makes physical work really hard." As Marian pushed her hair away from her eyes, Vivien felt sorry for her. She had the impression that Marian was perpetually weary. The house was large, and there didn't seem to be many labor-saving devices in it.

"Do you have any help here?" she asked.

"In the house, do you mean, or the plantation itself?"

"Both."

Marian sat down in the cane chair in the corner of the room and stretched out her legs, glad to take a quick break. "Occasionally, if we have a busy season with guests, I get some help with the breakfasts and the cleaning, but usually I do it all myself. We really can't afford to pay for help." Her face brightened. "But we're hoping that will all change soon."

Vivien recalled her saying something similar yesterday, but she didn't like to ask why.

"It can't be easy, living with your in-laws," she said tentatively, her innate curiosity getting the best of her.

"You can say that again." Marian glanced around nervously, as if she expected her mother-in-law to be standing in the doorway, listening. She didn't expand on the subject. Vivien had the impression that she was afraid to say too much in this house with the doors and windows open.

"What about the estate itself? Surely that's too big a job for your husband alone."

"His father still does a lot of the work with him, and we have temporary field workers for the sugarcane. But the gardens and grounds of the house are neglected. And in this part of the world, if you don't keep cutting it back, the vegetation takes over. I keep telling Paul that we'll soon be completely cut off from the road, but his father seems to like it that way. He tells me to stick to women's business and keep my nose out of men's work."

The senior Mr. Hendley sounded as charming as his wife. Vivien would have to be careful around him, too, it seemed. Oh, well, she could always move back to the hotel if it didn't work out. Besides, she really liked Marian and sensed that she was glad to have someone to talk to.

Marian got to her feet. "Speaking of women's business . . . I'd better get on. The bathroom's across the hall. Clean towels on the towel rack here." She indicated the white towels hanging on an old wooden rack beneath the window ledge. "I recommend you have a bath first thing in the morning, as we try not to keep the boiler going during the day. Makes the house too hot."

No hot shower when she came back after a long working day? Help! "Thanks for the tip. Oh, I meant to ask you about the phone. I need to make some long-distance calls. How do I pay you for those?"

Marian's face twisted. "Oh, dear, I should have mentioned that yesterday. They really don't like you making anything but local calls. Even then . . ." She didn't finish, but her expression was eloquent enough.

Vivien was ready to explode. This was the twenty-first century, for heaven's sake. If they wanted to run a bed-and-breakfast business, they had to be reasonably up-to-date, surely.

"There's a public phone at the rum shop near the crossroads. I think they might take a credit card."

"How far is that?" Vivien asked.

"About a mile and a half."

Vivien had already realized that it would be better if she rented a car. Now it became an absolute necessity. The thought of being cut off from the outside world without easy access to a telephone made her feel anxious.

"Sorry about that," Marian said with an embarrassed smile. "That's one of the drawbacks about living in a great house, I suppose."

" 'Great house'? That's an unusual expression, isn't it?"

"That's what they called all the old plantation estate houses in the olden days. Comes from England. They call them stately homes over there, but those are usually owned by the aristocracy. The large manor houses or estate houses are a notch below them, and they were called great houses. The name continued on in Barbados."

"Seems to me it's not the only hangover from England. I know they're also mad about cricket here."

"The settlers in Barbados were nearly all from England. No Spanish or Dutch or French, like some of the other West Indian islands. So the English ways have predominated, but it's changing now. They're even moving Nelson's statue from the center of Bridgetown. Better not bring that subject up with my in-laws!"

"What's so special about Nelson?"

Marian stared at her, openmouthed. "Don't tell me you haven't heard of Admiral Nelson, hero of the Battle of Trafalgar?"

"Sure I have, but if there has to be a statue of someone, I imagine Barbadians prefer to put up some more modern hero of their own."

Marian sat up straight, her back very stiff. "You're not English. You wouldn't understand."

Vivien suddenly felt hot and tired, and she wanted to unpack and get settled in. "I probably don't, but my parents would. They were born and raised in England."

Marian stood up and walked to the door. The weave of the cane chair had marked the backs of her legs with a crisscross pattern. "Better get on, I suppose. Let me know if there's anything you want," she said. "Anything at all," she added, her smile indicating that she didn't hold any ill will against Vivien for not understanding about her reverence for Nelson.

"I do need one thing as soon as possible."

"What's that?"

"A telephone, so I can make some calls. Just local ones," Vivien quickly added, seeing Marian's dismayed expression. "I have to let people know where I am. I also need to arrange for a car."

Marian sucked in her cheeks, chewing on the insides, and then shrugged. "I suppose they can't complain about that, can they?"

"They could," Vivien said firmly, "but I won't be able to stay if I can't make those calls." She was starting to think she must be nuts to stay anyway, with a family that seemed to have stepped directly out of the pages of a 1930s novel. Dealing with the elder Hendleys might be a bit of a challenge, she thought, recalling old Mrs. Hendley's icy welcome and her husband's averted back in the garden, but she wasn't going to let them stop her from enjoying this house. After all, what harm could two old people do her?

CHAPTER TWELVE

The request for a telephone resulted in Vivien's first encounter with Thomas Hendley. She was unpacking her bag and hanging clothes in the wardrobe tucked into a corner of her room. It was a beautiful piece of furniture, mahogany with a patterned inlay of scrolling stems and leaves in a pale gold wood, but there was a crack down the side and the door was so warped that it wouldn't shut properly. The climate here was not kind to furniture.

She was trying to get the lower drawer shut when someone rapped once on her door. Breathless from wrestling with the heavy drawer, she sat back on her heels and shouted, "Come in."

The door swung wide open and an elderly man with sparse gray hair, whom she guessed to be Thomas Hendley, stood there. The only time she had seen him before was in the garden, bent over the bushes. He was larger than she'd imagined. "Excuse me," he said. "You asked my daughter-in-law about using my phone." His voice was quiet but clear, with no hint of a Caribbean lilt.

Vivien scrambled to her feet. "Trying to get this drawer shut," she explained, wiping her hand on her shorts before holding it out to him. "I saw you working in the garden yesterday, but we haven't met. I'm Vivien Shaw."

He took her hand and then let it fall, giving her only enough time to register the dryness of his skin. It felt like shaking hands with a wad of tissue paper.

"So I understand." There was no welcoming smile, not even a relaxation of the thin lips. He must have been a handsome man once; the facial bone structure was patrician, but the lack of warmth in his expression had a chilling effect. She guessed that he must be about eighty or so. A proud, stubborn man, she gauged from the way he held his head, with no hint of the usual stoop of a man of his age. His head erect, he openly peered around the room, as if establishing that, although she was a paying guest, this was *his* domain.

"You wanted to use my telephone," he said, fixing his gaze on the window behind her.

"Yes, that's right. I need to let my contacts know where I am staying and also to arrange for a rental car."

His eyebrows rose. They were dark, unlike his hair. "Surprised you didn't arrange that before you came here."

Despite an urge to punch him in his arrogant face, Vivien smiled. "I have friends here who looked after me while I was staying in the hotel."

"Friends?"

One second, perhaps two, passed before she responded. "Yes, friends," she said firmly. "The friends I need to call."

"And the friends would be fellow tourists at the hotel?"

"No." Her tone made it clear that she considered this to be none of his business. "Friends who live in Barbados."

"Who are they?"

She didn't even try to hide her astonishment. "Excuse me?"

"I asked who they are. I know most of the people who live on the island."

"I'm sure you do." She waited for him either to leave the room or to tell her where to find the telephone.

"But we at Peverill Hall prefer to keep to ourselves." His tone and tightened lips were more than enough to clarify his meaning.

In another era, she might not have been quite so surprised to encounter such patent racism, but coming as it did from an aged white man living in the twenty-first century on an island with a population of about ninety-five percent Afro-Caribbean or mixed race, it was not only offensive, it was ludicrous.

Now she began to understand Wesley's reaction to her news that she was staying at Peverill. The Hendleys were obviously well-known for "keeping to themselves." She had the distinct impression that neither Wesley nor David, both probably infinitely better educated men than Thomas Hendley, would be welcome to cross Peverill Hall's threshold.

Her eyes narrowed. "Don't worry, Mr. Hendley. I won't be bringing any of my *friends* here."

"Good." He turned to leave.

"The phone?" Vivien reminded him.

He hesitated and then said, without turning back, "I will leave it on a table outside my bedroom. We charge for local calls. One dollar per call. Please make long-distance calls elsewhere." With this, he left.

"Thank you *so* much." Vivien went to close the door, tempted to slam it, but didn't want to harm the house. It wasn't Peverill Hall's fault that it had a moron for an owner. Marian had blamed senility for the behavior of Thomas Hendley's wife. Perhaps she was right, but Thomas himself was just plain obnoxious.

She heaved a disappointed sigh, knowing she'd probably have to leave sooner than she wanted to. Meanwhile, though, she'd take as many pictures of the house and grounds as she could. Itching to get started before it was too late, she shoved her bags under the high bed and got out her Nikon camera. Without easy access to a darkroom, it was simpler and safer to take digital pictures, although she still preferred the old-fashioned way and had also brought her 35 mm Leica with her.

"Better lock the door first," she told herself. But when she checked the antique metal lock, there was no key, only a small hook-and-eye type closure that could be opened from outside with a mere shove.

Something else to take up with Marian. She wasn't about to leave her door unlocked and have the Hendleys rummaging around in her things when she was out.

She dropped the hook into the eye. Flimsy though the lock was, at least she'd have some sort of warning if one of the Hendleys tried to repeat the same knock-and-enter routine that Thomas had.

A washstand stood in the corner of the room. The glazed white stoneware washing basin was decorated with a jade-green fern pattern, with a water jug and chamber pot to match. She took three pictures of it, from different angles, with a variety of light settings. Then the wardrobe, again with different settings, to avoid the light reflecting in the highly polished surface of the mahogany. She wanted to be sure of getting the intricate detail of the pale gold wood inlay. Then the bed, with its white counterpane of pulled-thread linen and tapestry pillow cover. A cane-backed chair with turned wood legs and a faded tapestry cushion came next. This room alone was a source of infinite treasure, never mind all the other rooms, the exterior of the house, and the grounds.

Vivien snapped picture after picture. Only when she felt she had covered everything, checking in the viewer to make sure each frame was exactly as she wanted it to be, did she feel satisfied. She had included even the simple plaster molding and cornices of the ceiling and the sash window with its window seat.

One room, at least, completed, she thought, sinking into the chair by the window.

When she had rested for several minutes, allowing her mind to empty and waiting for the trembling of her body—which was her usual physical reaction to the adrenaline rush of taking pictures—to lessen, she slid her camera into its special case and stowed it in her black cotton bag. Setting it on the bed so that she wouldn't forget it, she then unpacked the rest of her clothes, but her laptop and her other camera equipment she locked away in her suitcase, slipping the key into the small pocket of her wallet for safekeeping.

Only then did she slowly open the door, peering out first to make sure there was no one hovering nearby. This place was making her paranoid. Not the place itself, but the people who lived in it.

As promised, the telephone had been placed on a small table outside the master bedroom. Vivien noticed that the door was open about three inches. She shook her head. No doubt Mr. Hendley would say it was open to accommodate the telephone cord, but it was also a convenient way to eavesdrop. "Get a life," she said to herself.

"Are you okay?"

The male voice seemed to come from nowhere, startling her. She spun around and saw, halfway down the stairs, Marian's husband. He was kneeling down, which was probably the reason she hadn't seen him.

He straightened up. "Sorry. Didn't mean to scare you. I'm mending one of the newel posts. It's come loose. Damned termites chew away at everything. I'm Paul, in case you've forgotten. Welcome to Peverill."

"Thanks." Vivien gestured to the phone. "I came out to make a call."

Paul rolled his eyes. "Sorry about that," he said, lowering his voice. "Old people seem to think that using the phone for anything other than emergencies is some sort of crime." Fishing in his pocket, he drew out a small cell phone. "Use this. I find it easier than having to fight with him every time I want to make a call."

If his father was such a tyrant, why on earth did he and Marian stay here? Probably waiting for him to kick the bucket, Vivien conjectured, so that they could inherit Peverill.

"Thanks," she said. "It would be easier to call from my room."

"More private," Paul said, tilting his head toward his father's room.

"I'll pay you for the calls." They exchanged smiles as Vivien took the phone from him. "It's a beautiful house," she told him. "You must enjoy living here."

His tanned face abruptly clouded. "It's a constant battle with the elements and the termites. And it's hard to get help nowadays. No one wants to do laboring work anymore."

"Can't blame them in this heat, can you?"

"Suppose not, but it's a full-time job just keeping the vegetation cut back. I'm afraid it's winning the battle. Oh, well, doesn't matter." He sank back on his knees again to continue working on the stair post.

"Thanks again," Vivien said. "I'll bring your phone back as soon as I've finished."

"Make sure you give it back to me or Marian direct, okay?" He gave her a warning look.

"I will." She went back into her room and shut the door. Then, noticing the latch, she opened it and crossed the hall again. "Is there a key to the lock in my room?"

Paul stopped hammering. "You're not the first person to ask that, I can tell you. Sorry, the key was lost years ago."

"That means I can't lock my door when I go out."

"Don't worry. Nobody comes in here much, except us."

He smiled, but his smile didn't quite reach his eyes. "Your things will be perfectly safe."

"I have expensive camera equipment," Vivien protested. "I'd be happier with a lock on my door."

"Can't spoil the door by putting on a modern lock. That's the problem, you see." His shrug illustrated the fact that he wasn't going to do a thing about it. She could take it or leave it.

She shrugged in return. "Well, maybe I'll have to find somewhere else, then."

"Please yourself." He resumed hammering at the stair post, signifying that their conversation was at an end.

Once again, Vivien was tempted to slam the door when she went back into her room. The Hendleys were the most infuriating people. But at least she could now make her calls in private, without anyone listening in.

She dialed David Moreton's office number first and got his secretary. She was about to leave her number for David to return her call but hesitated. "I have a problem here about getting return calls."

"Are you at a hotel?" the secretary asked.

"No, that's the problem." Although she didn't think she could be heard, Vivien's voice automatically sank. "I'm afraid that a phone message for me might not be passed on."

"Oh, I see," the secretary said hesitantly, not seeing at all.

"Is Dr. Moreton out or in a meeting?"

"Well, he's in a meeting with a student." A pause. "Perhaps I can break in."

"That would be a real help. Thanks very much."

A moment later, David's precise, resonant voice came on the line. To her surprise, hearing him was a great relief. She had begun to think she was surrounded by alien beings. "Oh, I am glad you're able to speak to me."

"Well, that is a nice, warm greeting," he said, with humor in his voice.

"I'll explain later."

"Good."

"Thanks again for yesterday evening. I really enjoyed it."

"Good." David was all crisp and "get on with business" today. "Apparently Wesley wants us to have a meeting."

"Yes, so he told me, but if it's okay with you I'd prefer to make it tomorrow afternoon. I've moved and I wanted to give you my number, but I'm not sure that they'll pass on any messages."

"Why not?"

"I told you last night I was moving to this lovely old plantation house called Peverill Hall."

"You did. Wesley's not at all happy about it. He said there are rumors of strange goings-on."

"Did he give you any details? I can't get anything other than rumors out of him."

"No. He seemed rather cagey about the whole thing, but definitely agitated, which is not at all like Wesley."

"I have a good idea why he feels that way, but it may be something else."

"That's not at all clear." Dr. Moreton, pedantic professor of English, speaking.

"I know it isn't," Vivien said, her voice sharp. "I may be totally wrong. Anyway, I want to do some general research about Barbados. Wesley tells me that the university is probably the best place."

"Yes. Are you sure you can't make it here today? I had rather hoped we could get a start as soon as possible. If you came to the university around twelve thirty, I could introduce you to the staff, and we could have a talk about the book with Wesley over lunch. Then you'll be able to go there on your own without any problems."

"Thanks, David. But I have to arrange for a car and—"

"To drive yourself? You'll get lost."

"Thanks for the confidence in my driving ability."

"I am sure you are a very able driver. It's our signpost system I don't trust. Once you're off the main roads, it's like a maze. Far better to have a driver. I thought Wesley had given you one?"

"Yes. Spencer. But he balked at coming in to Peverill Hall. He was a great driver, apart from that."

"Well, I can take you around myself some of the time, so renting a car is a waste of money. Why don't you get Wesley to speak to the driver, ask him what the problem is?"

"I have a good idea what the problem is."

"What?"

Vivien hesitated. "Never mind." She didn't want to admit to him that she was staying with a racist family.

"Why don't I arrange to send a car for you right away?"

David certainly was a take-charge man. "Okay," she conceded. "I guess I can wait until tomorrow to explore Peverill." She knew she'd have to fight him on other more important matters connected with the project.

"I've had a thought," he said.

"What?"

"How far a walk is it from the road into the house?"

"Not that far."

"If Wesley's driver—what's his name?"

"Spencer."

"If Spencer would come to the end of the lane and sound the horn when he gets there, maybe you could walk down the lane and meet him on the road."

"That's a great idea, if he'll do it."

"I'm sure he will. He probably thinks the place is haunted. After all, an old house like that has plenty of history, and the people here know all the legends, real or imaginary."

"But you yourself haven't heard anything about Peverill, have you?"

"That doesn't mean a thing. I've lived away from here for a great deal of my adult life. Besides, I told you last night, I do seem to recall hearing something about Peverill."

"Is it common here?"

"What?"

"An irrational fear of certain places."

"Oh, yes. Bajans are a highly superstitious people. Despite their Christian background, they still retain certain vestiges of the old religions. Belief in restless spirits roaming in certain areas—or houses, that sort of thing. We shall have to find out from Wesley or from your research what it is about the place that is scaring your Spencer."

"Not just Spencer. I had the feeling that other local people don't like going there. On the other hand . . ." Again, Vivien hesitated.

"What?"

"The Hendleys seem to be rather racist."

"Oh," he said, as if that explained a lot of it. "There's a few members of the old white colonial families that still are, but most are not. We're big boys now, we can take it." He chuckled. "Makes quite a difference, you know, when you're running your own show. In what way were they racist?"

"This is awkward for me, David. I'm not used to talking about it with . . . I don't want to say something that will upset you."

"Despite our initial meeting, I'm not that squeamish, I promise you."

"I may be wrong, but when I said that I had Barbadian—" She broke off. "Should I say Barbadian or Bajan?"

"Either will do. Barbadian is more upper-class." He pronounced the word *class* with a superior English drawl.

"Okay, Bajan. When I told him I had Bajan friends,

Mr. Hendley asked me if they were tourists. I gather by tourists he meant white."

"Probably."

"And I got the impression he was warning me off bringing . . ." Vivien floundered.

"Sounds as if he didn't want you to bring in any of your new non-white Bajan friends to his house. How old is this guy?"

"Late seventies, early eighties. English accent."

"Ah, the old school. Most of us get along fine, but it's difficult for a few of the oldies to adapt to the new ways. Don't worry about it. It's the old leopard syndrome."

"What?"

"Cannot change his spots."

David's laughter rolled down the line, and Vivien smiled with it, her feelings of distaste ebbing away. "Thanks."

"For what?"

"For putting things into perspective."

"I don't think I helped at the start, did I? I set you on edge, so you thought you had to watch everything you say. I believe you will find Bajans have a great deal more self-confidence than that. They also have a buoyant sense of humor that can be most irreverent at times. You have been warned."

"Warning duly noted."

"Good. I have to get back to my student. I'll get your car there as soon as possible. Watch for it. If it's Spencer, he'll sound the horn and you will have to walk to the road."

"Thanks."

Before she could say more, David had severed the connection. She switched off the cell phone and set it down on the window seat beside her. Despite his occasional professorial manner, the conversation with David had made her feel less uneasy. It had been a reminder that she could escape to the normal outside world from the gracious but strangely disturbing atmosphere of Peverill.

A creak of floorboards from outside her room startled her. She jumped up to open the door a crack. As she peered out, the door of the main bedroom across the landing clicked shut.

CHAPTER
THIRTEEN

Vivien waited on the verandah, content to sit in the shade of the palm trees, their fronds blown gently by the ocean breeze. The heat was enervating. She knew she should be taking this opportunity to scout around the grounds, choosing which places were best for morning pictures, which for afternoon. But all she wanted to do was sit, rocking gently back and forth in the cane swing, in that soporific state between waking and sleeping.

From close at hand came three distinct musical notes. A small black bird, perched on the wooden rail, was watching her with bright yellow eyes. Again, it emitted its three notes, like a musician tuning up. She sat very still, not even daring to reach for her camera, delighting in the sound and feeling a connection to the little creature. Unlike many of the other birds she had seen since her arrival, this bird with its plain black plumage was not at all exotic, but its song was unique, exquisite. An instance of Mother Nature's compensation and sense of balance.

The sound of a distant car horn startled both Vivien and the bird, which flew off. Gathering up her bag and portfolio case, she hurried down the steps. The horn sounded again. It appeared as if David—or Wesley—had managed to persuade Spencer to come to the top of the lane. She felt a surge of relief. Now she could concentrate all her energy on her work and not have to worry about avoiding potholes, reading maps, or getting lost.

She didn't tell Marian she was leaving. She had told her earlier that she was going. She wanted to avoid having to check in and out with the Hendleys. They were intrusive enough already. Although Vivien had asked for a key to the front door, Marian had not given her one, telling her that someone was always at home and would let her in, whatever the time. It was not very satisfactory, but Marian explained that the house was filled with treasures and they would be very anxious if the key were to be lost.

She started off down the driveway, breathing in the myriad scents, the hum and buzz of insects in her ears. Hibiscus bushes covered with yellow and scarlet and coral blooms crowded in on her, their wiry branches reaching out to touch her hair, her bare arms. The path beneath her feet was dry and dusty. The heat had already dried up the puddles of water from the heavy rainfalls that seemed to suddenly turn on like a tap and then, just as suddenly, turn off again, particularly around noon or during the night. No wonder everything was so fecund here. Perspiration sprang out on her forehead, and she wiped it away with her forearm.

Spencer's van was waiting for her at the side of the road.

"Mornin', Miss Shaw," he said.

"Hi, Spencer," she replied. "No need to—" But it was too late. He was already getting out of the van to slide open the side door for her.

"You all right?" he asked her, with a hint of anxiety, when they were both seated.

"I'm absolutely fine," she said.

"Glad to hear it." He cast a quick glance down the lane to Peverill and sped off, obviously eager to get away. "Mr. Marshall tells me to take you to the university. Faculty of English, right?"

"That's right. I'm meeting Dr. Moreton there."

"And Mr. Marshall."

That was news to her, but she accepted that Spencer would know. They'd probably decided to have their meeting at the university.

"Your parents are lookin' for you," Spencer said. He glanced at her in his rearview mirror.

"My parents?" What on earth did he mean?

"Yes'm. Seems as how they called the hotel and you wasn't there." Again, the glance. "Seems you forgot to tell them you was movin'."

Oh, God! She felt a familiar mixture of guilt and annoyance. "I was going to call them later to let them know I'd moved," she found herself explaining to Spencer. "Trouble is it's not easy to use the phone at Peverill."

Spencer said nothing.

"How did you know about my parents' call?" she asked him.

"Mr. Marshall told me. The hotel called his office. Seems you didn't say where you was goin', so the hotel people couldn't tell your mother. Mr. Marshall will tell you the rest of it when he sees you."

"Okay. Thanks. I'll be sure to call them later," she added, feeling Spencer's censure from the rigid set of his neck and shoulders.

She sat back, watching the scenery go by but seeing almost nothing. All she could think of was the unassailable fact that, wherever she went, she couldn't escape from her parents. She felt hot anger flush up her neck and into her face. Here she was, thirty years old, with her mother calling around the world to check on her and a driver silently reprimanding her for her lack of filial duty.

Blindly, she watched fields and bushes and buildings pass, feeling stifled.

"Here we are." Spencer's voice broke in on her thoughts. "The University of the West Indies," he announced with pride as they drove past a jumble of different-size buildings, many of them painted in bright colors.

"Your two sons went here, didn't they?" Vivien said, recalling what he had told her yesterday.

"That's right." He grinned back at her over his shoulder. "And my granddaughter's studyin' geology in Jamaica."

"You must be very proud of your family."

He smiled at her and nodded, and then drew up before a two-story brick and glass building. The large sign announced it to be the DEPARTMENT OF LANGUAGE, LINGUISTICS AND LITERATURE. Rather a mouthful for such a simple-looking building.

Spencer got out to slide the door open for her. "Mr. Marshall said someone would call me when it was time to drive you back there."

Vivien marked the hesitant emphasis on the *there*.

"Dr. Moreton said you were to go straight to his office," a friendly woman at the information desk told her when she went into the building. "I will call up first." After a brief interchange, she told Vivien, "Mrs. Simmons is coming down."

Mrs. Simmons, an older woman dressed in a voluminous cotton dress imprinted with large, bright flowers, announced that she was the head secretary for the literature department. "Dr. Moreton hasn't finished his class yet," she told Vivien as she led her upstairs. "He should be with you in about half an hour. He said Mr. Marshall also would be here in about half an hour."

Vivien glanced at her watch. It was a little past twelve. "Thank you."

"You can wait in Dr. Moreton's office." She opened the door into a blessedly air-conditioned room, which was small but very tidy, with papers and books neatly set in rows on the shelves. A computer with a contemporary free-standing screen sat incongruously on an exquisite antique desk with turned pedestal legs. One stem of pale yellow orchids in a slender stone vase stood on the window ledge.

The effect of the entire room suggested someone of an orderly nature with a love of fine things. This was yet another side of David Moreton. As Vivien ran her gaze along the books she felt like she was intruding, prying. People's private offices were their inner sanctums, a reflection of themselves.

"Can I get you some tea or fruit juice?" Mrs. Simmons asked.

"I'd love a fruit juice."

"Passion fruit?"

"Perfect."

The secretary returned with a frosty jug of the pink juice, ice tinkling against the jug's sides. She poured some into a tall glass and set both on the table in front of a small couch.

"That looks great. Thank you." Vivien sat down and took a drink, the cool liquid sliding down her parched throat. "Oh, that is good. I'm still trying to adjust to the heat."

"And it is rather humid at this time of the year. Better to come in February when the trade winds blow." Mrs. Simmons hovered in the doorway, half in, half out. "Dr. Moreton said you are staying at Peverill Hall."

"That's right. I moved in there this morning."

"He was asking me if I knew anything about the place." She gave an arch smile. "Me being much older, of course." Her face grew solemn again. "I told him I knew little but rumors. However, after he mentioned it, I ran a check through the computer in the reference department of the library."

Vivien shifted to the edge of the couch and waited, her neck and shoulders tensing.

"Apart from the fact that it is one of the oldest of the great houses, centuries old, I knew there were rumors of some terrible happening at Peverill years ago, but I was not sure what was rumor and what was truth. We do go in for rumors a great deal in Barbados. Possibly because it is such a small island."

Like a professional storyteller, Mrs. Simmons was building this up slowly. Vivien waited, wanting, and yet not wanting, for her to get to the point.

"My search first found details of a trial in 1951."

"What kind of trial?"

"A murder trial."

Mrs. Simmons was enjoying spinning out the story. *Get on with it,* Vivien wanted to scream.

"There were several newspaper reports. I've printed off a few of them but didn't have time to finish them all." Mrs. Simmons nodded to the envelope file on the table. "They're in that file."

Vivien's hand went out to it. "Thanks very much. That was very kind of you."

"I didn't do much. Just let me know when you want to look something else up, and I will take you to the library. Dr. Moreton said you were to be given access to anything you wanted to see, so I've had a special laminated library card made for you. It's in the file." She still hovered.

Vivien guessed she was waiting for her to open the file, wanting to see her reaction to its contents. "Thank you," she said again.

Mrs. Simmons hesitated, and then took a step outside. "If you need me, I will be in my office down the hall," she said and closed the door.

Vivien sat, unmoving, gazing at the innocuous-looking file. Murder. That was Peverill's secret, the reason for Spencer's reluctance to go near it. A murder that had happened long ago, more than fifty years. Spencer would have been a boy then, perhaps a teenager. On a small island, it must have been a topic of discussion for many years thereafter.

She picked up the file but didn't open it, reluctant to
taint her image of the ancient house with a story of
violence. Then she opened it. Inside the file was a manila
envelope containing several sheets of paper. She slid out
the top page. It was a photocopy of the front page of a
newspaper from 1950, featuring a fuzzy but identifiable
picture of Peverill Hall. What dominated the page, however, was the stark black headline in inch-high letters:
MURDER AT PEVERILL.

Vivien closed her eyes for a moment, not wanting to
read on. Then she forced herself to read the column
beneath the headline and picture.

> *Police were called late last night to Peverill
> Hall, where they found the body of Lillian Hen-
> dley, the wife of Mr. Robert Hendley, whose
> family have resided at Peverill since the begin-
> ning of the nineteenth century.*
>
> *A spokesman for the police would confirm
> only that Mrs. Hendley had been brutally mur-
> dered. He said that an intensive investigation was
> in progress and that no further details would be
> given out until later.*

Robert Hendley. Who would he have been? Vivien
wondered.

She turned to the next page.

HOUSE SERVANTS BEING QUESTIONED IN PEVERILL MUR-
DER was the headline for the following day. She read on.

> *All the servants at Peverill Hall have been
> rounded up and questioned by Detective-
> Inspector Martin Williams during his investiga-
> tion of the shocking murder of Mrs. Lillian Hen-
> dley. Two house servants, in particular, have
> been taken to the Bridgetown police station for
> questioning. Their names have been released by
> the police. They are Clarence Spooner and Flor-*

*ence Smith. Detective-Inspector Williams would
say only that these two servants are helping in
the investigation. It is thought that Mrs. Hendley
interrupted a burglary in progress and was killed
because she recognized the perpetrators of the
crime.*

This was accompanied by a picture of a woman. The
photocopy was dark and rather blurred. Hard to say if
the woman was Caucasian or Afro-Caribbean. But on
reading the caption, Vivien saw that it was a picture of
Lillian Hendley, not one of the suspects, so obviously
she was white.

She read on.

> *It was also reported that it was Mr. Thomas
> Hendley, Mr. Robert Hendley's cousin, who re-
> ported the crime to the police.*

So Thomas Hendley was living at Peverill when the
murder happened. If, of course, it was the same
Thomas Hendley.

Vivien was about to read the next page when Mrs.
Simmons returned. "Everything all right, Miss Shaw?"
she asked, having knocked at the door and opened it
simultaneously. "I see you're reading about the murder," she went on, not waiting for Vivien's reply. "Fascinating, isn't it?"

Fascinating was not the word Vivien would have chosen, but she guessed that to some people scandals and
crimes were a turn-on.

"How far have you got?"

"The second page," Vivien said. "Don't tell me anything about it," she added quickly. "I'd rather find out
for myself."

"Of course." Mrs. Simmons's shoulders lifted in a little shiver of excitement. "It's like reading a mystery

novel, isn't it? Only it is more exciting because it's in your own backyard, as it were. Since I was a child, I had heard all the rumors, of course, but until now I didn't know the details."

Vivien gave her a thin smile.

"I suppose this will make you feel nervous about staying at Peverill, won't it?" Mrs. Simmons was positively enjoying this. "It would certainly make me feel nervous."

"Are we talking about ghosts?" Vivien asked, hoping her cool tone would get through to the secretary.

Mrs. Simmons advanced farther into the room, until Vivien could smell her overpowering perfume. "Oh, yes. They do say that she haunts the place."

"Mrs. Hendley?"

"That's right. Mrs. Hendley, the poor woman who was hacked to death with a cane cutter."

A small shudder like a trickle of ice ran down Vivien's spine. She had to return to Peverill, to sleep there. Where had the woman been murdered? It could even have been in the room in which she'd be sleeping tonight, she thought, sick horror creeping over her.

Replacing the page in the file, Vivien closed it and set it down firmly on the table. "Fortunately, I don't believe in ghosts," she said, as much for her own benefit as for Mrs. Simmons's. She sat up straight, pouring herself another glass of juice. "Thanks so much for your help, Mrs. Simmons," she said, glancing up at the secretary. "I'll read the rest of it later. Now I must get on with reading my own notes before the meeting."

She reached for her portfolio case, effectively dismissing Mrs. Simmons, but the door opened before she could leave, and David came in.

"Everything okay?" he asked with a slight frown.

Mrs. Simmons opened her mouth to speak, but Vivien got in first. "I'm sorry. I've kept Mrs. Simmons from her work for far too long."

But the redoubtable secretary was not so easily out-maneuvered. "I did some research for Miss Shaw about Peverill Hall, Dr. Moreton. I thought she'd like to know about the murder before she decided to stay there."

"Murder?" David's eyebrows rose.

"I am already staying there." Vivien's eyes met David's.

Whether he interpreted it as a plea for help or not, he realized that his secretary was getting to her. "Thank you, Mrs. Simmons," he said firmly and stood back, holding the door for her.

Taking the hint at last, she left, but then turned and said, "Can I get you some coffee?"

"No, thank you." He timed the closing of the door so that it eased her out of the room without actually touching her.

Vivien had to put a hand to her mouth to hide a smile.

"What was that all about?" David asked. "I could feel the tension in the room as soon as I opened the door."

Vivien's smile disappeared. "Your helpful secretary decided she'd start my research for me. I don't blame her," she added quickly, not wanting him to think she was complaining about Mrs. Simmons. "But it was quite a shock." She opened the file and handed him the top page, watching his face as he scanned it.

"Lord," he breathed, "no wonder your driver was scared to go near the place."

"Exactly." Vivien sighed. "After reading that, I'm surprised he agreed to come even to the top of the lane today."

"So am I. He obviously feels, as many would, that the place has evil vibes." He handed the page back to her. "Well, that decides it. We have to find you a new place to stay."

Vivien felt a sense of irrational panic. "I don't want to move again."

"Why not? You're obviously shaken by what you've read about the place. Why would you stay there?"

"Because . . ." she hesitated. "There's something about the place that intrigues me."

"Even when you know a murder took place there?"

"A murder that happened more than fifty years ago. I imagine there are few houses that old where something nasty hasn't happened." She knew she wasn't making much sense, but something told her she must remain at Peverill.

They were interrupted by a knock at the door and Mrs. Simmons filled the doorway. "Mr. Marshall," she announced, and Wesley came into the room. It was beginning to feel very claustrophobic, with the two men, both tall, and the large Mrs. Simmons all packed into it.

Wesley accepted Mrs. Simmons's offer of refreshment with a request for another glass to share the rest of the juice with Vivien, then sat in the chair behind the desk that David offered him. David took the small chair beneath the clock on the wall, stretching his legs out into the center of the room.

When Mrs. Simmons had brought two more glasses and another jug of juice and closed the door, David told Wesley, "We were discussing Peverill Hall."

Wesley tensed, his jaw visibly tightening.

Vivien turned on him. "Why didn't you tell me? You must have known why Spencer reacted so strangely to the place, yet you never said anything about someone having been murdered there."

"I told you not to go there. You should have taken my advice."

"All you told me was that it didn't have a good reputation. Naturally, I thought you were talking about now, the present, not the past."

Wesley's tongue ran over his lips. "You're right. I should have told you, but it is not something you want to spread around a small island whose main source of income is tourism, is it?"

"Oh, I don't know," Vivien said with a wry smile. "I would think some of those British tourists would go for it in a big way. I'm surprised the Hendleys haven't put up signs on the main road advertising it as the site of an infamous murder and arranged for the bus tours to stop there for a visit."

Wesley winced and took out a white handkerchief to mop his gleaming forehead, then leaned across David's antique desk. "Please reconsider your decision to stay there," he begged Vivien.

"Why? I don't like the Hendleys much, but I do like the house," she said, trying to sound nonchalant. "As I told David, the murder happened fifty years ago. How does that affect me now?"

"People have long memories."

David intervened. "I can think of other reasons why she shouldn't stay there. Apparently they won't let her use their phone."

"Paul Hendley lent me his cell phone," Vivien explained to Wesley. "That's how I was able to call. But I can't make long-distance calls from their phone."

"That reminds me," Wesley said. "Your mother called the hotel and was apparently very concerned when they told her you had moved and they didn't have your new number or address."

"Oh, don't you start." Vivien rolled her eyes. "Spencer's made me feel guilty enough as it is."

"Spencer?" David looked a question. "What has he got to do with it?"

"You have to meet Spencer to understand. Never mind, it's not important." Vivien fanned herself with the file. "Phew! It's very hot in here." But she knew it was the tension emanating from Wesley that was getting to her.

"I'll see if there's a larger room available," David said and left the room.

As soon as the door closed behind David, Wesley confronted Vivien. He sat forward in the chair, his large hands clasped tightly. "I know you like Peverill Hall, but I beg you to reconsider," he said in a low, impassioned voice. "The Hendleys have a bad reputation. That is why Spencer didn't want to drive you there."

"He also knew about the murder, didn't he? Does he think Peverill is haunted?"

"I imagine so. In a way, I suppose it is. Haunted by terrible memories."

"I don't believe in ghosts, Mr. Marshall. And, despite the fact that Mr. and Mrs. Hendley senior are a little weird, I infinitely prefer Peverill Hall to the Ocean Sands. I want to take pictures of the place. There can't be any danger in that, can there?"

"Who knows?"

"After all, I haven't read the rest of the file, but from what I saw it appears the police caught the killer—or killers—almost immediately, didn't they?"

Wesley slid his finger around the inside of his shirt collar, as if it were too tight for him.

"Tell you what," Vivien said, seeing his anxious expression. "Once I've taken all my pictures, if the Hendleys are getting to me in any way, I'll move out. But you'll have to find me another B-and-B. I don't want to stay at a resort, okay?"

Wesley cleared his throat. "I will start looking for one today. Meanwhile, I want you to take my cell phone."

"I can't take your phone," Vivien protested.

"I have another one. You cannot be left without a phone."

He didn't need to press her too hard. "Thank you," she said. "I must say I'd feel happier with it."

"Good." He reached into his briefcase and handed her his cell phone and power plug.

"How do I pay for my calls?"

"It's a government account."

"I can't have the government of Barbados paying for my personal calls."

Wesley gave an impatient wave of his hand. "Let's not worry about that now. I will take care of it." Again, he bent forward toward her. "You must promise to contact me, any time, night or day, if you have any problems, all right?"

Vivien's hand went to her throat. "I wish you wouldn't worry so much about me," she said with a little laugh. "Please don't. I'll be fine."

"Any time," he repeated, as if he hadn't heard her, "night or day." He struggled to his feet. "I must go," he said distractedly, moving to the door.

"But I thought we were going to have a meeting about the book over lunch?" Vivien jumped up.

Wesley shook his head. "No. I find I don't have the time. Please tell David I will call him." He stood staring at her, his breath coming so fast that she was concerned he might be ill. "I will look for a new place for you to stay," he said vehemently and strode from the room without a backward glance.

CHAPTER
FOURTEEN

As she rode back to the east coast in Spencer's van, Vivien kept going over Wesley's violent reaction to her staying on at Peverill. It had been disquieting to see such a calm, rational man behave so unreasonably. When David returned to his office to find that Wesley had gone, he, too, considered his behavior quite out of character.

They'd shared a hurried lunch of fried chicken, discussing—sometimes arguing about—their ideas for the book, agreeing to meet again the next afternoon for a visit to Bridgetown. Now that Vivien had a cell phone she could be easily contacted. When David had to leave for his next class, he promised to talk to Wesley before they met again.

"Have you eaten anything?" Spencer's voice broke into her thoughts.

"Yes. I had lunch. Why?"

"Better not eat with *them*."

"For heaven's sake, Spencer. Do you think they're going to poison me?"

"Never know," he muttered.

She was tempted to ask him what he knew about the murder but decided to wait until she'd read the file Mrs.

Simmons had given her. "I haven't arranged any meals there, apart from breakfast."

"Not any restaurants near that place."

"Oh."

"Want to stop at a Chefette, get some food? They got good fried chicken there. You could keep it for your dinner."

"No, thanks. I had fried chicken for lunch." She thought for a moment, realizing she had nothing to eat for this evening. "Tell you what. Would you have time to drop me off at a grocery store so I could maybe pick up a few things? Rolls and cheese, cookies, cold drinks?"

"Glad to. There's a small market about a mile down the road here. Don't want you to go hungry."

There wasn't much choice in the grocery store, but the owner was happy to show her where everything was and recommended the new delivery of local mangoes she'd just received. Vivien was amused to see that the stick of Black Diamond cheddar cheese she bought was made in Canada. She also got a six-pack of Banks beer and a copy of the *Nation*.

She came out of the store to find Spencer slumped in his seat, straw hat tipped over his eyes. He opened his eyes, as if he could tell she was there without looking, and climbed out of the van. "Thanks for waiting," she told him.

"No problem." He took the bag of groceries from her and put it into the van, making sure it was secure. "Any place else you want to go before you go back there?"

"No, that's fine," she said.

He waited until she'd done up her seat belt before starting the engine and turning out of the parking lot. "You call your parents yet?"

What was this? She seemed to be surrounded by people worrying about her.

"It will be the first thing I do when I get in, I promise you. Mr. Marshall has given me a cell phone."

He beamed at her over his shoulder. "Good." He fished in his glove compartment and handed a card back to her. "That's my number."

"Thank you, but you gave me your card yesterday."

"Well, here's another one. You call me any time, night or day, if you need me, see?"

Wesley had told her the same thing when he'd given her the cell phone. All this protectiveness was making her feel decidedly nervous.

"Thanks for all your help," she told Spencer when he pulled up at the top of the lane to Peverill. She got a reproving look for having lifted the grocery bag down for herself before he could get out of the van. "Spencer," she said firmly. "Let's get this straight, shall we? I really enjoy having you drive me. But if you want to keep driving for me, you're going to have to put up with me lifting things in and out of the van and opening my own doors. Or else . . . Understand?"

He stood there, a half smile on his face. "I understand."

She gave him his money and an affectionate grin.

"If you was to stay somewhere else, there'd be no cause for you to carry those heavy bags—"

"Spencer!"

"—all the way down the lane to *that* place," he finished. He tipped his hat to her. "Good day, Miss Shaw." He raised his hand to her and climbed carefully into the driver's seat. All his movements were slow and deliberate. Although he never complained, she realized from the way he moved that he must be suffering from arthritic pain.

The afternoon heat hung heavy in the shaded lane. By the time she'd walked halfway to the house, she could feel sweat dampening her waistband and trickling down her spine. The high-pitched buzz of the insects filled her ears, a continuous accompaniment to the chorus of birds trilling and chirping in the trees that closed in on her on both sides.

Unfortunately, mosquitoes were also buzzing around her. A couple landed on her arm, but she could do nothing about it, without setting down her portfolio, bag, and groceries. She was used to mosquitoes in Manitoba, but they didn't carry dengue fever. Silently cursing her mother for that particular warning, she put down her bags and swatted her arm, leaving a smear of blood. Too late. They'd already injected her with whatever venom they might have carried. She gave an involuntary shudder at the sight of the blood. Spitting on a clean tissue, she rubbed it away.

She continued down the lane, thinking about all the warnings she'd received, but when the house came into view, golden in the afternoon sunlight, it looked so benign that she couldn't help chuckling at everyone's anxiety for her safety.

"Ah, there you are." The disembodied voice made her jump. It was Paul Hendley startling her again. "We wondered when you'd be coming back." He came out of the bushes, holding garden shears. "You seem loaded down. What happened to your taxi?"

She hesitated, searching for an explanation. "I told him I'd enjoy the walk," she ended up saying, knowing it sounded false as soon as the words came out of her mouth. "I didn't realize how hot it would be."

"Here, let me help you." He took the grocery bag from her and walked beside her on the pathway of cracked earth.

"Thank you. It's just a few groceries for tonight," she explained.

"Groceries? You don't need them. Didn't Marian tell you?"

"Tell me what?"

"That our guests usually take dinner with us, as we're not near any restaurants. That's one of the problems with being so far off the beaten track, but some people like it that way."

"No, she didn't tell me."

Paul scowled, looking very much like his father. "Honest to God," he muttered. "I sometimes wonder where that woman's brains are." Then his face and voice lightened perceptibly. "Sorry about that. She's got a nice jerk chicken and rice dinner planned."

"Great," Vivien said. Spencer's warning crept into her mind. *Don't be so ridiculous,* she told herself.

"We charge extra for meals, of course," Paul added.

"Of course." She was happy to reach the verandah and be able to sink down on a cane chair in the shade. "But let's say that in future I won't need a meal unless I ask for it, okay?" She'd prefer to sit in her room, eating her roll and cheese, than have to eat with the family.

Paul shrugged. "Suit yourself." He set the groceries down. "But you'd better speak to my wife about tonight's meal."

"Oh, tonight's fine. I'm not going anywhere. What time will dinner be?"

"Six." He wiped his sweaty forehead with his arm. "My parents like to eat early."

"Fine." That gave her more than enough time to finish settling in, read about the murder, and explore the grounds. She gathered up her bags and went upstairs, longing to get her shoes off her sore, dusty feet. Serve her right for wearing her fancy sandals with the heels today.

When she reached her room, she kicked them off and sank down on the side of the bed, with an accompanying creak of springs. What she'd give for a good shower to wash off the dust and refresh her. "No shower, no airconditioning. What I've given up for you, you rotten old house," she said beneath her breath.

As if in reply, she heard the musical tinkle of the chimes that hung on the verandah below as a fresh gust of wind blew upon them.

Having taken a long drink from one of the bottles

of beer, which was still deliciously cool from the store refrigerator, she reluctantly picked up Wesley's cell phone and sat in the chair by the open window, her feet propped on the edge of the washstand. Time to call her parents in Winnipeg.

"Hello?" Her mother answered after the first ring.

"You must have been standing right beside the phone," Vivien said.

"And who could blame me," shrieked her mother. "Where the hell have you been?"

"That's nice."

"How could you do that to us? Leave your hotel without calling to let us know where you are! When you know how much your father worries about you."

"It's time he stopped worrying about me. I'm a grown, independent woman. I shouldn't have to check in with you every day."

"That is so unkind. You know how much—"

"Yes, I know," Vivien said, with a heavy sigh. "I'm here now, so you can tell Dad to stop worrying. I'm fine." She could hear her father's voice in the background.

"He's so upset he says he can't speak to you at the moment."

"Whatever." Vivien closed her eyes, feeling the little breeze soothing the back of her neck. "Tell him I'm sorry."

"That's easily said, but—"

"I've got a cell phone. Have you got a pen to take the number down?"

"You know I have, the one on the string that you gave me in my Christmas stocking last year."

Vivien rolled her eyes. "Okay." She gave her mother the number. "Got that?"

"Yes." Her mother repeated it. "Where are you staying?"

Vivien was about to tell her but then realized if she

did, her parents might try calling her on the Hendleys'
line. "It's just a small hotel. Cheaper and nicer than the
other place."

"I thought the Barbados government was paying for
your expenses."

"They are, but the other place was too noisy. Lots of
tourists. This place doesn't have a phone, so that's why
Wesley Marshall lent me a cell. I'll take it with me whenever I go out. It also has voice mail, so you can leave a
message for me any time."

"That's good . . . if you return our call."

Vivien sighed. "Let me speak to Dad."

"I'm not sure he—"

"Just put him on, Mom."

A whispered exchange and then her father's voice.
"You gave us quite a scare, Viv." She could tell by the
slight slur in his voice that he was on heavy medication.
"We didn't know what to think."

"Are you okay?" She was genuinely concerned.

"I was worried about you. Where are you?"

"A little bed-and-breakfast place."

"What's the name of it?"

"I gave Mom my cell phone number so you can get
me any time, wherever I am. So please stop worrying,
okay?"

A long pause, then, "I wish you'd come home. I can't
stop worrying that something will happen to you. You're
all I've got."

"No, I'm not, " she said firmly. "You've got Mom and
your friends. How's the weather there?" She knew from
experience that talking about the weather sometimes
helped to get his mind off his worries. "Any snow yet?"

"Too early for snow," he scoffed. "Won't come until
after Halloween."

"Oh, I don't know about that. I can remember going
out collecting candies with my witch costume over my
bunny snowsuit and my snowboots crunching through
the snow."

That made him laugh. "There's a picture somewhere of you that year."

Probably in one of the countless albums that were piled up in the basement closet. There was hardly a day of her life that she hadn't been photographed . . . until she left Winnipeg for Toronto.

"Have you been working in the yard?" she asked him.

"Raked lots of leaves. We had a heavy wind this morning, blew most of 'em down. My back's killing me."

"Take a good rest, then. Watch some television."

"Nothing on, except one of those endless *Law and Order* reruns. They seem to be on every day."

"I must go, Dad. Have to change my clothes."

"But you only just called," he protested.

"Sorry, but I'm going out this evening," she lied. "I've got another meeting with the author of this book."

"Okay. You take care of yourself."

"I will, Dad. I promise. Love you."

"Love you, too, sweetie. Take care."

"Bye." She pressed the off button before he could say any more. Their prolonged good-byes could sometimes take as long as ten minutes.

She unlocked her suitcase and got out her trusty compact 35 mm Leica. It would be good for some pictures later this afternoon when the sun started going down. She also took out her loose-leaf daybook. She liked to keep a regular diary when she was working on a project, together with a log of all the photographs she'd taken, the lighting and settings she'd used. Despite the advent of digital photographs, it was a habit she'd continued.

She smiled down at the daybook. VIVIEN CARLTON SHAW read the label on the green cover. She took it with her wherever she went. She'd kept the daybook for years, a diary of her working days. Of course, she didn't drag around all the past records. They were piled in a box on a shelf in her closet at home. She liked to leaf through them to remind herself of all the things she'd done, the places she'd been. Photography had opened up—no, it had *saved*—her life. Living at home had often been so miserable, she believed that losing herself in her photography had saved her sanity.

She placed the daybook on the bedside cabinet. She'd catch up with it later in the evening. Now she wanted to read the rest of the pages Mrs. Simmons had photocopied for her.

Settling herself in the chair by the window, she opened up the file and was about to reread the top page when she heard the tinkling sound of the cell phone from the depths of her bag. "Hello?"

"Is this Vivien Shaw?" A woman's voice.

"Yes," Vivien said, wondering who it could be.

"This is Celeste. Celeste Beaton. You remember we met at—"

"Of course. At the Marshalls'." Vivien waited for her to say more.

After a little pause, Celeste said, "I hope you don't mind me calling you. Wesley told me you had his cell phone."

"Of course not."

"You said you would like to come to tea with my mother and family."

Vivien groaned silently. "I would love to," she said brightly. It wasn't that she didn't want to visit Celeste and her family, but the woman's intensity got to her.

"I was wondering if you could come tomorrow afternoon," Celeste said.

"Oh, I am sorry. I've made plans with Dr. Moreton to show me Bridgetown tomorrow afternoon. What a shame."

"Shall we say Wednesday afternoon, then?"

"Wednesday would be great. What time?"

"Why don't you come at noon for lunch and then we can have a really good visit together," Celeste said eagerly.

"I'm not sure I can take that much time from my work—"

"Don't worry," Celeste chimed in. "I'd be happy to take you places you might be interested in seeing. We could do that after lunch."

"Sounds great."

"My husband, Joseph, will come for you at eleven."

It was getting earlier and earlier.

"Will you still be at Peverill Hall?" Celeste's voice sounded strange, husky as she spoke the words. Almost as if she were afraid to speak the name.

"Yes."

Another little moment of hesitation. "Wesley told me you'd . . ." Her voice died away altogether.

"You mean finding out about the murder at Peverill? To be honest, Mrs. Beaton," Vivien said firmly, "if you don't mind, I'd rather not talk about it, considering I'm right here in the house."

"Yes, yes, I understand. But . . . we have plenty of room in our house, and we would love to have you stay with us. When Wesley told me he was looking for a place for you to stay, I said he need look no further, you must stay with us. You would be most welcome." Celeste laughed nervously. "And please do not call me Mrs. Beaton. Celeste. Please."

Vivien was taken aback by her kindness. "That's more than kind of you, Celeste. Shall we say that if Peverill doesn't work out, I will take you up on your offer?"

Another pause. "All right. But, don't forget, Joseph and I are here if you need us."

Not more people being here for her night and day, Vivien thought wryly. It was like having extensions of her parents everywhere on the island.

"Forgive me," she said, determined to wrap up the call, "but I must go and get on with making notes before I forget everything that happened today. Thanks so much for calling me. I look forward to seeing you Wednesday. Does Joseph know how to get here?"

"Yes, he knows."

"My driver prefers me to meet him on the main road.

He's a bit superstitious, I think. I'm sorry to ask, but will Joseph come to the house for me?"

"Oh! Oh, yes. I'm sure he will. It's not the same for him."

"Great. Thanks, Celeste."

"Thank *you*. My mother and grandmother will be so excited to meet you. See you on Wednesday." Celeste rang off.

Vivien wondered what she'd meant by "It's not the same for him." Did she mean Joseph wasn't superstitious? Probably, she conjectured. Joseph certainly hadn't struck her as the kind of man who would be afraid of ghosts.

With a long sigh of relief, she switched off the cell phone and dropped it back into her bag. Now, at last, she could get on with reading the rest of Mrs. Simmons's file. Settling back in the chair by the open window, she started from the beginning again and then turned to the page after the part about the two house servants being held for questioning. Next came a lurid and distressing description of the murder scene. The woman had been hacked several times, probably with a cane cutter. *A frenzied attack* was how the police described it. Blood had stained and spattered the walls and the floor and soaked into the bedclothes and patchwork quilt on the bed where the body had been found.

Vivien stopped reading for a moment and closed her eyes. Lillian Hendley had been murdered in what the report called the "great bedroom," which she imagined was the largest bedroom across the hall, the one the elder Hendleys now occupied. It was disturbing to think that a human being had been brutally murdered in a room only a few feet across the hall from where she now sat. She imagined that much had happened in the more than three hundred years of Peverill Hall's life: many people must have died, given birth, made love in these rooms, but murder was different. Murder was an

unnatural act, not a natural one. To kill another human
being was an aberration. And there was no doubt that,
although fifty years had passed, this murder still lingered
in people's minds. People who had nothing to do with
the Hendley family. Wesley, Spencer, Celeste Beaton . . .
all were unable to hide their horror of this place. Even
David had seemed uneasy about her staying on at
Peverill.

Vivien knew intuitively that she must not allow herself
to dwell too much on the actual murder, particularly its
location, or she might be unable to finish reading the
newspaper reports. She took a drink from the bottle of
beer and started to read again.

After the description of the murder site, the reports
seemed to have skipped a couple of weeks. Perhaps Mrs.
Simmons had missed something. Vivien would be able
to fill in the gaps later. In the next page, suspicion
seemed to be swinging away from the servants and
pointing in the direction of the murdered woman's husband, Robert Hendley. It was all written very carefully,
and as Vivien read it, she had the impression of a small
but dominant society protecting its own. However, there
were suggestions that the couple had been heard quar-
reling. Mr. Thomas Hendley had reluctantly admitted,
on being questioned, that he had witnessed his cousin
striking Lillian Hendley in anger more than once. But
he must emphasize, he had added in his statement, that
Mrs. Hendley had not been at all easy to live with recently, because of her condition.

Despite the intense heat in the room, Vivien suddenly
felt very cold. The murdered woman had been pregnant.

Not one death but two.

She was moody and irritable, Thomas had told the
police. *She made my cousin's life very difficult. She
nagged him and was abusive to him in front of me and
the servants. It must have been very embarrassing for him.*

The faded photographic image showed Thomas Hendley as a handsome young man with a mustache, dressed in white trousers and a blazer.

As she continued to read, she was surprised at how quickly the police had built up a case against Robert Hendley, but in fact when she checked the gaps between dates, she realized that they must have been reasonably thorough in their investigation. The evidence they'd amassed seemed overwhelmingly to indict Robert Hendley. There was evidence of quarrels between husband and wife, instances of displays of violent jealousy by Robert, of fear of her husband by Lillian.

Most of the evidence against Robert came from his cousin, Thomas, who had lived with the family since he had come from England almost a year before the murder. Yet Thomas supported his cousin wholeheartedly and vehemently stated that he was incapable of murder. But then he'd added that *if* Robert had killed her, it was because he had been provoked by his wife's irrational behavior.

In making excuses for his cousin, Thomas Hendley seemed to have provided the one thing the police did not have, a motive for Robert to kill his wife. But, at the same time, Vivien realized that she would not have been suspicious of Thomas had she not known the man he'd become. Although she was trying to think of him as the handsome, smiling young man in the picture, it was hard to see beyond the cold, arrogant man she'd encountered this morning.

There were delicate suggestions that Lillian Hendley had been not *"as good a wife and mother as she should have been."* The newspaper actually put quotes around the phrase to emphasize what it really meant.

Vivien felt a surge of anger. She had never seen a more blatant example of *she deserved what she got.*

A significant gap ensued between this and the next couple of pages. Several months, it seemed. Robert Hendley was on trial for the murder of his wife. Vivien scanned down the page. Robert continued to protest his innocence, saying that he loved his wife, that he was devastated by her brutal murder, that he had no idea why she had been killed.

Turning to the final page in the pile, she found that it was a cutting about a break-in at Peverill Hall in 1996, when a man had been discovered in the master bedroom one afternoon. It had nothing to do with the murder.

Vivien riffled through all the pages again, but there was nothing else about the murder. She was left high and dry, not knowing what had happened to Robert Hendley. Had he been found guilty? If so, how many years had he served in prison? How ironic that the one family who could give her all the information was right here, under the same roof as she was, but, naturally, she could never broach the subject with them.

She was so frustrated that she was tempted to call Wesley to ask him if he knew what had happened to Robert Hendley. But she wanted to avoid contact with Wesley at present, knowing that he would try to pressure her to leave Peverill and move in with the Beatons.

She tidied the papers, slipped them back into the file envelope, and then sat there, no longer able to escape the images of the brutal murder that had happened in the room across the hall.

CHAPTER
FIFTEEN

Vivien knew she had to get away from the house and her overactive imagination. She grabbed her small backpack and stuffed into it her Leica, book, bottled water, and some bug spray. She pulled down the blind to keep her room as cool as possible, then crammed on her straw sun hat, and ran downstairs and out the front door, the screen door springing shut behind her.

The moist heat was overwhelming, hitting her like a wall as soon as she stepped outside. Thoughts of going for a long hike were instantly forgotten. All she wanted to do was lie in the swing on the verandah and read— or sleep. How on earth did people do physical work in this heat? But she knew that she needed to do something physical to banish the malaise created by reading about the murder of Lillian Hendley.

She stood at the foot of the steps, sprayed her skin and clothing with bug spray, and then started off down a narrow pathway to the left of the driveway. It was sheltered on both sides by tall oleander bushes, filtering out the fierce sun. The carpet of leaves beneath her feet was still moist from the last downpour.

The pathway led to a clearing of cushiony turf, at its center a round, open wood building with a railing.

Eager to check it out, she started to mount the steps but felt the top step slacken alarmingly beneath her weight. Clutching the railing, she gingerly balanced on the edge and from there stepped onto the floor of the summerhouse. But now she could see that the entire wood floor was rotten, the planks crumbling away. In fact, there was a gaping hole in the center. The place was an accident waiting to happen.

"They should put up a sign or a barrier," she murmured, intending to tell Marian that the next time she saw her.

Retreating to the path, she moved farther away from the house until she came to a break in the oleander hedge that led to an open door in the stone wall dividing the front of the property from the rear. She walked through the doorway and found herself facing a dilapidated small stone building. Some kind of barn or stable, she conjectured.

Looking around to make sure that no one was nearby, she pushed open the wooden door. It was dark inside, the only source of light a sunbeam piercing the gloom from the doorway. Dust motes danced in the narrow ray of light.

As her eyes became accustomed to the darkness, she saw a large flashlight hanging on a hook by the door. She took it down and switched it on. The barn sprang into life. It appeared to be a storehouse for a wide variety of discarded things. As she swung the light around, its beam caught a rusty tin bath, shelves filled with pickling and jam jars, several pieces of broken furniture. On one wall hung an array of rusty farm and garden implements: scythes and forks and a heavy type of machete. Cane cutters? she wondered with a shudder.

Retreating hurriedly to the doorway, she was about to switch off the flashlight and leave when the beam of light caught a glimmer of color in a far corner of the barn. Stepping carefully, she made her way across the

straw-covered floor to halt in front of what turned out
to be a small rocking horse lying abandoned on its side,
the red and blue paint on the saddle faded but still dis-
cernible. The sight brought a melancholy smile to her
face, but also piqued her photographer's instinct. It
would make a perfect picture. But was there enough
light? She'd jack it up as much as she could.

She swung her backpack down to the floor and
grabbed her camera from it, hoping that some mouse—
or worse—wouldn't decide to take up residence inside
it. Once she'd set the camera—wishing she'd brought
her portable tripod—she juggled it and the flashlight and
took several pictures of the rocking horse. When she'd
finished she gazed down at it for a while, wondering
about the small girl or boy who'd ridden it when it was
brightly new.

Behind the rocking horse were a couple of old cabin
trunks with broken brass locks. Sometime in the past
they must have been very fine. They were covered with
a veneer of rotting leather and bound with metal bands.
She moved closer and stared down at the trunk nearest
to her, hesitating. Where did healthy interest stop and
snooping begin? she wondered.

Holding her breath, she strained to discern footsteps,
voices nearby, but all she could hear were rustlings in
the straw and, from outside, the chatter of birds.

She lifted the lid of the trunk and it rose slowly with
a protesting screech of rusty hinges. The acrid smell of
mildew and damp arose as she removed the top layer of
protective paper. Floral wallpaper, she saw, when she
looked more closely. Beneath the paper were stacks of
old books in various stages of decay. She ran her fingers
over the half-eaten leather binding of a copy of *Rob-
inson Crusoe*. There must be dozens of books in the
trunk. What a waste, she thought, hating to see books
neglected, destroyed this way.

Again, she set up the camera and flashlight and took

photographs of the open trunk with the books stacked inside. Rummaging around, she found a small red leather edition of *Kidnapped* that was in better condition. She opened it, looking for colored illustrations, but there were only a few small black-and-white ones. She was about to put it back, but something stopped her from returning it to the decaying pile. Hurriedly, she stuffed the little book into her backpack, feeling guilty but glad that she'd rescued at least one of the condemned books from its fate. Heart pounding, she scrabbled around further and found a tattered copy of a *Daily Mail Annual.* She riffled through the pages, found a double-page spread of colored butterflies, and shot another two pictures.

That's about it, she thought, glancing nervously at the door. One more, then she must leave before someone found her here. She picked up the *Annual* to look for another colored section . . . and something fluttered from its pages to land on the floor. She bent down to retrieve it. It was a small black-and-white photograph.

"What the devil do you think you're doing?"

Startled by the voice, Vivien spun around. It was Thomas Hendley. She could see him in the doorway, against the backdrop of light from the outside.

Heart galloping, she palmed the photograph, praying he wouldn't see it. Bending down to pick up her backpack, she slid the photo into the open pocket. "I was exploring," she said lightly. "You have a fascinating place here."

He stepped forward, blocking the entrance. "You have no right to be in here. You are trespassing."

"I'm sorry. I didn't realize. I thought it was just an old barn. I was walking and saw the door was open so came inside to take a look."

He strode forward, remarkably upright for his age. Marcus, the dog, followed him, panting heavily. She tried not to flinch when he came sniffing at her legs, so close that she could smell the dog's rank breath. "Give me the torch," Thomas demanded.

She handed him the flashlight and found herself blinded as he shone it directly into her face. Then he focused its beam on the trunk of books. She was terrified that he would search her backpack and find the book and photograph. The photo she might be able to explain away by saying that she was interested in it for professional reasons and intended to return it, as she did. But the book was another matter. Discarded or not, she had stolen it.

But it was her camera he'd fixed his furious gaze on. It stood in full view on the stack of books.

"Excuse me," he said icily, coming even closer.

She stepped away from the trunk, and he lifted up the camera. "You were taking photographs."

"I'm afraid not," she said with a little sigh. "It's far too dark in here." She prayed that he wasn't conversant with modern cameras and their ability to see in the dark. "I was looking at these old books. I love books, and there are some old favorites in here. It seems such a shame to—"

"You had no right to come snooping in here." He emphasized this by raising his left arm, fist clenched. Immediately, the dog started barking. She recoiled from Thomas, thinking he was going to strike her or set Marcus on her. Now that Thomas was no longer between her and the doorway, she would have grabbed the opportunity to get out, but he was still holding her camera. Despite her fear of him and the dog, she was damned if she was going to give it up without protest.

He saw her looking at the camera. "I've a good mind to smash this," he said.

"That would be very inconvenient," she said, trying to sound nonchalant, "but it is fully insured."

He came closer again, and she had to fight her instinct to rush out the door. "I don't like intruders," he said coldly, his upper-class English accent even more pronounced, "but my son and daughter-in-law choose to ignore my wishes and bring strangers into my house. However, I still set the rules here, and one rule is that there will be no photographs taken of my house or my property, you understand, Miss Shaw?"

"I understand, Mr. Hendley. Now may I please have my camera back?" She was trying not to show her fear of him, but the man gave her the creeps. She could sense the contained fury behind the icy veneer.

But he was not about to let her go that easily. "How do I know you're not one of these people who take pictures to identify valuable objects for professional thieves to steal?"

She took a couple of steps backward toward the door. "I don't think there's anything very valuable in here, do you? I assure you, Mr. Hendley, I discovered this place by chance when I was out for a casual walk."

"With a camera?" He held it up.

"I take my camera everywhere with me. I'm a professional photographer."

"Exactly. That's what I said."

The man was paranoid. She held out her hand. "My camera, please."

"Why don't I take out the film?" His thin lips formed an unpleasant smile. "That way I could be sure you weren't in possession of pictures of Peverill."

"Because you would destroy some very important pictures I've taken for my upcoming book," Vivien told him, struggling to keep cool. "Pictures I took at the Ocean Sands and elsewhere. It would mean the loss of two days' work."

He gave a little shrug signifying that was of no importance to him, but he handed the camera back to her.

"Thank you." She tried not to show her relief.

"Now please get out of here, and don't let me find you taking pictures anywhere on my estate. I don't like intruders," he repeated.

As Vivien left the barn, she could feel the icy gaze of

those gray-blue eyes fixed on her all the way. The short distance between him and the entrance felt like a mile. It was a tremendous relief to step outside. Swiftly, heart still racing, she retraced her steps down the pathway to the front of the house.

She was halfway up the stairs when Marian came into the front hall, her face beet-red and glistening from the heat. "Oh, there you are. I was looking for you. Would you like some tea?"

"I'd love some, but I have to put my things away." Vivien hesitated, wondering if she should say anything about her meeting with Thomas Hendley. She might as well. No doubt he'd say something to Marian. He'd made it clear he objected to her taking in outsiders. She came down to the hall again. "Your father-in-law found me in the old barn at the back," she said in a low voice, in case Mrs. Hendley senior was nearby. "I hadn't realized it was off-limits to visitors."

Marian squeezed her eyes shut, shaking her head. "What did he say to you?"

"He wasn't very pleasant. Threatened to break my camera."

"Oh, God! I'm so sorry. He's absolutely paranoid about people taking pictures of Peverill, I should have warned you."

"I certainly know now."

"I am sorry." Marian lowered her voice. "He doesn't like us doing bed and breakfast, but Paul told him we can't continue here without some extra income, so he has to accept it or we'll go." She sighed heavily. "I wish we could go, but there it is. This is Paul's home and, like it or not, the old man needs his help." She put her hand on Vivien's arm. "Please don't leave because of this. It's not just the money. Without people like you coming here, I'd never see a soul."

"I must say I really felt like packing up after the way he behaved."

"I can understand that. Please, don't," Marian begged her. "I hate being alone here. I'll get Paul to speak to him, okay?"

"Okay. But I think I should skip dinner. I'm not sure I would be comfortable eating at the same table with him."

"Oh, but you must come for dinner. I'm making a really special meal for tonight. My time would be all wasted if you weren't there."

Talk about pressure, Vivien thought. Marian looked so disappointed that she felt she'd no option but to accept. "Okay, but it's not going to be easy."

"I promise to get Paul to talk to him. It'll be fine."

"Okay." Not convinced, Vivien started up the stairs again.

"Tea on the verandah in half an hour," Marian called up to her. "That okay for you?"

"That's great. Thanks, Marian."

"Thank you. Please stay," she begged again.

As soon as Vivien got to her room, she unlocked her suitcase and stowed her camera in it. Then she took the copy of *Kidnapped* from her backpack and held it in her hands, still feeling that mixture of guilt and pleasure about having taken it. She opened it to the title page, which was foxed with brown spots from the dampness. On the flyleaf opposite was a name, written in a child's rounded handwriting: *Trevor Hendley of Peverill Hall, 1949.*

Who was Trevor Hendley? 1949 was the year before Lillian Hendley was murdered. Had there been mention of a child in the newspaper report? She checked the file again. All she could find was that vile reference to Lillian Hendley not being a good wife and mother. So she must have had a child. Could Trevor have been her son?

How could she find out? Probably by researching the rest of the newspaper and police reports about the murder. *You've got less than a week,* she told herself. *Don't*

*waste time on something that has nothing at all to do with
the Barbados project.* But the confrontation with Thomas
Hendley had made her even more eager to learn all she
could about the murder.

Reluctantly, she set the file aside. From her backpack
pocket she drew out the photograph that had fallen from
the children's annual. Now she could see that it was a
faded picture of what appeared to be a family of three:
a woman seated on a bench beneath a large tree, a small
boy perched on the back of the bench, held safely by
his father, the tall, handsome man looking out at the
camera with laughter in his eyes. The man's other arm
lay around the shoulders of the woman.

Vivien peered more closely and then opened the file
again, seeking the photocopied picture of Lillian Hendley. Yes. Although the photograph had faded, the
woman was undoubtedly Lillian Hendley. When she
turned it over, this was confirmed by the inscription on
the back. *Robert, Lillian, and Trevor—July 1946.*

Tears pricked her eyes as she registered what she held
in her hands. Evidence of what had once been a happy
family. What on earth had happened to destroy this happiness? With a heavy heart, she reverently placed the
photograph inside the little book, against the boy's signa-
ture, and closed it. Sliding the book and photo into the
manila envelope, she added it to the papers in the file
and put the entire file at the bottom of her suitcase,
beneath a sweater she'd packed for traveling home, and
carefully locked the case.

As she stood there, looking down at the suitcase, the
memory of Thomas Hendley's raised fist swung into her
mind. The thought of having to share the dinner table
with this man made her shudder.

CHAPTER
SIXTEEN

Dinner with the Hendleys was a strange mixture of old-fashioned ritual and shabby informality. It was presided over by the senior Hendleys, seated at opposite ends of the gleaming mahogany table, both dressed in ancient clothes of faded gentility.

In fact, when seen up close, Vivien realized that everything was faded and shabby. Most of the sparkling crystal glasses were chipped, the silverware tarnished, the china dishes covered with little nicks and cracks.

Marian seemed to do all the work in the house without much help from anyone else. Paul made a half-hearted attempt to help, carrying the serving dishes from the kitchen, but Vivien had the feeling that they expected Marian to do most of the "woman's work" herself. Vivien's offer to help her was shot down by Thomas Hendley. "We don't expect our guests to serve themselves," he said. He emphasized the word *guest* with a sneer.

Before long she realized she'd made a big mistake by caving in to Marian's pleas to have dinner with them. Throughout the meal she could feel Thomas Hendley's gaze upon her, and whenever she looked up she found him staring down his aquiline nose at her, his piercing eyes filled with hostility.

Mrs. Hendley sat with her mouth pursed, except when she snapped at Marian to complain about something missing from the table or the rice not being hot enough. *If I were Marian,* thought Vivien, *I'd throw the whole lot in her miserable face.* Why on earth did she take it from them? And why didn't Paul stand up for her against his parents? But he didn't. He sat there, eating his food, saying little, drinking beer from a glass mug, ignoring the barbs that flew about him, like a man ducking arrows.

The food was far too heavy for a hot night, but Vivien supposed they were used to hot nights. She would have been happy with a light salad and some fresh fruit. The jerk chicken was tasty but very spicy. It was served with the rice and peas that seemed to be a compulsory accompaniment to Barbadian meals. Dessert was a heavy bread-and-butter pudding, flavored with cinnamon and brown sugar and spoiled by a dollop of thick yellow custard. Vivien had great trouble eating more than two spoonfuls.

Although Vivien thanked Marian at the end of the meal, no one else did. When they'd finished, they all got up and left the table, only Vivien attempting to clear the dishes from it. Covered by the squeak and rattle of Mrs. Hendley's ancient wooden wheelchair, as Thomas pushed it out onto the balcony, Vivien whispered, "I'm going to help you do the dishes. No arguments."

Marian wearily pushed her hair back from her damp forehead. "Okay. I won't say no, but we all have coffee on the verandah first. Then they go up to their bedroom."

"Fine. I'll wait until then."

Vivien turned to find Paul standing by the sideboard, watching them intently. Marian gave him a defiant look but said only, "I'm off to get the coffee."

"Your wife works very hard," Vivien said when Marian left.

"She does. Too hard."

"Can't you get some help?"

His mouth twisted. "My parents don't like having help in the house. They're afraid someone might steal something."

"Your father seems to think the same of me."

Paul's face flushed bright red. "Sorry about that," he muttered. "Marian told me what happened in the barn. We'll understand if you feel you can't stay on."

"Oh, no, don't get me wrong," Vivien protested. "I wasn't complaining. I love this place. Besides, I've paid you in advance for four days, remember?"

He looked flustered before giving her a taut smile. "Fine. Excuse me, I have to check on something with my father."

Vivien felt a little sorry for him. He'd obviously landed in trouble with his parents for having taken her in as a guest and was now trying to get rid of her. She hesitated, wishing she could go up to her room, but decided she'd better be polite and join them for coffee.

She remained in the dining room for a while, to allow the Hendleys to get settled. When she stepped out onto the verandah, she had the feeling they'd been talking about her and had halted in midstream when she appeared.

"Come and join us," Paul said, indicating the vacant chair beside his.

"Thank you." Vivien sat down opposite the senior Hendleys, who sat side by side, she in her wheelchair, he in the large, high-backed cane chair, puffing on a small pungent cigar.

"Well, how do you like Barbados, Miss Shaw?" Thomas asked her, with an attempt at a smile. "This is your first visit, I believe?"

"Yes, it is. This is only my third day, but I love the island, and its people are so friendly." Except you, she added in her thoughts.

"What do you do again?" The question came from Mrs. Hendley.

"Miss Shaw is a professional photographer, my dear." Thomas spoke before Vivien could reply.

"In a newspaper?"

"No, I'm more of an artist with the camera," she said. "I have gallery exhibitions and I've had books of my work published."

"Haven't seen them," Mrs. Hendley said dismissively.

"No, I don't suppose you have. They were published in Canada and the United States."

"Don't read much anymore. My eyesight's not so good." But the pale eyes looking at Vivien over the steel-framed glasses were sharp enough.

"That's too bad." This conversation was going nowhere fast.

"How long have you lived here at Peverill?" she asked Thomas Hendley, although she knew the answer already.

He jerked up his head. "Why do you ask?" Even in the semidarkness she could see that his face was suffused with a mottled red.

She'd obviously touched a nerve. "I just wondered if you'd lived here all your life, that was all."

He stared at her, then scraped back his chair, half rising. "Where the devil has your wife got to with that coffee?" he asked Paul.

"You sit down, Father," Paul said, jumping up. "I'll see to it."

But Marian was already crossing the hall with the large tray bearing a silver coffeepot, cups, and saucers and a plate of biscuits. She set the biscuits down on the table, with tiny white lace napkins. As she watched Marian pouring out the coffee, adding cream and sugar where needed, Vivien felt as if she were in an Edwardian play, or something by Oscar Wilde perhaps, with after-dinner coffee being served in the conservatory. But there was also an element of Tennessee Williams, with the exotic location and the characters with their warped personalities.

As soon as she'd finished one cup of coffee, she pushed back her chair and stood up. "Thank you so much for the meal. I'm going up now."

"One minute," Thomas said, getting to his feet. "How long are you planning to stay here?"

"I haven't decided, but probably a few more days. I've paid for the four nights," she reminded him.

"We've had another request for a room."

"Then I'll let you know tomorrow, okay?"

"Of course," chipped in Paul. "You let us know if you want to stay longer than the four nights, and we'll extend it for you." He seemed to be trying to offset his father's blatant rudeness.

Taking a strong draw on his cigar and then blowing smoke out in her direction, Thomas subsided into his chair.

"Good night," Vivien said, receiving only grunts in reply from Mr. and Mrs. Hendley.

"Sorry about that," Paul said in a low voice as he followed her into the hall.

Vivien paused at the foot of the stairs. "I can let you know about the room tomorrow." She gave him a rueful smile. "They don't like people staying here, do they?"

Paul sighed and shook his head. "You can say that again. They haven't a clue about the cost of everything nowadays. They live in the past as far as money's concerned."

He was waiting for her to go upstairs, and Vivien decided she'd better do so. Once he'd gone outside, she could come down again to help Marian.

She went to her room and slipped the steel hook into the eye. She'd wait a while and then go down to the kitchen. She picked up Carol Shields's latest book, *Unless,* which she'd started reading last night, but she'd read only a couple of pages when the sound of raised voices came to her from the verandah. First she heard the men's voices. Thomas's arrogant, accusatorial. Paul's defensive, belligerent. Then the women chimed in. Mrs. Hendley screeching abuse like a fishwife. Marian shouting back. Then another sharp, unidentifiable sound, followed by Marian sobbing.

"She will have to go," said Thomas Hendley, the words coming to her quite clearly, and Vivien knew that they were fighting about her.

She also realized that the sound she hadn't been able to place was a slap. Marian was still sobbing, but exactly who had slapped her was impossible to discern. Vivien was tempted to storm down immediately to support Marian, but something stopped her. After all, it was her own presence in the house that was fueling this fight. Better that she keep out of it for now, leaving Paul to deal with the parents from hell—and his poor wife.

CHAPTER SEVENTEEN

Vivien's first night at Peverill was not a good one. Although she read for a while, when she turned out the light her mind was filled with images of Lillian Hendley's murder, combined with the memory of her encounter with Thomas in the barn, and then the argument on the verandah after dinner. When, eventually, she was able to fall asleep, the thoughts remained with her in the form of disturbing dreams, which hovered uneasily in her mind even after she awoke.

Unwilling to face any of the Hendleys, Vivien did not go down to breakfast. She had plenty of food left from the groceries she'd bought, and Marian had given her a cooler to keep them in.

She was munching on a cheese roll when Marian knocked. "Can I come in?" she said from the other side of the door.

"Hang on. I'll unhook the door. Don't know why I bother to put this stupid hook on," she said to Marian when she'd let her in.

"I don't blame you. Everyone likes their privacy." Marian was bearing a tray, which she placed on the table by the window. "Thought you'd like breakfast up here," she said. "Just fruit juice and fresh rolls, okay?"

"That's really kind." Vivien noticed Marian's face was turned away from her. "Are you okay?"

"I'm fine."

"Sure?"

Marian's averted shoulders quivered. Vivien went to her and put her arm around her. "Sit down."

Marian shook her head. "No, I can't. I have to—"

"Sit down for a minute . . . and look at me."

Marian heaved a sigh and turned her face. Her eyes were red and swollen from weeping, but more important, her right cheek bore a large dark bruise.

"Someone hit you. Who was it?" Vivien demanded. Marian's hand flew to her face to cover the bruise. "It was Thomas, wasn't it?"

Marian gave her a rueful smile. "Let's not talk about it."

"You can't let him get away with it, Marian. He assaulted you. Why didn't Paul stop him?"

"I don't want to talk about it." Marian got up from the chair and went to the door. She said lightly, "I wasn't sure if you preferred tea or coffee in the morning, so I brought hot water in a jug with some tea and instant coffee. That way you can choose for yourself."

"Thanks." Vivien hesitated. "Would it help if I spoke to Paul about this?"

"No! No, you mustn't get involved," Marian said vehemently. "It's family business, nothing to do with you."

"Okay, but I can't help feeling involved when I'm the cause of you getting beaten up."

Marian gave a little laugh. "You do exaggerate, don't you?"

Vivien was about to protest but kept her mouth shut. There was no point in upsetting Marian even more.

"Thanks for caring," Marian said softly. "But it's not you, in particular. It's anyone who dares to invade their home. They've been that way for as long as I've known them."

"Have you lived with them since your marriage?"

"No, Paul and I lived in England for the first few years of our marriage, while Paul was finishing his estate management degree in Newcastle. Our daughter was born there. But then his father needed help here and persuaded Paul to come back to Barbados." Her expression grew bitter. "That was the end of our happiness and our independence."

"Couldn't you persuade Paul to leave?"

"I've been trying. For a while he was even checking out jobs in Britain, but now it's too late." Marian opened the door. "I must go."

"Would it help if I left this morning?" Vivien asked.

"No, not at all. It's not you, it's them." Marian slipped out, closing the door behind her.

For Marian's sake, Vivien spread one of the fresh-baked rolls with butter and guava jam, but she was so upset that she had no appetite. She poured herself some mango juice and sat down, trying to decide what to do. She was starting to think that she was crazy to stay on here. But now she was also concerned that, if she left, Marian would have no one but her chicken-hearted husband to take her part against his parents. Still, eventually she would have to leave, and Marian would have to work things out—or not—with her in-laws.

The question now was: Did she want to stay here for another night? The answer was yes—and no. Something still drew her to the place. A feeling of unfinished business. Perhaps if she could take some more pictures, she'd be happy then to leave.

She glanced at her watch. A few minutes before eight. Was it too early to call Celeste? Probably not. Wesley had told her that everyone started work early here, because of the afternoon heat. Not wanting to dither around any longer, she picked up the cell phone and punched in Celeste's home number.

Celeste answered, stating her telephone number in a formal voice.

"It's Vivien Shaw," Vivien told her. "I hope it's not too early."

"Vivien! How lovely to hear from you," Celeste said in her high, girlish voice. "No, I was about to leave for work. You just caught me in time. What can I do for you? I hope you're calling to say you are able to come for lunch today, after all."

"No. A little more than that, actually. I was thinking I'd take you up on your offer."

"Offer?" Celeste sounded puzzled.

"Of a room at your place," Vivien said, grimacing to herself. Perhaps this had been one of those customs where you ask someone to stay with you, but don't really mean it. "It's okay," she said quickly. "I can find somewhere else. I just thought—"

"I'm sorry, Vivien." A long pause. "It might be better if we discuss it when we meet at my mother's place tomorrow."

"Of course."

"It's—it's a little awkward to explain over the phone."

"No, please don't worry about it. I can stay on here. No problem."

"All will be explained tomorrow," Celeste said. "I feel very badly about this but—"

"Please don't."

An awkward silence ensued.

"So," Celeste eventually said, "unless I hear from you the arrangement stays the same: Joseph will pick you up at Peverill Hall at eleven o'clock tomorrow morning, right?"

"That's great," Vivien said brightly. "Bye." She clicked off the phone, feeling extremely embarrassed. Stupid! she told herself. You should have known Celeste was just being polite when she asked you to come and stay.

Well, that decided it. She was staying on at Peverill for another night. Then she could see how things went. Perhaps Paul would talk to his father and tell him to get his act together, but she doubted it. That was probably what had started last night's quarrel. And look how that had turned out, with Marian's face bruised.

Whether she stayed on at Peverill or not, she knew she must get away this morning and start working in earnest. She had a few hours before she was to meet David at the university. She'd check on guided tours, get a taxi into Bridgetown, and do some touristy stuff, and then David could show her the other, off-the-beaten-track things this afternoon.

But when she met David at the university, he told her that he wouldn't be able to take the afternoon off after all.

"There's been a huge blowup here about funding. The usual administration mess, but it has to be dealt with before tonight's faculty dinner, so I will be locked in meetings all afternoon. Sorry."

Vivien tried to hide her disappointment, but David sensed it. "Tell you what. Did you bring your camera?"

"Of course I did. I was out most of the morning doing a tour of Bridgetown."

"Good." He glanced at his watch. "I can manage an hour. Let's drive into town, see if we can find somewhere quick to eat that's in a photogenic area."

"You don't have to come with me," she assured him. "I can manage by myself. I saw plenty of places on the tour that I was itching to spend more time in, like the Jewish synagogue and the cathedral—"

David cut in impatiently. "You can tell me all about it while we're eating. Let's go."

He took her to the Waterfront Cafe, which overlooked both the Careenage—the natural harbor—and, across the water, Trafalgar Square. Here, they sat outside, eating deep-fried flying fish sandwiches for lunch, drinking Banks beer, and watching an endless stream of people passing by.

When they'd finished, Vivien rinsed her greasy fingers in a nearby water fountain and then took out her Nikon camera. David watched with great interest as she set out to capture the anchored yachts with their brightly colored sails and the hucksters selling gaudy souvenirs and all kinds of sliced fruits—guava and mango and pawpaw, which David explained was the Bajan name for papaya—from roadside stalls.

"I hate to do this," he said eventually, looking at his watch, "but I have to go. Do you want to come back with me or—"

"No, I'll stay here in town." She grinned at him. "I'm on a roll."

He grinned back. "So I see." He hesitated for a moment . . . and then squeezed her hand. "Call me in the morning, okay?" he said. "We'll set up something really special to make up for this."

"This was special," she said.

Their eyes met, then he glanced away. "See you. Bye."

As she watched him leave, she heard laughter and whistling from behind her, but when she turned around, the curbside traders appeared to be totally immersed in their wares. Smiling to herself, she set off on the walk back across the bridge to the center of Bridgetown, still glowing from the excitement of sharing new experiences with this unpredictable man.

Several hours later, she got a taxi back from Bridgetown to Peverill Hall and limped into the house, footsore and weary.

Marian caught her as she was about to go upstairs, as if she'd been waiting a long time to speak to her. "Are you having dinner with us tonight? You didn't say this morning, so I took it that you were. I'm making roast beef and my special Yorkshire pudding. The way they're supposed to be made, not these airy-fairy things those packets make." Her eyes silently pleaded with Vivien.

"I'm sorry, Marian. I think it's best if I stay in my room. I'm probably going out later."

Despite her disappointment, Marian nodded. "I understand. I'll bring you up a dinner tray."

Vivien summoned up a grateful smile, even though the thought of roast beef in this heat was revolting. "Thanks. I'm going to have a bath. I've been walking for hours."

"I'm not sure there's any hot water."

Vivien was halfway up the stairs. "That's okay. I'll manage."

As soon as she went into her room, she kicked off her sandals, dumped her heavy camera bag on the bed, and flung herself down beside it. What a day! Despite her aching feet and the yucky feeling of her clothes sticking to her body, she felt exhilarated. She'd taken hundreds of pictures. Her mind was still spinning with images of this stimulating island. Most of all, she felt that she and David had established a better basis for their future work together.

As she lay there, she scanned the room, checking to see that everything was the way she'd left it. Damn! She'd forgotten to pack her daybook away. It was still on the bedside cabinet, where she'd left it last night. She picked it up and opened it at yesterday's entry. Thank God she hadn't yet written down her impressions of what had happened last night in the barn! If anyone had been snooping in here, they'd have read only her first impressions of Peverill, most of which were glowing.

Seeing that the sun was starting to go down and the light rapidly disappearing, as it did so early in the tropics, she decided to postpone catching up with her notes.

A quick bath, change—in case she decided to go out this evening—and then perhaps her last chance of taking a few secret pictures of Peverill. The thought saddened her. When she'd moved in here yesterday, she'd had such high hopes of capturing the beauty of the lovely old rooms and their fading treasures. Now all she could do was perhaps add a few exterior pictures of bougainvillea climbing the old limestone wall and of the summerhouse in the shadowy dusk to those she'd taken yesterday. She'd have to hide her compact Leica in her black cotton bag. Old man Hendley could hardly demand that she turn out her personal bag, could he?

The water in the bathroom washbasin was barely tepid. When she turned on the bath faucet, it coughed and spluttered and only rusty water dribbled out. She decided to have a quick wash at the porcelain basin instead. Then she returned to her room and hurriedly changed into a sleeveless cream linen top with linen pants the color of cappuccino. Although David wasn't available this evening, she was determined to get out for a few hours.

As she came down the staircase, stopping to run her fingers over the intricately turned stair rods, she imagined all the women whose feet had walked on the polished stair treads over the past three hundred years. Women in silk and satin and damask, with hoops and panniers and crinolines—but also women on their knees scrubbing and polishing before dawn, then scurrying away to the kitchen belowstairs to avoid being seen.

Vivien looked around. The front rooms were empty. Tiptoeing across the hall, she glanced into the dining room and saw that it had already been set for dinner.

Deciding she'd better get out quickly, before someone saw her, Vivien went out onto the verandah. The late afternoon was glorious. It was still fairly hot, but the ocean breeze had cooled it down a little, and the eastern sky was already turning to a light navy-blue.

Aware that it could be dark soon, she'd packed a

small flashlight in her bag. There were two coach lights on the verandah, but that was all. No floodlighting in the grounds. That was okay. She didn't intend to go too far.

Nighttime usually held no terrors for Vivien. She'd learned how to move around quietly and easily in the darkness, so that she could take pictures of nocturnal creatures. But as she stepped down from the lowest step onto the driveway, she had to admit she felt a little wary. There might not be black bears prowling about or a moose playing chicken with you on a narrow path by the lake, but what was out there was the unknown. For instance, she'd stupidly forgotten to ask if there were dangerous snakes in Barbados. Or how about scorpions?

She started off down the narrow pathway. Then she turned to look back. The remaining natural light, plus the interior lights shining from the verandah and through the windows, were enough to show off the perfect symmetry of the house, the balanced position of the tall sash windows on the upper floor, the gabled roof, and the paneled door with its exquisite glassed fanlight. Perhaps this was the ideal time to look at the house, when you could see the shapes but not the details. Impossible in the dusk to see the lack of paint, for instance, or the rotting wood, the cracks in the coral limestone walls.

She slid her camera out of her bag and took three pictures of the house. She saw a shadow move across an upstairs window and hurriedly slid the camera back into her bag, wanting to avoid another confrontation with Thomas Hendley. Better to wait awhile.

She returned to the verandah and sat swinging back and forth in the swing, enjoying the evening sounds of the frogs and birds. Then, when all seemed still in the house, she set off down the side path, pausing to take some shots of the summerhouse. How strange that they would call it a summerhouse, she mused, when, really, it was summer year-round here.

She continued on, following the path as it twisted

away from the main house, past the opening that led to the old barn. In the semidarkness, the overgrown hedge seemed taller, the pathway longer. All of a sudden it came to an abrupt end, fetching up at a high barbed-wire fence. The fence appeared to surround a clearing, which was a stark contrast to the untamed growth in the rest of the grounds. In the increasingly fading light, she could see a stretch of flat earth dotted with several piles of branches and tree stumps, as if the land had been bulldozed clear recently. She tried to follow the wire fence around the clearing, but the vegetation became too heavy for her to get through.

What could the clearing be for? Maybe some land the Hendleys had sold for development. Might even be for a hotel, although surely the beach was not close enough for a hotel's needs. Possibly a condominium development? The thought horrified Vivien. She hated to think of an apartment block in this secluded, unspoiled spot.

She drew out her camera again, adjusting the settings for the semidarkness, and shot several pictures in quick succession. She was concentrating so hard that she didn't hear the footsteps until it was too late. She smelled cigar smoke. An arm reached over her shoulder, grabbing the camera from her hands, and she spun around to confront Thomas Hendley.

"This time you have no excuse."

"Give me back my camera," she demanded, trying to hide her fear.

His gaze locking with hers, he sprung open the camera and, fingers locating the film, ripped it out.

"You have no right," she said, her hands clenching into fists.

"Oh, yes, Miss Shaw, I have every right. This is my land. You were warned yesterday not to take photographs. I am confiscating your camera. You will get it back when you leave Peverill Hall tonight."

"I've paid for four nights," she said, jutting her jaw out belligerently. "I don't intend to leave tonight."

"We'll see about that." He stepped back and, with a laughably courtly little bow, gestured to her to go ahead of him. "Let me escort you back to the house, Miss Shaw. It is not safe for you out here in the darkness."

Mind and heart racing, she stalked ahead of him, well aware that she'd been a fool to risk the chance of being caught taking pictures again. Damn him! He'd destroyed those perfect shots she'd taken of the front of the house in the dusk. Thank God she'd taken out yesterday's film and locked it away, or she would have lost those shots as well.

When they went into the house, he slammed the front door shut behind them. She held out her hand for her camera, but he shook his head. "I said you'd get it back when you leave. Not before."

"I'm supposed to find somewhere new to stay even though I've paid for four nights? I wonder what the tourist board would think about that . . . or about you stealing my camera."

His sucked in his cheeks, his lean face becoming cadaverous, and stiffly handed her the camera. "I'll refund your money," he said disdainfully, as if discussing money was beneath him.

"I'm not leaving because you say so. And if you force me to leave, I'll report you." She turned from him and ran up the stairs, aware that he was watching her all the way.

Breathing fast, she slipped the steel hook into the eye and stood with her back to the door, surveying the room. Then her eyes narrowed. Where was her daybook? All she could see on the bedside cabinet was her traveling alarm clock and book. She crossed the room and looked around the cabinet. As she moved, her foot brushed against something on the floor. The daybook lay there, facedown, under the bed. She bent down and picked it up.

Could she have knocked it off the cabinet before she'd gone out? she wondered as she placed it back on the table. No, she clearly recalled seeing it there when she left. Someone had been in her room. She remembered seeing the shadow on the blind. She hadn't realized at the time that it could have been the blind in her room.

She slumped into the little chair beside the window, nerves taut. *Face it,* she told herself. *Whether you want to or not, it's time to get out of here.* The heat was stifling, the ceiling pressing down on her, but a slight breeze stirred the rose chintz curtains. She'd open the window fully and let the air fill the room while she got her things together.

Then she'd call Spencer to come and get her.

The lower half of the old sash window was very heavy to lift; the wood had roughened and splintered over the years. She struggled with it, trying to push hard on both sides to slide it upward. Gradually, inch by inch, it lifted. She had to jiggle it back and forth at the same time as she lifted it, and the weight made her shoulders ache. It stuck about an inch from the top, but at least now she could feel the cooler air flowing into the room.

She leaned out, hands on the window ledge, sadness enveloping her at the thought of leaving this lovely house. Despite the hateful Thomas Hendley, it was a lovely evening. Although more rain was forecast, the strong evening winds had swept away the clouds. She leaned out farther, so that she could see the navy sky, now speckled with stars.

The breeze carried the acrid aroma of Thomas Hendley's cigar up to her. She could hear his voice talking to someone else, but not what he was saying. Not wanting to be seen, she abruptly drew her head in.

She was about to lift her hands from the ledge to lower the window a little when, with the speed of a guillotine blade, the window crashed down.

For a suspended moment, Vivien felt nothing, only a stunning sense of shock. Then came the pain, wave upon wave of pain that made her feel sick and faint. As the full weight of the window bore down on her wrists, trapping them, she cried out in agony. The world started darkening around her. She gathered as much strength as she could and screamed, "Help! Help me!"

Silence.

"Help!" she cried again. She tried to draw her hands away, but they were tightly pinned down by the weight of the window, crushing her wrists.

Again, blackness closed in on her. She tried to support her body with the chair to avoid falling down and damaging her hands even more. "Help!" she cried, but this time her voice sounded faint in own ears.

She felt herself slip away into unconsciousness for a moment and then, to her enormous relief, she heard someone try to open the door. "Help me, please," she whimpered.

The door burst open with a splintering of wood. "My God, what's happened to you?" It was Marian.

"My hands," Vivien whispered. "The window fell . . ." Her voice trailed away.

Marian appeared beside her, struggling with the window, but she couldn't budge it. "Paul," she bellowed. "Paul!"

Hurried footsteps, voices . . . then the blessed relief of the lifting of the window, followed by such excruciating pain, as the blood again circulated through her hands, that Vivien found herself spiraling into blackness.

CHAPTER
EIGHTEEN

She was lying on a strange bed in a strange room, with two strangers standing beside her and a lighting fixture shaded by frosted glass in a white ceiling above her. Panic swept over her. She struggled . . . and then came the sickening waves of pain again.

Oddly enough, this time the pain brought her to her senses. She tried to lift her hands but could not. "My hands hurt," she whispered.

The woman leaned over her. "I've wrapped them in towels filled with ice," she said. As her pinched face came into focus, her hair hanging in damp strands about it, Vivien realized that she was Marian Hendley.

Paul Hendley looked deeply concerned. "The sash cords must have been rotten," he told her apologetically. "Everything's falling apart in this bloody house."

"My hands. I can't move my hands," Vivien told them. She desperately wanted to have someone with her she knew. "The bones might be broken."

"I don't think so," Marian said. "Just nasty cuts and bruises."

"I should go to the emergency room and have them checked," Vivien whispered, the right words coming slowly to her mind. She sounded like her father, she thought, disgusted at herself.

"You'll be fine," Marian said, rubbing her shoulder. "Lie still, and I'll make you a cup of tea with sugar. You're probably suffering from shock."

Vivien's voice rose. "I'd like to have them checked, to make sure."

"You rest now. You don't want to go to the hospital at this time. If you're still in pain tomorrow, Paul will drive you into Bridgetown, okay?"

Panic started in the pit of Vivien's stomach and spread into her chest, making her heart race. She was trapped here, with no one to help her. Then she remembered the cell phone. "Fine," she heard herself saying.

Marian hovered over her. "I've got some painkillers and a glass of water. Let me help you take them."

"I—I can manage."

"You shouldn't be moving those hands," Marian warned.

"I'm fine. I'd like to try to rest for a few minutes." Vivien's heart was pounding. She must get rid of them so she could use the phone.

"I'll bring you up some tea and biscuits."

"Thank you."

They both went out, but there was no lock on the door. One of them could come in at any time. Where was that phone? Had she left it by the window? Or had she put it away somewhere out of reach? Her mind was too fuzzy to remember. Holding her hands in the air, so that the melting ice trickled down her arms into her armpits, she struggled up onto her elbows. Slowly and painfully, she dragged herself to the far edge of the bed. She had a faint recollection of having put her bag there when she'd found the daybook on the floor last night.

Last night? No, that must have been only a few minutes ago. She felt as if hours had passed since she went to the window and opened it. *Don't think about that now. Concentrate on finding the phone.*

Once she'd gained the edge of the bed, she looked over the side and to her great relief saw her bag on the floor. But, the question was, had she replaced the phone in the bag or left it by the window? She couldn't remember.

"Why the heck don't you just ask one of the Hendleys to call Wesley for you?" she said aloud. But she didn't want them to know she had a phone. Clearly, they were reluctant to take her to the hospital. They were concerned that they might get into trouble over the accident. Afraid she might sue them, perhaps. But all she cared about was getting in touch with someone who could help her, to find medical attention. Anything else, such as the attachment of blame, was unimportant to her at this moment.

She painfully freed her right hand from the wet towel, leaned over the edge of the bed, and slowly eased her arm downward. The rush of blood into her hand made her cry out, but she muffled the cry by pushing her face into the pillow. Fortunately, she'd left the bag open. The room reeled about her as she moved her fingers around inside. She had to pause, taking several deep breaths, to avoid fainting again. With the window now tightly shut, the room was stifling, airless.

She tried again. This time her fingers encountered what definitely felt like the small cell phone. Whimpering with relief, she closed her fingers about the phone and slowly lifted it, hanging on, terrified she might drop it on the floor, out of reach. When she had it safely on the bed, she fell back, exhausted, onto the pillow, sweat pouring down her face.

But relief quickly ebbed away when she realized that she didn't have Wesley's phone number. It was in her wallet at the very bottom of the bag. Tears welled into her eyes, running down her cheeks and into her ears. She wasn't sure she had the strength to go through that again.

Feeling sick to her stomach, she sat up and was about to lean over when she suddenly recalled that she'd tucked Spencer's card into the little side pocket of her bag.

"Oh, thank God," she breathed. Her fingers reached down into the pocket and encountered the card. When she drew it out, she saw for the first time the swelling and lurid bruising starting to form around her wrists and the lower part of her hands. The sight of it made her feel even more nauseated, but she swallowed hard and focused on the number.

Please, God, let it work, she prayed as she painstakingly punched in the number.

To her relief she got the ringing tone. She pressed the phone tighter against her ear, listening with the other for any sign of Marian coming back with her tea. "Come on, come on," she whispered in an agony of impatience.

A woman said, "Hello," at the other end of the line.

"I'd like to speak to Spencer, please." The niceties of telephone etiquette came automatically. She could hear children's shouts and laughter and music in the background.

"Spencer's busy," said the woman. "It's his granddaughter Elsie's birthday party. Sorry. Try another taxi."

"No, no," Vivien cried. "Don't hang up. I don't want a taxi. I want help. Please tell Spencer it's Vivien Shaw. I need help."

"Shaw?"

"Yes, that's right. I've had an accident."

"Wait, please."

Vivien leaned her head back against the pillow. The pain was coming at her in black waves now. Marian's two pills sat on top of the bedside cabinet with the glass of water, but Vivien needed to stay awake, just for a little while longer, to get help.

Minutes ticked by . . . or seemed to. Then Spencer's slow, deep voice said, "Miss Shaw? What is wrong?"

"Oh, Spencer, thank God." Vivien released a sob and then controlled herself. "I've had an accident. I may have broken bones in my hands. Can you get Mr. Marshall for me? I can't get hold of his number." She had to stop talking to fight the pain again but added a heartfelt "Please."

"You hold on there. I'll have someone there as soon as I can. Mr. Marshall, he's too far away, 'cross the island. Dr. Moreton live closer."

"I don't want to bother Dr. Moreton. He has a faculty dinner—"

"Leave it to me. Want me to call you back?"

"No. I trust you to get someone."

"That's good. You called the right person."

"I know." Vivien didn't want to tell him that he was the only person whose number she could get to. In retrospect, she realized she could have asked the operator to call the ambulance service, but her brain wasn't functioning very well. "Thanks, Spencer."

When the connection was cut off, she felt desperately alone again, but she knew that Spencer wouldn't let her down.

She heard the door handle turn and quickly dropped the phone into her bag. Marian came in with a tray laid with a small floral teapot, jug and sugar basin, china dishes, and a plate of cookies.

"You're looking a bit better." She bustled around, pulling up a table and setting the tray on it, close to the bed, within reach. "You'll feel even better when you've had some tea."

"I'm not sure I should have anything to eat or drink in case they need to operate."

"Operate!" Marian's laugh was brittle as broken glass. "What a pessimist you are. Of course they won't need to operate."

Vivien saved her breath. She needed her strength to ward off the pain until whoever it was came to help her. Sweat broke out on her face, yet she felt chilly at the same time. She swallowed hard. "What I need most is a bowl," she managed to say. "I'm feeling really sick."

Marian hurriedly removed the tray and fetched the bowl from the washstand, setting it beside Vivien. She stood looking anxiously at her. "Can I help?"

Vivien shook her head. "No, thanks," she whispered. She laid her head back on the pillow, fighting the waves of nausea.

Marian waited for a time, her face pale. Someone, probably Paul, called to her. "Back in a minute," she said and left the room.

Vivien lay there, eyes closed, concentrating on breathing slowly through her nose.

She must have dozed for a while. She awoke with a start to the roar of a high-powered engine approaching fast and then the screech of brakes as the vehicle came to a halt outside.

Hammering on the door, loud voices. She could distinguish Thomas Hendley's, raised in anger, and Paul Hendley's, protesting.

And, above them all, David Moreton's. Footsteps bounded up the stairs. "Is this her room?" she heard him ask outside the bedroom door.

"How dare you barge into my house without my permission!" Thomas Hendley shouted. "I'm calling the police."

"You do that. Is this her room?"

Vivien raised herself on one elbow. "David, I'm in here."

The door opened and in the doorway stood David Moreton, dressed in black jacket and pants with a white silk turtleneck top. He seemed to fill the room with his presence.

He came to her side, his gaze quickly assessing, taking in everything. "What happened?"

"It was an accident," Marian said.

"I asked Miss Shaw what happened," he said without turning around.

"She's right," Vivien told him. "It was an accident. The window crashed down on my hands. The sash rope must have frayed." She held out the unwrapped right hand to show him, and he flinched. "Fortunately, it missed the finger joints and hit the lower part of the hands, mainly my wrists."

Marian stepped forward. "I've put ice on them. I think the swelling's going down." But her attempt to make less of it was ignored.

"You could have fractured bones in your wrists," David said. "They'll have to be x-rayed."

"That's why—" Vivien was about to say that was why she had called Spencer, but clamped her mouth shut. His eyes meeting hers, David frowned but said nothing about her call.

"Can you walk?"

"I think so," she said shakily. "Trouble is I can't use my hands."

"No problem. I'll lift you off the bed and then support you downstairs. I'd carry you down, but I wouldn't want to risk any more broken bones." His wry grin did more than any medicine to help make her feel better.

She glanced around the room. "My things . . . my camera . . ."

"Don't worry about those. We'll just lock them in the room."

"There's no lock."

"Ah." He turned to Marian and Paul, who stood in the doorway. "As you have not provided your guest with a lock on her door, I take it that you will give a guarantee that all her belongings will be taken care of and that no one will be permitted to enter her room until she returns?"

Paul bristled. "I'm not about to give guarantees to—"

"Yes, of course we will," Marian said, putting a restraining hand on her husband's arm. "We just want to make sure Miss Shaw's hands are okay, don't we, Paul?"

Still glowering at David, he nodded.

"Is that your bag on the floor?" David asked Vivien.

"Yes."

"We'll take that with us." He picked up the bag and drew the drawstring tight, so that nothing could fall out. "Would you carry that down for Miss Shaw, Mrs. Hendley?" He handed it to Marian and then turned back to Vivien. "Ready?" he said softly.

She nodded but couldn't hide her apprehension from him.

"I'm going to slide you off the bed. Don't try to hang on or use your hands at all. Keep them in the air. Just let me take your weight, okay?"

She nodded, fear making her feel nauseated again. "I'm feeling a bit sick," she told him, embarrassed.

"I'm not surprised. Shall we take the bowl?"

"Hang on. Get an old plastic one from the kitchen, Paul," Marian said to her husband. "Hurry."

David arched his eyebrows at Vivien, and she couldn't help smiling in return. He bent over her, and she caught a hint of his cologne, something lightly spicy, without being too heavy. His arms slipped around her back and under her knees and lifted her easily from the bed, then he set her on her feet.

Breathing fast, she stood, swaying, trying to stop the room from spinning around her.

"Take it easy," he said in her ear. His arm slid around her waist. "One step at a time, mind. If you do pass out, you won't fall. I'm supporting you."

He was. She could feel his strength through his arm around her, his side pressed against hers. Taking a deep breath, she started to walk around the bed, holding her hands up, crossed over her chest. He walked with her, very slowly, pace by pace, across the room and out the door to the top of the staircase. To Vivien, standing at the top looking down, it looked like more than a hundred steps. She caught sight of Thomas standing at his bedroom door, watching them.

"One step at a time," David reminded her.

Legs shaking, she took one step down—and he was there, his long legs keeping pace with her. She was tempted to grab the banister rail, but she kept her hands crossed. Slowly, they descended the staircase together, until she was standing, knees trembling, in the main hall.

"The worst is over," David told her.

"We've still got the outside steps."

"They'll be a breeze. Not so many and no polished wood to slip on."

He was right. In unison they easily descended the tiled steps, Marian bringing up the rear with Vivien's bag and a green plastic bowl.

David's Mustang waited for them in the driveway, this time with its roof covering the interior.

"Nice car," Paul breathed, a hint of envy in his voice.

"Not so nice for the present situation."

Vivien knew what David meant. The seats were low, and she wondered how she was going to get in without being able to hold on to anything.

"Who's this?" David said as he was about to open the passenger door for her.

Another vehicle was driving down the lane. Vivien peered into the darkness and then recognized the van. "It's Spencer." Braving the dangers of Peverill Hall, she thought, with a rush of affection.

He drew the van to a halt, clambered down faster than usual, and came across to them. "You okay, Miss Shaw?" His voice and expression registered deep concern.

Vivien would have hugged him if she could. "I don't know what I would have done without you," she said in a low voice. Knowing he wanted to ask what had happened to her, she told him quickly. "A window fell on my hands. Dr. Moreton's taking me to the hospital to have them x-rayed. It was an accident."

His wary glance slid from her to the Hendleys standing at the top of the steps. If he'd been a Catholic, she imagined he might have crossed himself.

"I must get her off to the hospital," David said. Maintaining his grip on Vivien, he held out a hand to Spencer. "Thanks for calling me, man, and for coming to see she was okay."

Spencer nodded.

"Go back, enjoy your party," Vivien said. "I'm so sorry to have taken you away from it."

"You let me know how she is," Spencer said to David and then turned to walk back to his van.

"He's really taken to you, hasn't he?" David said, watching him climb into the front seat.

Vivien had to smile. As Spencer drove off, she turned back to David's car. "How am I going to get in?"

"Easy." He slid the seat as far back as it would go. "Turn backward, parallel to the side of the seat."

"Like this?"

"Right. Now I'm going to let you go and you lower yourself onto the seat sideways, then swing your legs in—or I can lift them in for you."

He was right. In an instant she was sitting down in the passenger seat. "How did you know that?"

"Experience. When my mother had knee surgery, I drove her home. The nurse told her how to get into the car." He leaned over to do up her seat belt, his face almost touching hers. "I'll go get your bag and the bowl."

He was back with both in a moment, also carrying a blanket. "Mrs. Hendley said you might be cold from the shock." He tucked it around her knees, careful not to touch her hands.

As they sped along the dark lanes and then onto the main highway, Vivien felt as if she were in some sort of weird dream, being rescued from danger by an avenging angel. She chuckled.

"What's so funny?"

"You. All you needed was to be swinging one of those huge swords when you came into my room. The Hendleys must have wondered what hit them."

"Them Hendleys sure didn't like a black Bajan boy comin' into their house and takin' over."

"I did warn you."

"You were right."

"What did they say?" She was furious at the thought that they might have insulted him.

"Not important."

"It is important."

"Not now it isn't. All that matters is getting you to the hospital. You won't have to wait, by the way. I called a friend who's an excellent orthopedic surgeon. He's going to meet us there."

Vivien didn't know what to say. Her eyes filled with tears.

"What's wrong?" David asked, glancing at her.

"You."

"What have I done now?"

"That's the thing. I haven't thanked you, because I don't know how I can. You've missed your dinner."

"That's no great loss."

"Which reminds me. Why were you at home when Spencer called, and not at the faculty dinner?"

"Had to go home to change."

"Oh. Anyway, I can't thank you enough. You've been so kind to a stranger who—"

"What stranger? I've insulted you in public, dined with you, danced with you, argued with you? Some stranger."

"I'm not so good with words tonight. Thanks, David." It sounded so inadequate, but she sensed that anything more would have embarrassed him.

"Don't worry. As soon as you're patched up, the real me will be back again, arguing and fighting with you. It'll be a miracle if we ever get this book done."

She glanced down at her wounded hands. "It will be," she whispered. "A photographer needs her hands."

He groaned. "Shit! My mother always told me I had a big mouth."

She wanted to reach out to him, to reassure him. Good thing her hands were not to be used. She kept having these urges to touch him. "Don't worry. Once I know what the damage is, I'm going to do my best to heal quickly."

"That's the spirit." He glanced at her again. "You okay?" he asked softly.

"Pain's bad again." Eyes closing, she tried to breathe through her nose.

"I meant to ask you if you took painkillers."

"No. Marian offered me some, but I thought I'd better wait until I saw a doctor, in case I need surgery."

"That's good in one way, but rotten for you." He hesitated and then asked, "Why didn't you want them to know you'd called on a cell phone?"

"I don't know. Stupid, isn't it? They must have guessed I'd used a cell phone. Otherwise, how would you have known I needed help?" She tried to think back. "It may sound paranoid, but I guess I was so shocked from the pain that for a while I thought they might not want anyone to know about the accident in case I blamed them for it and maybe sued them for negligence."

"You may be near the truth. From the little I saw of it, that house appears to be falling apart."

"It's a beautiful house," she protested.

"It might once have been beautiful, but it's been sadly neglected."

"Don't blame the house because you don't like the people."

"I would remind you that all those houses were built with the sweat of black slaves for the glory of white plantation owners."

Pain washed over Vivien and she couldn't stifle a groan.

He struck himself on the forehead with the palm of his hand. "Oh, Lord, there I go again. The last thing you want now is another Moreton lecture on the colonial history of Barbados."

"That's true. But that doesn't mean I wouldn't like to discuss it sometime with you. Just not now, please."

"Lord, I hate to see you in such pain," he said fervently. "What can I do to help?"

"You've done more than enough just by being here with me," she said softly.

CHAPTER NINETEEN

Martin Jones, the surgeon, was a large man, almost as tall as David but not as lean, with a soft voice and gentle manner. She seemed to have two guardian angels tonight, Vivien thought.

She had asked that David come into the examining room with her, but having glanced at her hands after the doctor had fully unwrapped them, he studied the charts on the wall while she was being examined.

"Very nasty," the doctor eventually said. "Broken skin, soft tissue and flexor tendon contusion. Painful, I'm sure, but I do not believe there are any actual fractures. We will know once we have the results of the X rays."

"When will that be?" Vivien asked anxiously.

"I'm sending you to be x-rayed immediately. As soon as they've been taken, come back here and we can look at them together. If there are no fractures, we can give you a shot of morphine for the pain."

"Want me to come with you?" David asked her.

"No, you go get yourself a coffee or something."

"She'll be fine," Dr. Jones assured him. "I'll send an orderly with her." He looked from David to Vivien with open interest, trying to determine their relationship.

David must have come to the same conclusion. "Vi-

vien is a professional photographer from Canada. We
are collaborating on a book," he explained, with rather
more emphasis than was necessary.

The doctor rose from his revolving stool. "I'll come
with you. I'll send the orderly in right away," he told
Vivien. As the two men went down the hall, she could
hear him ask David a question about the latest cricket
match at Bridgetown Oval. This made her think of her
father. He still liked cricket, even though he hadn't
played the game himself since he was a boy. He loved
to watch the summer cricket matches in Assiniboine
Park and used to take her with him when she was small.

"Oh, Daddy, I wish you were here with me," she whispered, tears forming, but she blinked them away.

When she was wheeled back from the X-ray department twenty minutes later, the two men were waiting
for her. She felt stupid sitting in a wheelchair, but she
still hadn't had any painkillers and was shaky from tension and the constant throbbing pain.

The surgeon slipped the X rays, one by one, into the
viewer on the wall. "As I thought," he said, after examining them carefully. "Severe contusions, but no fractures or disruption of tendons."

"That's great," she said, relieved but now feeling guilty
for having made such a fuss when nothing was broken.

"These things are often far more painful than fractures," he said, reading her mind. "But now you can
have something for the pain. I'm going to give you a
shot of morphine right away and then some Tylenol 3s
to take until the pain recedes."

"Morphine makes me sick."

"I'm sure it does, but that's better than suffering acute
pain. I'll give you some Gravol as well for the nausea."
Once he'd applied dressings and carefully wrapped her
hands in tensor bandages, he gave her an injection of
morphine. "There you are. I hope you were not planning
on being alone tonight."

"Well, I was—"

"No," David said decisively. "She will not be alone tonight."

"I won't?" Vivien said. "You have a—"

"We'll make some arrangement."

Grinning broadly, Dr. Jones clapped David on the back. "That's good. The hands should be elevated, Miss Shaw. Lie down on your back or side and pile up some pillows or cushions and put your hands on those. Apply ice bags or packets of frozen vegetables wrapped in towels to ease the swelling, for no more than half an hour at a time." He turned back to David. "If the pain gets worse, call me again tomorrow and I'll give her another morphine shot, but the pills should suffice. Are you planning to stay in Barbados for a while, Miss Shaw?"

"I intended to stay for a few more days." She glanced at David and saw his lips twist in a wry response.

"I would recommend you not travel until the bruising has dissipated. It should not take more than a week. You must also avoid carrying anything heavy."

"I have a heavy camera bag," she said, dismayed at the prospect of not being able to take her full equipment out when she was working.

"No lifting," he warned her. "Get someone else to do your carrying. Or, if you must work alone, slide the bag over your shoulder or preferably across your body to spread the weight. Avoid straining your wrists. We want to get those tendons back into shape."

"Thank you so much for coming out to the hospital to see me," Vivien said.

"My pleasure." The doctor stood up and shook hands with David. "Good to see you, man." Then he turned back to Vivien. "Do not hesitate to give me a call if you are concerned about anything, Miss Shaw. Otherwise, come to my office in a few days and we shall see how the healing is progressing."

She struggled to get up from the wheelchair but found it impossible without using her hands.

"No, no," the doctor warned. "No walking out of here tonight, especially after the morphine shot. You can wheel her, David. Leave the chair with the security guard at the front."

It was humiliating to have David push her in a wheelchair, but Dr. Jones was right. The pain was easing a little, and although she was totally conscious, she felt as if she were floating in another dimension. The morphine must be kicking in.

"Okay?" David asked as they waited at the desk for the pills.

"I think so. Bit woozy from the shot. Less pain."

"That's good."

Once the nurse at the desk had given her the painkillers and the Gravol, together with instructions on when to take them, David started off down the corridor to the elevator. The bright overhead lights blurred as she gazed up at them.

"David."

"Yes?"

"I hate you having to—to do thish." Now her words were getting blurry as well.

"I hate having to do it. I'd rather we were out dancing again and we could erase what happened to you this evening, but we cannot, so be at peace."

"We should call Wesley."

"I will." He halted by the elevator. "Would you rather I took you there, to the Marshalls'? I'm sure Sarah would be happy to take care of you."

"I don't want anyone to take care of me."

"Fine, but you can't be alone tonight. If you would prefer it, we could—"

She twisted in the chair to look up at him. "You've been s-so kind to me, David. I trust you." She was getting all mushy and maudlin.

He smiled down at her. "I would like that in writing. I have the feeling you will soon be adamantly denying you ever said it."

"I hate to cause you all this trouble."

"Then just shut up and let me get you home."

"But what about the faculty dinner thish evening?" Her tongue seemed too large for her mouth.

"I will be very happy to have an excuse to get out of it."

"Then you don't mind?"

"No, I don't mind . . ."

Vivien closed her eyes. Everything swirled about her, the hospital announcements booming and echoing in her brain, and she was caught up in a vortex of sound and bright lights, whirling, whirling about her. Then she felt herself in motion again, until she found herself standing beside a pile of bloodred hibiscus blossoms several feet high on an open expanse of cleared land. This time she was on the other side of the barbed-wire fence, surrounded by tree stumps and silver coffeepots sticking out of the ground as if in a Salvador Dali painting. All of a sudden, a wind whipped up the pile of red hibiscus blossoms, tossing them into the air, and she found herself deluged with the flowers, but then the deluge became fluid, liquid. A torrent of sticky, bloodred liquid pouring down on her.

She awoke with a gasp and a choking scream to find herself beside David in his car, speeding along a deserted road.

"Are you okay?" he asked, slowing down a little.

"What happened? I don't remember getting into the car."

"You fell asleep in the hospital. The nurse said it was okay for you to leave, so I thought it best to get going. You were out of it when I got you into the car. I had to put the top down to get you in. You okay?" he asked again.

"I was having a strange dream, a nightmare, really."

"What about?"

"I don't know." She shook her head, trying to clear it. "Peverill, I think, and hibiscus blossoms." She shivered. "Sounds nice, but it wasn't." She was still shaking.

"Cold?" he asked. "I can put the top up."

"No, don't. I like the wind blowing through my hair."

"What hair?" He put up his hand and ran it over her head. "Are you sure you don't have some African blood in you, with all those curls?"

Vivien had to laugh. "That would make you happy, wouldn't it? Sorry, no luck. My mother and father both come from dull, middle-class white English families. Typical examples of the 'nation of shopkeepers.' My father's father was a grocer in Kent. My mother's father was a farmer."

David laughed. "I can try, can't I?"

Vivien slumped despondently in her seat. "Besides, I don't think you have to worry anymore about me not being able to understand Barbados. With these hands, I don't think I'll be using a camera for a while."

"Rubbish! What sort of strength do you need to press a button?"

"It's not the button part. It's holding the camera, setting up tripods, that sort of thing. And getting into wild locations."

"Not too many wild locations on this island, apart from the northern section."

"I don't think it's going to work," she said despairingly. "I'd be better to go home tomorrow."

"You cannot go home. You heard Martin, you must not lift or carry anything for a few days. So, no travelin' for you, Miss Shaw. You're going to have to stay put and enjoy exploring Barbados for a while."

"Where are you taking me?"

"My place." David glanced at her. "Is that okay? I called Wesley and Sarah. No answer, but I left them a message."

"What did you say?"

"That you'd had an accident but were going to be okay. I told them I was taking you to my place so you wouldn't be alone tonight." His voice ended on a rising note, as if he were asking her again if it was okay.

"Thank you" was all she said. Her mind was too confused for her to say much more. All she knew was that if someone had told her this morning that David Moreton would be taking care of her, she would have laughed out loud. She closed her eyes for a few minutes, lulled by the drone of the engine.

She was woken from a half sleep by the throbbing in her wrists, particularly the right one, which had taken more of the window's weight. A low moan escaped her.

"Pain back?"

Vivien nodded, biting her lip. "A bit," she admitted.

"The morphine must be starting to wear off. We're nearly there."

"Where's there?" She could hear the swelling surge of the sea now. They were driving uphill, the wind from the coast buffeting the trees lining the road. She could see in the headlights how their trunks were bent from the constant onslaught of the winds blowing in from the Atlantic.

"My house is above Bathsheba."

"You mean one of those lovely places with the huge windows overlooking the sea?"

"Ah, I'd forgotten you've been to Bathsheba already."

"I went with Spencer." She thought of him, leaving his granddaughter's party to drive to Peverill Hall to make sure she was okay. "I don't suppose you called him?"

"You suppose wrong. I called him while you were sleeping. He was pleased to hear you were okay and relieved that you weren't staying at Peverill Hall tonight."

She half sighed, half laughed. "Poor Spencer. I think he believes Peverill is haunted by ghosts."

"Maybe he's right."

"Oh, come on. Don't tell me you believe in ghosts."

"Not ghosts, per se. Unsettled spirits."

Unsettled spirits. Yes, that was a good description of what she herself felt at Peverill.

David's car was slowing down, turning into a short driveway that sloped up to the garage at the rear of a two-story house. He pressed a door opener, the garage door lifted, and they were inside, parking beside a black Jeep SUV.

"Two cars? On this small island?"

"I'm going to sell it. Waste of money. I bought it on impulse."

Must be nice, Vivien thought. Obviously his university work plus his writing were fairly lucrative. The next thing she knew, he was around on her side and his breath was on her cheek as he bent to undo her seat belt and help her out. His arm slid around her waist, and he half lifted her from the low car seat so that she didn't have to use her hands.

"I can walk," she protested when he kept hold of her.

"Good for you, but there are two steps up, so I'll be right beside you."

Vivien had never realized how much she used her hands for balance. She found herself tottering on the two steps, put out a hand to grab the door frame—and gasped. The mere motion of her hand and the curving of her fingers sent pain knifing up her arm.

"I'm right behind you," David said, "so try not to grab hold of things. Sorry, there are more steps inside the house, but I'll stay behind you, and you can take it very slowly. Don't try to hold on to the railing."

With David supporting her from behind, she maneuvered the steps up from the kitchen. When they reached the top, David switched on the lights, and she found herself in a vast room with a high floor-to-ceiling window, a virtual wall of glass. To the side was an exit onto the balcony that surrounded the house. The entire structure was designed to observe the wild Atlantic Ocean that surged below them. The rear of the house, she guessed, overlooked the wooded hillside.

It appeared to be a large multileveled open space. The bedroom was on a mezzanine overlooking the living room, accessed by a narrow staircase, with a railing across the full width of the room for safety.

Vivien stood, leaning lightly against David. "It's magnificent," she breathed. It was more than that. She had never before seen a house that seemed to be so much part of the wild natural beauty surrounding it. "No wonder you don't want to share all this with anyone."

She felt an increase of tension in the arm around her waist, but all he said was "Come and sit down." He led her to a comfortable chair covered with a slipcover of black-and-white cotton with a simple design.

She sank down into the chair with a heavy sigh of relief, propping up her feet on the black footstool. "That feels so good." She inspected the fabric of the chair. "Is this local?"

"I bought the fabric in Ghana when I was in Africa last year."

"It really works in here." She wanted to ask him about Africa, but her eyes fluttered shut. "Sorry. I'd love to look at everything, but I don't think I could take it all in tonight."

"Would you like something to drink or eat?"

She wanted only two things: to find the bathroom and to lie down on a bed and sleep. Neither request was an easy one in the circumstances, but David continued to surprise her.

"Time you got more sleep, but I imagine you'll need the bathroom first."

She grimaced. "Sorry."

"What's to be sorry about? Just goes to prove that

black or white, brown or yellow, we're all basically built the same way." His mouth twitched into a broad smile, showing his wonderfully white teeth. "Apart from the male-female thing, of course."

She ignored that.

"Come on. I'll help you upstairs. There's a loo there."

"Loo?"

"I spend part of my year in England, so I have to be bilingual."

He helped her up the staircase, which was higher and steeper than the other one, and then opened the door to the bathroom.

"I'm fine now," she said firmly.

"Don't lock the door."

"Excuse me?"

"You're half out of it with morphine and shock. Please do not lock the door," he repeated firmly. "I don't want to have to break it down because you've crashed onto the floor in a dead faint."

Vivien released a long sigh, but she left the door unlatched.

"I've left some pajamas outside," he called to her a few minutes later.

She opened the door a crack. "*Your* pajamas? You must be kidding. You're well over six feet tall. You want me to trip over the legs and do another injury to myself?"

He put up his hands defensively. "Okay, okay. Just trying to help."

"I can manage, thank you," she said haughtily.

He shrugged and turned away.

"David."

He turned back. "What?"

"Sorry. That sounded so ungrateful. This is—is kind of embarrassing."

"I know. What else do you need? I've never been a

nurse before, so you need to tell me. Water? Your painkillers?"

"That sounds good."

She heard his footsteps go down the stairs, envying his agility. She felt so lethargic she doubted she'd ever be able to run or jump again.

Picking up the pajamas gingerly with her stiff fingers, she went back into the bathroom and closed the door. She looked in the mirror and was appalled to see a pale-lipped, tousle-haired woman, with dark circles like bruises beneath her brown eyes. Her linen top was crumpled and creased as if she'd slept in it. What a mess!

She managed to splash water on her face, which felt good. She didn't even attempt to dry it off, but she wished she had some moisturizer.

She looked at the pajamas again and, on impulse, stripped off her top and pants and slipped on the avocado green silk pajama top over her bra and panties. It took some time, and the pain made her wince. The top swamped her, reaching down to her knees. Something told her that these were new pajamas, kept solely for show or, perhaps, for when his mother visited him. David Moreton probably didn't wear anything to bed. The thought sent heat rushing into her face.

She came out of the bathroom and sat on the side of the king-size bed. What she needed most of all was sleep. She felt exhausted, as if she'd been awake forty-eight hours. Yet she also feared sleeping, afraid she might slip again into that surrealistic nightmare world she'd descended into before.

"Are you decent?" David called up to her.

"Sort of." His head appeared and then the rest of him followed, bearing a tray. "Hey, you put on the pajamas."

"Only half."

"Looks great on you—better than on me." Their eyes met, then they both glanced away. He set the tray down on the bedside cabinet. "One pill, one bottle of water, one glass. Biscuits and some fruit juice. Ice wrapped in towels. Shall I give you the pill and a glass of water for it?"

"Please." To her annoyance, tears suddenly welled into her eyes. She tried to brush them away, wincing at the sudden movement.

"What's wrong?" he asked, looking up from the pill container.

"I hate being so bloody useless."

"Won't be for long." He helped her get into bed, plumping the pillow, holding back the sheet for her. "This is a new role for me, you know. David Moreton, R.N."

"It's not funny!"

"I know it's not, but enjoy it while it lasts. Take your pill."

She did as she was told, gulping the pill down and then drinking some juice to get some flavor into her mouth, which was bone-dry and tasted like she'd smoked one of Thomas Hendley's foul cigars.

"Now lie back and I'll put a couple of extra pillows here, on your belly, so you can elevate your hands and rest them on the ice. Martin's orders."

"Okay, nurse."

"That's better." He gave her a wide grin. "Anything else?"

"Wesley. I don't want him to be worrying."

"That's my next job: checking my messages. I'm sure he will have called me while we were driving back from the hospital. Are you comfortable?"

"As much as I can be. I hate sleeping on my back."

"Martin said your hands will be better in a few days," he reminded her.

She sighed. "What a waste of valuable time."

"Get some rest. I'll come back to check on the ice. Sleep well."

"Thanks, David," she murmured, already half asleep. "I don't know what I'd have done without you."

"Go to sleep."

Her eyelids fluttered shut. She felt his fingers brush her forehead and adjust the ice bags around her wrists . . . and then she heard him go quietly back down the stairs.

CHAPTER TWENTY

David waited until he was sure Vivien was asleep before going downstairs to the kitchen to check the machine. Wesley had left two messages. The anxiety in his voice was palpable in the first message. "Please call me as soon as possible and let me know what's happening," he finished. The second message was quite unlike the usually unflappable Wesley. "David! Where the hell are you? Where's Vivien? For the Lord's sake, don't tell me you've taken her back to Peverill. I called there but no one answered. Call me back, whatever time it is."

David was about to switch off the machine when another voice, this time female, came on the line. It was muffled, but clear enough to be understood.

"Tell Vivien Shaw she is in great danger. The accident proves it."

David stared at the machine and then replayed the message. Just those words and then a click when the call was ended. He had the feeling that he knew the voice. He played it back once again. Yes, a high voice, like that of a child. But whose was it? And was it a threat or a warning? He couldn't tell, but whichever it was, it was disturbing. How did the caller know Vivien was staying at his house? Had someone from the hospital told her that he'd checked Vivien out?

It was a mystery, and he didn't like mysteries. Maybe Wesley would be able to explain it. He poured himself a beer and sat on the counter stool, punching in Wesley's number.

The phone was answered after the first ring. "David?" said Wesley's voice.

"Yes, I—"

"Thank God. We've been worried out of our minds. Where's Vivien?"

"She's here, at my place."

"Is she okay?"

"She's fast asleep."

"But is she all right?"

"She was in a lot of pain, but Martin gave her a shot of morphine, which helped. I wish Sarah had been home."

"She *was* home, but she had a meeting and turned off the ringer. That's why you got the machine. Tell me what happened."

David told him as succinctly as he could about the window at Peverill, Vivien managing to call Spencer, and then Spencer calling him.

"You mean the Hendleys didn't call you?" Wesley said.

"No. Vivien said they tried to downplay what had happened. She had the feeling that perhaps they were worried about her suing them for negligence."

"I wonder," Wesley said slowly.

"That's one weird family. I thought they were going to throw me out of the place, or at least order me to go to the servants' entrance. Talk about throwbacks to another era. I didn't know there were people like that left in the island. They should be put in a museum."

Wesley was silent.

"You still there?" David said.

"Yes, I'm here. Do not let Vivien go back to Peverill Hall."

The warning jarred David. "Something's going on here. What is it?"

"I blame myself wholly for what has happened." It sounded as if Wesley were talking to himself. "We should have known—"

"Known what?" David demanded. "That a window with rotten sash cords would drop on Vivien's hands? It was an accident, Wesley."

"I am not so sure about that."

"Now who's the writer? Wesley, you're imagining things that are not there. Like many of these old plantation places, Peverill Hall has been neglected. I should think a lot more of it could be crumbling and dangerous. It was an accident," David repeated, but even as he spoke, into his mind came the woman's whispered message, which was still on his machine. "That reminds me, someone else appears to be as paranoid as you, my friend."

"What do you mean?" Wesley seemed as jumpy as a cat with fleas.

"Someone left an anonymous message on my machine after you called me the second time. I have the feeling I know the voice, but . . . Yes," David said triumphantly. "Of course. It was Celeste Beaton. Here, let me play it for you." He switched on the machine and played the woman's message for the fourth time, holding the phone receiver close so that Wesley could hear it. "That is Celeste, isn't it?"

"Perhaps." Wesley was being cagey.

"Listen up." David's voice dropped low, but not too low for Wesley to understand every word he said. "I have a woman here in my house who is a comparative stranger to me. A woman you saw fit to bring from Canada to Barbados to work with me on this book. I have been called out on a rescue mission because you were not available—"

"Not so. Vivien did not call me."

"That's beside the point. I have engaged a doctor friend of mine to treat Vivien Shaw, and then I have been forced to bring her home and act as a nurse for her because I could not get you on the phone. The very least you can do," David said, his voice rising, "is tell me what the fuck is going on."

A long silence, then Wesley said, "I'm sorry, David. I cannot. All I can say is that I have made one hell of a big mistake in bringing Vivien here and the quicker we can persuade her to go home the better. I never thought that she would go to Peverill."

"What has Peverill got to do with it?"

"It has everything to do with it."

"You are not making sense."

"I know that. David, I wish I could tell you, but this is not my story to tell."

"Whose is it?"

"I cannot tell you that, either. There could be all kinds of repercussions."

"Okay, I've had enough." David took a swig of his beer and slammed the glass down so that the beer slopped over onto the counter. "I'll keep Vivien here for tonight. Tomorrow, you come and collect her, and I wash my hands of the whole affair."

"Sarah and I can come for Vivien tonight, right away."

"No, you're not disturbing her just when she's got to sleep. She's exhausted. She's staying here tonight."

"Right. We'll come and get her tomorrow, then. But you have to promise me that you won't breathe a word of this to her."

"Of what?"

"Of what we've been talking about."

Wesley sounded exasperated, but not as exasperated as David, whose patience was long gone.

"You may know what we've been talking about, but I haven't a clue. I can't very well tell Vivien anything when I don't know what the hell's going on. But *you* could tell her. She's a mature woman, not a kid. Don't you think, if it involves her, she should be let into this little mystery of yours?"

"No!" Wesley shouted. "She must not know. All we have to do is get her away from Peverill and everything will be fine. The best way to help her is to work on making sure she does not go back to that place."

"Fine." David had had enough. "Be here for her first thing tomorrow."

"Nine o'clock?"

"Make it eight. I have a class at nine." David slammed down the receiver, not caring that it might have damaged Wesley Marshall's ear. What the hell was the guy going on about?

David wiped up the spilled beer, made himself a chicken sandwich, and went out on the balcony, leaving the glass door half open. This was where he could usually find peace, sitting here and looking out over the ocean, far from the bustle of Bridgetown or the crowded beaches that brought both prosperity and overdevelopment to the island. Here he could imagine himself back in a Barbados before time-shares and all-inclusive resorts. But then his practical side would usually click in and he would have to remind himself that if you went far enough back, you'd find a Barbados where black folk were little more than indentured servants and didn't have the vote.

As he sat there, long legs stretched out before him, listening to the constant pounding of the ocean as it swept into the shore below him, the feelings of serenity the surging ocean usually elicited seemed to elude him.

And he knew why.

Ever since he had walked into the Marshalls' room three nights ago and been introduced to his photographer for the Barbados book project, his comfortably compartmentalized life had been set on its head. It wasn't only because she was neither from Barbados nor black. It was her attitude that he would play second fiddle to her that had riled him. Even now he squirmed in his chair, recalling his fury when she talked about him writing captions for her pictures.

Yet before long he had realized that behind the confident woman who was proud of her work there was an aching vulnerability. He had sensed during their meal at Brown Sugar that her success and independence had been hard-won, and that she still wasn't quite sure it would last. "I was always afraid that someone might suddenly snatch it away from me," she'd told him, "and that I'd be back where I'd started, taking pictures of car accidents and lottery winners for the *Winnipeg Free Press.*"

But what disturbed him most of all were his own feelings. His father had died when he was only twelve. Everyone expected that David would go into the family printing business when he left school. But David didn't leave school at sixteen. In fact, he had never really left school. It was his sister and his younger brother who had helped his mother maintain the business. Later, they, too, had gone back to school, and now Colin was a computer whiz and in great demand with the hotels and restaurants moving into the twenty-first century, and Sally was married with two children and expecting a third, and a very active member in her church and its community outreach programs.

David had steered clear of matrimony so far, despite his mother's never-ending complaint that a man should be married and settled down at his age, not still fooling around. David had been very happy to fool around, but he did agree with his mother about one thing: that he should "stick with his own kind" as far as the women in his life were concerned. It wasn't that he didn't have plenty of friends of all races; he just preferred to keep his love life confined to his own. He found black women

sexy and vibrant and frequently less inhibited than
women of other races. Perhaps his mother had been a
big influence on him there, as she herself had been
courted by many men after his father had died, but she
preferred to remain independent.

Then, only three short days ago, Vivien Shaw had
crashed into his life and, despite all his precepts, he had
found himself attracted to her. This made him feel bewildered, irritable, and wary of both himself and her. He'd
asked her to dance that second night and then cursed
himself for doing so, because being close to her aroused
him, and this made him feel he was somehow betraying
all he believed in. What bothered him even more was
that he sensed she was attracted to him and that she
wasn't sure how to deal with these new feelings. She'd
never even dated anyone other than white men. So, here
they had been for the last couple of days, taking one
step forward and two or three hurried steps back . . .
until this evening, when he had been called to her aid
and had instinctively reached out to her, because how
could he leave her alone when she was suffering such
pain with no one else but him to help her? And then he
had taken her to his home, where very few women had
penetrated. Even his mother and sister rarely came here.
It was his fortress and his refuge from the outside world,
a place to retreat and regroup.

And now, Vivien Shaw, a white woman, was sleeping
in his bed, and he had to take care of her.

Only for tonight, he reminded himself.

Yes, but something else was going on, and unless Wesley was going to tell him what it was, and he had seemed
adamant about not doing so, David was going to continue to worry about Vivien.

For a long time he sat there, gazing out, his ears filled
with the ebb and flow of the ocean, the chicken sandwich
on the plate, uneaten.

Then, suddenly, a sound from inside the house merged

with the pounding of the ocean. David sprang to his feet and dashed up the stairs. Vivien was sitting upright in the bed, eyes staring, bandaged hands held out in front of her, screaming, "Blood! Blood! There's blood everywhere."

"Vivien!"

She continued screaming, but this time there were no words, just short piercing screams. He sat beside her on the bed. "Vivien, wake up! You're having a nightmare." He took her shoulders and shook her gently. "Vivien, wake up!"

The screams stopped, her eyes focused, and she shrank from him with a gasp of terror.

"It's me, David. Remember me? The guy who's going to write captions for your photographs."

"David?" Her eyes filled with tears, but at the same time she was laughing. Weeping and laughing, she leaned her head against him, and he stroked her damp hair away from her forehead. "Oh, God, I was having such a terrible nightmare again. There was blood everywhere, all over the walls and the—"

"Don't think about it. I'll put on the reading lamp so you can see where you are."

"I was looking for you, but I couldn't find you anywhere. Where were you?"

"In your dream or in reality?"

She put up her hand to brush it across her forehead and winced. "I'm not sure which is which."

"Well, this is real. You are in my bed, and you awoke from a bad dream. I was sitting on the balcony, listening to the ocean, and I heard you so I came in to wake you."

"Was I screaming?" she whispered.

"You were."

She turned her head to press her face against his shirt. "I was screaming in my dream. I couldn't stop."

He had never been more tempted to kiss a woman in his life . . . but he didn't kiss her. He knew he would be

taking advantage of her vulnerability. Instead, he laid
his cheek on her head and held her, gently rocking her.
"You're okay now. It was a dream, that's all."

"I'm so tired, but I'm afraid to go to sleep again. Will
you stay with me?"

"I'll be here all the time, right beside you." He lowered her down onto the pillow again and stood up.

She lifted her head. "Don't go."

"I'm just going to the other side of the bed. I'm tired,
too. It's been a busy evening."

She released a long sigh and let her head fall back on
the pillow.

David thought about putting on the bottom half of
the pajamas but decided against it. Lying in such close
proximity to Vivien was going to be difficult enough.
Better to have two layers of clothing between him and
her. He lay down beside her.

She was so quiet, he thought she'd already fallen
asleep, but then she said, "David?"

"Yes?"

A rustling, as her head burrowed into the pillow.
"Nothing. I just wanted to make sure you were there."

He reached out his hand to brush her cheek with his
fingers. It was the next best thing to kissing her. "I'm
right here beside you. Sleep well."

"Thank you. You, too."

Before long David felt her body relax beside him, and
her breathing became slower. But sleep eluded him. It
was far too early. In fact, the longer he lay there, the
more wide awake he became. He was disturbed not only
by lying so close to her, breathing in her fragrance, but
also by his conversation with Wesley.

Not to mention the woman's message about Vivien
being in danger.

He was pretty sure that it had been Celeste. If so, she
must know something more about this whole Peverill
Hall thing. Otherwise, why would she leave a warning
that Vivien was in danger? First thing tomorrow, he'd

call Celeste and see if he could find out from her what the hell was going on.

Now his mind was spinning round and round, seeking to get a grip on his weird conversation with Wesley. Eventually, he couldn't lie there any longer. He carefully slipped out of the bed, determined not to waken Vivien, and tiptoed barefoot down to the kitchen, sliding the door closed so she wouldn't hear him. He looked up the Beatons' number in the telephone book and dialed it.

Joseph answered. "Sorry to bother you," David said. "It's David Moreton. Is Celeste there?"

"Celeste?" Joseph repeated.

"Yes, she called me, left a message."

"Oh, right." Joseph sighed. "I told her you'd guess who it was."

David smiled grimly to himself. He'd been right. "I'd like to speak to her."

"I imagine so. I will get her for you."

David could hear their voices, Celeste probably berating Joseph for having given her away. Then she said, "Hello, David," sounding very tentative.

"Good evening, Celeste. How are you?"

"I'm fine. What can I do for you?"

He felt like saying, "You can cut all this mystery crap, for one thing," but he knew that would not go down well with the ladylike Celeste. "You called me earlier— about Vivien."

A long pause.

"I recognized your voice, Celeste," David said impatiently.

"I was worried about her."

"How did you know she'd been hurt?"

"Wesley called me, after you called him about the accident. Can you tell me what happened?"

David gave her a capsule version.

"I feel so much to blame." To David's surprise, Celeste started crying.

"You? How could you be responsible?"

Celeste didn't answer, and he could hear Joseph's voice again, this time trying to comfort her. "Celeste," he said insistently, "can you please tell me what's going on? Wesley's talking in riddles about not allowing Vivien to go back to Peverill, but he won't give me any more information. Celeste, are you there?"

"Yes, I'm here."

"Did you hear what I said?"

"Yes, I heard. Do you want to bring Vivien here now?"

"No. She's fast asleep."

"All right. We had plans with her tomorrow. Can you bring her to our place in the morning? My family and I can take care of her. I will explain everything to her then."

"But you're not going to explain it to me?"

"No. If Vivien wants to tell you, that is her business, but I cannot tell you."

David cursed to himself. "Well, at least if Vivien knows what's going on, I suppose that's what matters. I have a class at nine o'clock. I will have to bring her—"

"Don't worry. I will take the day off. I can fetch her from your place."

"Wesley was coming over to get her, with Sarah."

"I know. He called me."

It struck David that there must be some sort of bond between Celeste and Wesley other than the fact that he and Celeste's sister worked together in Toronto. Barbados was a tight-knit community with a great many familial connections, not all of them up-front and public. Perhaps this was one that he didn't know about.

"Okay," he said, seeing that she wasn't going to add anything more. "I will tell Vivien you are coming for her in the morning. Will you call Wesley and let him know he doesn't need to come?"

"Yes, I will. And, David?"

"Yes?"

"Please tell Vivien how terribly sorry I am. I did not mean for this to happen."

"It was an accident, Celeste," he insisted.

"I very much doubt that."

CHAPTER
TWENTY-ONE

Vivien awoke when she turned onto her left side, crushing her hand beneath her. Groaning, she turned onto her back, lifting her hands onto the pillow again. She hated sleeping on her back, but it had been the only way to be able to keep her hands elevated. Although they were throbbing again, the pain was a little easier than it had been. She remembered David giving her a pill around five o'clock, when she'd grown restless. Then, slowly relaxing, knowing he was there beside her, she had fallen asleep again.

Now, as she lay in David's bed, staring at the sunshine filtering through the slats of the blind over the huge window, sunbeams dancing on the wall across a brightly colored mural, she thought about last night. The vivid nightmare, David waking her up, holding her, tenderly rocking her, his cheek against her hair. As she remembered, she was engulfed in such radiant warmth that she closed her eyes, wanting to embrace the feeling forever.

"How about some breakfast?"

Startled, her eyes flew open to find David standing halfway up the stairs.

"Sorry, did I wake you?"

"Not really. I was kind of dozing."

"Could you manage a little breakfast?" He sounded different this morning, more crisp and businesslike. "How about pumpkin fritters?"

"Sounds great, but I'm not very hungry. Coffee would be good. Coffee and fruit juice."

"You have to eat," he said. "Those pills are rough on an empty stomach. How are you feeling?"

"Sore, but much better than last night."

"Good. Would you like to take a shower?"

"I can't." She held up her hands.

"Oh, of course. Sorry." He seemed distracted, as if something else was on his mind. "Do you need some help?"

"No, thanks. I think I can manage." Vivien got up slowly, swinging her legs over the side of the bed. She needed to go to the bathroom. Her head was swimming, making her nervous about standing up. As she slowly unfolded her arms, letting them hang by her sides, the blood rushed down into her hands, and she felt even more light-headed.

He vaulted up the remaining stairs and put his arm around her. "Here. Hang on to me." He helped her get up from the bed and into the bathroom. "Okay now?"

She nodded. "Thanks."

Embarrassment hung between them this morning, an acute awareness of last night's forced intimacy. As she closed the bathroom door, she felt a pang of disappointment. She'd probably read more into what had happened last night than had actually been there. David had merely been kind and supportive when she needed help. Nothing more. *What more can you possibly want?* she chided herself.

That was the trouble. She wasn't sure. Her emotions were on a roller coaster, up and down.

As she was dressing—which involved a great deal of improvisation—the aroma of freshly brewed coffee wafted up to her. An incentive for her to get moving.

When she was ready, she slowly descended the stairs, one at a time, trying to hang on to but not clutch the railing too tightly.

When she reached the foot of the first staircase, she was exhausted and had to stand for a minute, catching her breath, before she tackled the stairs down to the kitchen.

She put her foot down on the top stair, then felt her head swimming again and paused.

"Where do you think you're going?" David's voice came from behind her.

She halted on the second step without turning around. "To the kitchen."

"Breakfast is out on the balcony. You were faster than I expected."

She turned cautiously, putting one hand on the railing to balance herself. As she stepped up, she kept her gaze fixed on the steps.

David was watching her intently. "Well done. You're doing really well," he said with a smile and turned to lead the way out to the balcony.

The table was set with bright yellow pottery dishes: bowls of sliced mango, a plate with slices of banana bread, one empty coffee mug, one half-full mug. He poured her coffee for her, but when she tried to pick it up, the mug tilted and she slopped some of the coffee onto the table.

She bit her lip. "Sorry about that." She made an attempt at mopping it up with a crumpled tissue from her pocket but seemed to be making even more of a mess.

"Don't worry about it. I'll fix it." He glanced at his watch.

"Do you have to go somewhere?" Vivien asked, recognizing the signs.

"Sorry. I'm due to teach a West Indian Lit. class at nine."

"You don't have to worry about me. I can—" She stopped, wondering what she was going to do. All her things were still at Peverill, but she certainly didn't want to go back there. Not for now, at least. She swallowed a lump in her throat, suddenly feeling desperately alone.

David gently squeezed her arm. "It's okay," he said. "I've made arrangements for you."

"What arrangements?" she asked sharply, hating this feeling of not being in control.

"It's okay," he said. "You can change it if you want to. Celeste Beaton is coming over to pick you up."

Vivien had forgotten about Celeste. "Oh, no. I was supposed to be having lunch with Celeste and her family."

"That's what she told me. She'll be over soon."

Vivien groaned. "Oh, David. I don't feel like meeting people today."

"I meant, she wants you to move in with her."

"Oh, I see."

"Would you rather stay here today? I can cancel my class."

Her mouth trembled into a smile. She suspected that he took his work very seriously and that his offer didn't come easily. "Thanks, but I wouldn't allow you to do that. I have to get my act together, decide what I'm going to do."

"I'd say stay on here, but I don't want to leave you on your own. Why not let Celeste take you back to her place for now? I think it would make her feel better as well."

"Celeste? Why?"

"She blames herself for the accident."

"But that's ridiculous. How could she be to blame for what happened at Peverill Hall?"

David shrugged. "Don't ask me. But I have a feeling she knows more about that place than we do."

"Then I wish she'd tell me what she knows," Vivien said heatedly.

David gave her one of his enigmatic looks. "That's

what she intends to do, apparently. She wouldn't tell me anything. Said it was up to you to pass it on to me, if you wanted to do so."

"Sounds weird. Are we talking ghosts or superstitions or what here?"

"You mean like a duppy?"

"What's a duppy?"

"A restless spirit." David shrugged. "I have no idea, but from the way Celeste was talking, I think it is something far more substantial than a duppy." He glanced at his watch again. "Better eat something. She should be here in a few minutes."

And then this fleeting time they'd spent together would be at an end, Vivien thought, a wave of regret washing over her. She felt tears welling in her eyes and forced them back.

He stood up and came to crouch down before her. "Don't worry. Remember, the doctor said you have to stay at least another week." He hesitated, then bent forward to kiss her, but at the last instant his lips avoided hers and brushed across her cheek.

"Thanks for everything, David."

He sprang up, suddenly all energy. "It was nothing. Eat," he ordered. "Or you'll be passing out and Celeste will think I've starved you. Excuse me, I have to gather up my stuff."

Vivien toyed with a piece of banana bread and sipped some juice. She also toyed with the questions spinning through her mind. Was David attracted to her or not? She thought he might be. Was he attracted to her, but repelled by the fact that she was white? That was more likely. This morning in particular she'd felt that back-and-forth sensation she'd experienced with him at Brown Sugar and the blues club.

She had to be honest to herself, at least. In some ways she felt the same. Attracted to him but wary, knowing that relationships between people of different cultures could be fraught with difficulties.

She heard the hum of a car negotiating the hill and steeled herself to meet Celeste.

David came out to the balcony. "That's Celeste driving in," he said. He hurriedly cleared the table and piled the dishes on a tray. "I will get your things from the bedroom."

She followed him inside. "My bag's by the bed. That's all I had."

"Sit down," he told her. "I'll be back in a minute." He went down to the kitchen, reappeared a short time later, and then loped up the bedroom stairs two at a time.

When he returned, she was still standing, looking around at his home, wondering if she would ever come back here again. "There you are," he said. "One bag." He was about to hand it to her but hesitated.

"What's wrong?"

"You can't carry it. Is the strap long enough to hang across you?"

"I think so."

"Okay." He came close to her. "Lift your left arm," he ordered. Vivien did so. His breathing was ragged, but that was probably from running up and down the stairs. She was holding her breath, trying not to breathe in the clean male smell of him. He lifted the strap over her arm and head and then settled it across her body. As he did so, his hand brushed against her right breast, sending a jolt like an electric shock through her. "There," he said, straightening the bag on her right hip. "That should be okay."

She stepped back and took a deep breath. "Thanks." She opened her bag and checked inside. Anything to avoid looking at him. "I think I've got everything," she said distractedly.

"Your cell phone is the same make as mine, so I was able to recharge it last night. It's in your bag."

"Thank you."

"If you've left anything behind, I can drop it off at Celeste's place."

"David!" Celeste's voice called from below.

"And here she is," David said. He ran down the stairs again and then reappeared with Celeste. She was dressed as if she were going to church, in a floral dress and a beribboned straw hat.

Oh, God, Vivien thought. *This is difficult enough without having a stranger here.*

"Sorry to rush out of here, but I don't want to be late for my class." David handed Celeste a key. "This is the spare key. Stay as long as you like, but lock up when you leave."

Celeste looked bewildered. "But don't you have a security system?"

"Yes, but don't bother about it. Delia is coming to clean up today. I've left her a note. She'll see to it." He was halfway down the stairs, then turned around. "Hope your hands get better soon, Vivien. You keep in touch now." He gave her his special smile. "Thanks, Celeste." Then he was gone.

They soon heard the door into the garage crashing shut, followed by the engine's roar as he drove down the hill like the proverbial bat out of hell.

The two women stood eyeing each other. "You should be sitting down," Celeste said.

"Yes, I guess you're right." Legs shaking, Vivien sank down on one of the cotton-covered chairs, feeling as if David's leaving had sapped all the energy from the room.

She was surprised when Celeste came to her, kneeling down beside her. "Are you okay? How are your hands?" Her soft high voice sounded deeply concerned. Tentatively, she put out her hand but stopped short of touching the bandaged wrists.

"Better today. They were pretty painful last night. Fortunately, David's friend looked after me well and gave me painkillers."

"David's friend?" Celeste looked puzzled.

"Dr. Jones," Vivien explained.

Celeste sat down on the long couch. "No broken bones, David told me last night."

"No, I was lucky. Just nasty cuts and badly bruised tendons."

"Any particular treatment, apart from the bandage?"

"Ice and keep my hands elevated. I slept with them on a couple of pillows last night."

Celeste jumped to her feet. "I'll get you some cushions." Before Vivien could protest, she fetched a couple of yellow cushions from the end of the couch and put them on Vivien's lap.

"Did David look after you well?"

"He was wonderful. I couldn't have managed without him."

"I wanted to come over right away last night, but he said you were asleep. Did he tell you that?"

"Oh, yes." Vivien wasn't sure he had but seeing Celeste's nervous, restless hands, thought it best to say yes.

"Can you tell me what happened?" Celeste asked. "Or is it too painful to talk about it?"

Vivien didn't want to talk about it. All she wanted was to be left alone, to rest somewhere quiet and safe. "I was leaning on the windowsill, the sash cords broke, and the window fell on my wrists, that's all."

"And you are sure it was an accident?"

Vivien looked at Celeste's anxious face. "Of course," she replied. "Why wouldn't it be? Surely you're not suggesting these people attack their boarders and rob them, are you?" She gave a little laugh, but it froze when she saw the solemn expression on Celeste's face. Vivien brushed her forehead with her bandaged hand, wincing as the blood rushed down to her wrist. "I'm feeling a bit tired."

Celeste jumped up. "Of course you are. Here I am asking you stupid questions when I should be getting you home and into bed."

Vivien sighed inwardly. Kindhearted though Celeste was, she wondered if she'd be able to stand being in the same place with her. She'd probably fuss around her until she felt like screaming. Oh, well, what alternative did she have?

"Can I help you?" Celeste asked, hovering above Vivien.

"Thanks, I think I can manage."

"Shall I take your bag for you?"

"It's okay. I'm comfortable with it slung across me." Vivien hesitated. "I've been thinking. Would it be possible to go to Peverill Hall?"

"To Peverill?" Celeste repeated incredulously. "Now?"

"To pick up my clothes and cameras and things," Vivien explained.

Celeste looked disconcerted. Her mouth opened and closed again. Then she said, "Would you mind waiting until later?"

Of course, Vivien thought. She doesn't want to go to Peverill. "That would be fine. It's only that I don't want to leave my stuff there. My camera equipment is pretty valuable."

"I am sure it is. It must be wonderful being such a great artist. My sister, Janice, was so impressed with your exhibition in Toronto."

Janice? It took a moment for Vivien to realize Celeste was speaking of Wesley's friend Janice Greene. Come to think of it, Janice had had the same earnest, intense quality as Celeste when she'd talked to her in the gallery in Toronto. "I hadn't realized Janice Greene was your sister."

"Oh, yes," was all Celeste said. She settled Vivien into her comfortable car and then went back to lock up David's place. "There, that is all done," she said when she returned and then started the engine.

She drove surprisingly well, quite fast. Vivien had

imagined she would be a slow, cautious driver. She wondered if she should broach the subject of the Hendleys, but Celeste's reaction to her suggestion about going to Peverill deterred her. It was Celeste who raised the subject.

"I feel so guilty for not having you to stay in our home last night," she said, her gaze fixed on the winding road ahead. "I am responsible for your injury."

"Of course you're not. It was an accident. Nothing to do with you."

"I understand," Celeste said, "that the younger Hendleys are pressed for money. Thomas Hendley and his wife are very much against having strangers staying in the house." When she spoke, her mouth seemed stiff, as if it pained her even to talk about the Hendleys.

"Yes, that was perfectly obvious." Vivien looked at Celeste. "Are you suggesting that the old man set up this so-called accident to get rid of me?"

"That is possible."

"If he did, he must be out of his mind." Anger welled up in her. "If he did, I should get the police onto it."

Celeste did not respond.

"Wesley warned me. So did Spencer. That was the problem. Everyone seemed to warn me about the place. But despite the Hendleys, I loved it. I was longing to take pictures there." She gave Celeste a glimmer of a smile. "My mother would tell you I can be very stubborn."

"They are not good people," Celeste said.

David said Celeste knew more about Peverill than they did. But was it going to be just another regurgitation of the rumors connected with the murder?

"I certainly wouldn't call them friendly, apart from Marian, and Paul's not too bad," Vivien said. "When I go back to get my things from my room there, I intend to check the window cords."

Celeste cast a glance her way.

"What?" Vivien said, growing impatient with Celeste's silences.

"If it wasn't an accident," Celeste said, "they've probably destroyed them."

CHAPTER
TWENTY-TWO

Vivien slept for most of the journey to Celeste's home. The painkiller she'd taken after eating some of David's banana bread had knocked her out.

She awoke with a jolt when the car stopped. She was surprised to see that Celeste's home was a large house fronted by a curving, white-paved driveway and well-kept garden. She'd been expecting a little wooden house like those she'd seen on her way into Bridgetown yesterday.

"What a lovely house," she said as Celeste helped her from the car.

Celeste beamed. "It is my pride and joy," she said, leading her to the front door. She nodded to the Toyota RAV in the driveway. "Joseph must be back. That's good."

Vivien was too weary to ask why it was good. All she wanted was to lie down and sleep.

"Joseph, we're here," Celeste trilled as she walked into the house, her voice backed by the door chime that issued a peal of bells when the door was opened. The large hall—a combination of glass, gilt, and marble—was deliciously air-conditioned.

Joseph appeared, dressed in his white cricket gear, the

knees of his white trousers smeared with green grass stains. He was holding a fried chicken leg. He strode forward, emitting a smell of healthy sweat, holding out his other hand to her. "Welcome, Miss Shaw."

"Joseph! You have not showered yet," Celeste complained. She shook her head at him, but he didn't seem to care.

"I was starvin' hungry so fetched me some chicken."

"He just returned from cricket practice," Celeste explained.

Vivien smiled at Joseph and held up her bandaged hands. "Sorry I can't shake hands. Thank you for having me to stay."

"You are welcome, welcome, welcome."

"What would you like to do?" Celeste asked. "There is plenty of time before we have to leave. Would you like to rest in your room or outside by the pool? And what can we get you to eat or drink?"

Vivien had latched on to only one thing. "Leave? Are we going somewhere?"

Celeste looked surprised. "Yes, of course. To my mother's."

Joseph looked from one woman to the other. "Darlin' girl, Miss Shaw might not feel well enough to go."

"Oh." Celeste looked stricken. Her hand went to her mouth. "I am so sorry. How thoughtless of me!" She looked as if she were about to burst into tears. "Mummy and Nanna were so excited and . . . How could I be so stupid?"

Joseph came to her and put his arm around her, and she buried her face against his chest. His eyes pleaded with Vivien above his wife's head. "Excuse her, Miss Shaw. She's not thinkin' straight today."

It was not difficult to sense that this meeting Celeste had planned between Vivien and her family meant a great deal to her. Vivien couldn't understand why it was so important, but obviously to Celeste it was. Perhaps she felt Vivien was some big celebrity she'd bagged and wanted to show off. Yet, despite her nervous excitability, Celeste seemed too sincere to create such a buildup merely for a visiting photographer.

A frisson of apprehension ran across Vivien's shoulders. Something was going on here that she couldn't understand, and she was determined to find out what it was.

"Celeste?"

She lifted her tearstained face from Joseph's chest, and he handed her a tissue from the box in the frilly cover on the hall stand. "Yes," she said, sniffing.

"If I could have a good sleep this morning," Vivien said, "I think I might feel strong enough to meet your family."

Celeste clasped her hands, a look of ecstasy spreading across her face. "Oh, Miss Shaw, could you? We could make the meal really, really late, about two o'clock, maybe?"

"I'm afraid I won't be at my best," Vivien said wryly. "I'm taking heavy painkillers."

"If you don't feel well enough to come, Joseph can call me at my mother's home and let me know. You don't mind staying here without me, do you?" she asked. "I have to help prepare the food, you see. Joseph will be here to look after you."

Joseph grinned. "I make a good nurse," he said.

Vivien smiled back. "Then I'm in good hands." She liked Joseph. He was a solid, straightforward man who adored his wife. He also evidently made a great deal of money as one of Barbados's top-ranking cricketers. She'd heard of wealthy baseball and hockey players, but wealthy cricket players?

When Celeste took her into the guest room, Vivien had to hide a smile. Pink ruffles everywhere—on the bed, the dressing-table skirt, and the lamp shades—but the bed was large and inviting. Celeste fussed around her for a few minutes and then, having been assured Vivien had everything she needed, tiptoed from the darkened room.

She slept soundly, no nightmares, for almost three hours and awoke feeling remarkably refreshed. Something had woken her. A tinkling sound. There it was again. She suddenly realized it was her cell phone, deep at the bottom of her bag. She leaned down and tried to open the bag, which was at the side of the bed. Her fingers were all thumbs, and the thumbs weren't much help either, but she managed to open it. "Hello?"

"Vivien!"

"Oh, hi, Mom. Can I call you back?"

"Tried to get you all last evening. Where on earth were you?"

"I was out. My phone was turned off."

"I left a message, but you never called back."

"Sorry."

"You promised you'd keep your phone on so we could get in touch, remember? When are you coming back to Canada, Viv? Your dad isn't well at all. I'm really worried about him."

"I'm with some people at the moment, Mom. Call you back later, okay?"

"Okay. Don't forget. Love you."

"Love you, too," mumbled Vivien. "Tell Dad I'm fine." She switched off the phone, dropping it back into her bag. No point in telling her mother she wouldn't be coming back to Canada for at least another week.

She washed in the adjoining bathroom and got dressed again. What a mess she looked, she thought, surveying herself in the bathroom mirror. Hands bandaged, clothing all creased. She knew that linen was supposed to crease, but this was ridiculous. Oh, well, if Celeste insisted on her meeting her family today, she'd have to put up with her as she was.

*   *   *

Joseph drove fast most of the way but had to slow down when he joined the highway north of Bridgetown, where the lanes were jammed and drivers fruitlessly leaned on their horns. It was not the most relaxing of drives, but once Vivien started asking Joseph about cricket, he was eloquent in describing what was, to him, not just a profession but a passion, an obsession. A religion, David had called it.

Joseph was still trying to explain all the particular positions on the field to her—silly mid-on, slips, gully—when they arrived in a small area outside Speightstown, and drew up before a pretty chattel house with several attractive additions, each with a separate roof.

"This is the original chattel house where Celeste's mother was born," Joseph told her, "but the family has added several rooms since then, includin' a full kitchen and bathroom."

"I thought it was a chattel house, but it seemed too big."

"Lots of people have kept their old homes but modernized them and added on rooms to make them more comfortable."

"And they don't have to be mobile anymore?"

He shook his head. "Not so easy now to move them because of the water pipes and electricity lines. 'Course, in the old days, before runnin' water and electric, they could be folded down and packed up. That way, if you couldn't pay the rent and had to move on, or you had a new place to work, with a little parcel of land to set up your home, you could move your house along with you."

The house boards were painted lime-green, the ornate ironwork around the roof and the window frames a glossy white. It looked like a gingerbread house with extensions.

Joseph opened the little wooden gate and ushered her
down a path through a small, neat garden with two trees,
one of which was laden with round green breadfruit.
The front door opened and Celeste and an older woman
appeared. Celeste came to hug her. Vivien could feel
her body trembling. Celeste turned to introduce her
mother, an older version of herself. "This is my mother,
Verna Boyd," she announced proudly.

Her mother was as light-skinned as Celeste, her hair
gray-streaked black curls. She didn't hug Vivien, but she
looked as if she would like to. She held out her hand.
"Welcome to our home, Miss Shaw."

"She cannot shake hands," Celeste gently reminded
her mother.

"How stupid of me! Celeste told me about your accident. How are your hands?" Mrs. Boyd asked jerkily.

"Better today, thank you." Vivien had taken another
painkiller before she left to get her though the afternoon.

"You come on in and sit down, make yourself at
home," Mrs. Boyd said, sliding a hand through the crook
of Vivien's arm to help her over the doorstep into the
house. She smelled sweetly of a light floral scent, and
the house was filled with the delicious aroma of spicy
food. For the first time since the accident Vivien actually
felt a pang of hunger.

"Well, I'll leave you ladies alone," Joseph said. "You
won't be needin' me any longer." With that he disappeared down the hallway.

Vivien was shown into a small room that she supposed
would have been called the front parlor in earlier days.
It was crammed with an abundance of dark furniture and
little knickknacks, all family treasures, Vivien imagined.
Treasures in the truest sense.

"Welcome to our home," Mrs. Boyd said. "You sit
down now, Miss Shaw, and rest yourself." She indicated
a cushioned chair that was like a folding deck chair,

made of dark mahogany, and then sank down on the small couch against the wall, fanning herself with a small painted fan. "This heat is real bad. There's a storm risin', they say."

"Do you get many storms at this time of the year?"

The question seemed to fluster Mrs. Boyd. "You forgot to offer Miss Shaw some drink, Celeste. It's too hot in here for her."

"I'm fine," Vivien assured her, wishing that Celeste's mother were more relaxed.

Celeste offered Vivien refreshments, including beer and rum punch, but after the hard, hot drive and the dusty road, Vivien was happy to accept a tall glass of fruit juice.

"How you enjoyin' our island, Miss Shaw?" Mrs. Boyd asked her. Then she looked flustered again, her hands fluttering in the air. "Silly me. Here's you, with your hands all messed up, and I'm askin'—"

"I think your island is beautiful," Vivien said, her smile designed to put Mrs. Boyd at ease. "You can have an accident anywhere. The only thing about it is that it stopped me from getting on with my work today."

"Your work?" Mrs. Boyd looked puzzled.

"Taking pictures, Mummy," Celeste reminded her. She sat down on the couch beside her mother, her body obviously tense.

"Oh, yes," Verna Boyd said. "You a famous photographer, right?"

Vivien grimaced at the word *famous*. "I love my work. Would you allow me to take some pictures of your lovely home?"

Mrs. Boyd beamed. "I'd like that," she said. "No one but family ever took pictures of my house before." Vivien caught a glint of tears in her eyes and looked down at her glass, embarrassed by this open display of emotion. "Good," she said briskly. "Once my hands are a little better, I'll come and take some pictures."

"You must feel the heat here, right, bein' from Canada, where it's so cold?" Mrs. Boyd asked. "You were raised there all your life?"

Celeste intervened. "I don't think Miss Shaw wants to answer a lot of questions, does she?"

Vivien shook her head. "I don't mind."

"We will eat soon," Celeste said abruptly, "but first we want to talk to you."

Vivien sensed the air of urgency in the room. Now her suspicion was confirmed. This *was* something more than a hospitable invitation to a meal. She looked expectantly from mother to daughter . . . and waited.

Celeste studied her nails and then the pale palms of her hands. "It is hard to know where to start," she said. "So it is probably best just to plunge right in." This was a very different, far more businesslike Celeste than before. She gripped her hands together in her lap. "You know about the murder of Lillian Hendley that happened more than fifty years ago at Peverill Hall."

"Yes?" Vivien tried to sit forward, but it wasn't easy in a chair that sloped backward. "Could I move to another chair?"

Celeste looked annoyed, as if she'd been thrown off her stride. "Of course." She rose to help Vivien move to a straight-backed Windsor chair.

"Okay now?" Celeste asked as she resumed her seat beside her mother, trying to hide her impatience. Vivien nodded. "As I was saying," Celeste continued, "you know about the murder. Have you had time since the accident to read all the details? Wesley told me that you had some research notes from the university."

"Yes, I've read them at least twice. I ended up feeling really frustrated because the information David Moreton's secretary gave me only went as far as the trial, and so I never found out what happened to Robert Hendley. I don't know if he was found guilty or—"

"He was hanged."

The bald statement, coming so starkly, hit Vivien like a fist in the stomach. "Hanged? I guess they had capital punishment back then."

"The West Indies still has capital punishment." Celeste's voice lacked any emotion.

"Oh! I hadn't realized that. I thought because Canada and Britain had abolished it—"

"After he was found guilty, there were appeals, of course, all the way to the Privy Council in England. And several petitions."

"When was he hanged?"

"In 1952. The appeals dragged on for more than a year."

"Robert Hendley was the sole owner of Peverill Hall, right?" Vivien asked.

Celeste nodded. Her mother sat on the couch, watching them intently.

"His wife, the one who—"

"His wife, Lillian Hendley, was my great-aunt. My mother was her niece."

A stifled sob came from the small, tense figure beside Celeste. She clasped her mother's hand in hers.

"Oh, my God," Vivien breathed. "I didn't know. How terrible for you."

"I was not alive then, of course," Celeste continued, "but my mother was. She was only ten years old when it happened. The person who still remembers all of this very clearly is my grandmother, Lillian's younger sister."

"My mother," Mrs. Boyd added in a whisper.

It was so quiet in the room that Vivien could hear them breathing.

"She's eighty now," Celeste added, "but, as I said, she remembers that horrible time more clearly every day."

"She is here," Mrs. Boyd said.

"Here in Barbados?"

"No, here in the house. We didn't want to upset her

by having her here when we told you 'bout our relationship to Lillian."

Vivien didn't know what to say. It explained Celeste's horror of Peverill Hall, but it didn't explain why they were sharing their tragic story with a stranger.

Celeste must have read her mind. "We are telling you this because you are the first person we've known who has actually stayed in Peverill Hall."

"Oh. Oh, I see." But Vivien didn't really see at all.

"We want to know the truth," Mrs. Boyd said.

"The truth about . . . ?"

"About Aunt Lillian's death. She was my favorite aunty. Everyone loved her." Mrs. Boyd's eyes filled with tears. "But the one who loved her most was her husband, Robert." She dabbed her tears with the wad of tissues Celeste handed her from the box on the table.

"You don't think he killed her?"

"We don't think so, but we cannot be absolutely sure."

"What we want to know is the truth of what happened at Peverill that night," Celeste said.

"Yes, that's right," Mrs. Boyd said eagerly. "We want to find out the truth."

"I'm sorry, but—but this all happened more than fifty years ago. How can you possibly find out anything more now, after all this time?"

Celeste stood up. "I think it's time to bring Nanna in, don't you?" she asked her mother.

Mrs. Boyd nodded. "I'll get her." She started to get up.

"No, Mummy, I'll get her. You sit and rest." Celeste left the two of them alone, with Vivien totally lost for words.

"We hate to do this to you," Mrs. Boyd said. "But we feel you were sent by the Lord to help us." She spoke with such fervor that Vivien knew she meant it.

"I don't know what I can do to help," Vivien mumbled, wishing herself anywhere but here.

"Don't you worry yourself 'bout that. We will tell you."

That was what Vivien was afraid of. She was saved from having to respond by the appearance of Celeste with a small, white-haired woman who walked into the room with the help of two canes.

Her bright eyes fixed upon Vivien. "Is this her? Is this Vivien?" she asked.

"Yes, this is Wesley's friend Miss Shaw," Celeste said, taking her arm. "My grandmother's name is Ruth," she told Vivien. "Ruth Fletcher." She seated her in the other high-backed chair beside the couch.

"We've told Miss Shaw about your being Aunty Lillian's sister, Nanna." Celeste spoke in a loud voice close to her grandmother's ear.

"Yes, Lillian is my big sister. I should say, she *was* my sister, but the older I gets, the more she seem to be here, beside me. And I know she will be there waitin' for me when I gets to the other side."

Emotion vibrated in the room. It was so overpowering that, coupled with the heat, Vivien felt she was being stifled.

"My mummy did not want Lillian to marry a white man. 'Didn't you learn your lesson from your daddy?' she told Lillian, when Lillian up and said she was goin' to marry Robert Hendley of Peverill. See," Ruth explained to Vivien, "our daddy, Lillian's and mine, was a white man. An upstanding lawyer from Bridgetown. But he never married my mother, so we was all bastards." The pride with which she spoke the word took the sting out of it, but Vivien could only imagine the difficulties of growing up half white and illegitimate in the Barbados of the 1920s and '30s, part of—and yet not fully accepted by—both societies. "He was generous with his money and educated us well in the church schools, but he drew the line at a wedding ring for our poor mother. That was why she did not want Lillian to marry a white man. But Robert was different. He treated Lillian like the lady she was from the day he first laid eyes on her. And you should have seen Robert when their little son, Trevor, was born. He was over the moon with happiness. And so it continued . . . until the day that his cousin, Thomas Hendley, arrived on the boat from England."

"Excuse me, Mrs. Fletcher," Vivien said. "You're talking about the Thomas Hendley who still lives at Peverill, right?"

"The very same one." The old woman's lips thinned so that they almost disappeared. "From the day he set foot in Peverill, things started to change. Wait!" She turned to Celeste. "Where did you put those notes of Lillian's that I gave you?"

"I have them right here, Nanna." Celeste opened a drawer in the desk in the corner of the room and took out a box of polished mahogany. "In your daddy's old cigar box."

"You've put them in order like I told you to do?" Celeste's grandmother was of the old school. Vivien could imagine her wielding a wooden spoon if she were disobeyed.

"Yes, Nanna."

"Give Vivien the first one so she can read it for herself. Read the parts I have circled. You unfold it for her, Celeste."

Vivien took it carefully in her bandaged hand. It felt as light as air, a mere scrap of paper, scored by lines where it had been folded for half a century. The beautiful copperplate writing was faded but legible.

Vivien bent her head and read the note to herself.

Peverill, 1950
. . . He has just left me. He likes to get up before dawn to catch the coolest part of the day in the fields overseeing the cane cutters. It will be good for him to have help, he works too hard, but I do not like the thought of having a stranger about the place.

"You have read it?" demanded Celeste's grand-mother.

"Yes," Vivien replied.

"My sister and I were very close. We lived 'cross the island from each other. She would write to me once a week, sometimes more. One of the field-workers at Pev-erill had a family near here. He would bring her notes to me. The stranger she talks of in the note is her hus-band's cousin, Thomas. Give her the next one, Celeste."

Celeste handed Vivien another note, taking the first one back from her, then reverently folding it and replac-ing it in the cigar box.

"Read it," commanded Mrs. Fletcher.

Vivien read the circled part of the second note.

> *Peverill, 1950*
> *. . . He arrived yesterday, with two trunks and several boxes. He is quite the gentleman. But . . . I'm not sure about him. He keeps looking at me in such a strange way as if I am some exotic animal in a zoo. He finds the heat troublesome and complains about it all the time. We shall have to wait and see if he can settle in.*

" 'I am not sure about him,' Lillian tells me in her note." Ruth Fletcher knew these notes by heart. "She did not like the man from the very start."

"Were these notes given to the police?" Vivien asked.

"Wait until you have read all of them," she was told. "Have you given the girl something to eat, Verna?" Mrs. Fletcher demanded of her daughter.

"I don't need anything, thank you. I wouldn't mind another glass of fruit juice, though."

"Give her the juice, Celeste. Then give her the next note. I wish I had kept more of her notes," Mrs. Fletcher told Vivien as Celeste was pouring the juice, "but these few is all I have."

Vivien took a long drink of juice and then clumsily

accepted the next note that Celeste handed to her. Why on earth were they showing them to her? She found it intensely disturbing to be reading the private notes written to her sister by a woman who was murdered by her husband. *If* she was murdered by her husband. And what made it even more disturbing was having the murdered woman's family watching her as she read them.

> *Peverill, 1950*
> *. . . R. is v. pleased with him. They sit on the verandah at night, smoking and talking about England and things I know nothing of. Sometimes, it makes me feel like I'm left out.*

"That is the one where she feels 'left out,' right?"
Vivien nodded.
"See, he makin' her feel inferior to her husband, 'cause *he* think she's inferior. Give her the next note, Celeste."
Celeste did so, again carefully unfolding the delicate paper for Vivien.

> *Peverill, 1950*
> *. . . I know I should like him, because he is family, but I do not like him. He is all smiles with R. but keeps coming close to me when R. is not here. And yesterday he touched my body and called me a bad name. But I'm going to keep my mouth shut, because R. needs his help. I know Mamma thinks I should tell, but I can deal with him by myself.*

Despite the uncomfortable heat, Vivien sat frozen in her chair. "She's still talking about Thomas Hendley, isn't she?" she said at last, her voice not much louder than a whisper.
Mrs. Fletcher's hands were clasped tightly in her lap. "The good Lord forgive us our sins, she is. I should have

gone to Robert and warned him, but my mummy warned me not to come between a wife and her husband. And Lillian, she say to me and Mamma, 'You keep out of this, both of you. It between Robert and me.' So we did what she say. A short while later she was dead. She and her unborn child."

Vivien swallowed hard. "Yes, the newspaper report mentioned she was pregnant."

"Four months gone." Mrs. Fletcher choked, coughed, and could no longer hold back her grief. "My beautiful Lillian was dead," she sobbed, "she and her baby hacked to death in her own bed."

As the two women went to hold her, Celeste kneeling before her, clutching her grandmother's knees, Ruth Fletcher's sobs rose to a muted wailing. Despite the arms holding her tightly, she rocked violently back and forth, crying out her sorrow.

Vivien felt utterly helpless. Their grief bombarded her yet shut her out. "What can I do to help?" she asked of the three women when Ruth had quietened a little. "Please tell me what I can do."

Celeste released her grandmother and scrambled to her feet. "The police told our family that the notes were not sufficient evidence to suggest that Thomas, not Robert, was Lillian's killer. They only proved she didn't like Thomas, nothing more. By this time, you see, they were convinced that Robert Hendley had killed his wife. They asked my grandmother if she'd had any more notes since that last one."

Mrs. Fletcher pushed her daughter aside. Breathing hard, her hair awry, she sat up in the chair, her eyes like glowing coals. "I knows my sister. She would have sent me a note that week if she could have." She leaned forward in the chair. "But what if she wrote one, but had to hide it from *him*. What then? I asked that inspector of the police and he says to me, 'Show me that note, if you can, and I will see what I can do.' But I didn't have no more notes to show him, and none of us was allowed into Peverill even to get some of her own things. They gave us nothin' to keep that was hers. Not even one of the handkerchiefs I stitched for her wedding."

Were they asking her to steal some of Lillian Hendley's things, so they could have them as keepsakes? Vivien wondered. It was hard to say no to such an appeal, but she wouldn't even consider doing such a thing.

"Aunty Lillian had three favorite hiding places," Verna said, sinking onto the couch again. "She showed them to me once when I visited her at Peverill. She said it was a secret between her and me."

"And Verna, she didn't tell me nothin' about this until long after the trial was over, when it was too late to do anything 'bout it." Mrs. Fletcher darted a scathing look at her daughter, who shrank back against the couch.

"It was not her fault, Nanna," Celeste said. "She was only a child at the time, and everyone must have been so upset, no wonder she didn't remember."

"I know, I know." Mrs. Fletcher slowly shook her white head. "But, oh, Lord, what a world of difference it might have made if Verna had told me."

Verna hung her head like a child who'd been reprimanded. Vivien could tell that this wasn't the first time she'd been chastised for something she'd done—or omitted to do—fifty years before.

Celeste turned back to Vivien, who was mesmerized by the three pairs of dark eyes, all fixed upon her now. "If we tell you where these hiding places of Lillian's were, will you look in them for a note she might have left before she died?"

But I'm not going back to Peverill to stay, Vivien wanted to tell them. She hesitated, then said, "That depends on what or where these hiding places are."

"We will tell you that," Celeste said.

"The good Lord sent you to help us," said her mother. "He will show you the way."

"The good Lord helps those who help themselves," said Mrs. Fletcher dryly. "If you take this on, my child, you will need to take great care."

"Oh, yes," breathed Verna. "You must. We cannot have you harmed in any way."

"You have already been harmed," Celeste said, nodding at her hands still wrapped in the tensor bandages.

"That was an accident," Vivien said. "I knew nothing about all this when it happened." But then she recalled that she had not locked away the file about the murder in her room at Peverill the afternoon she'd discovered the old barn.

"I wouldn't be so sure. Perhaps Thomas thought we had sent you to search his house," Celeste suggested. She smiled a bittersweet smile. "After all, over the past fifty years our family has never let anyone on the island forget Lillian's death. Each generation of our family has taken it upon themselves to keep the stories and rumors going. The Hendleys have found it very hard to get people to work their land or in their cane fields."

Vivien suddenly remembered something she had read in the file. She'd thought it had nothing to do with the murder, but now she was not so sure. "There was a piece in the newspaper, dated sometime in 1996, about a break-in at Peverill—"

Celeste made a face. "We arranged that, but the man who did it for us was an amateur. They caught him as soon as he'd broken into the house. Paul Hendley beat him up before he handed him over to the police."

"So I guess you didn't try that again."

"No, the Hendleys accused us of being responsible, but the police didn't take it any further."

It sounded as if the police might be taking sides, Vivien thought. Although accusing people of spreading rumors wouldn't be easy to prove, conspiracy to commit the crime of breaking and entering might. "But what if Robert did kill his wife?" she asked, her sense of fairness rising at this seeming persecution of the Hendley family.

"Robert loved Lillian," Celeste said firmly. "The only reason he might have killed her was because of the lies Thomas was pouring into his ears about her. Thomas Hendley would still be guilty, even if Robert's hand had done the actual killing."

"But we think it was Thomas did it," Ruth interjected.

Vivian shivered. Somehow it wasn't too difficult to think of Thomas as a killer. "So, for the past fifty years your family has persecuted all the Hendleys."

"Oh, no, not all. Just Thomas and his brood."

Vivien shook her head. "It's a horrifying story. If it's true, a terrible wrong has been committed."

"A wrong that needs to be put right. And, in you, we have the chance to do that."

Vivien shook her head, more in an attempt to make sense of all she had been told than to deny that she could help them. "Even if I was able to find these hiding places, after fifty years the Hendleys would have made sure that nothing incriminating could be found."

"That is for you to find out, missy," said Mrs. Fletcher, her eyes bright. "And if you find nothin', at least then we know there was nothin' there to be found. Will you do it?"

Vivien thought hard for a long time. She could hear their breathing and the wooden carriage clock on the corner table ticking the minutes away.

"Yes, I will," she said at last. She heard a long exhalation of breath. "But if Thomas is as dangerous as you suggest, I'm not willing to risk my life to do this, you understand."

"Of course not," Mrs. Fletcher said. "We don't want no harm to come to you. Take no risks, child. Be careful, careful, careful. But the good Lord will be with you, for it was He who sent you to us."

CHAPTER
TWENTY-THREE

Vivien did not feel at all like someone heaven-sent to fulfill a family quest. On the return journey, as Joseph chattered on about how much it was going to mean to the family to have someone search Peverill for a long-lost note or any clue to what had happened to Lillian Hendley on the last day of her life, Vivien was berating herself. She had allowed the three women's heartrending emotion to sway her.

"It might be better if they put it out of their minds and moved on with their lives," she told Joseph.

He drew in a deep breath and blew it out again, puffing his cheeks. "You are tellin' me," he said. "But those women, they pass this burden on from one generation to the next, and they are never at peace. They will only be happy when Thomas Hendley has paid the price for his sins."

"I can understand that." She thought of her confrontations with the man and felt cold at the thought of having to see him again. She must have been mad to agree to their entreaties. "He's an old man now. They won't have to wait long for him to go."

Joseph slapped his hand hard on the steering wheel. "That is the problem, Miss Shaw. If he die in his bed, then he has never paid the price, has he? And Nanna, she's eighty years old. She want to see justice done before she goes to her maker."

It all made sense in a twisted way. Except for the fact that they'd picked a stranger, and a damaged one at that, to do their dirty work for them. Still, after hearing how they'd kept the rumors going for fifty years, Vivien could understand their frustration. There wasn't much chance of the Hendleys letting any member of Lillian's family come near Peverill land. No wonder Thomas Hendley was so paranoid.

Vivien was determined not to get caught up emotionally in the family's long, sad search for justice. It had nothing to do with her. All she was going to do was look for the three hiding places Verna had told her about and see if anything was hidden in them. And if she couldn't find them inside the house—or it was too difficult to get at them without arousing suspicion—then that would be that. Lillian's family would have to count her out as an accomplice in their vendetta against the Hendleys. The possibility of another confrontation with Thomas made her feel physically sick.

A wind had blown up, its force buffeting Joseph's RAV. "That's a strong wind," Vivien said. Almost immediately, there came a sudden squall of rain, lashing down.

"There's a big storm comin'," Joseph said, switching on his fast windshield wipers.

A storm. That was all she needed. She fervently hoped she could search Peverill this afternoon and get out of there before the night came. "How often do you get hurricanes?" she asked Joseph.

"Real ones, not just storms?"

"Yes."

"Oh, 'bout every ten years or so. But tropical storms can be pretty strong as well. Got a torch?"

"You mean a flashlight?"

"Right."

"Yes." It was in the bag she had with her, she realized. "Why?"

"In case the power goes. The real storm is not supposed to hit until tomorrow, but you never know."

"I've got some candles as well." She always traveled with the essentials.

"Good." Joseph cast a glance at her. "That searchin' they've asked you to do . . ."

"Yes?"

"Don't you go doin' it unless you feel it is safe, okay?"

"I won't."

"I don't want those crazy women leadin' you into some danger, and you all alone with those Hendleys."

"I'm used to being by myself."

"That Thomas is a piece of work, and his wife is not much better."

"I know, but Paul and Marian are okay."

He grunted at that. "Just you be careful."

"I will. Thanks for the warning." The rain was easing off a little, and Joseph switched his wipers to the slower speed. They drove for a while in amicable silence, apart from the whining wind and the rustle of the trees as they bent westward before its strength.

By the time they reached Peverill, the rain had stopped and the sun had come out again, but there were still heavy black clouds about. Talk about changeable weather. Joseph pulled in to the side of the lane, a little way from the house. "This okay?" he asked.

"Fine." Even Joseph was nervous about getting too close. She couldn't blame him. But it wasn't Peverill Hall that was evil.

He helped her out of the RAV. "You need help to get inside?" he asked, casting an apprehensive glance at the house.

"No, thanks. I'll be fine."

"How you goin' to manage with those hands?" He nodded at the bandages.

"I'll manage. They're feeling better already. Besides, all being well I'll be finished here by this evening."

Joseph got back into the RAV. "You take care," he called out of the window. "Call me when you need me to come, okay?"

"I will. Thanks again." She felt an impulse to jump back into the RAV before it moved away, but she'd promised Celeste and her family. Something told her she must not break that promise.

She watched as Joseph slowly drove away, wishing she still had his solid presence there. The sun beat down, steam rising from the ground. The moist heat was oppressive. A weight bore down on her chest, making it difficult to breathe. Bracing herself, she turned and walked toward the house. As she came nearer, she caught the acrid smell of smoke and burning vegetation and saw a plume of dark smoke rising from behind the house. She climbed the steps slowly and then rang the bell.

The door opened immediately. Marian stood there, dressed in cotton shorts that were too tight for her and a bright pink T-shirt that had been discolored in places by bleach. "You came back." She seemed surprised, perhaps apprehensive as well. "When we didn't hear from you last night, we thought you weren't coming back." She held the door half shut, blocking the entrance with her body.

"Can I come in?"

"Yes, of course." She opened the door wider and let her in. There was a decided awkwardness between them. "How are the—the hands?" Marian asking, glancing at them.

"Very painful, but no broken bones."

"I'm glad." The flush in Marian's face deepened. "You might have called us. We were worried about you."

"Were you? Sorry about that, but they gave me a morphine shot at the hospital. I was out for most of the night." Vivien glanced nervously around the hall, dreading the sudden appearance of Thomas.

Paul came in from the back of the house, his face grimy and stained with smoke. "I thought I heard a car." He eyed Vivien warily. "How are you?"

She held up her bandaged hands. "Sore, but I'll survive." She hesitated, then said, "Did you check the sash cords?"

"I certainly did. They were absolutely rotten. I replaced both of them with new ones this morning. I also spent over an hour repairing the door frame where Marian had to break it in, because you had the hook on."

Vivien couldn't believe her ears. It sounded as if he were blaming *her* for what had happened. She forced herself to breathe slowly to keep calm. "What did you do with the old sash cords?"

"Burned 'em. They were rotten, no use for anything."

"Burned them?"

"That's right. On the bonfire. We have one going most days."

"Must be hot."

"Oh, it is, but it's the best way to get rid of rubbish. It's a never-ending battle the way stuff grows here. We also got rid of all those moldy old books you found."

They'd burned the books. Now she was even more glad that she'd rescued one of them.

Paul rubbed his soiled hands together. "So, what can we do for you, Miss Shaw? Oh, I suppose you're here for your things. I'll get them for you."

She tilted her head to look at him. "I paid in advance for four nights, remember?"

"Yes?"

"I've only had two, if you count last night."

"Well, that was hardly our—" He stopped suddenly, realizing what he was saying.

"Hardly your fault, were you about to say, Mr. Hendley? I don't think a court of law would agree with you, do you?"

"It was an accident," he said, baring his teeth like an aggressive terrier.

"Even if it was, you advertised for people to stay with you, which, I imagine, would presume a certain degree of safety in your home." Vivien held up her hands. "I have suffered considerable pain, loss of ability to work . . ."

Paul shuffled his feet. "Yes, well, we know all that. What do you want from us? We'll refund your money, of course."

"I don't want the money."

"You mean you want to stay on here?" His voice registered surprise, but something else stirred at the back of his pale blue eyes. "And that will be it?"

"If you mean that I won't make any complaints to the tourist board about negligence, that depends on how quickly my hands heal and how soon I can get on with my work."

"I've already warned you, my father doesn't like people staying here."

"And how does this dislike manifest itself?" Their eyes clashed.

"My father's not bloody insane," Paul said, his face flushing.

"I'm sure he's not, but just make sure he keeps away from the room I've rented, okay?"

Marian quickly interceded. "You look ghastly," she said. "You should be resting. I take it you've had lunch?"

"Oh, yes." Celeste and her mother had laid on a feast, but Vivien had found it hard to eat anything after what they had told her.

"I'll make up a jug of lemonade for you and there's a piece of jam sponge. You want it outside or in your room?"

"My room, please. I think I should go and lie down for a while. Thanks, Marian."

"I'll take your bag for you. You go ahead."

Vivien started to tackle the stairs, using her elbow for balance, but was so slow that she told Marian to go ahead of her.

"You really did get clobbered, didn't you?" Marian said. "You can't even use your fingers."

Vivien bit back a sarcastic response. "I can use them," she explained, "but it is difficult to grip with them."

She was immensely relieved to get into "her" room and to see, as her gaze quickly scanned it, that everything appeared to be there, including her daybook on the bedside cabinet.

Marian set her bag down on the bed, then hesitated by the door. "I'm so sorry this happened." Her face was mottled pink.

"I know. Let's not talk about it, okay?"

Marian nodded. "I'll bring the lemonade." She closed the door.

Vivien was trembling with fatigue and tension. She longed to lie down but doubted she could sleep in this place, with the man she now suspected of committing a horrific murder lurking somewhere nearby.

She closed the door and was about to latch it but remembered that Marian was coming back. She ran her fingers down the newly repaired door frame. Hard to believe it was only yesterday it had happened. It seemed like an age ago. She smiled as she recalled David's appearance in the doorway and wished with all her heart that he was here with her now. One call from her and he'd be there in a flash, she was sure of that. Her smile faded. David thought she was safely settled with Celeste and Joseph. If he knew she was back at Peverill, he'd go berserk. God willing, she'd be gone from here before he found out.

She quickly checked to make sure that her cameras,

equipment, and laptop were still safely stowed away in
her suitcase. Then she took out the Peverill file, leaving
the envelope containing *Kidnapped* hidden away. Kicking off her sandals, she padded over the wooden floor
to her bedside cabinet to pick up her daybook, thinking
how much she had to add to it to catch up with all that
had happened.

The window was open a few inches, but the air coming
in was hot and humid, and the room was like an oven.
Vivien checked the sash cords and saw that they were
white and stiffly new. She recalled that the old ones had
been brown, discolored with age, contrasting with the
white paint of the window frame. She would never know
now whether the old cord had broken accidentally—or
been cut deliberately. Maybe the old man hadn't intended to harm her, only to scare her. After all, to be
woken up during the night by a window falling like a
guillotine would have been quite a shock. Perhaps
enough to make her move out.

On the other hand, having seen the state of disrepair
in the lovely old house, the crumbling stonework and
the worm-eaten furniture, it was possible that the old
cords had been rotten and both had snapped when she'd
lifted the heavy window.

She drew down the blind to ward off the sun and
transferred her daybook and the Peverill file to the other
side of the bed, within easy reach. She also put David's
book there, turning it over so that she could see his
picture. He looked out at her with that enigmatic little
half smile, and she felt such a wave of longing to have
him there that it was hard to bear.

She turned away from him and, sitting sideways on
the high bed, swung her legs up onto it, lowering her
head onto the pillow with a sigh of relief. How difficult
it was to do the simplest things she usually took for
granted. The fresh lavender scent from the bedclothes
tempted her to sleep, but she knew that she was back

here for a purpose. It was time she considered how she was going to go about the investigation.

She would have to explore as much of Peverill Hall as was possible beneath the watchful eyes of the Hendleys. She was looking for three things. The first two would be fairly easy to find, if they still existed: an old blue-and-white Staffordshire vase, and a large mahogany sewing box with a handle and brass hinges that had been made by Lillian's grandfather. It had been his gift to her for her wedding, and therefore doubly precious to the family.

The third, although probably easy to locate, would be the most difficult to access. There had been, according to Verna Boyd, a loose board in the floor of the master bedroom. Verna said she remembered that Lillian had to lift the small coconut mat from the floor to lift up the board and show her the aperture beneath it where she used to hide things. She said she thought that Lillian had to move the bed to get at the board, but couldn't recall exactly where the bed was located in the room.

Vivien had never even seen inside the bedroom of Thomas and his wife, never mind being able to get into it. Marian had told her they kept it locked even from her, allowing her in only to clean it once a week. And Mrs. Hendley senior spent much of her time in there. That bedroom was going to be Vivien's greatest challenge.

She was staring at the decorative plasterwork around the central ceiling light, trying to find the energy to get up, when she heard a knock on her door, followed by Marian's voice. "Are you awake?"

Vivien leaned up on her elbow. "Come in. It's not locked."

Marian came in, carrying a tray. She put it down on top of the bedside cabinet. "There you are: lemonade I made fresh this morning, cake and some fruit."

"You're spoiling me."

Marian's sunburned face flushed. "Least we can do," she murmured. "There's some raspberry jelly to go with the cake. A jelly's nice and light when you're not feeling too good."

"Sounds perfect. Thanks, Marian." Vivien sat up, with her back against the pillows. "I should really get up, but I'm still feeling tired."

"No wonder. Staying all night at the hospital." Marian looked at her over her glasses. "You were at the hospital all night, weren't you?"

"That's right," Vivien lied.

"Noisy places. You just rest there and I'll put the tray on the bed beside you." Vivien saw her glance at the file as she laid the tray down on the bed. Fortunately, she'd closed it up. "Working?" Marian asked in a friendly tone.

"Just reading some papers I need for the project."

Marian perched on the side of the bed nearest the door. "This project of yours, remind me what it's about . . . if you don't mind me asking?"

"It's a book about Barbados in general," Vivien replied, deliberately making it sound vague.

"You mean a history book?" Marian asked. "Or a book about Barbados as it is now?"

"To be honest, I'm not quite sure. That's up to the author. I'm only the photographer." David would love to hear her say that.

"And who's the author?"

"David Moreton."

"Never heard of him."

Vivien was not about to tell her that David Moreton and the angry young man who had stormed into the house yesterday were one and the same.

"And you're from Canada. Toronto, I think you said, right?"

"That's right." Marian knew most of this already. Where was all this going?

"I should have realized from the start that you were Canadian. Your accent sounds almost English."

"That's because both my parents were born in England. I guess I've picked up their accents."

"Right, that would explain it." Marian nodded to the food on the tray. "Don't let me keep you from eating."

She seemed to enjoy watching people eat. Vivien, on the other hand, didn't like to be watched when she ate. Her mother tended to do that, and it made Vivien feel self-conscious.

"What part?" Marian asked.

"Part?"

"What part of England are your parents from?"

"My mother was born and raised in Somerset. We flew over a couple of times to visit her and Grandpa, but Dad's not keen on flying. Grandpa died several years ago."

"And your father?"

"He came from a small town in Kent. We never visited his parents. They're both dead now."

Marian got up from the bed. "I think I told you, I come from the north, Yorkshire. I don't know southern England very well." She glanced at her watch. "Well, must be going." She walked to the door and then turned back. "Almost forgot to ask. What would you like for supper?"

"Supper?" The question took Vivien by surprise. She hoped to be gone from this place before dark. "A sandwich would be plenty. I don't have much of an appetite at the moment."

"Okay, then. I'll let you rest."

"Thanks for the lemonade and food. Looks good."

"Hope so. I won't come for the tray until I hear you up and about."

"Thanks, again."

It was a relief when Marian left the room, shutting the door quietly behind her. Vivien noticed that the door

hinges no longer squeaked. Paul must have oiled them
when he repaired the door frame. She slipped out of
bed and padded to the door to hook it up, then managed
to fill the glass half full with lemonade, although the
weight of the jug made her wrist start throbbing again.
She ate a little of the cake and jelly and then lay down
again. Her eyelids were heavy. She fought sleep, but it
won in the end.

She was woken with a start by a peal of thunder and
lightning illuminating the room through the blinds. Immediately the rain spilled down, beating on the roof
and pouring down the nearby drainpipe. She glanced
at her watch and saw that she'd slept for almost forty
minutes. She was wasting precious time. If she was
going to find anything before nightfall, she'd better
start looking now. Damn this weather. It meant there
was less chance of the Hendleys working outside. Still,
she had to check.

She slid off the bed, slipped her shoes on, and went
to open the door. Now that the hinges were oiled, it
swung open easily, but she heard the dog barking and
so shut it again. Moving to the chair by the window, she
lifted the blind and looked out at the rain streaming
down the glass. It made her feel even more cut off from
the outside world. Her mind started racing.

Why had they suddenly decided to oil the door
hinges? She'd have preferred to hear if someone opened
her door. She had to leave it unsnibbed if she was out
of the room. Anyone could come into the room then.
When she was in the bathroom, for instance. She
scanned the room. If someone came in and wanted to
hide, where would he—or she—go? The wardrobe was
large enough for someone to hide in, wasn't it? And
the bed was high enough off the floor for someone to
slide under.

She felt the walls of the small room closing in on her.
She had to restrain herself from racing down the stairs

and running full speed down the driveway to the safety of the road beyond it. Instead she decided to harness the adrenaline rush and use it in a positive way, by starting her search for Lillian Hendley's hiding places.

CHAPTER
TWENTY-FOUR

Around the same time that Vivien had returned to Peverill Hall, Wesley received a call from Celeste telling him what had happened during Vivien's visit.

"I thought we had agreed not to involve her in this," he said when she'd finished, furious that Celeste had gone against his advice. "It is far too dangerous for her to go looking for nonexistent clues to what might have happened to Lillian."

"Nanna says she's been sent by God to help us."

"Nanna's a stubborn old woman who won't give up this quest to get to the bottom of Lillian's death. You should know better than to encourage her."

"She says Vivien's staying at Peverill, so she might as well do the best she can. And I agree with Nanna about that. She's the first one we've known to get inside the place in fifty years. Apart from that useless idiot we hired to break into Peverill."

"For the Lord's sake, Celeste, are you wanting to bring about another tragedy in the family?"

"No, of course not."

"Well, you are going about it the right way, that's all I can say. I wish I had never listened to you and Janice. Vivien would be better off where she was, safe and sound in Toronto." He heard a clicking on his line, signifying a call coming through. "Hold on, I have another call."

"Leave it! Vivien is our blood, Wesley, yours and mine. We all wanted to see her."

"Well, that blood might well be on your hands. I think it is time she knew the truth."

"No! Don't you dare tell her. She knows nothing about that. So don't you dare tell her. Imagine what a shock it would be for her if she were to find out!"

"Better shock than something far, far worse."

"Rubbish! Hendley's an old man. What could he do to her?"

"I pray to the Lord I don't have to find out. Someone else is calling me." The clicking on the line was getting on his nerves. "I will get back to you." He rang off with Celeste still protesting in his ear, but it was too late. The other caller had given up.

At times like this, Wesley wished he spent one hundred percent of the time in Toronto, away from his many relatives. But even there he couldn't get away from them. After all, that was how all this had started, with Janice Greene—his cousin Verna's daughter and Celeste's sister—telling him she'd met Vivien Shaw at the Royal Ontario Museum, where Janice worked as a curator. They both knew who Vivien was, of course. His aunt, Nanna Fletcher, and her daughter, Verna, had painstakingly created a detailed family tree, incorporating those members of the family who were scattered throughout the world. Vivien herself had made it all remarkably easy when her expressive gifts had genuinely moved him at the exhibition.

If not for Peverill, the reunion would all have gone fine. Celeste would have taken her to meet her family. Verna and Ruth would have had the pleasure of seeing Vivien without her actually having to know the truth. She would have spent a week, perhaps two, taking preliminary photographs for the Barbados book and then gone home none the wiser. Everyone would have been happy.

If not for Peverill.

Vivien had discovered Peverill. Or had Peverill discovered her? Wesley wondered if it was fate, God's will. How else to explain that Vivien had found Peverill Hall, despite the fact that it was tucked away off the road, unseen by most inhabitants of Barbados, never mind visitors to the island.

Now all he could hope for was that the falling window had indeed been an unfortunate accident. After all, there was no reason for the Hendleys to suspect that Vivien was connected to Lillian's family. She was known as Vivien Shaw, not Carlton. He had made sure of that before he engaged her to come out to Barbados. As long as the Hendleys never found out who she was, she would be safe.

The phone rang, startling him. It was probably Celeste, calling him back. He picked up the receiver.

"Wesley, it's David."

Lord in heaven! Who else was going to call him? "Yes, David."

"Where's Vivien? I called Celeste, and Joseph said she was on her cell phone speaking to you. He also told me that Vivien has gone back to Peverill Hall. I couldn't believe it."

"Unfortunately, it is true. But Celeste tells me she plans to pick up her things and then leave again."

David cursed beneath his breath. "I wish you'd tell me what the hell's going on."

"I wish I could," Wesley said, "but I cannot."

"I've been reading about the murder. Mrs. Simmons made a second copy of the papers she gave Vivien. That was a very strange case."

"It happened fifty years ago." Wesley tried to make his tone as disinterested as possible. Fortunately, David was not one to concern himself with the intricacies of Bajan family connections, or he would have been aware of Wesley's relationship to Lillian Hendley and her family.

A long pause. "Are you absolutely sure she will be safe in that house?" David asked him.

Wesley hesitated.

"Because if there's any doubt," David said, "I will go there right now and drag her out of it. She shouldn't be alone. Her hands need ice and the bandages—"

"I will get Sarah to call her right away to make sure she's all right. Will that make you happy?"

"Happy? No. But it will make me feel a little better."

Long after David had rung off, Wesley sat at his desk, staring at the telephone. What had he done? To satisfy the vengeance of a group of women, it was possible he'd put Vivien's life in grave danger. As long as the Hendleys don't know who she is she will be safe, he assured himself, striving to ease his conscience.

But what if they did discover who she was? What then?

CHAPTER
TWENTY-FIVE

Vivien waited for the rain to ease a little before leaving her room. Slowly, almost imperceptibly, the drumming on the roof lessened. Eventually she judged it to be sufficiently quiet for her to be able to hear clearly, and she stepped out into the upper hallway. Although it was not yet evening, it was very dark, the lights not having been switched on. She leaned over the railing, straining to hear voices, but couldn't distinguish any. However, she was still cautious. She knew that the heavy doors in Peverill shut out sound.

She tiptoed down the broad staircase, wincing whenever the stairs creaked, and was about to cross the hall when Marian suddenly appeared, carrying a basket of clean cutlery.

"You didn't sleep long," she said.

"The thunder woke me up."

"Yes, it was pretty noisy out there."

"When do they expect the weather to improve?" It felt strange not having a television to check the weather report. "Is there a radio somewhere?"

"I've got one in the kitchen. I'm afraid it's going to get worse before it gets better. They're expecting the eye of the storm to hit earlier than they'd first forecasted, probably tonight, so it's best if we all stick close to home for the rest of the day."

Vivien sighed inwardly. There went her idea of searching the house when everyone was out. "I hope it's not going to be a hurricane."

Marian shrugged. "Who knows?"

"What do you do if it's really bad? Do you have special shutters?"

Marian gave a dry laugh. "Not us. Modern places have steel shutters, but the old houses just have to weather it the best they can. This old place has been knocked about quite a few times, I believe, particularly the hurricane in 1955. But it's still standing after three hundred years, so they must have built it right to start with."

"Good craftsmen."

Marian smiled wryly and shook her head. "More like good design." She seemed different, more edgy, not so friendly. "What do you plan to do?" she asked, taking out the cutlery and putting it away.

"Sort the photos I've taken, catalogue them, so I know exactly where and when I took them. Do some more research. I was going to go back to the university library, but maybe that's not a good idea."

"With this weather . . ." Marian shrugged and bent down again to sort the cutlery into neat piles in the felt-lined drawers. "You could end up being stuck there, with no electricity."

Vivien could think of worse fates. "You probably have some books about Barbados history, don't you? I think I saw some bookshelves in that little back parlor when I met Mrs. Hendley. Would it be possible to take a look through them?"

"Depends on whether she's in there or not." Their eyes met and Marian grimaced. "If you know what I mean."

Vivien nodded. "Thanks, Marian. Apart from that, I think I'll take it easy."

Marian began using an old carpet sweeper, running it back and forth across the rug beneath the dining table. "I'll go and check the back room," she said when she'd finished.

"Thanks." Vivien started to make her way to the front door.

"I take it you're not planning to sit outside?"

"No, just looking."

"Everything on the verandah is soaked. I took in all the cushions, but the furniture out there is sodden, and there are wet leaves and twigs everywhere. Paul said he'll wait until the storm's over before he clears it up. He and his father are checking to make sure everything's tied down tight. And I've got to see how the chickens are doing out in the back. That chicken house isn't too sturdy."

Vivien was left alone in the front room. Standing there beneath the crystal chandelier, she made a hurried visual check of the room's contents. No sign of a blue-and-white vase. She wished she'd asked Verna what size it was. For all she knew, it could be massive and easy to see, or tiny and hidden away . . . She sidled over to the glass-fronted cabinet in the corner of the room, but there was nothing blue among the little curios and crystal pieces on the glass shelves.

"It's empty at the moment." Marian's voice coming from directly behind her made Vivien jump.

"Sorry. I was looking at this lovely collection."

"I think it's mostly junk, but I wouldn't know. I said, the room's empty." Marian's voice dropped. "You should go in right now, before the old battle-ax comes downstairs and takes it over."

"Are you sure?"

Marian nodded. "Take any book you want—she won't notice. But put it in a drawer in your room, out of sight. They don't like anyone to touch their things." She raised her eyebrows, a wealth of meaning in her expression.

Vivien nodded in understanding. As she walked quickly back to the parlor, her stomach cramped; she was sure now that one of them had probably been into her room, snooping. Or worse.

She hadn't really taken much notice of the back room when she'd had that first unpleasant encounter with Mrs. Hendley. Now she was under duress to look hard for two things. But while she was looking, she must pretend to be interested in the books on the bookshelves on either side of an incongruous pseudo-fireplace. It had obviously been incorporated into the house's original plans to give the place the appearance of a cozy room more suited to the chilly climate of England's winters than the intense heat and humidity of Barbados.

Again, no sign of a blue vase, but as she was looking, her eye caught sight of what could be a wooden sewing chest in the corner, partly hidden by a high-backed cushioned chair, and she recalled that Mrs. Hendley had been doing some sort of needlework when they'd met.

Heart beating fast, she pulled the chest out, wincing with pain as she did so. Handle, yes. Brass hinges, yes. This certainly looked as if it could be Lillian's sewing chest. Breathing even faster, Vivien opened it up and carefully lifted out the three trays. They were filled with an assortment of old wooden spools of thread, darning wools of every color, needle cases, scraps of leftover fabrics . . . but when she'd reached the bottom, feeling around with aching fingers to see if there might be a hidden compartment, there was not one sign of a scrap of paper. Disappointed, she was about to put the trays back in again when she heard the *thump, thump* of a rubber-footed cane on the floor.

"What the hell do you think you are doing?"

Scrambling to her feet, Vivien turned to see Mrs. Hendley in the doorway, leaning on a black cane. Behind her stood Marian, eyes staring, hair more disheveled than ever.

"I—I am sorry, Mrs. Hendley," Vivien stuttered, "I was looking at your book collection. I happened to see the sewing basket and remembered that I had to sew a button on a blouse, so I was looking for some—"

Vivien recoiled from the stark hatred darting from Mrs. Hendley's eyes. "How dare you!" she spat out at Vivien. "How dare you come in here and touch my things!" She raised her stick as if intending to strike Vivien with it.

"Now, Mother," Marian said. "Calm down. You know what the doctor said. Getting excited is bad for your heart."

Mrs. Hendley swung around, her raised stick not more than a foot from Marian's face. "And you, you slut, you let her in here to my room."

Vivien strode forward. "Excuse me, Mrs. Hendley, but I came in here and opened your sewing box by myself. Keep Marian out of it. I can't believe you'd make such a fuss about someone looking for a needle and thread."

The stick was still raised, but now Mrs. Hendley had turned to focus on Vivien again. "You're a liar, just like all your kind."

"Say what you like to me," Vivien said coldly, "it won't bother me, but I find it unbelievable that you would treat your son's wife the way you do. She works like a dog for you all and never gets a word of thanks for it."

"Please, don't . . ." Marian whispered, her face twisted.

"It's true. So you'd better sit down, Mrs. Hendley, and I'll take the stick from you and put it somewhere safe." The old woman was staring at her, openmouthed. "I would like to borrow a needle and some thread. Then I'll tidy away your sewing box just the way I found it, okay?"

Mrs. Hendley was so astonished she allowed herself to be maneuvered into a chair. Her stick was taken away and set by the door, out of her reach. As Vivien clumsily tidied the sewing box, she tried to hide the fact that she was shaking. "Thank you for these," she said once she'd finished, holding up the needle and spool of ivory thread. "I'll return them as soon as I've finished."

Mrs. Hendley's face was mottled red with anger. "You'll be sorry," she hissed. "You're filth, that's what you are. Filth!"

"Come on," Marian urged. "Let her alone and get out of here."

Vivien followed her out. As soon as Marian had shut the door, she grabbed her arm, practically dragging her into the front room. "What the hell are you playing at? You don't realize the risk you took. I warned you. Now look what you've done."

Vivien shook herself free. "I'm sorry, but I refuse to be talked to that way by a miserable old woman. I know she's your husband's mother, but she's—"

"Nuts. That's what she is," Marian shrieked. She dragged her hand through her hair. "Nuts from being shut away in this godforsaken loony bin of a house, cut off from normal people, and that's the way I'm going, too."

"Marian, I'm sorry. I didn't mean to cause you more problems. It was just that—"

"You said you wanted to borrow a book, not rummage in her things. You should get out of here, Miss Vivien Shaw. Get out of here now and forget you ever saw Peverill and its inmates. Get out before it's too late."

Vivien stared at her. "What do you mean?"

The squeak of hinges from the back door startled both of them. "Hello," Paul shouted. "What's going on?" He walked down the hallway. "I could hear you yelling from outside, Marian."

Marian took a couple of deep breaths. "It's your mother again, having one of her fits."

Paul sighed. "What about this time?"

"It was my fault—" Vivien started to explain, but Marian's hand gripped her upper arm so tightly that it shut her up.

"It was nothing," Marian said. "I'd gone in to get some thread for Miss Shaw, and your mother caught me in there."

"You should be more careful." Paul looked from one to the other of them, then turned away. "The roof's coming off the chicken house. I'll need your help."

"Coming," Marian said. She narrowed her eyes at Vivien. "Don't you forget what I just said," she hissed before following Paul out the back door.

Vivien slowly made her way upstairs, her breathing shallow and fast. She paused at the top, drawing in a deep breath to calm herself. Damn Celeste and her family! For a moment there she'd thought the old woman was going to slash at her with her cane.

She was starting to think that Celeste's family had put some sort of hex on the house and all its occupants. "I can't say I'd blame them," she said in an undertone, opening the door to her room.

She was so agitated that she didn't trust her own eyes when they told her no one was in the room. She went to the small wardrobe and opened it, feeling around the back and sides to make sure old man Hendley wasn't hiding inside.

Was it her imagination, or had Marian hinted that someone had been snooping in here? She wasn't sure. *Oh God,* she thought, *I really am starting to get like my father.* What she was perfectly sure of was that Marian had warned her to leave. "Get out before it's too late," she'd said. What did she mean? If not for Celeste's family, Vivien wouldn't have needed a second warning. She'd be out of here like a shot, happy to call David or Joseph to come and get her. But she'd given her word she would try to find Lillian's hiding places. On the other hand, she wasn't sure she could face the thought of spending another night here.

By sundown, the skies were almost black and the wind had picked up, swirling above an angry sea. When the invisible sun had set, the coastline was pummeled by heavier rain bouncing off cars and houses like a hail of bullets.

Wesley was due to return to Toronto the next morning. Now it looked as if he wouldn't be able to go. Besides, how could he possibly leave, with Vivien still at Peverill? Perhaps this storm would persuade her to give up her senseless quest and leave the house.

The thought energized him. If she didn't call him or Celeste very soon, he'd give her a call and suggest he or David or Joseph come and get her before the storm worsened. Looking outside, he saw it was more than just an excuse. The sky should have been bright with stars tonight, but it was mired in black, rolling clouds, and the thunderclaps—followed by jagged flashes of lightning—were so loud they seemed to shake the building. It looked damned dangerous out there, and the forecast was even worse. As if to confirm his suspicions, the telephone rang. It was the caretaker to say that they were putting up the steel shutters right away, and that the emergency generator was primed and ready to go in case it was needed.

Thank heaven Sarah had decided to cancel her lecture and stay home tonight. He was about to warn her that the storm shutters were going up when the telephone rang again.

"Mr. Marshall?" A man's voice, vaguely familiar.

"Yes. Wesley Marshall here." He clicked into professional mode immediately.

"This is Matthew Carlton. You may recall that we met at my daughter's exhibition in Toronto."

"Jesus Lord," Wesley whispered to himself, the blood

draining from his face. "Yes, Mr. Carlton, what can I do for you?" he asked. "You'll have to speak up. We have a bad storm blowing up here."

"You can tell me where my daughter is staying. My wife called her this morning and she said she was with people, but she'd call her back. That's the last thing we heard from her. I—we are worried about her. My wife said she didn't sound at all like herself when she spoke to her. Please tell me where she is, Mr. Marshall, so I can call her."

Wesley sat there, his heart pounding so hard he felt he was about to go into cardiac arrest. He heard footsteps. "Who is it?" Sarah whispered from the study door.

"Mr. Marshall?" Matthew was saying in Wesley's ear, raising his voice.

"One moment, Mr. Carlton." He heard Sarah's sharp intake of breath when he spoke the name. "My apologies. My wife has just come into the room. Excuse me." Placing his hand over the mouthpiece of the phone, he swiveled around in his desk chair to face Sarah.

"Matthew Carlton?" she mouthed at him.

He nodded. "He wants to know where Vivien is staying."

"Oh, Lord!"

"If I only knew how much he knows, but I don't. Obviously Vivien hasn't a clue about her background, but that might only mean that he kept it from her, which would be understandable, wouldn't it? If he doesn't know, telling him she's at Peverill would mean nothing to him. However, if he does—"

Sarah's eyes darted fire at him. "I told you, Wesley Marshall. I warned you not to open this Pandora's box."

Wesley could hear Matthew shouting down the line. "What shall I tell him?" he appealed to Sarah.

"Tell him the truth," she said, her tone flat. "It's time someone did. You know how I detest secrets, particularly in families."

He stared at her, his eyes not fully registering her face in the shadowy light. Although the windows were tightly closed, he could hear in the lull between thunderclaps the sound of clinking tackle as the wind lashed the yachts anchored in the harbor below them. There was likely to be some damage there tonight.

He drew in a deep breath, releasing it slowly, and then took his hand from the mouthpiece. "Sorry about that, Mr. Carlton. My wife was relaying a message to me. You were asking about Vivien. She has moved into a private house that does bed and breakfast."

"I know that already. Is there a name for this place?"

"Yes." Wesley screwed up his face as if he were in pain. "It is called Peverill. Peverill Hall."

Silence for the space of one heartbeat, then, "Oh, God! Oh, my God!" It sounded more like an extended groan than words.

A loud crash sounded in Wesley's ear and then . . . nothing. He turned to Sarah.

"What did he say?"

"He knows, Sarah. The poor man knows."

Hearing Matthew's cry, Ellen rushed into the living room and found him doubled up in the chair. The cordless phone was on the floor where he'd evidently dropped it, its battery case loose.

She dropped to her knees beside him, trying to see his face. "What is it, Matt? Is it your heart? Tell me!"

"She's there! She's at Peverill." He rocked back and forth, his arms folded tightly across his stomach. "She's at Peverill."

"Who is?"

"Who do you think, you stupid woman?" he shouted. "Vivien, of course. Vivien's at Peverill."

Ellen clamped a hand to her mouth and sank back. "Oh, no. How could she be there? She doesn't know anything about the place."

He leaned over and grabbed her wrists. "Don't you

see? He must have found out who she was and lured her there." His dark eyes blazed into hers. He was breathing so fast she was terrified he was going to have a heart attack.

She tried to put her arm around him, but he shook her off. "How did you find this out?"

"I called Marshall. Said we couldn't get through to her. Asked him where she was staying. He told me."

"Now, you must try to calm down, Matthew." Ellen spoke slowly, as if to a child. "Tell me what Mr. Marshall said. Did you tell him anything about . . . you know?"

"Of course not. What good would that do?" He gripped her wrists so tightly it felt as if he were cutting off her circulation. "Don't you understand? As soon as *he* finds out that she's Vivien Carlton, he'll realize she's my daughter."

"But why should he want to harm Vivien? She knows nothing whatsoever about . . . the past."

"That's the trouble, Ellen. You were right. I should have told her, like you said, then she never would have gone to Barbados. Or certainly never to Peverill. Oh, God, I should have warned her." He started to gag.

"I'll fetch a bowl." Ellen jumped up.

"I don't need a bowl," Matthew said, still gagging. "Get me some tissues." Ellen grabbed the box from the table and gave him a handful of tissues. He held the wad to his mouth and lay back in the chair, his face ashen. "Oh, God," he groaned.

"I'll get you some water." Ellen ran to the kitchen, poured water from the bottle into a glass, and brought it back for him. He took a small sip from the glass and handed it back to her.

"I'm sorry I yelled at you," he whispered. "I'm so afraid for her. My beautiful girl. She doesn't deserve this." He grabbed her hands again. "I can't lose her as well."

"You're not going to lose her." Ellen's knees were shaking so hard that she sank down on the footstool beside him. "Tell me what you told Mr. Marshall."

He dropped her hands. "To hell with Marshall. Vivien's in danger. I have to go to Barbados."

Ellen was bewildered. "You'll never get a flight tonight."

"I can damn well try. There's bound to be an overnight charter. I'll tell them it's a medical emergency."

"Why don't we call Vivien?"

"We tried that already and couldn't get through, remember?"

"Then we'll call Mr. Marshall again and ask him to send the police there. You should have thought of that when you were speaking to him."

"Don't you understand? Marshall said there was a bad storm blowing up. The phone lines probably won't work in the storm. I know what those storms are like." He buried his head in his hands. "Lord, do I know," he groaned, his voice muffled. "There was a hurricane the night my mother was murdered."

CHAPTER
TWENTY-SIX

A few minutes after seven o'clock, the lights flickered . . . and then went out, plunging Peverill into absolute darkness. For a moment Vivien panicked, then she calmed down. Thanks to Marian's warning earlier, she'd already put the flashlight and two long-life candles in her backpack, where they would be easily accessible.

She felt her way to the other side of the room and was relieved to find both flashlight and candles still where she'd put them. She was about to strike a match when a particularly loud crash of thunder shook the house. It was followed by a blinding lightning flash that illuminated the entire room before it went dark again. But it was no longer entirely dark. A crackling sound and a flickering light came from outside. She hurriedly drew up the window blind and saw that one of the massive mahogany trees had been hit and was on fire, the flames leaping up, sending sparks into the air. The rain had abated a short time ago, but the strength of the wind had increased. If the fire wasn't checked, it could spread, perhaps even to the house itself.

Vivien stared out the window, mesmerized by the orange brightness of the fire against the black sky. She could hear voices shouting: first Paul and then the deeper voice of his father, yelling to Marian to "get the bloody water hose from the shed." And then she saw the three of them, bent against the power of the wind, the men dragging a metal ladder to the tree next to the one that was on fire, Marian uncoiling the hose.

Vivien switched on the flashlight, not sure what to do first. Should she rush down to offer her help? Or should she grab her backpack and stuff her precious cameras and computer and her daybook into it, and get out of the house right now, in case it, too, caught fire? The latter would take only a few minutes, so she decided to do it first.

The only thing she couldn't find was her cell phone. She tried looking for it, but it didn't seem to be in the room. Determined not to be trapped in the house because of a phone that was probably at the bottom of her bag anyway, she continued packing the essentials. When she'd finished, she put the backpack beside the door, ready to be grabbed if necessary, and then she went back to the window to check outside.

The Hendleys were working as a team, Paul up the ladder directing the powerful spray of water on the fire, his father holding the weight of the heavy hose, and Marian working at the water source. They seemed to be getting the fire under control, with the help of the rain, which was heavier again. Vivien went to her door and peered out, wondering where Mrs. Hendley was. A candle flickered below on the hall table. In its wavering light, she suddenly saw that the elder Hendleys' bedroom door stood open. Her heart started to race. This might be her one opportunity to get into the bedroom. But what if Mrs. Hendley were in there?

Vivien tiptoed across the landing to peer over the banister. The commotion of shouting against the roar of the wind was still coming from outside. Inside, the house was mute. As quietly as possible, Vivien made her way to the open bedroom door. "Are you okay, Mrs. Hendley?" she asked in a low voice. If the woman was in there, Vivien would say she was just checking on her. But there was no answer. Indeed, in contrast with the noise outside, the house seemed very still, as if it—like Vivien—were holding its breath.

She was about to switch her flashlight onto low beam when the silence was broken by the jarring sound of the phone ringing downstairs, making her heart leap in her chest. She paused, hardly daring to breathe, waiting to hear if it would be answered, but it wasn't. It rang several times and then stopped, leaving the house as silent as it had been before.

Strange, she thought, the telephone was usually plugged in upstairs. Probably Mrs. Hendley had taken it down with her, but why hadn't she answered it? Vivien remained frozen in the doorway, waiting, waiting for someone to come in the back door or move around down below, but all she could hear was the pounding of her own pulse and the wind howling. Vivien's heightened senses likened it to the sound of lamentation echoing down the years.

Enough imagination, she told herself. If she was going to do this, it was now or never. She switched on the low beam, keeping it down on the floor, and entered the room. Apart from the beam of light from the flashlight, the room was very dark. Its large window overlooked the front of the house, but it was tightly shuttered and the blind was closed so that the glare from the burning tree did not illuminate it. In addition, some kind of heavy drapery covered the window, shutting out the world, so that no one could look into or out from the bedroom.

Despite the sweltering heat, Vivien shivered. It was hard not to think about what had happened in this room. If it had not been so dark, she knew that, despite the span of intervening years, her eyes would have intuitively sought evidence of bloodstains on the walls or the floor.

Get on with it! she admonished herself. She lifted the beam of light to check the Hendleys' bed. It was large, with a dark mahogany headboard and turned mahogany posts at the foot. Vivien tiptoed across the floor, but when she pushed the bed gently she found it wouldn't budge. Not only was it heavy, there were no casters.

"Idiot!" she muttered under her breath. How could she have forgotten that she was still incapable of pushing heavy objects? She was about to get the hell out of the room when a noise made her freeze. It was the same *thump, thump* that she'd heard this afternoon heralding Mrs. Hendley. Moreover, the noise was nearby, out in the upstairs hallway.

Determined to avoid another confrontation, Vivien didn't even stop to think. In one awkward but swift movement, she knelt, turned over, tucked her knees in, and rolled under the bed. Thank heavens there was just enough space between floor and bedsprings to accommodate her. Her heart was beating so hard she was sure Mrs. Hendley would hear it, but she kept her breathing shallow and tried to remain as still as possible.

"Is someone in here?" Mrs. Hendley called out in her sharp voice. The beam from a high-powered flashlight swept across the room. In an agony of tension, Vivien held herself rigid. She was relying on the probability that Mrs. Hendley couldn't bend or kneel to peer beneath the bed.

Please, dear God, let her leave, so I can slip out, she prayed, but the woman seemed to be standing there like a stone statue. By stretching her neck just a little, Vivien could see the hem of her long black skirt and the clumpy, black lace-up shoes beneath it, and she could hear the old woman's heavy breathing, with an occasional wheeze mixed in.

It was dusty under the bed, and there was a smell of mold from the mattress. As Vivien breathed it in she, too, felt like wheezing. She tried to hold her breath but couldn't sustain it. The dust gathered in her chest, in her throat, in her nose. She instinctively put up a hand to pinch her nostrils to stop the coming sneeze and, to her horror, the flashlight fell from her grasp onto the floor. The noise seemed magnified a thousandfold in her ears.

"So you are there! I thought so."

Vivien waited for Mrs. Hendley to say more. She was poised to roll out and even tackle her if she had to, so she could get out of this accursed house. But, to her surprise, she heard Mrs. Hendley's cane thumping back to the door. Vivien held her breath, unable to believe her good fortune. Obviously, the old woman didn't want to deal with her by herself. She was going for help. That would give Vivien the chance she needed to dash out of the house. Her hands might be damaged, but her legs, thank God, were not. Despite the storm, she would run down that driveway like she'd never run before.

"Marcus!"

The shout reverberated through the house.

"Come here, boy."

The skitter of nailed paws on the wood stairs, heavy panting.

"That's my boy. You go get her, Marcus. There, under the bed."

The dog flattened himself so that he and Vivien were on the same level. She could smell him, hear his panting breath, and then he started barking, sharp, loud barks that filled her ears. Oh, God, was this to be her fate, to be torn apart by the Hendleys' Doberman?

She heard the woman chuckle. To Vivien, it sounded like a witch's cackle. "Good dog, Marcus. You stay there and keep Miss Carlton company," Mrs. Hendley told the dog. "Stay, Marcus."

As she thumped slowly away, the dog stayed, lying flat less than a foot away from Vivien's head, his rank breath hot on her face. She lay still, barely breathing, terrified to move, knowing that if she came out from under the bed, those bared, sharp teeth would fasten on some part of her body. As she lay there, she became aware also of a board that was sticking into her spine, as if her weight had shifted it a little. And she wondered, as the hot tears stole down her cheeks, if there was indeed a loose board beneath the bed as Verna had thought. How ironic that would be.

She could hear Mrs. Hendley's voice screeching from one of the windows. Marcus pricked up his ears at the sound, but when Vivien moved her hand, his ears flattened and a growl issued from his throat. She was trapped, and there was absolutely nothing she could do about it.

But as she lay there, her courage returned. What could they do to her? Turn her over to the police on suspicion of stealing? At this moment, she'd welcome being arrested. She thought about her defense. *I didn't touch anything. All I was doing was checking on Mrs. Hendley to make sure she was safe. I was worried in case the fire spread to the house and she'd be trapped.*

Any further conjecture was cut short when she heard voices and footsteps, saw a beam of light, followed by Thomas Hendley's peremptory "Come out!"

Vivien started to move, but Marcus growled and inched forward, his muzzle almost touching her.

"Heel, Marcus!" The dog backed away and stood up, going to his master.

Grabbing the flashlight, Vivien rolled out from beneath the bed. She had to lean on her elbow to lever herself up onto her feet. Feeling extremely vulnerable, she faced the Hendleys . . . to find herself staring at a shotgun pointing directly at her.

"That's hardly necessary, considering I was wanting to see if I could help—"

"Shut your mouth. We know exactly what you're doing, Vivien Carlton, and why you're here." He sounded more English than ever, with his old-fashioned public school accent. "What we don't understand is how you could be so stupid as to come here on your own, without any kind of protection. Or were you expecting us to welcome you as a long-lost member of the family?"

His wife thought that was funny, but he didn't join in her laughter, his expression remaining as stony as always.

"I've no idea what you mean, but I do have plenty of friends in Barbados, so I think you should put the gun away . . ."

This time he did smile. "And let you walk away, is that right?"

"Why not? I haven't done anything. And if you think I have, then call the police."

"Ah, poor Miss Carlton, you chose a bad night if you thought you might have police protection, didn't you? Electricity down, traffic accidents, fires, robberies . . ." Still smiling that wolf smile, he shook his head. "Alas, the police will not be coming to this remote part of the island tonight. I always said my cousin was stupid. It seems his genes have been passed on."

Vivien hadn't a clue what he was talking about. And why was he calling her Miss *Carlton?* "Look, Mr. Hendley, I know you don't like strangers coming here, so just put away your gun, let me get my stuff, and I'll be out of here in a few minutes."

"No, I don't think so. You'd just be back again with a barrage of lawyers. What I would like to know is how the hell you found out about the oil."

"What oil?"

"Oh, please don't play the innocent with me. It's making me very impatient." He turned to his wife. "Why don't you go rest and let me deal with this?"

"Oh, no. I'm enjoying it too much. Besides, I don't trust her. You know how wily her kind can be."

What was it with this woman talking of *her kind?* What kind was that? Did she mean Canadian?

"Don't you worry. She's not going to get away."

Mrs. Hendley settled into the cane chair near the window, propping her stick against the wall. "Want me to fetch Paul?"

"No, he and Marian are making sure the fire's out."

Vivien's heart lifted. Paul and Marian. They'd rescue her from this couple of maniacs. That was, if they came into the house in time.

"What are you planning to do with me?" she asked.

"Kill you."

He really was insane. Vivien wanted to run but knew that Marcus would catch her, if she wasn't shot first.

"Then we'll bury you somewhere on the property, away from where they'll be drilling, of course. It might be a little embarrassing if the oil company were to dig up a corpse on our property next year."

Vivien forced herself to smile. "You have quite a sense of humor, Mr. Hendley. But tell me, what's all this talk about oil? Have they really found oil on Peverill land?"

"Stop wasting my time. You wouldn't be here if you didn't know that."

Vivien was about to reply when she heard footsteps coming up the stairs. "Everything okay?" It was Paul. Unable to contain her relief, Vivien called out, "Paul! Help me." Before she saw it coming, she felt the butt of the shotgun crash into her breast and she doubled up in agony. Clutching herself, she screamed to Paul again. "Help me, Paul."

When she was able to straighten up, she saw him standing solid in the doorway. She also saw the handgun in his hand. "Please help me," she appealed to him. "Your father's gone insane."

"Sorry." Paul actually looked sorry, but she saw now that his gun was pointing directly at her.

"Why?" she whispered. "I don't understand."

"Let's not play games. We gave you plenty of chances to leave." Paul shook his head sadly. "But you stupidly came back after the so-called accident and insisted on staying on here."

So-called. "So you did cut the window cords," she said, turning to Thomas.

"No, actually, I did not." He parted his lips in a saturnine smile. "Paul did. I told him it wouldn't be enough to get rid of you, but he didn't want to kill you."

"My father was right," Paul said. "You just wouldn't go away. Let's get this over with." He motioned to her with the gun to come to the door, but Vivien didn't budge.

"If you're going to kill me, I think I should at least know why, don't you? Whatever happened to the English sense of fair play?" She was not only stalling for time. She genuinely wanted to make some sense of this incomprehensible nightmare situation.

"I'll tell you why," Paul said, angrier than she'd ever seen him. "This fucking place has been grinding us all down for years. We owe money everywhere, and our credit's run dry. Then last year they found oil nearby. You probably saw the rigs. They're conspicuous enough. We put the last bit of money we had into engaging surveyors and cleared some land, and what do you know? They found oil on Peverill land, too." His smile resembled his father's. "In a short while, Peverill Hall, as we know it, will be no more, and we will be rich."

So that was what the clearing she'd found was for. They were going to drill for oil. "I see. But what have I got to do with this?"

"Give it a break, Vivien, and admit you've lost." Paul shrugged. "Okay, if we have to spell it out. You and cousin Trevor somehow found out about the oil, but being his father's son, he sent his daughter down to spy on us and confirm it. Before long, there'd be lawyers taking over, telling us that Peverill is his, not ours, and we could lose everything. Everything." He stepped forward and grabbed Vivien's arm with his left hand, jabbing the gun hard into her side. "Do you realize how many bloody years Marian and I have put into this place, with no reward? How many fucking years we've worked our butts off? My wife's so exhausted she's near a breakdown because of this place. If I kill you, it's as much for her as for anyone."

Vivien knew she had nothing to lose. "Please," she begged, looking from Paul to his father. "I don't even know who Trevor is. You've mixed me up with the wrong person."

"Matthew," Paul Hendley said. "Your father, Matthew. His first name was Trevor." He stared at her and then at Thomas, his blue eyes filled with surprise. "I do believe she's been telling the truth and that her father never told her."

Vivien felt as if her entire mind had gone to mush. "My father is Matthew Carlton. His family came from England. He's never lived in Barbados." She knew she was pleading for her life now. "He didn't even want me to come—" Her hand flew to her mouth as she remembered her father's extreme reaction to her news that she was coming here.

"Oh, yes, he has lived here," Thomas replied. "He lived here for the first seven years of his life, until his father—my cousin, Robert—murdered his wife, Matthew's mother. Before Robert was hanged, I sent young Trevor—sorry, Matthew—to England and he was adopted by my sister and her husband, Joan and Edward Carlton. They lived in—"

"Kent," Vivien whispered. "My father's parents lived in Kent. But now you say they weren't his parents at all."

"His real parents were my cousin, Robert Hendley, and his wife, Lillian. My stupid cousin actually married the woman when he didn't need to."

Paul was watching Vivien's face closely. "You really didn't know, did you?" he said. "But now that we've told you, we definitely can't let you go."

"Of course she knew. She's been in cahoots with Wes-

ley Marshall since the start of this farrago. All this nonsense about bringing her in for a book project!" Thomas
scoffed. "Just an excuse to get her here and into
Peverill."

Vivien felt as if she were wading through quicksand.
"Wesley didn't want me to come and stay here. He was
afraid for me. Now I know why."

"You should have listened to your good friend Wesley." Thomas gave a harsh laugh. "Of course, you knew
that you were related to him as well?"

"Wesley?" she repeated incredulously.

"She didn't know," cackled his wife from her chair by
the window. "She's so stupid she didn't know. Wesley
Marshall was that woman's nephew," she told Vivien.

"Which woman?" Vivien asked, totally bewildered.

"She really doesn't know, does she?" Mrs. Hendley
said, enjoying the joke even more. "Lillian, of course.
Lillian, your half-breed grandmother. Haven't you ever
looked in the mirror and seen yourself? Your skin may
be white, but that hair gives you away. You really are
stupid, aren't you?"

Now, too late, it was all falling into place. "You are
all wrong, you know," Vivien told them, painfully aware
of Paul's gun biting into her side. "I don't think my
father knew anything about this. He was too young to
remember."

"He knew, all right. He knew that his father had murdered his mother and that he was later hanged for it."

Vivien was so close to Paul she heard the hiss of in-
taken breath. "Enough!" he said. "Let's get this over."

Her father knew about his mother's death, his father's
execution. But what else did he know? Had Thomas
bundled him off to England, hidden him away with the
Carltons, solely to gain the Peverill estate for himself,
or was there another, more sinister reason for hiding the
grieving boy away?

"Get her out of here," Thomas told his son. "We
don't want to do anything in the house."

Her eyes darted fire at him. "No, that might be too much of a coincidence, right? To kill Lillian's granddaughter in the same room as Lillian was killed. Perhaps the police might put two and two together and come up with the right answer this time." She swung around on Paul. "Your father's a murderer. Now he's making you one as well, to cover up what he did fifty years ago. Don't be a fool, Paul. You don't have to copy him."

"If you don't shut your mouth, I'll kill you right here."

"And then there'll be more blood to add to Lillian Hendley's, right? And what then? My father will come here to find out what happened to me. Will you kill him, too?"

"Your father's a weakling, a coward," Thomas said. "My sister used to write and tell me how he had nightmares every night, waking up screaming for his mother and father, wetting the bed."

"And did you tell your sister the truth?" She knew immediately from Thomas's expression that his sister had been told only that Matthew's father had killed his mother. Her heart ached for her father. No wonder he'd found it impossible to face life. The son of a brutally murdered mother and a father who had been executed for the crime, cut off from the family and the land that had been his since birth.

Thomas ignored her question. "I notice Matthew sends his daughter to do his dirty work. I don't see him here, coming to your rescue, do you? He always was a feeble excuse for a boy. That's what mixing blood does."

Vivien had never hated anyone as much as she hated Thomas Hendley. Perhaps the Hendley blood was rising in her now, because, if she'd had the means, she would happily have killed Thomas right then and there.

Don't panic, she told herself. *Keep cool.* "What about Marian, Paul?" She was fighting for her life, clutching at anything to stall them. "What will she think of you committing murder for your father?"

"I'm not doing it for him. I'm doing it for us. For Marian and me."

"Where is she?"

Paul didn't answer her.

"Where is Marian, Paul?"

"She's not coming to your rescue, that's for sure."

"You mean she might have, right? Because she doesn't want you to do this?"

"You're asking for it." He dug the gun even farther into her side, and she imagined for a horrible moment his finger squeezing on the trigger, blowing a gaping hole in her. "Well, she won't be rescuing you," Paul said. "I can promise you that. She's safely locked in the tractor shed."

For one swift moment Vivien felt a leap of gratitude that Marian had not been part of this, at least not when it came to killing her. But it also meant that one of her last sources of hope was gone. The storm still raged outside. She was totally cut off, with no one to help. Like her grandmother before her, she was going to her death.

And, like Lillian, she suddenly realized, the reason for her oncoming death was Peverill Hall. She was never going to discover if there had been some peripheral reason for Thomas killing Lillian, but she was convinced that his main reason had been to gain Peverill for himself by pinning the murder on his cousin, Robert. It was a wonder that he'd left Matthew alive. *Oh, Dad, if only you had told me, together we might have been able to bring this man down and regain Peverill for ourselves.* But she knew that, in a way, Thomas was right: her father would never return to Peverill or Barbados.

And there, of course, went her last source of hope. Her father had never been there for her when she needed him. Any other father would have swallowed his pride and told her why he didn't want her to go to Barbados, but her father was too much of a coward to tell her the truth.

"Enough!" Paul's gun jabbed harder in Vivien's side. "Let's go. You and I are going to take a walk."

"You've seen too many gangster films, Paul," she said with a shaky laugh. She was desperate to retain the tenuous sense of camaraderie they'd had. When it came to the crunch, she still wasn't convinced that Paul was capable of killing another human being.

"Need help?" Thomas asked him.

"Later," Paul replied.

Later, when they dug her grave. Was this her fate, to be buried on the estate whose beauty had lured her to her death?

"Take Marcus with you, just in case."

"Good idea. Here, boy," Paul called, whistling the dog to his side. Marcus stood beside him, growling at Vivien. Any hope she might have had of getting the better of Paul physically was now gone.

Paul took her arm and shoved her ahead of him, out of the room and across the hall, his parents watching them from the doorway of their room. As Vivien set her foot on the top step, the telephone rang.

Paul turned back to his parents. "Why's the phone downstairs?"

"Your mother must have left it there. Doesn't matter," Thomas said. "Don't answer it. You never know who it might be."

It could be someone for me, Vivien thought with a rush of hope. Someone who couldn't get through on her cell phone. Wherever it was.

The telephone kept ringing: six, seven, eight, nine, ten rings . . . and then it stopped, as it had earlier.

"Keep going," Paul said. Vivien started down the stairs. "Can't you go any faster than that?"

"I don't want to fall," she said in a small voice, thinking how ludicrous she must appear, afraid of falling when she was about to be shot. She continued on, sliding her hand down the banister rail but not gripping it.

She had just reached the hall floor when, suddenly, the place was flooded with light. At first she thought the electricity had come back on again, but then she realized that the light was coming from outside, a beam from a searchlight, and she and Paul were standing there, blinking, in that pool of light.

Paul jabbed the gun into her side again. "Get over there, out of the light," he ordered her urgently, jerking his head to the far corner of the hall, but it was too late. They'd been seen.

"Police!" A voice came booming over a megaphone. "We want you to come out, one at a time, with your hands on your head."

"Go to the back door," Paul told her, shoving her ahead of him. She could smell his sweat; like a frenzied animal, he was sweating profusely.

The beam of light caught them again.

The augmented voice reverberated around the house. "We have police surrounding the house. Put down your weapons and come out the front door, hands on your head. We don't want anyone to be hurt."

Paul stopped moving. His gaze swiveled from the back to the front of the house, trying to assess his chances of escape. Vivien heard a creak on the stairs. She looked up and saw Thomas Hendley creeping down.

"Use her as a shield," he hissed at his son. "Go out the back with her in front of you. The van's there. Here's my keys. Tell them you'll shoot her if they don't let you through."

Paul stared at his father as if he hadn't understood one word.

"Give me the gun," his father ordered him. "You take the shotgun. We'll blast—"

"It's over," Paul shouted at him. "Don't you see? It's

over." Vivien felt the gun slide down her side, and then Paul pushed her away. "Go on, get out." He shoved her again. "Get out before I change my mind." A sound like a sob came from deep in his throat.

Vivien ran, skittering across the polished floor. She knew instinctively what would happen. As she ran from them, she could sense Thomas raising the shotgun and already imagined the impact exploding in her body. A crash came from somewhere in front of her. Glass breaking. "Get down!" someone yelled. As she flung herself on the floor she heard the whine of the bullet and a loud grunt from behind her.

She didn't stop to see what had happened. Scrambling to her feet, she scuttled to the front door, screaming to them to open it for her. Then, with a great *whoosh,* the door flew open and she was outside on the verandah, wind tearing at her, rain instantly soaking her. Someone grabbed her. She froze in fear and then saw the police uniform: white shirt, navy pants with a red stripe.

"Who are you?" he yelled at her, trying to be heard above the wind.

"Vivien Shaw," she yelled back. "Vivien Carlton."

"Who's still in there?"

"The Hendleys. Thomas and Paul are armed, shotgun and handgun. Mrs. Hendley's upstairs."

"I think we got the man with the shotgun." He pushed her away from him. "Take care of her," he yelled to another policeman at the foot of the steps. Two policemen in helmets bearing plastic shields rushed by her and entered the house. She heard a woman's shrill scream and then felt herself being lifted bodily from the verandah and carried past two police cars to the car parked behind them.

She was set on her feet and a blanket wrapped around her. She peered at her rescuer's face through the deluge of rainwater. "David?"

"Get in the car before we both drown."

Yes, it was definitely David. Tears of relief poured down her cheeks, mingling with the rain.

"Get in!" he shouted, shoving her into the passenger seat of his SUV, and then slamming the door. He sprinted around to the other side and flung himself in, shutting out the rain and the wind, which buffeted against the Jeep, rocking it.

Then she was in his arms, squeezed so tightly against his body that she thought her ribs would crack, but she didn't care. He was pressing kisses all over her wet face. "Jesus Lord," he said between kisses. "I thought I'd lost you."

She was trembling violently, more from relief than cold. "He was going to kill me, David," she said, in a pause between his breathless kisses. "He was going to kill me."

He stopped kissing her and gazed into her eyes, breathing hard. "Bastard! Was it the old Hendley or the young one?"

"Both. Thomas had a shotgun. Paul had a handgun. They were going to kill me and bury me on the estate."

He stroked her wet hair back from her face. "Forget them. You're safe now. No one's going to hurt you anymore."

It was true. It was really true. She was safe now. She turned and buried her face into his chest, feeling his heart beating fast beneath her cheek. Then she lifted her face up, and he held it between his warm hands, bending his head to kiss her. Her eyes fluttered shut as she felt his mouth sweet and warm on hers. As one hand slipped beneath the blanket, her lips parted to meet his and—

They sprang apart as someone rapped on the window. David rolled it down an inch.

"Dr. Moreton, sorry to bother you, but—"

"Get in the back, Peter, or we'll all be drenched."

The policeman jumped in and slammed the door. "Lord, what a night. Sorry, I am drippin' all over your car seat."

"No problem, so are we," David said. "What's happened?"

"My name is Sergeant Peter Bond," the policeman told Vivien. "I need to ask you a few questions, Miss . . . is it Shaw or Carlton?"

"It's both. I was born Carlton but use Shaw professionally."

"So we should use Carlton for official purposes?"

"I suppose so." The name seemed somehow tainted for her now.

"Forget questions and taking notes," David said, waving an impatient hand. "Tell us what's happened in there."

"I am not sure I should—"

"They were going to kill her. She deserves to know what's going on."

The policeman leaned forward. "You are right." He hesitated. "The old man, Thomas Hendley, is dead. Shot through the heart by one of our men." He sounded proud. "The old man was going to shoot you in the back."

"I know." Vivien released a long sigh. She hated the thought of anyone being killed, but this man had been evil, she was convinced of it, even though they might never be able to prove everything. "What about Paul?"

"Arrested on weapons charges. But that's where we need your statement, to determine what else he should be charged with."

Vivien nodded. "Mrs. Hendley?"

"The old woman?"

"Yes."

"They will be takin' her to the hospital, if they can get through. Appears she had some sort of heart attack when she heard her husband was dead."

Vivien wondered if the old woman would survive without Thomas. It seemed to have been a strange but loyal relationship. "Is Marian okay? Paul said he'd locked her in the tractor shed."

"Marian Hendley is one of the reasons we got here in time. She rang us from the shed to tell us what was happening."

"Rang you? How?"

The policeman chuckled. "She told us that her husband had ordered her to steal your cell phone when you were in the bathroom. She did, but she kept it in her pocket, so when he locked her in, she still had it."

David laughed. "Talk about 'hoist by his own petard.' "

Vivien was dumbstruck by the strangeness of fate. If she hadn't established a relationship with Marian, would she have taken her side against Paul and his family? *Thank you, Marian,* she thought to herself. There would be time to thank her properly later. Although, if Paul were facing serious charges, Marian might not be prepared to listen.

"Her call was the final one of several we received about you this evening," Peter said. "Dr. Moreton's, of course." He nodded at David. "But also your father."

"My *father?*" Vivien stared at him.

"Yes, Miss Carlton. When he rang you from Canada and could not get an answer, he rang Mr. Marshall, found out where you were, and realized you were probably in danger. I spoke to him myself on our special line. He is on his way here now."

"Mr. Marshall?"

"No, not Mr. Marshall. The roads are blocked with fallen trees down his way, so Mr. Marshall could not get through. No, your father and mother are on a plane to Barbados. Should arrive early tomorrow, if the storm's died down by then."

Vivien hardly heard a word of what he was saying.

All she could think of was that her father had been so worried about her that he had taken action to help her and was now facing what must be a traumatic return to Barbados—all for her.

"What's wrong?" David asked, seeing her turn away. She sniffed. "I need tissues."

"There is a box back here." Peter handed them to her and she dragged out several and blew her nose.

"I'll explain later," she told David, who was watching her anxiously.

"What we need to know is why the Hendleys wanted to kill you, Miss Carlton. That is the big mystery to all of us."

"It's all very complicated. There were a couple of reasons, I think, but I can't prove one of them. Anyway, the chief reason was that they aren't the rightful heirs to Peverill."

"Then who is?" David asked.

"My father and, I guess, after him, me."

"I don't understand," David said.

"I said it was complicated."

"Why would they be prepared to kill someone for this place? It's only worth the land it's on, and there's not much value in land for hotel development on the Atlantic side of the island, because there are few safe beaches."

"Oil," Vivien said.

"Ah!" said David and Peter in unison.

"Oil was discovered on the Peverill estate."

"Ergo, the land is very valuable," David said.

"Exactly."

"Well, that explains it," Peter said, although he still looked puzzled. "May I ask where you will be for the next twenty-four hours, Miss Carlton?"

Vivien hesitated.

"She will be with me," David said.

Peter frowned. "Is your house safe in this storm?"

"Yes, it's perfectly safe, if a little claustrophobic and noisy with the rain beating against the storm shutters."

"Can you make it back there?" Peter asked. "There are several roads flooded and trees down."

"I made it here all right, so we should be able to get back."

Vivien thought of the floorboard beneath the Hendleys' bed. "We do need to come back here in the morning. There might be important evidence of another crime."

"Oh?"

"Tomorrow," she told the policeman. "I'll explain everything tomorrow. Meanwhile, it might be best to put Marian Hendley into a hotel or something and lock up Peverill Hall until you've finished your investigation."

"Exactly what we had planned," Peter said officiously. "I will speak to you tomorrow, Miss Carlton. Good night, David." He leaned forward to shake hands, steam rising from his uniform, and got out of the Jeep.

She and David sank back into their seats, releasing a united sigh of relief. Vivien's neck was sore from having to turn her head for so long to speak to the policeman.

"Let's get out of here," David said, switching on the engine.

Vivien didn't even ask if he was sure it was safe to drive in this weather. She was content to put herself in his hands. Besides, she wanted to set some distance between her and Peverill. For tonight, at least.

David's driving was slow, from necessity. The SUV was rocked by the wind, but it held the road well. It was the poor visibility and the debris on the roads that slowed them down: not only tree branches and palm fronds but empty cans and rolling bottles, planks of wood and whole breadfruit and coconuts, plastic garbage bins lifted by the wind from somewhere else and dropped onto the deserted road. On a couple of occasions David had to stop the Jeep, get out, and drag heavy debris to the side of the road: an entire tree, roots and all, and a galvanized steel roof from someone's home or barn.

Above the noise of the storm, David told Vivien he had read Mrs. Simmons's file and asked her to explain to him what had happened back at Peverill Hall. Shakily, she recounted the terrifying, but illuminating events. "So, my father is actually the son of Robert Hendley, the rightful heir to Peverill. Lillian Hendley was my grandmother," she said sadly in conclusion.

They drove for a while in silence. As they passed Bathsheba, she could hear the angry ocean roaring with the wind, but David told her that the storm seemed to be abating, probably moving farther out into the Atlantic. "Could be gone by morning," he said as the car climbed the road to his house on the cliff.

When they entered the house and went upstairs to the living room, Vivien paused, looking around in the dim light provided by his backup generator, taking it all in again.

His arms went around her, drawing her close. She looked up at him. "Did you know," she said, "that Lillian was Wesley's aunt and Celeste Beaton's great-aunt? Her—that is Lillian's—father was white, but her mother was black . . . which makes me . . .?" She tilted her head, waiting.

His eyes widened, then he started to laugh and couldn't stop, tilting his head back, the laughter coming from deep down. "The joke's on me, right? I thought you were lily white, and yet it seems I got me a black woman, after all."

She joined in his laughter. "Well, one-eighth black."

"Here in Barbados, they call it being Bajan white."

"Bajan white," she repeated, liking the sound of it.

"You guessed all along, didn't you?" she said, delighting in challenging him. "You said I must have African blood because of my hair, remember?"

"No, I was joking. Cross my heart. You had me completely fooled."

"Fooled?" she said playfully. "I didn't know myself until tonight." Her laughter died away. "This is serious stuff, having to take on another side of me I've never known."

His eyes glowed. "I can help you."

Vivien's reply was to lift her head and kiss him. "Thank you," she whispered against his mouth, profoundly moved by this intimation of a more serious relationship between them.

The kiss deepened. "I think it's time we got these wet clothes off," David said with a shaky laugh. "We're both dripping on the floor." Reluctantly, Vivien drew away from him. "Can you make it upstairs? I'll find your pajama top."

He helped her up to the bedroom at the top of the narrow staircase. There they both stood, looking at each other, waiting . . . Then, as if they had been given some hidden signal, they both started stripping off their wet clothing.

"Help me take these bandages off, please," she begged.

He did so, bending to press a tender kiss on each bruised wrist when he'd finished. "I wish I'd been there to deal with the Hendleys."

"Shut up," she said softly.

"Turn around," he said. He unhooked her bra for her and she felt his hands slip around to caress her breasts. She tried not to flinch when his fingers touched the place where the butt of Thomas's gun had bruised her. With a low moan, she turned and pressed herself against him, sliding her hands down his flanks, dragging his briefs halfway down. He hurriedly completed undressing himself and her, and then they were both on the bed, their bodies slick and wet, sliding against each other. Tongues and hands and bodies, hot and moist.

There were few preliminaries; they were too desperate. But David did take the time to whisper that he would be careful of her hands and that, this time, she could be submissive. "To hell with that," she whispered against his mouth, her hands across his back, drawing him down as she opened herself to him. When they merged in the primal movements of love, she forgot everything that had happened, losing herself as they became one with the undulating ocean, pulsing in unison to its pounding rhythm.

CHAPTER
TWENTY-SEVEN

Vivien's father and mother arrived early the next morning. They were greeted at the airport by what could best be described as a family delegation, accompanied by two young musicians, who might or might not have been members of the family, playing joyful calypso on portable steel pans. Not only had Vivien and David come, but also Wesley and Sarah, Celeste and Joseph, Verna and her siblings and their children of all ages, and Ruth Fletcher, the regal matriarch in her red silk dress. And all of them wanted to embrace the long-lost son of their beloved Lillian.

Vivien could see that her parents were overwhelmed. Her father looked particularly bewildered by this outpouring of familial affection. "Poor Dad," she whispered to David. "He's not sure what's hit him."

David took charge. "Come along, Mr. and Mrs. Carlton. Let's get you to your hotel. They need some rest after their long journey," he explained to the crowd of relatives, who looked disappointed at this swift curtailment of their rejoicing. David grinned. "We'll all party later on," he told them. They shouted agreement to this, and people turned in the airport arrival hall to see what was going on.

Her mother and father were still looking stunned after David had driven them to the Ocean Sands. Vivien had to decline all the offers of accommodation for her parents from everyone, particularly Wesley and his wife, who had been hurt when she'd insisted that her mother and father be booked into the hotel. "They'll need space and privacy for a while, especially my father," she told Wesley firmly. "I have to rely on you and Sarah to help me with that. He's not going to adjust overnight. It's going to take time and patience on everyone's part."

Once they were in their hotel room, she answered a few of her father's questions, but she could see both her parents eyeing David, trying to work out if there was any relationship, other than that of professional partners, between them. Even that could wait a while, she decided.

The first thing she did tell them was that Thomas Hendley was dead. "Dead? How?" asked her father.

"He was shot by a police marksman last night."

"Why? I don't understand."

"It's not that important now. He was threatening me, that's all, and your phone call alerted the police." She squeezed his hand. "Thanks, Dad."

She knew that neither David nor Wesley would resent this oversimplification, designed to make her father the hero. Which, to her, he was.

"So he's dead at last." Matthew released a long, deep sigh as if a great weight had been lifted from him.

"Yes, Dad. What's more, we're pretty sure that it was Thomas, not your father, who killed your mother."

Tears welled in Ellen's eyes. "Oh, Matt." She put her arm around his shoulders.

He sat there, unable to take it all in, his hands hanging between his knees. "But there's no evidence, is there? They bundled me out of Barbados quickly, but I know that everyone thought my father had murdered my mother. Even I believed it after a while. I hated him," he suddenly said, his voice no longer lethargic.

"Your father?"

"No. Thomas. Cousin Thomas, they made me call him. I loathed him. He was cruel. I remember that. Sarcastic to me and vicious with all the servants. And when my father wasn't there, he spoke to my mother as if she were even less than a servant. But whenever my father was there, he treated her like a fine lady."

"I want you to know," Vivien said firmly, "that your father loved your mother to the very end, that he never stopped loving her. He protested his innocence and his love for Lillian to the day he died."

"How do you know that?" he asked in a quavering voice.

"Through the newspaper clippings we've already gathered, and there are many more. You'll also hear from Lillian's family that Robert loved Lillian. They've been trying to prove it for decades."

"They did that for him, for my father?"

"For him and for Lillian . . . and for you. I know it must seem strange to you, Dad, but they are your family. Your own flesh and blood. Lillian's legacy to you."

He seemed dazed. "It's all too much."

"I know, I know." She hugged him. "I'm sorry. I didn't mean to overload you. I just wanted to explain why they were all so excited to see you at the airport. You see, they've kept track of us all over the years. Even Wesley's offer to me to come to Barbados was made because of an encounter I had with Celeste's sister, Janice. She's a curator at the Royal Ontario Museum." Vivien laughed. "For all I know, she might have been responsible for getting me that first important exhibition way back when. I haven't checked on that one yet. The thing is, Dad, although we knew nothing about them, they knew a great deal about us, because we were Lillian's child and grandchild."

Her father looked up. "I want to go there."

"Where? Peverill?" Vivien was surprised.

"Yes."

"I thought—"

"It's time I faced up to the bad memories. If I go there, there might be some happy memories as well. I want to find out."

"We have to go there anyway," Vivien said. "There's something I have to do, and I wanted you to be there with me, but I wasn't sure you would want to come."

"I do."

By the afternoon, the sun was hot and bright in a brilliant cornflower-blue sky, and the entire island was clearing up after the storm.

When they drove down the driveway to Peverill Hall in David's Jeep, Vivien was surprised to see that most of the mess created by the storm had been cleared away. She suspected Wesley and David of a conspiracy to arrange this before her father arrived at Peverill. Not only had the debris of plants and branches from the storm been swept away from the driveway, but also the heavy growth of vegetation had been cut back and the verandah and its roof cleared. As they drew to a halt before the house, they saw two men on ladders repairing the shutters.

Vivien squeezed David's knee. "Thank you," she mouthed to him. He smiled back at her and nodded.

They remained seated in the Jeep, saying nothing, as Matthew gazed at his former home. "It's even more beautiful than I remember," he said at last. "But far more shabby, too," he added.

Vivien released her breath, relieved that his first sight of the house hadn't traumatized him. "It can easily be repaired."

"Repaired? Oh, Lord. I should imagine it would cost a fortune to repair it."

You might have a fortune, she wanted to say. Was it

too early to tell him? She glanced at David, and he answered her silent question with a nod.

"Dad, before we go inside, there's something else you should know."

"Oh, no. I don't think I can take any more," he said, with a shaky laugh. "Okay. What is it?"

"I believe that Thomas killed your mother and pinned it on your father mostly because he wanted the Peverill estate for himself. In recent years, though, it's been more a liability than an asset to him. Marian told me what a strain it's been for them all, trying to keep it going. But I found out that they've discovered another possible resource here, far richer than sugarcane."

"What?"

"Oil. Petroleum. You remember you asked David about the rigs we passed a few miles back? They think there's oil on Peverill land as well. If there is, once you've proved your right to Peverill, you could be a very wealthy man."

"Oh, my goodness," Ellen said, her hand going to her throat.

Matthew seemed to be digesting it slowly. "Would it mean having to destroy Peverill?" he asked, addressing David. "The house itself, I mean?"

"I don't think so. There's another plantation house that's successfully drilled for oil without tearing down the original building. Of course, it would mean losing the fields and much of the land."

"Were you thinking of moving into Peverill Hall, Matt?" Ellen asked him, eyeing the house a little nervously.

Matthew chuckled. "I don't think it's quite your style, dear, is it?"

Ellen shook her head. "Not really. It's hard to believe this was your home." Her remark left a feeling of awkwardness.

"Why don't we go inside and take a look?" David suggested, breaking the silence.

"Good idea," Vivien agreed. There was no point in putting it off any longer.

Wesley was there already. He came out on the steps with Sergeant Bond to greet them.

David introduced her father to Sergeant Bond. While they were talking, Vivien took the opportunity to draw Wesley aside. "I have a bone to pick with you."

Wesley looked suitably chastened. "I know, I know. I had ulterior motives for bringing you here to Barbados."

"I still can't make out what you intended to do. How were you planning to break the news to me that my father's father was hanged for murdering his wife?"

Wesley sighed. "That was what I kept telling the rest of the family, but they said they only wanted to see you, meet you, that there would be no reason to tell you that you were related to them. I thought it was a crazy idea from the start, but, as you know, they are an extremely determined group of women. Of course, none of us thought there was even the slightest chance of you being in any danger. Your finding Peverill changed everything. You may recall that I warned you not to stay here."

Vivien shook her head at him. "I still don't understand how you knew so much about us. I gather the family was keeping some sort of dossier on us."

"In a way, yes. I can explain," he said eagerly.

"Not now," she said, seeing that Sergeant Bond was waiting to speak to her.

"I would like to take your statement now, Miss Carlton." He took out his notebook.

"Could it wait just a little longer?" Vivien asked him. "You remember I mentioned evidence of another crime? I'd really like to see if we could find it, so that if we found anything you could confirm it officially."

Peter put his notebook in the pocket of his short-sleeved white shirt. "If you think it might be of some importance, I see no reason why not, Miss Carlton."

The repetition of her name raised a question that had been bothering her since yesterday. *Miss Carlton*. Frowning, she shook her head, striving to pin it down.

"What's wrong?" David asked.

"I've just remembered something. How did the Hendleys know I was Vivien Carlton, when I called myself Vivien Shaw?"

"I have no idea."

"Where to, Miss Carlton?" Sergeant Bond asked.

"Upstairs, to the main bedroom." She saw her father flinch. "Would you rather stay down here with David?" she asked him, taking his arm.

"No. I must—" He swallowed hard.

"Okay. What about you, Mom?"

Her mother was very pale, her hand tightly gripping Matthew's, but she shook her head. "If your father's going upstairs, so am I."

Matthew turned to Wesley. "Please come with us." Wesley nodded and followed behind them.

As they walked down the front hall, Vivien saw dark stains on the polished wood floor, the area cordoned off with yellow tape. She glanced away.

All kinds of memories raced through her mind as they slowly mounted the stairs. She thought back to her first sight of the house and the way it had drawn her in, enticing her, welcoming her, as it had welcomed her father today.

Was it possible for an inanimate object, such as this house, to become a living entity, capable of love and hate and desire? Could the souls of all those who had lived and worked for three centuries at Peverill—not only masters but also slaves and servants—be imprinted, like photographic images on film, upon wood and mortar and coral limestone, their spirits working together to cast out evil and bring about good in the house and estate that they had created?

Vivien shook her head, smiling at such fanciful

thoughts but still filled with wonder at how beautiful Peverill Hall looked and felt today, with soft winds blowing through the open jalousie windows cooling the interior and dust motes dancing in the rays of sunshine.

"Where do you want to look for this possible evidence?" Sergeant Bond asked briskly when they reached the upper hallway.

"The main bedroom," Vivien said, "but I'd be grateful if you could allow us a few minutes on our own first."

He nodded and he and the other man moved away while Vivien led her parents and Wesley to the room where Lillian Hendley had died. Matthew stood in the doorway, peering inside. "I always had to knock on the door before I could go in," he said in a low voice. "I'm sure that's the same dressing table, there beneath the window, where my mother would sit and braid her long, dark hair. I loved to sit on the bed and watch her reflection in the mirror. She was very beautiful. I loved her very much. She didn't deserve . . ." He turned away blindly, and Ellen put her arms around him, soothing him with soft words.

"Are you sure you wouldn't rather wait downstairs, Dad? We can always come back tomorrow when the police have gone."

"No," he said firmly. "I want to be here to see justice done." He gave a small sob. "It helps to be here."

"Okay." Vivien ran her hand over her mother's back and then went to the door to get Sergeant Bond and the other men, including David. "We'll need help to move the bed," she told him.

Although the sunlight shone in the two windows, Vivien's memories of the place were dark. "This was where it started last night," she told Sergeant Bond, but her gaze took in everyone crowded into the room. "The room was empty. I thought it was my only chance of getting into it, but I hadn't realized Mrs. Hendley

was upstairs—and that Marcus was nearby." She
glanced around nervously. "Where is Marcus, by the
way?"

"The dog? Shut in his kennel outside," Sergeant
Bond replied.

"Good." She looked around the room, seeing it in
the daylight for the first time. It must once have been
a beautiful room, with its delicate plasterwork ceilings
and cornices, mahogany flooring and ornate woodwork,
but now it was shabby, the walls and ceiling stained
brown from Thomas Hendley's cigar smoke. "Lillian's
niece, Verna," she continued, "said that when she was
a little girl her aunt Lillian showed her her favorite
hiding places for treasures. I've checked one of them—
Lillian's sewing basket. There was nothing unusual hidden in it. I couldn't find the second one, which was
a blue-and-white vase, although I suppose it could be
downstairs in the kitchen somewhere. The last place
was a loose floorboard beneath the bed in this room.
Right, Wesley?"

"Absolutely right," Wesley agreed. "My cousin could
not remember exactly where the bed was placed in the
room when Lillian showed her."

"But when I hid under the bed last night, I could
feel something sticking into my back, through the mat.
Of course, if it's noticeable, I'm sure Thomas would
have had the floorboard up and checked by now, so I
don't hold out much hope."

"Let's get on with it, then," David said, pushing the
bed toward the window with Peter's help. Then the two
men rolled up the dusty coconut mat to reveal the old
floorboards, which were badly in need of cleaning.

As Vivien stood beside her father, watching them,
she slipped her hand into his and squeezed it. She
knew that this could prove to be the final piece in the
puzzle.

Kneeling down, David and Peter ran their hands over

the boards. David looked up. "There's one that's slightly raised, as Vivien said it was, but if it was ever loose, it certainly isn't now."

"We'll need a crowbar." Sergeant Bond stood up and went to shout down his request to one of his men.

While they waited, Vivien leaned against the wall, recalling what had happened in this room last night and thinking how much had happened since then: Thomas Hendley's death, Paul's arrest, and making love with David. Smiling to herself, she looked up . . . and caught David watching her as he sat back on his heels, waiting. When their eyes met, he grinned, his eyebrows lifting in a silent salute.

The other policeman arrived with a toolbox. He took out a small crowbar and began to lever the board up with it. With a screeching and popping of old nails, the board came up.

Peter reached down into the gaping hole beneath. "Careful, sir," the police officer said quickly. "Watch out for those rusty nails."

Vivien felt her father's hand grip hers. She held her breath.

"There *is* something there," the sergeant said excitedly. He drew out a battered tin box and held it up for everyone to see. Its surface was eaten away by rust, but it was still possible to read HUNTLEY AND PALMER BISCUITS on the lid.

The men scrambled to their feet. David took a magazine from the nearby rattan stand. He opened it and placed it on the bed, so that Sergeant Bond could set the tin down without harming the delicate white linen bedcover.

"I think you should open this, Miss Carlton," the sergeant said.

She hesitated, her heart racing. "Perhaps my father should—"

Matthew shook his head. "Oh, no. You must open

it." He released her hand with a little nod of encouragement.

The tin was so badly rusted that it was hard to ease it open. The policeman took a small screwdriver from the toolbox and pried the lid open for her. Inside were two folded pieces of paper. Vivien recognized instantly that they were of the same stock as the notes Celeste had shown her.

"Good thing they were put in a tin," the sergeant said. "Else there would be nothin' left of them, with termites and rodents and dampness."

Dampness? Vivien was terrified that when she opened them she would find that the ink had faded so that there would be no writing left. Or perhaps the paper would disintegrate in her hands the moment she touched it.

"Go on, child," Matthew said gently. "Read it."

With extreme care, she opened the folded note and started to read it aloud.

Peverill, 1950
There's a storm blowing up. I hate that feel-
ing, everyone's edgy and it is sticky hot. I tried
to tell R. about T. when we went to bed, but he
said I was imagining things because of the
baby. I know he loves me, but he has so many
worries with the cane yield bad this year, he
doesn't need me telling him more bad things.
But I'm afraid, Ruth. I'm really afraid of
HIM. What can I do? He waits for R. to go
out and then he comes and presses up against
me and says really bad things to me. Says it is
what I really want and he is going to do it to
me. (Promise me you won't show this note to
ANYONE, especially Mamma, it would only
worry her. R. is probably right. It is just the
baby making me nervous. But how can I get
him to believe what I tell him about T.? It is

*like he doesn't want to hear any bad things
about his precious cousin.)*

When she finished reading, she handed the note to
Wesley. Her father was behind her, and his arms went
around her. She leaned against him, gaining solace from
the very solidity of him. "Your poor mother," she
whispered.

Tears swam in his eyes. "Read the other note," he
said.

She dug out a tissue from her pocket and blew her
nose. She scanned the note first. There was no heading
this time, very little punctuation, and the scrawled writing was almost illegible.

*Dearest Ruth, you may never see this or my
last note I haven't been able to send it to you
because of the storm. Robert has gone to the
fields to see what he can salvage. Thomas made
some excuse to stay home. A few minutes ago
he told me he wasn't going to take no from me
anymore and that he'd kill two birds with one
stone whatever that means. There's no one else
in the house except Trevor everyone's gone to
help salvage the crop I told Trevor he must stay
very quiet downstairs and lock himself in the
little parlor and do his new jigsaw·puzzle whatever happens. I'm in the bedroom with the door
locked   the lights are gone   I hear his footsteps
on the stairs   I will try to hide this from him
and hope you will find it   Take care of my
precious, darling son   Pray for me. Oh, Jesus
Lord save me he is at the door . . .*

When she'd finished reading the note aloud, Vivien
handed it to Wesley and turned to her father. She felt
his arms close about her, holding her tightly against

him. "She was thinking of me before she died," he murmured.

"Oh, Dad." She lifted her head and pressed her damp cheek to his, and then he opened his arms to include Ellen, and the three of them clung to one another. Everyone else in the room was silent.

Eventually, Sergeant Bond cleared his throat. "Was there evidence of sexual assault in the Hendley trial?" he asked.

"Not now," David snapped at him.

"I agree," Wesley said, carefully placing the two open notes on the bed beside the biscuit tin. "But this will be crucial evidence when we instigate an inquiry into the trial and wrongful execution of Robert Hendley." Matthew looked up at him. "We will clear your father's name."

"That is all I ask." Matthew went to the bed and gazed down at the notes. "Would it be possible for me to take these notes so that I can read them for myself?"

"I should take them and lock them away as evidence," Peter Bond said apologetically.

"Verna has some other notes that your mother wrote," Vivien told him.

"I would like to read these for myself," her father insisted. "When I can be on my own."

"If I undertake to keep them safely until Mr. Carlton has read them," Wesley said, "will you release them into my care?"

Peter hesitated. "I would give you copies—not the originals—but I sent my photographer back to the station."

"I'm a professional photographer," Vivien said. "And, unless you've taken it away, my equipment should still be in the room where I left it."

"It should be. We had hoped to lock everything in, but there was no lock on that door."

"Tell me about it," she said wryly. "I have a digital camera and a laptop. If it's okay with you, I can photograph the notes and print them off the computer for my father."

The sergeant nodded. "Fine."

Vivien crossed the upper hall to go to her room. David followed her. "You may need some help." Her hands were still very sore but improving steadily. David had made her sit with them wrapped in ice this morning, and then he rebound them with the bandages, which were grubby and frayed.

Her parents came to stand in the doorway, as if they couldn't bear to lose sight of her for a moment.

The room looked as if it hadn't been touched since she'd left it in the darkness last night. Her backpack was still by the door, packed with the precious things she'd gathered together when she'd planned to flee the house. She caught sight of her daybook and drew it out.

"What's that?" her mother asked.

"My general all-purpose diary and daybook. I use it to record what pictures I have taken, when, where, and which settings, et cetera." Vivien looked down at the slick green cover of the book, the white label declaring it to be hers in large black letters: VIVIEN CARLTON SHAW.

"Oh, my God!" She clamped her hand to her mouth.

"What?" her mother asked.

"Oh, my God. *That's* how they knew who I was. How stupid could I be? I left the evidence on my bedside table for everyone to read. They knew me as Vivien Shaw, but they obviously read the name on the book. That's what gave me away. And, come to think of it, it was after they'd been snooping in here that the little episode with the window happened. Once they found out who I was, they were determined to get rid of me in one way or the other."

"I imagine this book will constitute more evidence," her father said. "If one of the Hendley family touched it, the police will probably be able to lift some fingerprints from it."

"What good will that do? Thomas Hendley is dead."

"But his son is not," David said.

"I won't get any satisfaction from Paul being convicted," Vivien said. "To me, he was just one more of Thomas Hendley's victims."

Once Vivien had finished photographing the notes, Sergeant Bond gave permission for her and her parents to explore the house, as long as they avoided the places surrounded by yellow tape. Then he, David, and Wesley left them alone, but not before Wesley had reminded them to be sure not to be late for the huge family party at Celeste's home. "You and your wife will be the guests of honor," he warned Matthew, who still looked stunned by all that had happened.

After they'd gone, Vivien stood in the upper hallway with her parents. "Despite all that has happened here," she said, "I love this house."

"Perhaps you'd want to live here, Viv?" her mother said. "I have the feeling there's a chance you might be settling here in Barbados."

Vivien could feel her cheeks burning. "Who knows? It's early days yet. David and I might not survive doing this book together."

"But there is something between you, isn't there?"

"Let her alone, Ellen," Matthew said. "She's only known the man a few days."

"Dad's right," Vivien said, knowing that he needed to be eased into everything gradually.

When they'd finished exploring upstairs, they went down and found David sitting on the verandah, looking very relaxed, chatting to the men who'd been working on the shutters. They exchanged pleasantries with the repairmen, who then went back to work.

David motioned to them to sit down. "I found some lemonade in the fridge. Hope it was okay to help myself."

"Marian made it," Vivien said, with a pang. She wondered what was going to happen to Marian. Nothing, if she had anything to do with it. If it hadn't been for Marian, she could very well be dead by now. She hoped she'd go to live with her daughter in North Carolina or make a new life for herself in England.

"You can't have seen everything yet," David said.

"No, we're just stopping for a break en route to the lower level." Vivien sat down, fanning herself with her straw hat, which she'd retrieved from her room. "Dad was just asking if I'd like to live in Peverill."

"And would you?" David gave her one of his enigmatic looks.

"David doesn't approve of plantation great houses because they were built by slaves."

"Now, forgive me, but that is an extreme oversimplification of my opinion, Miss Carlton."

Vivien grimaced. "Sorry. But that's the gist of it."

"He's right, of course," she was surprised to hear her father say. "But now these houses are here, rather than just tear them down, perhaps they can be used as a tool to explain the history of Barbados to all, from every aspect, colonial and African. After all, Dr. Moreton, I think you must agree that it is also the history of tremendous achievement as well. To have come from your ancestors' transportation on slave ships to running your own country in three centuries is quite an achievement."

"Respectfully, sir, I think you should have said 'our.' "

Her father frowned. "Sorry?" he said, his voice puzzled.

If Vivien had been near David, she would have pinched him, hard. Did he have to lecture her father, today?

"They were *your* ancestors on those slave ships as well as mine," David said quietly.

Vivien exchanged glances with her mother, who looked troubled. Vivien was about to jump in and change the subject, when her father cleared his throat.

"You are right, of course," he said, his eyes steadily meeting David's. He blinked away tears. "I'm very much a hybrid, I'm afraid. And reminding myself of my mother wasn't something I chose to do too often. It brought too much pain."

David looked ashamed. "I was wrong to—"

"No, no. You were quite right." Matthew smiled. "I seem to have suddenly acquired a large family of various hues. By denying them I'd deny my mother, whom I adored. Thank you for reminding me." He held out his hand to David and they shook hands.

"My apologies, sir," David said.

"No need," Matthew said. "However, I don't think this is the time for philosophical discussions. We were talking about this house. I was asking Vivien if she'd like to live here, if it became ours."

Vivien thought about it. Would she? "Despite all that's happened, I love this house. I had the feeling that it welcomed me the moment I saw it." She turned to her father. "You know what I mean, don't you, Dad?"

He nodded.

"But I don't think I'd want to live here. It's too big, has too much sad history. On the other hand, I hate the thought of it being torn down."

"I agree with that," said Matthew. "Definitely not."

"If there is oil," Vivien said slowly, thinking as she spoke, "Peverill Hall could be repaired and made beautiful again, but what then? We wouldn't want to sell it and find it converted into a conference center or something like that, would we?" She turned to David. "Sunbury has been beautifully restored. It's on view to visitors. Do you know anything about it?"

"Sunbury is privately owned, but there are some old great houses that have been turned over to the Barbados National Trust. You have to endow them with funds for them to take it on, but it seems to be working well. That way both local people and tourists can see these places."

"That sounds perfect." Vivien turned to her father. "What do you think of it, Dad?"

He wasn't convinced. "I'm concerned that it might become a place for ghouls to come and see where my mother was murdered."

David grinned. "From what I know of them, the people of the National Trust would be appalled at the thought. I don't think they'd do anything tasteless. Vivien's right, it would be better than turning it into a hotel or a conference center and changing its whole character."

"Well," Matthew said. "That's all up in the air at present. There may be no oil, and then we'll have to sell it. I certainly don't have the money to take care of it."

"There's oil, all right," David said. "Wesley told me they're pretty certain. As for your right to the place, you were heir to Peverill Hall when your parents died." He frowned. "Unless your adoption canceled that out."

Matthew waved away the issue. "I was never legally adopted. The Carltons pretended I was, but when I sent for the certificate and it couldn't be found, they confirmed that they hadn't bothered to go through adoption legalities, although they'd told Thomas they had. So I've always remained the son of Lillian and Robert Hendley."

Vivien sprang up and slid her arms around her father's neck, from behind his chair. "I'm so glad," she whispered, kissing his cheek. She suddenly remembered something. "Come into the house with me a minute, Dad."

"Why?"

"It's a little secret. Come in." She took him by the hand. "Excuse us a minute," she told the others. She led her father into the front hall, closing the door. "Wait there," she told him. "I'll be back right away."

"Do I have to close my eyes?" he asked, conjuring up memories of old childhood games.

"Why not?" She dashed upstairs to the room that had been hers for a brief but immensely eventful time.

Her backpack and suitcase were still open on the bed, with her cameras and equipment lying beside them. She reached down into the case and, lifting up the heavy sweater with which she'd covered it, drew out the manila envelope containing the old leather-bound copy of *Kidnapped* and the photograph she'd carefully placed inside it.

She ran down the stairs again. He stood waiting for her, eyes still closed. "Hold out your hands. No peeking." He held them out, and she placed the envelope in them. "Okay. Now open your eyes."

He did so, glancing down at the envelope and then up at her. "What is it?"

"Open it and see, Daddy."

He drew the book from the envelope, read the title, then opened it to the title page. His eyes widened when he saw the carefully scripted name on the opposite page. "Trevor Hendley," he whispered. He looked up from the book to stare at her. "This was mine."

She nodded, hardly able to speak. "I know."

"My father used to read this book to me. Where did you find it?"

"I rescued it."

"What do you mean?"

"I'll explain later." She came to stand by him.

"There's something else here." Hands shaking, he removed the photograph. He stared down at it for so long that she thought, for a heart-stopping moment, that perhaps the faded image had completely disappeared and it was now blank. But when she looked at it she could see quite clearly the picture of a happy family, which she now knew was her father as a young boy with his mother and father.

A shuddering sob came from deep within him, and he turned and buried his face in her neck. She held him close until he drew away. "I'm sorry, sweetie," he said, wiping his eyes with a white handkerchief.

"Don't be. I understand. I understand everything now, Daddy."

"It's all been . . ." he couldn't finish.

"I should have kept them for another time. It was too much for you."

His fingers caressed the photograph. "It is the greatest gift you could have given me. I had nothing left of my parents. Nothing at all. It was like—like they never existed. As if they'd been nothing but a dream. From the time I left Peverill, no one ever mentioned their names to me again. It wasn't until I married your mother that I was able to speak about them and what had happened here. Even then I wasn't even sure if it had actually happened or whether it had been a nightmare."

"I wish you'd told me."

"When I heard you were at Peverill, I cursed myself for not having done so."

The front door opened, and Ellen peered around it. "Everything okay?" she asked anxiously.

"Everything's fine." Matthew smiled down at Vivien. "We'd better get on with seeing the rest of this place. Then we've got some sort of family party to go to." Half turning his back, he closed the book on the photograph and slid it into the manila envelope. "I'll show her these later," he whispered to Vivien. "Put them away safely for me." He handed her the envelope and went to join Ellen and David on the verandah.

A few minutes later, as they all prepared to start out on a tour of the rest of the house, Vivien fell back with her father, linking her arm in his. "Are you still sorry I came to Barbados?"

"How could I possibly be sorry?" he asked her, his dark brown eyes shining. "By coming here, you have given me back my life."

Squeezing his arm, she walked into the house beside him, eager to explore places with him that even she had not yet seen.

SUSAN BOWDEN

BITTER HARVEST

0-451-20237-6

When aging Eleanor Tyler begins to suffer a series of terrifying incidents (such as catching a glimpse of her dead husband and finding her dog on her bed, murdered), her rigid control over her family, its multinational food business and even her sanity are jeopardized. Her family insists that she is hallucinating, but Eleanor knows her experiences are real. More frightened than she'll admit, Eleanor attempts to make an ally of Michelle Tyler, the granddaughter she's never met. Michelle has heard nothing good about the family that rejected her late mother as a pregnant teenager, and she has enough to cope with given a brand-new pregnancy she's not sure her restless reporter husband will welcome. Still, she reluctantly agrees to visit the Tyler mansion for Thanksgiving and receives a hostile greeting from her new aunts, uncles and cousins.

To order call: 1-800-788-6262

S645/Bowden